GHOSTS OF THE ARBUCKLES

Aurion du Preez

Anaphora Literary Press

Quanah, Texas

ANAPHORA LITERARY PRESS
1108 W 3rd Street
Quanah, TX 79252
https://anaphoraliterary.com

Book design by Anna Faktorovich, Ph.D.

Published in 2024 by Anaphora Literary Press

Ghosts of the Arbuckles
Aurion du Preez—1st edition.

Library of Congress Control Number: 2024925136

Library Cataloging Information
Preez, Aurion du, 1946-, author.
    Ghosts of the Arbuckles / Aurion du Preez
    330 p. ; 9 in.
    ISBN 978-1-68114-615-7 (softcover : alk. paper)
    ISBN 978-1-68114-616-4 (hardcover : alk. paper)
    Kindle (e-book)
1. Mystery, Thriller & Suspense—Thrillers & Suspense—Historical.
2. Literature & Fiction—Genre Fiction—Small Town & Rural.
3. Mystery, Thriller & Suspense—Mystery—Private Investigators.
PN3311-3503: Literature: Prose fiction.
813: American fiction in English.

Prologue

Late one night a ghost went wandering. Her impulsive course took her along streets and sidewalks, and eventually to the stately three-story building where she had received her earliest education. Unimpeded, she passed by the guard at the outer gates and stole through locked metal doors to explore the dark and silent corridors within. Whimsically, she wafted up and down staircases, in and out of vacant classrooms, and through walls and ceilings in a game of hide-and-seek with no one. Pausing curiously in the library, she observed an open book of poetry by Lloyd Jacobs, called *Last Flight Out*. She was intrigued by a few succinct lines that expressed sentiments she herself felt, and an inexplicable yearning arose within her as she read.

> *Sometimes when dusk is well away,*
> *permission is given by your leave, Sir,*
> *to walk again among the living as in old time,*
> *again in peregrino ephemerally,*
> *to walk the farmstead where I toiled my years,*
> *to see the incursion of Queen Anne's Lace*
> *into our field of vetch and rye,*
> *to see the blossoms of columbine.*

After a moment's reflection a determined soliloquy slipped from her cerulean lips: "I think I too should linger among the living. Not to satisfy my own nostalgic yearnings, nor to critique their foibles or frustrate their plans, but rather to nurture and advise them, as would a personal mentor. I shall whisper softly in their ears during moments of quiet meditation, or better still, while they slumber. Thus, wisdom and discernment will survive my departure, nestled discreetly among their temporal thoughts and dreams, embedded in myriad memories. How else can those with only mortal eyes perceive what is not readily visible? How else can they learn what only the dead know with certainty?"

Part 1: The Memorial

One

At seventy-six, Luke Greenwood was incomparably spry and independent. He had lived alone since his wife Dovie passed away, ten years earlier, although her life and death remained something of a mystery to everyone but himself. On a balmy Saturday evening in September 2015, he decided to walk to the grocery store six blocks away. Wearing his favorite ball cap with the US Navy Veteran logo, he twisted the key to latch the front door dead-bolt, stepped off the porch, and headed down Third Avenue SE.

The Sooner Mart on Lake Murray Drive was operated by a Pakistani immigrant named Amir Bukhari, whom Luke had befriended. When Luke arrived, there were cars at both gas pumps and another three waiting. The store itself looked commendably busy. He was glad, for Amir's sake. Business had been slow all through the summer months, despite the claim by the previous owners that the location was ideal for traffic to and from the lake all through the year.

Once inside, Luke picked up two packets of Hostess cupcakes and a quart carton of Colvert's milk before meandering from one aisle to the next, eyes scanning the shelves for anything else that might strike his fancy. Finding nothing he couldn't do without, he returned to the counter and eased up behind three other customers waiting to pay.

Amir acknowledged him with a broad grin, a crisp salute, and a jaunty *Hey, Luke Skywalker*. Luke beamed and nodded. Faces turned his way, assuming he was a celebrity in town for some special event. Their expectations were visibly dashed, and Luke's smile faded to reality. At the same time, Amir scanned a six pack of Michelob Lite for a large man with a full beard and a dusty mop of white hair. Wearing baggy shorts and a floral sort-sleeve shirt, he had the appearance of a department store Santa Claus on vacation. Luke smiled furtively at the thought.

Next in line, a thin, middle-aged woman with a bad cough and loosely fitting dentures asked for a carton of Benson and Hedges cigarettes with the special filters. She pointed them out on the shelf immediately behind Amir. He turned and laid his hand on the correct packet, as if her finger had painted it with a laser beam.

After her, and immediately in front of Luke, a husky woman with tattoos and a nose ring purchased an assortment of lottery tickets, including five Cash Fives and one Mega. Handing them to her with a bright smile, Amir wished her good luck. She grinned, dragging fingers through tangled strands of partially bleached hair: "If I win, I'll give you a hug and a happy meal from McDonald's." Amir had heard such empty promises before. But he nodded politely, shuddering at the thought of her beefy arms squeezing the breath from his lungs.

When she stepped away, Luke bellied up to the counter and laid out his few items. He tugged his wallet from a snug hip pocket and began thumbing through a neatly arranged assortment of bills. Two other customers had filed in behind him.

According to Amir's report to the police, what happened next was surreal. Yet, he remembered flashing segments with stunning clarity. As Luke handed him a five-dollar bill and three ones, a lanky youth appeared from nowhere and shouldered his way toward the counter. Amir inhaled to tell him to wait his turn at the end of the queue, but his words were cut short. The spry youth lunged, bumping Luke off his feet and into a rack of Wrigley's gum, Tic Tacs, and Lifesaver breath mints. At the same time, the youth's long-fingered hand snatched the wallet from Luke's grip, and he loped out the door with the wallet clutched firmly against his chest. Luke pushed himself up from the floor, skating on a lake of broken plastic and loose mints.

In similar circumstances, some people would have cowered on the floor, paralyzed by fear. Not Luke Skywalker. Amir sensed Luke's intentions and yelled out *"No, no! Don't do it!"* Luke ignored the warning. Gripping the counter to recover his balance, he propelled himself forward and bolted out the door after the young thief. Well ahead of Luke, he leaped into the passenger seat of a waiting Ford Crown Victoria. No doubt a former police cruiser, very popular in certain circles, the getaway car was black with white doors, and a spotlight hung loosely above the driver's side mirror.

The motor revved and tires spun in gravel. Undeterred, Luke lunged onto the hood like Dirty Harry and hung on with the tenacity of a pit bull gripping a postman's leg. Teeth gritted and face distorted, Luke's angry wide eyes locked onto the terrified face of a young female in the driver's seat. Amir said she was no more than a kid, maybe sixteen. Her tightly braided hair sported some kind of shiny threads twisted into the ends. Both hands gripping the wheel, she let out a long scream as she accelerated backwards. The car reversed in a long arch before sliding to a halt. Luke adjusted his grip along the back edge of the hood and spread his legs wide, bracing himself for a rough ride. The girl dropped the gear shift into drive. Again, rear tires spun, sending a spray of gravel against the storefront windows. The girl rotated the steering wheel hand over fist to make a tight left turn. The Crown Vic tilted and rocketed forward onto the street, tires screeching on solid pavement. Luke lost his grip and went flying. He rolled several times before slamming against a heavy wooden electric pole.

Brandishing a small caliber revolver, but never aiming it toward the vehicle, Amir ran to Luke's aid. He found Luke conscious, but severely injured. Blood gushed from a head wound, matting Luke's thin silver hair. His eyes fluttered and roamed. He groaned incoherently. Amir stuffed the pistol into the back of his jeans as he hunkered over Luke. Immediately, he heard tires screech. He looked up to see taillights brighten and the rear of the Crown Vic lift as it skidded to a halt. Amir's face froze in fear as the car reversed toward them. Slowly it approached, quiet and menacing, until it stopped next to him and Luke. Amir's heart leaped into his throat. The dark glass of the rear passenger window eased down. Amir expected to see the muzzle of a gun and a flash that would end his life. Instead, out the window flew Luke's wallet, fluttering like a pigeon's wings and landing open across Luke's chest. Grimacing, Luke picked it up with quivering fingers and flipped open the pockets to reveal his Oklahoma driver's license, a photo of his beloved Dovie, and a Discover card, which was his one and only means of credit purchase. The cash was gone.

The dark window glided up and the Crown Vic accelerated away. On trembling legs, Amir shrugged under Luke's blood-coated arm, gripped him firmly around the waist, and hoisted him to his feet. Together they hobbled across the street toward the storefront. Amir noticed only one customer still observing from the store entrance—the woman who had bought cigarettes. The other customers had fled. Amir shouted for her to call the police and request an ambulance.

As Luke's legs gave way, Amir dragged him across the gravel parking area to the storefront. Luke slumped down against an icebox and closed his eyes. By the time the paramedics arrived, he was dead. They assessed that he'd sustained a massive concussion and cerebral hemorrhage when his head struck the pole.

Two

A phone call at three a.m. is never a good thing. The boss doesn't wake you up in the wee hours of the morning to offer you a raise or a promotion. Your children don't call after midnight to say they love you and plan to come home for the holidays. Sadly, no. A chirping phone at zero dark thirty is always the harbinger of bad news.

This particular call shattered a pleasant and vivid dream. I was at the helm, sailing across San Francisco Bay, cool breeze in my hair and salt spray on my face. I had passed under the Golden Gate Bridge, bow pointing toward open water. My wife Meredith was perched on an elevated stern seat, gripping a stanchion and leaning pensively toward rolling waves. Suddenly, a god-awful intermittent chirping noise dropped the sails and dried up the entire Pacific Ocean. Groggy, I felt as if I had washed up on a flat volcanic rock on a dark and silent planet— starless, moonless, and soundless, except for an irate seagull squawking in my ear. My eyes stretched open as I rolled over, and one hand fumbled through a morass of fading incongruous images. Dragging the receiver to my ear, I heard a crackling voice that closely resembled that of my cousin Jordan.

"Russ?" Jordan cleared his throat. "Sorry to wake you at this hour."

"No problem." I paused, knuckling drooping eyelids. "I'm sure you have a good reason. I won't say I had to get up anyway, to answer the phone."

"Yeah, yeah," he said reflexively. "Old joke, number forty-seven. But you didn't really have to get up, did you? You just rolled over and lifted the handset."

I chuckled. "Yea. Busted."

Although Jordan lived in Georgia, and I in California, we had maintained contact over the years. Mostly by phone. We shared an off-the-wall sense of humor; sometimes crude, weird, or just plain silly. But we understood each other, and even with the portentous timing of this call, we easily masked tension with a moment of banter. However, I could hear that Jordan's voice was etched in distress. I found the switch to my bedside lamp before pushing myself upright against the headboard. I caught my breath and forced out an essential question.

"Is everything alright?"

Jordan sniffed. I waited through ominous silence. Then he said it, flat out and clear. "Uncle Luke is dead."

A chill skittered up and down my spine, halting my breath and speech. I threw my feet off the bed and sat straight up. "Oh, dear God, no. What happened? He seemed healthy and active when I last talked to him. I think he said he was busy with a Cub Scout project." I drew in a deep breath and blew it out slowly, waiting for details.

In logical and philosophical terms, Luke's passing was no surprise. Although healthy, he was in his twilight years. As anyone's life progresses into the eighth and ninth decade, death is imminent, and everyone knows it. To deny that reality is as senseless as not connecting a sunset with nightfall. Yet, the news hit me straight in the gut. I listened in silence as Jordan recited the story, no doubt just as Amir had reported it to the police. I never expected Uncle Luke to go out in that way. Ardmore was the quiet little town of my childhood. We seldom heard of any violence. Fires, yes. Car wrecks on the highway. But not armed robberies. And not my Uncle Luke.

The last of our mother's siblings, the capstone of two generations of ancestors whom I knew personally, Lucas Tatum Greenwood had seemed immortal. More important, he had played a unique and important role in my life. Jordan's, too. We and our other two close cousins, Terry and Christine, felt a deep and timeless connection with him. Almost spiritual. In fact, I'd have to say I dearly loved the man. Over the last several years I phoned him on his birthday, and he phoned me on mine. My own father didn't do that, and he had died suddenly, without an opportunity for me to say goodbye. But that was my fault, and I regret it. I should have been in closer touch. In contrast, whenever I spoke to Uncle Luke there was always a lilt in his voice that truly warmed my soul. I had learned a lot from him, and considered him a mentor and personal confidant.

I sank back into my pillow and slung an arm over my face. Uncontrollably, my lips tightened and my eyes misted as I pictured Luke's sparkling blue eyes, crinkled at the corners when he smiled. A tear found its way down my cheek, over my jaw to my neck, and pooled in the hollow above my collarbone. As certainly as I felt the movement of that tear, so I felt an emptiness in my gut, as if part of me had dissolved and disappeared. After his wife Dovie died, Luke remained single and childless the rest of his life. But he claimed hundreds of students at Ardmore High as his *kids* of heart and soul. And we four cousins, Luke's three nephews and one niece, believed ourselves to be special. Luke had tucked us under his wing, as if we were the children he never had. We were a tight-knit family within the family. In this moment, I felt as if Uncle Luke had been snatched away leaving a large and diverse progeny to venture on in life without him, like minnows released into a pond. His departure seemed like the ascension of Jesus before the bewildered eyes of his disciples, except there would be no promise or expectation of his return.

In recent years, Luke lived alone in a two-bedroom frame house in the southeast quadrant of Ardmore, Oklahoma, not far from Hardy Murphy Coliseum. I'm pretty certain he retired at sixty-eight, or maybe a year later; but after that he worked a concession stand at the fair every year, and at other events in-between. He also served, for nearly a decade, as the scout master for Troop 232. The last time I talked to him by phone, he was still going strong. He had no intentions of being confined in a nursing home. He wanted to make his exit while busy at something he loved. That might not have been precisely how it happened, but his death was newsworthy, to say the least.

Having conveyed sufficient details, Jordan whispered a goodbye and hung up. I returned the handset to its cradle and folded an arm behind my head as I tried to formulate a plan. Without a doubt, I needed and wanted to attend the funeral, which was scheduled for that Friday morning. It was now Wednesday. I needed to shuffle a few things around and take a couple of days off, but working freelance, that was not difficult. But first, I had to book a flight—this morning, if possible.

Among Luke's many relatives, I was one of the few who resided outside Oklahoma. And quite possibly, I was the last to receive the news of his death. But I felt intensely compelled to attend his funeral, not just because of what we had experienced together years earlier, but because of things I did not understand and could not explain— things my cousins and I had agreed to leave alone, like proverbial sleeping dogs.

I eased out of bed, trying not to disturb Meredith. Once on my feet, my thoughts congealed into a basic and logical *to do* list. I slipped on a T-shirt and baggy shorts, scooted my feet into a pair of flip-flops, and tiptoed along cool tiles into the carpeted study. *Tiptoe* is probably not the right term. Meredith often quipped that no one can walk quietly in flip flops. That's how they got their name: from the horse-on-cobblestone sound they make with every step. I countered that it wouldn't bother her if she didn't have the hearing of a timber wolf.

Meredith typically replied that even earplugs wouldn't shield her from the variety of rude and annoying noises I made around the house. She could list them effortlessly— grunting while I sat on the toilet, snoring that she compared to a thunderstorm rolling in from the Pacific, and explosive sneezes that sent Toby, our ten-year-old white Persian cat, scrambling for cover. I confessed openly to a couple of those, especially my visceral grunts on the toilet if I tried to push out too much business in a hurry. But I argued that it compared favorably to Meredith's growls and grunts on the tennis court, for which Maria Sharapova is famous. My flip flops thwacking across the kitchen tiles were mild compared to that. But still, Meredith found it annoying. I hoped she didn't hear me at that particular hour. Then I heard her soft voice.

"Hey, cowboy. What was that about?" She appeared behind me in the kitchen, knuckling sleepy eyes.

I hesitated, trying to rein in the emotions that stifled my breathing and churned in my stomach like a double order of street tacos. "Damn it all," I said forcefully, lifting my eyes toward the ceiling. "Uncle Luke is dead," I said. I choked up for a moment, and had to clear my throat before continuing. "He was killed trying to stop a robbery. Funeral's in Ardmore, day after tomorrow."

Meredith's face tilted into a compassionate frown. Her lips tightened. "I'm so sorry, sweetheart. That's terrible." Her arms reached out as she eased closer and drew me into her nurturing embrace. But she intuitively avoided questioning me for details. "Sad, regardless of the circumstances," she said. "I know you loved him. You spoke of him often. You should go."

I stood still for a moment before responding. My arms folded around her. I held tightly, knowing she knew the hard work of grief better than I. "Thank you. I knew you'd understand."

Perhaps in that moment I was reminded of our mutual mortality— that likely someday one of us would leave the other behind. For just a moment or two, those thoughts intensified my angst. However, Meredith's acknowledgment of Uncle Luke's value to me, and her permission to join my family in celebrating his life, somehow combined to brush the emotion aside and energize me to get busy.

Within moments after flipping on the coffeemaker, I plopped

down at the computer. A wiggle of the mouse awakened the monitor, and I clicked the Google icon to begin an internet search. I quickly found two flights from San Francisco to Oklahoma City, both that afternoon, but one had a two-hour layover at Albuquerque and the other a similar stop at Denver. Then I discovered a Delta direct flight to Dallas, but I would have to rush to make it. I booked a business class seat and paid with my American Express card.

Meredith couldn't go back to sleep. Maybe she didn't try. I heard her puttering around in the kitchen, and a few minutes later she brought me a cup of coffee and a toasted bagel laden with cream cheese. I carried them back to the bedroom, trying not to slosh coffee on the new carpet. I eased the cup down onto a coaster and nibbled the bagel while I one-handed socks and underwear into a carry-on bag. Figuring any funeral is a suit and tie affair, I zipped my only dark suit into a hanging bag, along with a tie and a starched white shirt.

Fortunately, from our place in Palo Alto it's a straight shot north to the airport—half an hour, in normal traffic. I parked in the short-term lot and hurried through check-in and security, moving as fast as I could without pulling a muscle. An attendant closed the forward door behind me and the plane was rolling by the time I buckled my seatbelt. Somewhere over southern Nevada I said no to another bagel, but yes to orange juice and coffee. The coffee failed to wake me up. I snoozed off and on during the rest of the flight, and I awoke with a jolt as we landed at the sprawling Dallas/Fort Worth International Airport. Avis had a rental car waiting. A new Honda Accord.

I had hoped my brother Spencer could pick me up at the airport so we could ride together from there up to Oklahoma. He lived in Dallas. But, as a lead engineer at Texas Instruments, he bore responsibilities he couldn't lay aside. He said he was conducting a training session all that week, flying solo because his partner was out sick. The best he could do was to send flowers, with his condolences. He said he would do that online and have them delivered to the church the next morning.

The weather was mild, being mid-September. I anticipated the drive from DFW to be less than two hours. Up Interstate 35 through the rolling hills of North Texas, then across the Red River to Ardmore, Oklahoma. But that gave me plenty of time to reminisce. Along the way, I unpacked memories that had been filed away for nearly half a century. Crossing the Red River, I spontaneously let out the opening line from the song in Rodgers and Hammerstein's famous play *Okla-*

homa: *"where the wind comes sweepin' down the plain..."* For the life of me, the rest of those lyrics would not surface. I promptly faded to *"La, la, la, la; la, la, la, la... hawk makin' lazy circles in the sky."* First stages of senility, I had to assume. From that point on, cruising along the Interstate, I kept an eye out for hawks. There were plenty of crows. And I caught sight of a lone scissortail, Oklahoma's state bird, rocking on a fence line as I passed. Squadrons of sparrows, lifting, circling, and resettling around a broken hay bale in a pasture. A few buzzards in the distance. But no hawks.

Ardmore had changed a lot since I was last there. The Interstate was now complete all the way from Laredo to Duluth, but it skirted the western edge of Ardmore as if it held no more significance than a prairie dog town. On the contrary, I found it to be growing with new developments already filling the gap between the old downtown and the new Interstate. Now called Commerce Street, Highway 77 had been expanded into a four-lane business corridor with adjacent service roads running both north and south. From my point of view, it was more complex than the runway system at JFK, festooned with a conglomeration of traffic lights and signs, and more challenging to navigate than Boston's tunnels. Strip malls, gas stations, and restaurants lay in random patterns up and down in either direction, with camouflaged entries only locals would recognize.

Approaching a split in the lane with a traffic light in the middle, I was uncertain which way to turn. I slowed almost to a stop, trying to decide. Behind me, an impatient young local in a bright yellow Camaro pounded the horn. Annoyed, I stopped, shoved the gear shift into park, flipped on the emergency blinker, and folded my arms across my chest while staring at him in the mirror. He poked his angry face out the window and let out a string of profanities, tromped the accelerator, and sped around me. I turned my head to see him lean towards me and shoot me the finger just before he plowed into the back of a Cadillac. I should have been ashamed to feel a sense of satisfaction, but I wasn't. Tugging the gear shift into drive, I smiled and waved as I cruised slowly past the fresh accident, leaving the young hothead and an angry, but rich, old fart about my age to sort out their problem.

Exploring the once-familiar northwest side of town, I noticed that the modest medical facility where my brother Spencer and I were born was now an enormous complex called Mercy Hospital, with several detached buildings and offices. Not far from there, I drove past the little rock house on G Street where Spence and I spent the first few years of our lives. The yard and house had shrunk considerably, now too small to accommodate my memories. I realized that growth from childhood to adulthood creates a natural warp in perspective. I scoffed at the numerous shoddy improvements made by perhaps several successive owners. The front porch was now enclosed by a sagging and dirt-laden screen. The garage had been converted to a room with a single entrance under a crude awning, and a second story had been added above it. The barn and horse lot behind the house had been replaced by a detached garage. I fought the urge to knock on the door and give the residents a good talking to. Silly me. I realized I was still pissed off about the hothead in the Camaro.

I turned back along 12th Avenue in a westerly direction. Within a few seconds I found my way to the La Quinta, which lay tucked away behind Lowe's Home Improvement, almost invisible from the highway. I opined that specific location to be another outrageously poor decision by the city planners. After checking in, I flopped down on the bed and started thumbing through messages on my cell phone. Delete. Delete. Delete. Then I came across one from my cousin Jordan, enquiring whether I'd be at the funeral. I texted that I was already in town.

After a short nap, I drove back down to the main drag, Ardmore's version of 77 Sunset Strip, to a buffet I had spotted earlier. A big sign, the Sirloin Stockade. And near the entrance, a huge faux Hereford steer stood on a cement slab, staring out towards traffic. I hadn't eaten anything since the morning bagel, so my stomach felt hollow and a buffet seemed inviting. Following two couples through the door, I collected a tray and utensils, and slid my Mastercard through the slot. At the center island I found roast beef, mashed potatoes and gravy, and pinto beans, which I recalled were more or less the staples for this part of the world. I grabbed a little coleslaw in the salad section. Nearly all the patrons of this place were cotton tops, some older than me, and I wondered if anyone among them had been in my first or second grade class. No one looked even vaguely familiar. But then, sometimes I hardly recognize myself in the mirror. Passing time tends to crash-land on our faces.

An hour later back in my room at the motel, I burrowed my head and shoulders into a stack of hefty pillows and watched *Dawn of the Planet of the Apes* until I fell asleep. Startled awake after midnight by a gunshot on some detective show, I fumbled for the remote and switched off the TV. I must have drifted off thinking about Uncle Luke. The details of his death swirled hauntingly in my head. The next time I opened my eyes, I heard the sound of footsteps, conversation, and a car door slamming just outside my room. It was eight a.m. I crawled out of bed, showered, shaved, and dressed for the funeral.

Three

By twenty past ten, I had found my way to the First United Methodist Church, located more or less in downtown Ardmore. The funeral was scheduled for eleven o'clock. When I arrived, the parking lot was full. I found a vacant spot on a side street about a block away and strolled along a walkway in front of white-framed, two-story houses dating to the 1940s. The front yards were all shaded by colossal pecan trees and live oaks that had never blinked during the hot summer. The sun was bright and the morning air fresh.

A black Cadillac coach and two limousines pulled up near a side entrance to the church. People I did not recognize stepped out of the limos and followed the casket through a door on ground level. I sauntered around to the front of the building with its classic columned entrance, pausing only to take a gander at the tall steeple pointing skyward. Merging with other guests, I ascended wide cement steps. A woman with a black lace veil over lacquered silver hair held the door open for me and returned my grateful nod with a soft smile. Once inside, I found a quiet corner of the foyer away from the growing crowd.

I assumed I was not the only person to attend a funeral after being more or less estranged from the family for decades, and for whom recognizing faces was virtually impossible. I found myself pondering what might be the thoughts and feelings of octogenarians who have survived nearly all of their friends. The last couple of years must be lonely. They leave behind virtually no one who knew them well. And it struck me that there is little sense of victory in being the last man standing— only solitude, perhaps certain regrets, and for some a few secrets gripped tightly right down to the moment of departure. The reality struck me that having resettled on the west coast far from my roots, my immediate family was comparably small and my list of good friends quite short.

In contrast, Uncle Luke's long residence in Ardmore and his stellar career as a school teacher drew a crowd of educators, city employees, business owners, and politicians; many of whom were true and loyal friends. In high school, Luke's best friend was Sam Daube, the golden child of the family whose department store, founded in 1888, was the oldest in Oklahoma. He also knew the Colvert family, whose dairy products were popular over several counties. At some point, Luke fell in love with Barbara Colvert, three years younger, but after a few dates she ditched him for Howie Kimball, the son of a local oil tycoon. After Luke came home from the Navy, Howie had married someone else. Luke and Barbara became friends again, although never became romantically involved. However, for several years she sponsored his geological research team. Perhaps she had hopes for a reconciliation. Who knows?

After a few minutes, my uneasiness dissipated and I merged into the fifty or more family members who overflowed the fashionable parlor and stood in small circles in the foyer. Immediately, I noticed a grinning face floating toward me from the curtain of dark suits and dresses. It was my cousin Jordan. Despite the bald head and fashionable Van Dyke beard, I knew him instantly. I realized he was among those I saw following the casket into the building, but from a distance he had not looked familiar. No one in that group did. Like me, he brandished the marvel of modern orthodontics. Our smiles were brighter and nearer perfect than those in our high school photos. We embraced warmly.

"Glad you made it," Jordan said, blue eyes sparkling.

"Sure. Uncle Luke was a special guy. I wish I hadn't let time and distance keep us apart."

"Well, it happens," Jordan said. "Come on in. Terry and Christine are here, and lots of relatives you've never met, I'm sure. Or maybe you did and don't remember."

I felt a rush of nostalgia, along with certain memories I had intentionally swept under the rug. Our large family now seemed to revolve around cousins with their spouses and children, among whom four of us—Terry, Jordan, Christine, and I—had a unique bond. Jordan and I were about the same age and we had spent a lot of time together as children. In certain ways, I felt closer to him than my own brother Spencer.

Within a few minutes an attendant escorted the family into the service where we were acknowledged by a standing congregation. We filed into vacant pews at the front. I sat between Terry and Jordan. After the undertakers closed the casket, the service formally began. Terry was the first to step up to the podium. He had been asked to read the obituary, which was fitting, since he was the oldest of Luke's nieces and nephews and a suitable representative of the entire family. Moreover, as far as I knew Terry and Uncle Luke were the last of our family members to have served in the military.

Terry read the abbreviated biographical data, composed by Christine, and the list of those who'd preceded Luke in death— his loving wife Dovie and all his siblings. Most of those details were common knowledge, published on the website of the Craddock Funeral Home, and were tedious both to read and hear. More importantly, Terry noted that over the years Luke had been an instructor, coach, friend, and mentor to many. No one knew of any skeletons in his closet. In that regard, Uncle Luke was unusual, I suppose, and he bore no shame.

Following the obituary, Amir stepped sheepishly to the podium. After an abbreviated version of Luke's death, he tearfully recounted the occasions when Luke had visited his home. One time, in early March, Luke brought gifts for Amir's four children, figuring that was appropriate for the season of Ramadan. He knew very little about Islam, but he respected the beliefs others held dear. That aside, Luke was fond of Amir, and they were more than casual acquaintances. They had watched televised soccer games together, and Luke consoled Amir after Pakistan's loss to Australia in the 1999 Cricket World Cup Final. Amir said he had told Luke that, since coming to Oklahoma, he and his wife Zainab often felt out of place, and at school the children struggled to fit in. In that regard, Luke wrote him a note which he had kept. It read: *America is the world's greatest theme park; people come here from everywhere, and together we wait in line to enjoy the rides, which are too expensive and always far too short. So, give yourself to those you love and what you believe in. Do your job well. Relax, and make yourself at home. Like the famous words in Desiderata, "as much as anyone, you have a right to be here."*

The minister's eulogy consisted of the same scriptures and poetry I had heard a dozen times, undoubtedly retrieved from a liturgical guide for honoring the dead. A buxom middle-aged brunette with a voice like a police siren wailed out *Eternal Father, Strong to Save,* a prayerful petition for divine mercy and deliverance for those in peril on the sea. Commonly called the Navy Hymn, the famous lyrics are thought appropriate in memory of deceased sailors. I must confess, on that occasion those lyrics struck my ears as a conundrum, since the dead sailor whose life was being celebrated had already perished; not at sea, of course, but trying to retrieve his wallet from a petit thief at a corner grocery store. He was dead nonetheless. He had not been saved from peril, on the sea, in a store, or at the side of the road. This, to my skeptical mind, illustrated the ultracrepidarian nature of many American beliefs and traditions, and the assertion of unverifiable propositions as irrefutable truth. I grimaced, but reminded myself that some people draw comfort from such words, however empty and meaningless they might seem to others. Living in a bubble of belief makes many people feel safe. Immortal, even invincible. But they're not.

Terry, being solo at this event, rode with me to the graveside service. He sat quiet along the route, his gaze turned toward the countryside. I suspected that standing before a congregation and reading the obituary before tearful eyes had rattled him. But there was something deeper. He had that thousand-yard stare common to combat veterans who had witnessed too much death and destruction. While Jordan and I were finishing high school and starting college, Terry joined the Army and did three tours in Vietnam. He was discharged in the summer of '68. By August, he had enrolled at Southeastern Oklahoma State for the fall semester. That was Uncle Luke's *alma mater*. In fact, our horrific camp-out in the Arbuckle Mountains was intended to celebrate his return home and immediate embrace of higher education. It didn't quite work out that way. That one week was a pivotal point for all of us.

Terry had made up his mind to major in pre-law and criminology, but it would become evident that he was struggling with post-traumatic stress. Looking back, I realize that Terry dealt with it admirably. He graduated at about the time I finished my master's degree. I thought he had the right stuff to be an attorney, but he said he'd had enough of school. He became a police officer, and after three years of stellar service he was recruited to work undercover with the DEA. He and his wife Sue had now retired, bought a mobile home, and were touring the country. At this particular moment, our mutual burden was grief, which he and I tried to stifle in our own distinct ways. But there were significant gaps in Terry's story which I did not yet know.

Many years earlier, Grandpa and Grandma Greenwood had organized a family plot at the Springer Cemetery. When we arrived at the open grave, Terry went immediately under the canopy and sat down while I strolled around, curiously studying gravestones. Nearby was a marker of pink granite for Jordan's folks, Matthew and Beatrice, right next to Christine's parents, Marcus and Hazel. My parents (Thurman and Phoebe Barnett), like Terry's, were buried in the town of Paul's Valley where the Barnett clan originated. I had not thought about it for a number of years, but large families are almost too complex to sort out.

I focused my attention on those closest to me. My mother had died at age 83. She wanted to be buried in Ardmore where she was married, and where Spencer and I were both born. But Spencer and I agreed that she should be buried next to Dad in Paul's Valley. That really didn't make much difference to me, at an emotional level. Spencer and I share certain personality traits that some psychologists might identify as OCD. We both tend to insist that things always match up, line up, and are squared away. When we replace a jar of jam in the fridge, we turn it so the label faces out. For that reason, as much as any other, we wanted Mom buried next to Dad. It just felt right.

Our father had died a decade earlier, and his funeral was quite well attended. He had made many close friends in the construction industry. In contrast, when our mother died most of her friends were gone already. And our family, I'm sorry to say, more or less let us down. Unintentionally, of course. Terry was on a special assignment, and couldn't get away. Jordan was in Israel with a tour group led by a Baptist pastor named Harold Kimberley. Christine was campaigning for the state elections. But a number of Mom's friends from church attended, and her pastor did the service. Since then, I have never felt the urge to visit my parents' graves, much less stand and talk to them as if they could hear. A lot of people do that. Spencer has mentioned it occasionally. I've never challenged or criticized him for that, but deep down it makes no sense to me. My sentiments are for the living, and I believe in communicating in the here and now, face to face.

I approached the open grave and laid my hand on the casket. A lump rose in my throat. I found myself mumbling an apology. It was as if by allowing him space for his dubious interaction with the spirit world, I had failed to support his connection with reality.

Uncle Luke's graveside service culminated with a traditional flag folding ceremony, and taps played flawlessly by a stoic ensign in full dress uniform. We had agreed that Terry should receive the flag. The first round of the twenty-one-gun salute caught me off guard. I flinched. The third volley was absorbed by the roar of four Navy F-4 Phantom jets that flew straight over the cemetery. One tilted upward and away with a stream of smoke—a maneuver called *the missing man*. I glanced at Terry as his chin quivered and he brushed away a tear. Such moments are ineffably moving.

Four

From the cemetery in Springer, Terry and I joined a line of cars eastward on Lumberman Road towards the Greenwood farm. In the hazy distance, I caught sight of a wind generator on the southwestern slopes of the Arbuckle Mountains, heralding Oklahoma's embrace of high technology. I could also faintly make out, on the hillside, the unmistakable white letters marking the *Lazy S Ranch*. Jordan was in the lead, driving along a vaguely familiar route. Although this was no longer a funeral procession, a farmer on a John Deere tractor stopped in the middle of a field, climbed down, and removed his hat. I had to assume he knew the family and was doing what he could to show respect. Terry noticed, but said nothing.

Driving along a gravel road between plowed fields, I was struck by the contrast of the hustle and bustle of Ardmore's Twelfth Avenue and this bucolic atmosphere worthy of a Norman Rockwell painting. We were unmistakably skirting the Oklahoma Hills of Woody Guthrie's lyrics. It was also the home of Wiley Post, the first pilot to fly solo around the world. And, of course, this region laid claim to Will Rogers, vaudeville performer and comedic social commentator, also remembered as "Oklahoma's favorite son." Rogers was born of Cherokee ancestry on the Dog Iron Ranch near a town called Oologah, back when Oklahoma was still officially Indian Territory. Post and Rogers were good friends, sadly killed together in a plane crash in Alaska in 1935. Truly, our grandparents associated with some famous people, and I recall them casually dropping such names in conversations long forgotten.

In the distance ahead, a cell phone tower loomed above a field of mature corn. I imagined the millions of signals it cast, like an invisible spider web connecting this rustic community with the rest of the world. That tower was a monument to the slow transition of one generation to the next; the Builders to the smaller Silent Generation and then on to the massive Boomers after World War II; then to the Yuppies; and currently the groups called Gen X, Y, and Z. If certain novelists are correct, looming ahead is a Zombie Apocalypse, or some kind of Armageddon, and possibly an escape to Mars by a resilient remnant of academics, technicians, and a few stalwart politicians.

Of course, there have been end-times prophets in every generation since Jesus, interpreting contemporary events as sure signs of a
catastrophic termination of the world as we know it. In contrast, scho-
lastic circles claim that such an event will not be connected to religious myth, but rather the result of ecological mismanagement or an
extinction-level impact by a comet, or possibly our annihilation by an
alien species. For Uncle Luke, the end resulted from an altercation with
a run-away thief.

I immediately recognized the farm house as we approached. One
by one, cars angle-parked in long stretch of gravel along the front. Towards the back, a brush-covered hill rose and extended east and west.
I remembered it well. I climbed out of the rental and moseyed along
behind Terry, up creaking wooden steps to the front door. Inside, the
connected rooms were alive with chatter and the clatter of younger
children playing chase. Clearly, over all these years this had remained
the family gathering place for special occasions.

Farming had changed considerably in the past couple of generations. During the 1800s, farmers used a crude plough of wood and
iron, fashioned by a blacksmith. They worked ten hours a day, following an ox or a mule churning up one furrow at a time and covering no
more than an acre or two before dark. Well into the twentieth century
a farmer raised crops and live-stock with the singular goal of feeding his
family. In only a couple of generations, farming had transitioned to big
business involving enormous loans for up-to-date equipment, manag-
ing leases and hiring specialized labor, and the creation of a system of
co-operation within numerous agricultural communities. Family subsistence had been rapidly displaced by corporate farming and complex
global marketing.

Following the trend, Jordan's son Jared leased out most of the
Greenwood land to other farmers who either grazed cattle or raised
alternate crops of wheat, rye, and sorghum. I remembered Jared as a
lanky lad, with long, stringy blond hair and a weary face. But now he
was a sharp-looking, blue-eyed businessman, well-groomed and wearing a Giorgio Armani suit. That was pretty upscale, for an Oklahoma
farm boy. As soon as I stepped through the front door, I spotted him in
the corner with a group of men whose appearance and manner flashed
their financial success like a neon light.

Part of the agreement with Jared was to carry on family traditions for as many as could manage to attend. That included Christmas, Thanksgiving, Easter Sunday, and, of course, funerals like this one. I was told that Jared's wife, whom I had not yet met, had more or less assumed the role of surrogate Grandma, coordinating the other women who handled the cooking and other duties of traditional farm wives. Through the crowd I could see several women back in the kitchen, sashaying around each other like square dance partners as they uncovered and laid out an assortment of potluck dishes. One woman, a little older than the others, flapped her arms like an irate goose and shooed the kids out into the back yard to play. Out they scampered, screen door banging behind them.

I surveyed the dining room, trying to imagine the faces that were no longer present, particularly our grandparents. I imagined Grandma among the women in the kitchen. Glancing through the window, I pictured Grandpa on the back porch, lighting up his pipe before stepping out on the patio to gaze across the back pasture toward the mountain.

Jordan and I were probably in the first grade when Terry informed us three close cousins there was no Santa Claus. As I recall, I took the news pretty well, but Jordan was sorely disappointed and displayed all the traits of confirmation bias. A week later, he presented Terry with pictures of Santa with his sleigh and reindeer, and written testimonies of a couple of adults who claimed to have met Santa in person. Christine, two years younger, was severely traumatized, and maintained a rather solid state of denial well into the third grade. Strange things happen when you are forced to confront childhood fantasies. Our individual journeys forward into multi-faceted reality had become too complicated for me to trace, but intriguing to acknowledge.

Grandma had been all about biblical names for her children, which she wanted to come from the New Testament because, according to Pastor Tinsley, the Old Testament had given way to the New, and the Law of Moses was nailed to the cross of Christ. So, she and Grandpa named their boys Matthew, Markus, and Lucas. I suppose they were hoping for a fourth, whose name would have been Johannes (or, more likely, the simpler form 'John'). But they had two girls instead, whom they named Dorcas and Phoebe. Terry and I were double cousins; our mothers being sisters who'd married brothers Harvey and Thurman Barnett from Paul's Valley. Double cousins were unusual, and we became a constant target of teasing, with kids comparing us to hillbillies, inbred and crossbred until (so the song goes) one day you discover you're your own grandpa.

My mother Phoebe often said that one look at our eyes was evidence enough that Terry and I were related. Both of us had hazel irises, one of the rarest eye colors in the world— brown around the pupil and a mix of green, blue, and tan at the edge. Terry claimed that his eyes and mine were equally complex, but honest. His were a bit darker than mine. From a distance, they appeared to be brown. As a teenager, I told my parents I was glad we had moved to Texas, because in a cluster of small Oklahoma communities I would never find a wife who wasn't a relative. That might have influenced my falling in love with a California girl.

Terry didn't care one way or the other. He lived in sublime detachment from his immediate surroundings. For that reason, it always seemed difficult to conduct any sort of meaningful conversation with him—at least until after his military service. He was never unpleasant. He just didn't have much to say. In high school, he'd dated several girls. But none steady.

A woman approached me and put out her hand. Now pushing seventy, I have often said that any woman under fifty looks like a girl to me. But those who appear a little older demand a measure of respect without any reference to age. This particular woman seemed close to my age, and she looked remarkably familiar. A broad grin stretched beneath a dozen freckles that peeked through a thin layer of makeup across her cheeks and nose. Her reddish-brown hair was pulled back in a tight bun, with streaks of grey at the temples. She must have read puzzlement on my face. Green eyes sparkled.

"You're Russ, aren't you? I'm Christine," she said. "You'd damn well better remember me."

Christine. Ah, there's another story. Frizzy hair, reddish brown. Each day a different look. Freckles across her nose and cheeks, and green eyes that publicized her mercurial disposition like the instrument cluster on a street dragster. As we matured, we three boys weren't quite sure how Christine could maintain a role in the cousin quadrangle. She just didn't seem to fit. With the onset of puberty, she was outraged that God had denied her a penis and testicles. Instead, she was cursed with burgeoning breasts that got in the way of free swinging on the monkey bars in the playground, and a monthly menstrual cycle that she interpreted as evidence that God, if there is a God, then HE... Christine always stressed that the Judeo-Christian deity was undeniably male with all the associated biases… HE was more like the Greek god Zeus, clearly a vengeful and self-righteous misogynist prick, undeserving of a woman's worship.

In her junior and senior years at high school, Christine won the regional debate competition. Commendably, she held no opinion without reason and forethought. She devoured books and essays in various genres and completed six high school courses beyond requirement. She graduated magna cum laude, which got her an academic scholarship to OU. She took extra courses to complete college with a double major in education and political science. I was eager to learn what she had done with it, since we hadn't talked in nearly fifty years.

"Oh, of course." I thumped my forehead, a little embarrassed, but my foggy memory cleared as I took her hand. "I should have recognized you immediately. Time changes us all, but you truly possess Cleopatra's eonian beauty and charm."

Christine grinned and her eyes widened. "You are so full of shit." She wagged her head, tossing my hand away before propping both fists on her hips. "I've always been as homely as Janice Joplin, and I'm getting frumpier by the minute. I wish I had her voice." She brushed the back of a finger under her nose. "I would have taken better care of it than she did. But I can't carry a tune in a five-gallon bucket. All that aside," she waved it away, "how the hell are you?"

"I'm fine. Healthy and still active." I paused, still reeling. "I've sort of lost track of all our relatives. I know your dad was my Uncle Mark."

Her head dipped solemnly. "Yes. He died young. I was thirteen."

"I do remember that. I'm truly sorry. I know that was difficult for you. Devastating, I imagine."

"It was, yes. But that's water under the bridge, now."

After her father's untimely death, Christine declared herself an atheist and non-conformist. She developed strong convictions on just about every topic, seldom traditional or within the parameters of conventionality. If it was commonly accepted, she opposed it; and if it was commonly rejected, she defended it; but with her own rationale and well-constructed arguments. She was incredibly bright and articulate. Her political and social views were so far left they nearly fell off the map, and while still in high school, she joined the Young Democrats of America. She mourned the assassination of JFK, RFK, and MLK Jr. as evidence of a great sickness within American culture. She challenged most conspiracy theories as hokum; the fabrication of highly imaginative minds. But, on the Kennedy and King assassinations, she was certain of a plot conceived by the far right and carried out by the CIA.

"I'm totally failing here," I said, gesturing toward the full room. "I've forgotten most of the names of people I just met. I suppose most of them are descendants of our great-aunts and uncles, like from Grandpa's family, and Grandma's siblings whom we seldom, if ever, saw. Like Uncle Hub. Do you remember him?"

Christine hesitated, staring incredulously into my eyes. "Yes, Dumdum. Uncle Hub was your great-uncle," she said. I felt the sting of her scolding tone and look. Then her face twisted as a puzzled thought hit her. "Well, that's not true, now that I think about it." She folded her arms across somewhat flattened breasts and shifted to a more relaxed stance. "He was my mother's brother, so he's no direct kin to you." She waved it off as unimportant. "His real name was Hubert." She said, with a smile and casual nod. "But somehow, everybody called him Hub. Not sure why."

"He drove a grader for the county, as I recall."

"How the hell would you remember that?" She wagged her head, frowning dubiously, but grinning widely at the same time.

"I can't explain it, but it's there, clear as a bell. You know, when you're a kid, certain things stick. Spencer and I both attended Charles Evans Elementary and our mom always picked us up after school. Well, one day, for some reason, she had to go up Mount Washington Road, which was gravel and they were getting ready to pave it. There was this ginormous yellow grader clearing and leveling, and it was tilted over slightly as the wheels on one side churned through a muddy ditch. A flagman waved us over to keep us at a safe distance. My brother and I were in the back seat, and Mom pointed and said, '*That man up there in the cab is your Great-uncle Hub.*' I remember he had red hair and a huge smile, and he leaned out the tractor cab and waved. We were like… awestruck, you know what I mean? So, believe it or not, over all these years, every time I see a big road grader, I think of him. I just forgot exactly who he was."

"Ahh, that's sweet, anyway." Christine dropped her arms and relaxed.

"And you…" I directed a finger loosely at her.

"What?" she said.

"I remember something in particular when you were in your early teens." As I stared at her, I pictured a bushy head of hair and the ruddy, defiant face of a radical feminist. But now, she was tastefully made up, presenting a mature and professional image.

"Not that winter of '68," she said, lifting her eyebrows. "We promised not to talk about that *ever* again."

"No, no." I threw up a hand. "Something else." I put a finger to my lip and deliberated. "Ah, yes, it had to be you. You didn't have a driver's license yet, but you were driving."

"Oh, hell. Here it comes." Christine folded her arms again. One foot began tapping as she stared at me, trying to stifle a smile.

"That *was* you." I leaned toward her, and I'm certain my eyes widened involuntarily as I smiled tauntingly. "You drove your mom's Buick into the front window of the Super Dog. That little event was in the *Ardmorite,* complete with a photograph. You nearly hit a server on roller skates. She threw a tray full of chili dogs and French fries all over the hood, and in the misting rain it dissolved into a sloppy mess. Your excuse was that your shoes were wet and your foot slipped off the brake and onto the gas pedal. I remember it now, like it was yesterday."

Christine turned her head with a self-conscious snigger just before her right fist shot forward and punched me in the ribs. I buckled over, not sure whether to console her with a hug or duck and cover. I had never been sucker-punched before by a sixty-eight-year-old woman. Or any woman, for that matter. Despite working out three times a week, my abs were not tight enough to sustain the impact of her knobby knuckles. But I knew she meant it to be funny, so I laughed and coughed simultaneously, searching her face for a little sympathy. Grinning ear to ear, Christine relaxed her kung fu posture and folded her arms casually. She was not angry. In fact, on the contrary, it appeared to be a re-bonding moment. She threw her arms around my neck.

"It's so good to see you, Russ." She relaxed, one hand resting on my shoulder. "That's about the only thing anyone remembers about me from back then," she said. "They never mention that I was top of my class, president of National Honor Society, or anything that really matters."

"That's how it is, Cuz," I said, my shoulders lifting spontaneously. "That's why I moved to California. No one out there knows the goofy things I did when I was a kid. In fact, they wouldn't..." I glanced left and right and leaned closer. "They wouldn't give a shit."

"Good for you. I would have fared better myself on the west coast, but for some reason I gutted it out here in Okie Land. I assure you, contrary to common perception, there is far more to life in Oklahoma than just slumping in a lawn chair by the trailer, and watching corn grow."

I grimaced. "I know. But people need a whipping boy. Somebody to pick on. Laying aside all our juvenile indiscretions, I guess we both have enough to account for as adults."

"Damn straight." Christine grinned and nodded vigorously.

Catching my intentional segue as a hint to get serious, she tilted her head, studying my face. I watched her green eyes shift from volcanic to glacial in a single breath. That was a trait I remembered. When she was angry, her corneas ignited in emerald and gold splinters and her look shot flames like a Medieval dragon. But when she smiled, they melted into tropical pools, as engaging as an island breeze and sparkling like gems in a treasure chest. And if she was bored or perturbed, the lights went out, as dark and vacant as Carlsbad Cavern at midnight.

"You're a writer." She blinked and smiled, and as distinctly as her eyes had chilled momentarily, they now warmed into an affectionate glimmer.

"I am, yes."

"I've read some of your work." She shifted her stance and her eyebrows lifted. "My second husband and I did a river cruise with Norwegian, a few years back. You wrote the travelogue in *Holidays Abroad*. I recognized the name Russell Barnett, so I looked you up. And, sure enough, the author was my dear cousin from yesteryear."

I chuckled. "How 'bout that. Yep, I did write for that magazine for a while. But they went belly up in 2009. I had to move on. I'm freelance these days, with an occasional short contract. But that kind of journalism has been good to me. Even now, I have more work than I'd really like. What about you? Still married, I assume."

"Yes, Howard's a consultant with JP Morgan Chase. Travels a lot."

"Is he here? I'd love to meet him."

"Nope. In Boston this week. How long did it take you to acclimate to West Coast liberalism?"

It struck me that Christine avoided more details about her husband. But I let it go. "Bout twenty minutes." I bobbed my eyebrows for emphasis, not certain she would catch the humor.

"Yeah..." she said, nodding and drawing her lips tight. "You probably wouldn't have been happy had you stayed around here."

"No doubt about it," I said. "For several reasons; not just religion and politics."

"Well, I'm enough of a church-goer to appease the Moral Majority, but that's not my focus. And I'd have to say that education has become a rung on my ladder into politics. I'm running for the Oklahoma state legislature. It doesn't pay much, but I can afford to retire from my current job if I win. And I believe I will."

"I'm impressed," I said, trying not to be gushy. "But not surprised. Thinking back to our younger years, I would have expected nothing less."

My conversation with Christine was interrupted by two younger women (Tammy and Karen, they said), whom I supposed were related to me, but I would never remember the connection unless I traced it on a genealogical chart. After introducing themselves hurriedly, they turned to Christine and launched a complaint about the principal at the Norbert Wilkins Middle School and his biased discipline policies. I was stunned to realize these two *girls* were talking about their grandchildren, not their own kids. It sounded like both had become matriarchs of their respective clans, poking their noses into the lives of their grown children instead of allowing them to discover responsible parenthood on their own. But I held my tongue.

"As superintendent," Tammy said firmly, glaring into Christine's face, "*you* need to do something."

Christine had not elaborated on her stellar career in education, and we didn't get far enough into our conversation for me to ask. In contrast with the angry teen I once knew, her maturity and self-actualization were now quite evident. I now surmised that when Uncle Luke was still teaching at Ardmore High, he might have been really pissed to be supervised by his niece. Anyway, it was clear that, by default, she had inherited complaints from all her junior relatives. I excused myself with a casual gesture. Christine acknowledged with wriggling fingers but turned her eyes quickly back to Tammy, who continued to shake a finger in her face. I slipped away while both women blathered in Christine's ears.

Moving into the crowd, I pondered the complexity of family consanguinity. Scattered through the house were brothers and sisters and aunts and uncles of various levels—first, second and third cousins, some once, twice, or thrice removed. I noticed a couple of middle-aged guys in blue jeans and boots; both with short cropped hair and tanned faces. They appeared to be the outdoors type—maybe construction workers. They were either part of the family or, at the very least, close friends. One was barking loudly about current politics, saying he was fed up. "If them bleedin' heart liberals try to take away our guns, they'd better brace theirselves for a war. That's for damn sure." I sneaked past without making eye contact, figuring that if Christine got wind of any antebellum racism or neo-Nazi rhetoric, she'd jump in the middle of it. And when she was done, those boys would know they'd been chewed up and spat out in fine chunks.

I ambled curiously through the house, testing my memory of this ancestral monument. In the hallway hung a gallery of family portraits, with a few ancestors dating as far back as the mid-1800s. At the top were faded black and white images of my grandparents, Bertram and Gertrude Greenwood (commonly called Bert and Trudy). Below them were all of us by family and a horde of children I did not recognize. The more recent photographs had unmistakably clearer resolution and brighter color.

My head brimmed with images from fifty years earlier, like Grandpa sitting in a rocker by the fireplace, pipe smoke circling his balding head. I remembered his coveralls, a sort of stonewashed blue and white pinstripe, and heavy work boots. I pictured his sparkling eyes and crinkled nose. Grandma was a plain woman with long hair always tied in a bun. She never wore any kind of makeup, as I recall. She worn proudly every line in her face. Both she and Grandpa had false teeth they kept in a dish by the bed at night. Grandma's uppers were accentuated with a single sliver of gold, and Grandpa's had a chip out of one upper incisor.

As I stood lost in memories, a young Indian woman brushed past me in the hallway, then stopped and wheeled around. "I'm Poloma," she said, extending a hand toward me.

"I'm Russ Barnett, I'm..."

She cut me off. "Yes, I know who you are. Pleased to meet you, and I want to talk to you later. I have a dozen questions."

I nodded as she scurried off in the direction of the busy kitchen. She seemed quite sophisticated, and very much at home. At the same time, I thought our encounter a bit odd. I felt a sudden chill on the back of my neck, and a wave of discomfort washed across my face. Strangely, although I did not know her, the encounter seemed a connection to long ago, like the things Christine didn't want to discuss.

I shook it off and meandered further through the house toward the back bedroom where Jordan and I had slept many years ago. The door was open, and I leaned in for a peek. A lanky kid with greasy hair and a cemented frown sat on the edge of the bed and flayed at the strings of an unplugged electric guitar. I assumed him to be Jordan's fourteen-year-old grandson Mitch. The muffled melody did not resemble anything I knew… nothing as familiar to me as Jimmy Hendrix, Eric Clapton, or Stevie Ray Vaughn. But he was in the zone, doing his musical thing. He looked up and nodded slackly in my direction. Above his bed, I could make out a large poster of a young black woman. I was not sure who it was, but the name Beyoncè came to mind. Her breasts peeked out beneath a torn-off football jersey, and something like a thong stretched tightly between her spread legs and over her hips. The caption read *Bootylicious*. I grinned, nodded, and moved on, trying not to imagine what took place each night in his bed beneath that curvaceous image.

Without a doubt, everything changes over time. Nearly half a century had passed since I was last in this hallowed house. Every family has its memories, good and bad. Some we cling to and some we're glad to leave behind. But all of it is like proverbial water flowing beneath a bridge on route to the sea. Or, maybe it's more like Samuel Goldwyn's twisted comment: "Since then, we've passed a lot of water under the bridge."

Five

Unlike the other three of us cousins, Jordan was an only child. He was also the only grandchild to carry the family name Greenwood. That made him special, but I never knew him to flaunt it. Trim, light skinned, with blue eyes and blond hair, Jordan bore a Nordic appearance inherited from his mother's side of the family, and which he touted as Viking. At age nine, Jordan had a life-threatening accident that, over time, assisted in defining his character. A car hit him while he was riding his bicycle to school, breaking both legs in several places. He spent his third-grade year in a lower body cast. Doctors speculated that he might never walk again, but they did not know his drive and determination. He fully recovered and became a star athlete in school—an energetic hotshot on the basketball court, and a competitive middle-distance runner.

Jordan's father, my Uncle Matt, had owned a gas station on Highway 77 in Ardmore, around the corner from the National Guard Armory. A very close friend, Hank Simpson, was the officer in charge. He allowed Jordan to skate there on the roller rink, since that was part of Jordan's therapy. Naturally, Jordan invited me and Spencer to join him. For about three years, before we moved to Texas, every Wednesday after school we rode our bikes to the Armory and skated until near suppertime.

However, the Armory held another fascination for us all. Out back, locked behind a chain link fence, there were several trucks and jeeps of WW II vintage, and the one Sherman tank. Jordan had found a key to the gate, so we sneaked in and played inside the vehicles (mostly the tank), bouncing in the seats and pretending to be in the heat of battle. The supply room had all kinds of injury-staging models and devices used for training, like broken arms and legs and stick-on gunshot wounds. We played war games in which one of us would be the corpsman patching up injuries on the others. I remember when Captain Simpson got onto Jordan for wasting bandages, because they were government property. Jordan blamed me, and I blamed Spencer. He had no one else to blame, and had to turn it back on us. The captain was impressed with Spencer's gutsy rebuttal and fined me and Jordan a dollar each, or an hour on cleaning detail. We each coughed up a dollar.

Later in college, Jordan completed a degree in American history at OU, with a keen interest in Native American tribal customs and ancestry. He married a girl he met there, named Janine. Because of their love for travel, they opened a travel agency and settled in a suburb of Atlanta, coordinating tours and cruises. Atlanta was home to Delta Airlines, with numerous overseas connections. Being at the heart of the Bible Belt, many church-goers were keenly interested in the Holy Land and the region of Paul's journeys. Jordan and Janine made a specialty of tours in Israel and western Turkey.

Jordan explained that his daughter Jennifer, well into her teens, would gag at the sight of a cat eating a mouse, or a trickle of blood from a scraped knee. She literally fainted when her brother Jared's nose bled after a hard smack in the face by a soccer ball. To everyone's surprise, Jennifer became a nurse. Jared, on the other hand, had a gift for profitable investments, and by twenty-three he was a burgeoning financial consultant and accountant. He now handled taxes and annual returns for fifteen large farms in central and southern Oklahoma.

For that reason, Jared was the right person to assume management of the family property. The Greenwood children, the parents of all of us cousins, had agreed to keep the land together as part of a trust, along with a sizeable investment in government bonds. When our parents had all passed on and Uncle Luke became the last surviving Greenwood sibling, he preferred not to assume the role of resident trustee. We of the next generation agreed to Jared's management if he committed to make a living on his own and not draw from the investments (other than an annual stipend). It was complicated paperwork, and some of the younger distant cousins on Grandma's side protested. They preferred selling the farm and divvying up the money. I was glad that didn't happen. The big issue now was that the land and investments were rolling forward through the generations with no one reaping any financial gains. Jared had worked out a proposal for annual distributions. I was eager to see details. Meandering through the crowd at this post-funeral gathering, roaring with the cacophony of conversation and laughter, my mind exploded with memories. Of course, with each recollection a few questions arose.

Amidst my ambling down memory lane, Jordan's distinctive and authoritative voice sliced through the noise, announcing chow time. He instructed everyone to file through the kitchen, grab a plate, load up, then find a place to sit in the dining room, living room, outside on the porch, anywhere. "Or, if you can eat standing and talking, that's okay, too," he said. He led a quick prayer, also remembering Uncle Luke and others of the family who had passed on. With a chorus of *amens* around the room, bowed heads lifted, eyes opened, and chatter resumed. My own thoughts leaped into skeptical mode. I wondered why a life of routine prayer had not protected Uncle Luke from robbery and untimely death. But I understood that belief of any kind is a powerful and resilient thing.

Not really hungry, I waited through the line, selected a small paper plate, and helped myself to a slice of apple pie. With coffee and pie in hand, I wandered back to the dining room where I caught a glimpse of Terry and Jordan huddled in one corner like a pair of pigeons on a barn rafter. Both had their wallets and cell phones out, sharing family photos and pointing slyly across the congested room to match up pictures with living individuals. I impulsively gravitated toward them, parked my pie and coffee on a side table, and dragged up a chair. Terry may have been more technically savvy than Jordan, but it wasn't evident with the latest cell phone applications. That explained Terry's plastic accordion of photos. He giggled as it unfolded like a slinky and dangled down toward the floor.

Most of the pictures were of his two children, of whom he was remarkably proud. My eyes lingered on one shot of Heath, a handsome young buck wearing a ball cap and a T-shirt with an image of an Alien (from the movie by that title), teeth dripping saliva. Heath worked for Haliburton and had spent a lot of time in Afghanistan. Terry's lovely green-eyed daughter Hanna was a flight attendant with American Airlines. Both Heath and Hanna were single, Terry said, devoted to their careers. I noticed that he had said "my children" and not "our children," which seemed strange. He didn't mention their mother. I assume they were divorced. Grandma Greenwood had been a font of wisdom and traditional church truisms, like marriages are made in heaven, and God always has a plan. But it would appear that even God's plans don't always work out.

Looking around the room, my eyes spun as I tried to recognize faces and link children to parents, or grandparents. Passing time really does a stunt with your head. The mendacities of most of the conversations I overheard ranged from nostalgic to nauseating. But I knew it to be the stuffing that filled common down-to-earth life, particularly in small town and rural communities. Turning back to Terry and Jordan, I knew we had a lot of catching up to do. Our last time together was the end of December in 1968. The three of us boys, plus Christine, had struggled nearly fifty years to forget those bizarre and terrifying events.

On a whim, Jordan suggested we get out of the family circus and drive up to our old campsite. Jordan escorted me and Terry outside to his black Ford Expedition. We climbed in and headed across the back pasture. I leaned toward Jordan from my safe nest in the back seat. "Did you think to invite Christine on this little jaunt?"

"Yep, I did." Jordan shrugged nonchalantly, his eyes lifting to the mirror. "She said she didn't care to dredge up that particular truckload of memories. So, I just let it go."

"Fair enough." I gave him a perfunctory nod. On the left, we passed a fairly new metal barn. Through the open door I caught sight of a stainless-steel car in the shadows. "Is that a DeLorean?" I couldn't help sounding intrigued.

"Belongs to my son," Jordan said. "He's been collecting those stainless-steel lemons for a while now. I think he's got five more inside, some not complete.

"What's he plan to do with 'em?"

"He's rebuilt a couple, but mostly he strips 'em down and ships parts overseas. Besides being a farm manager, he's an international wheeler-dealer."

"Every time I see one," I said, "I'm reminded of that scene in *Back to the Future*. You know, with the fiery tire marks through the street in downtown Hill Valley. Funny name for a town."

Terry snorted and nodded, twisting in my direction. "I'd bet John DeLorean made more money on that movie deal than he did selling cars."

"Maybe so," I sniffed.

"Plus, he's got a '59 Cadillac convertible," Jordan added. "Belonged to Jayne Mansfield." His eyes lifted to the mirror, and I could make out a twist of a smile. "Lord only knows what that's worth."

"I mean no disrespect to her memory," I said, "but I guess that's not the one that ran into the back of a truck." I glanced at Terry, who nodded and winked.

"I'm sure not," Terry answered. "But big trailers these days all have a metal guard on the back, because of that accident. They call it a Mansfield Bar."

After a moment of awkward silence, I leaned forward to change the subject. "Now, your daughter is Jennifer?"

"Yep. She's up in Muskogee."

"Who is the Indian girl I met at the house? Poloma, I think."

Jordan's eyes met mine in the mirror. "That's Jared's wife. Our daughter-in-law." He paused before adding, "She's Choctaw."

I hesitated, not sure what to say. "Very lovely girl."

"She is, yes. But I'm not ashamed to say it's been a challenge."

"Why's that? This *is* Oklahoma, after all."

"The problem ain't from our side," Jordan snipped. "We think the world of her. It's her parents. From their point of view, she shamed them, like *unforgivably*. They disowned her. They literally look the other way whenever Jared's around."

"So, why the tension?"

"Well, sir, it's like this. Her folks are very staunch Christians; the hellfire and damnation type. A lot more intense than Grandma and Grandpa. Real strict and straitlaced. Jared and Poloma had dated, but they wanted her to marry an Indian boy—the son of their minister at church, who is also a tribal leader. But, come to find out, she was pregnant. And she fessed up that it was Jared's. The pastor's son broke up with her, his parents' doing I'm sure, and the whole church disowned her. We encouraged Jared to marry her, since she was carrying our grandchild." Jordan turned and looked over his shoulder in my direction. "Her parents didn't come to the wedding."

"Wow."

Jordan was quiet for a few seconds, brooding. Then he huffed. "So, today we have two half-breed grandchildren."

Terry snorted. "You see? It don't matter where you go to church. Shit still happens."

Jordan waved it off. "Like I said. It's her parents. We love those babies. Don't see 'em as often as we'd like. Most of the Indians... sorry, *Native Americans*... here in Oklahoma have adopted white Christian customs. Of course, most tribes always had free courting, rather than the match-making and bride-price of some ancient cultures. Indian kids date just like whites do. There's a lot of mixed marriages around here."

I hesitated before speaking again. "None of that bothers me. I hope you know that. But when she introduced herself, I got this weird feeling. Spooky, if you catch my drift. She reminded me of White Dove, our Aunt Dovie. And, I don't know how else to say it, I just felt… a presence."

Terry shot me a glance, but said nothing. And Jordan did not respond at all. My eyes drifted toward the side window as Jordan steered the big Ford along a double rutted trail, across the back pasture through tall patches of Johnson grass badly in need of mowing. Still visible were remnants of a military shooting range from WWII. For at least a minute or two we were all quiet, gazing out the widows, our mental wheels churning like those on the Ford.

Terry's voice broke into the thick silence. "What happened to the airport over by Gene Autry?"

"It's still there," Jordan answered, clearing his throat. "There's a big Dollar General Distribution Center there, and a few other businesses. One called King Aerospace. Not sure what they do. Anyway, the place is a lot bigger and busier than it was back… well, you remember when."

Terry stared intensely across the pasture. "Yep, I sure remember that place." He seemed pensive and morose; his tone portentous.

Jordan pulled to a stop at a galvanized metal gate. I jumped out to open it. There was no lock. Just a chain wrapped a couple of times around the frame, with the last link hooked over a nail. It swung open without assistance and stopped when the corner dug into dirt. Jordan eased the big Ford through.

"Make sure that's latched," he said, head hanging out the window. "One of the neighbors has a few head of cattle in this pasture, somewhere. Can't afford to let 'em out."

"Got it." I closed the gate and replaced the chain the way I had found it. As I hopped into the back seat, rear tires spun in loose dirt and the door slammed shut on its own.

"Yee-hah!!" Terry whooped, looking over his shoulder with a grin. Jordan accelerated along uneven and overgrown humps. A covey of quail scurried away from our tires, taking flight and gliding momentarily like the Wright Flier before settling into the safety of tall Johnson grass. We rumbled along rugged twin lanes of farm trail, climbing steadily up the southeastern edge of the Arbuckle Mountains. Jordan steered skillfully around loose rocks and along the high ridges among eroded gullies. Easing to a stop, he switched to four-wheel drive. Tires dug in as we jostled up a steep opening between two large boulders. The Ford rocked spasmodically, steadily climbing past a rocky outcrop and a thick cluster of jack oaks. Squadrons of cardinals lifted and colored the sky with speckles of fluttering red.

In the ancient gritty soil of eroded limestone hills, varieties of flora were limited. Post oaks and blackjacks were small, many clinging tenaciously to rocky slopes or in hundreds of meandering gullies. Black daleas, shortlobe oaks, and ash junipers flourished. Over the years, mesquite trees also had invaded the lower ridges of this and other hills in the region, migrating from Mexico mostly in cattle manure laden with seeds. Otherwise, the striated slopes were, as they had been for millennia: home to a variety of wild grasses, sagebrush, and prickly-pear cactus.

As we ascended, scant groves of trees opened up to bare rocky slopes, with a view across sprawling farmlands. To the west arose a line of wind generators, facing the sunset like alien robots surveying the checkered plains. I had noticed only one earlier, on the way to the farm. Clearly, there were many— evidence of technological progress even in this rustic environment. Looking eastward, stretching toward Gene Autry, the terrain appeared much the same as I recalled. Still mysterious, a monument to historical events unknown to many, but remembered vividly by a few.

We all had a better understanding of it now than we did growing up. Jordan, in particular, because he took college courses in that area of history. He could yammer on for hours if you got him started. Or if a thought crossed his mind, and he couldn't suppress the urge to share it. "It remains a point of interest" he said impulsively, "that the five so-called civilized tribes practiced slavery, you know, back before they were relocated. And they had to sign an agreement not to keep their black slaves, on pain of forfeiture of their land. Here and there you can find communities descended from black slaves who were freed after the tribes settled here."

"Does anybody coon hunt around here?" I asked, changing the subject. "I can see lots of big trees in those gullies and all along the apron. I guess Cool Creek is still lined with cottonwoods."

"I would think so," Jordan said casually. "Jared don't hunt anymore. Hounds are just too expensive to feed and care for, unless you're really into that. I used to love it." His eyes lifted to the mirror. "You remember my old Chevy pickup with the dog box in the back?"

I smiled. "Sure do. And I'll never forget that weekend at your house when the dogs got out and ran for miles through the neighborhood. They chased anything that moved or had a scent. Knocked one little neighbor kid right off his bicycle. Skinned his knees and elbows. His mamma was *not* happy about that."

"You know what? It took about five huntin' trips to get them boogers back on task. That one little jaunt up and down the streets, around houses, through yards, chasing cats and all. Nearly ruined 'em. They turned to trashin'."

"What's trashing?"

"Means trackin' somethin' besides coons," Jordan said assertively. "You know, like possums, skunks, deer. Not supposed to do that. Anyway, next time I took 'em to the woods, they tore out barkin' through the brush chasin' a dadgum squirrel. Forgot all about coon scent. My folks blamed me for letting 'em out, but I told them it was you." Jordan shot me an interrogating glance. "It *was* you, wasn't it?"

I threw up my hands. "Not me. I thought it was the garbage man. I was in the house watching TV. How old were we then?"

"Oh, I can't remember. Thirteen; fourteen maybe. That was before I had a driver's license. I rode a scooter."

I leaned forward. "What about you, Terry? Ever into that hillbilly shit?"

"You mean, driving a pickup?"

"No, Sarge." I wagged my head and tried to mimic a country hick drawl. "I'm talkin' about coon huntin.'"

"Nah," Terry answered coolly. "I'm a deer hunter. Can't eat a coon. Well, you can, but they're kinda' greasy and tough. Lotta black folks eat 'em. Possum, too. One of my close buddies in Nam was a really tough dude from Valdosta, Georgia. He told me his favorite Thanksgiving meal was possum and sweet taters." Terry looked my way and sniffed. "I ain't never been that hungry."

My head bobbed spontaneously. "I guess if you're dirt poor, you'll eat just about anything. I'll bet your folks told you the same stories we got, about growing up during the Great Depression." I tapped Jordan's shoulder. "Our grandparents had a tougher life than we can possibly imagine. Often, a couple of families ate together to pool their resources. And at the evening meal, the working men always ate first, then the women, and the kids got what was left. My dad said he was twelve before he knew a roasted chicken had anything but a neck and two feet. He never saw the rest of the chicken on the table."

Jordan and Terry chuckled. "Grandpa still hunts squirrels," Jordan said. "He says fried squirrel is lip-smacking good. I'm a country boy at heart, but I have to admit I'd rather have a burger and fries."

Ahead, the road ascended in a steep curve, deeply scarred by erosion and speckled with loose rocks. The Expedition pitched and clawed for traction. Jordan managed the wheel deftly as we inched our way to the crest, where the road widened and leveled out into a wide circle. We eased to a stop. Jordan killed the engine, just as a squadron of crows lifted from the bare branches of a tree and went cawing off down the slopes toward the woods. That was a sight and sound that lingered in my memory through the years; the ambiance of America's heartland. Before us stood a white cliff encircling a small water-filled crater— the old abandoned rock quarry, just as I remembered it. The crystal surface rippled in the breeze, glistening in the afternoon sunlight. Jordan pushed buttons one by one, and windows glided down. I drew in the fresh, cool air. We sat for a moment, mesmerized. Our eyes lifted to the rocky ridge above the quarry.

Impulsively, I broke the silence. "I looked at this side of the mountain on Google Earth before I left home. The letters of the Lazy S Ranch are clearly visible from up there in orbit." I pointed toward an assumed satellite above. "I made out lots of game trails, like little veins running in all directions. But I couldn't find any cave openings. Probably lost in the shadows."

"Ownership has changed several times," Jordan said, "but the old ranch stayed the same. Like an old lady who outlived several husbands but held onto her maiden name."

"Funny thing," I said. "From high above, this little mountain range looks like the carcass of a dragon that just died and settled into the plains. The rocks are like fossilized spines, and the head twists down, nostrils sniffing at Gene Autry's butt. I mean the town, of course."

"It's really not what you think of as mountains," Terry said. "More like a cluster of hills, sort of compacted together. What's that old country song?" He hummed a bit, almost beneath his breath. "Those Oklahoma hills where I was born." His voice dwindled and he shook his head and looked away.

"Pardon me for so many questions," I said. "What ever happened to the old bus we camped in. You parked it right over there, if my memory serves me right." Jordan and Terry turned heads in the direction of my gesture.

"Yep," Jordan said, popping his lips. "That's the spot, alright."

"As I recall," Terry said ponderingly, "Dad sold that bus to a hippie on his way to Woodstock. It had more room that the VW he was driving. In better shape, too."

"That's a hoot," I said, a smile lifting. "Sold it to a hippie, on his way to Woodstock." My mind drifted back, and I tried to picture the blue bus, with horses tied nearby. Campfire by the rock overhang. "That was a long time ago."

Terry chuckled, suddenly struck with another thought. His smiling face rotated in my direction. "Dad told the hippie the bus was painted blue because of Jim Morrison's song, *The End*. Apparently, that made the sale. Ya'll remember the Doors, right?"

Jordan grinned as the lyrics seeped out. "*The blue bus is calling us.*"

Again, we sat quiet. Eventually, I asked the question I could sense swelled in the Broca region of their brains. A question that neither Jordan nor Terry would venture. "Do you think anyone else has found *the* cave? I'm talking about Ghost Cavern?"

For a moment neither of them responded. The silence was palpable. Then Terry spoke, turning to face me.

"I doubt it. Probably never will. It's covered up."

Jordan and I exchanged puzzled looks. "What do you mean?" Jordan said. "How would you know that?"

"I hiked up there a couple of years back."

"You did?" Jordan's face twisted toward Terry. "You never mentioned that to me."

"What are you? My mother?"

"Well, all things considered, I'd think you'd tell me something like that."

"I dunno. It just didn't seem important." Terry huffed. "That was after the divorce, and I was dating Sue. I brought her to meet Grandma. I needed a little personal time. I'm sure you both know that feeling. On a sudden whim, I hoofed it up top to have a look-see. The hole is totally covered with rocks. The pair of small mountain cedars that were there before are now a thick cluster. Nobody passing by would possibly think there could be a cave there."

"Ya'll wanna hike up and see it?" Jordan said, just above a whisper.

Terry glanced at me. "What do you think?"

I shook my head. "Nah, I'd rather not." I checked my watch. "Besides, I really don't have time. It's getting late. We need to get back."

"You know something weird?" Jordan said, his face darkening. "Jared told me that the last time he saw Uncle Luke, he was talking about dying, and he said the strangest thing. *Just throw me in the Ghost Cavern. Part of me is already there."*

Terry leaned forward and twisted in the seat, casting an ominous look first at Jordan, then me. "I guess our secret wasn't really a secret. Uncle Luke knew about that place. Maybe he knew more than us."

Jordan shrugged. "I don't know. I wonder how come Grandpa and Grandma never said anything."

"Maybe they were afraid," I said.

Terry's mouth twisted studiously. "You know, I don't think Uncle Luke ever mentioned where Dovie is buried. There was no funeral that I knew of."

Jordan shook his head. "Heck, I sort of assumed her family took charge of that. You know, tribal customs and all. But still, it's strange we weren't invited."

We sat for a minute or so, hearing only the occasional tweet of a lark and the sound of our hearts thumping. I leaned my head out the window, scanning the rows of jagged rocks that ran almost due east and west. I thought to myself how limited a person's scope becomes, living in a large city on the west coast. Often the only scenery is what you see driving down a freeway. But even viewed from a small mountain like this, the western horizon stretched out enigmatically toward the sunset. To the south, I imagined looking all the way across the Red River and over a few rolling hills to Dallas. So near, yet so far. And not one soul anywhere out there knows the secrets held tight in these little Arbuckle hills.

Back at the farmhouse, Terry and I exchanged phone numbers. I hurried through the house, saying my goodbyes and well-wishes. I found Christine and commended her for learning to drive after such a rough start. Wary of another punch in the gut, I folded my arms over my abdomen as I said it. She laughed and playfully jabbed my arm with a soft fist. Her green eyes glistened as she grinned big and hugged me.

"Let's stay in touch," she said.

"Sure. We need to."

From there I spotted Poloma at the kitchen table, nursing a baby. I felt awkward, but I maneuvered through the crowd and laid my hand on her shoulder. Next to her, a two-year-old eyed me from his high-chair.

"I just wanted to say goodbye. It was a delight meeting you."

She looked up with a broad grin. "I am so glad you came. My father-in-law speaks highly of you."

"Thank you. We've been good friends nearly as long as we've been cousins."

"We didn't have that chat," she said. "Maybe I'll see you again."

"Perhaps so. It would be a delight."

I took a final scan of the room before making my exit. The sun was rapidly disappearing in the direction of New Mexico, leaving a bright orange and yellow rim on the flat western horizon. Dusk settled gracefully upon the farm. I climbed into the rental and backed out onto the sandy road, just as a large plague of boat-tailed grackles descended into a bur oak to roost for the night. Christine emerged from the screen door and sidled up next to Terry on the front porch, slipping an arm around his waist. Terry glanced at her, smiling, and threw an arm over her shoulder. Jordan wriggled his fingers and Terry lifted his chin in a casual nod. I tossed them a jaunty wave as I drove away.

The route back to Springer was intuitive. I turned left on Highway 77 and sighed nostalgically at the sight of the old stand pipe that marked the approach to Ardmore from the north. I had seen it many times when I was a child. Ten minutes later, I eased up in front of room 112 at the La Quinta. My flight out from DFW was at one o'clock the next afternoon, so I was under no pressure to rush. I found a bar within walking distance and had a couple of drinks in a corner booth. Then I shuffled back to the motel and went straight to bed. The next morning, I woke up at six thirty. I settled for coffee and a small dish of pineapple yogurt at the buffet, and I was on the road before eight.

Six

Driving south toward the Red River, I passed the WinStar Casino in Thackerville. Some people consider it a monument to the Native American gambling enterprise in Oklahoma. However, the sight of it took me back to our inauspicious outing up in the Arbuckles, for reasons that are hard to explain. Chills tickled my spine as a litany of memories ignited in my head— vignettes of various experiences I had tried to forget, and which Terry and Jordan were still reluctant to discuss. Christine too, I'm quite certain. Nonetheless, there was nothing I would or could have done differently, and over all these years I have felt no remorse. But I was fully aware that some of it had impacted my perception of reality and left me with questions yet to be answered.

Impulsively, I took the next exit, made a U-turn under the freeway, and headed back to the casino. After cruising around through the parking lot, I found an empty space near an entrance and eased tentatively to a stop. I sat for a while, thinking, remembering. When the urge hit me, I swung out of the Honda and marched toward the casino door. There were numerous gambling centers within a few hours' drive from Palo Alto, where I lived. However, Las Vegas was our favorite, and occasionally Meredith and I flew there for a weekend getaway. My game was blackjack, and both of us played the machines. But we had a strict rule that when either of us reached a net five-hundred-dollar loss, we would walk away and call it quits for that trip. However, in this particular casino, and on this particular occasion, I had no real urge to play. I just wanted to see the place.

Inside, I strolled around somewhat timidly, perusing rows of one-armed bandits with blinking lights, incessant mechanical tunes, and intermittent clinking as small winnings spat out rhythmically into metal trays. Most of the patrons had the appearance of my age and older, retirees with nothing better to do than waste their money hoping for the elusive big win. A heavyset man with a bald head, sandaled feet, and a floral shirt fed quarters into a machine, two and three at a time, while sipping a Mai Tai through a straw.

On a different row, a thin woman with a wrinkled face, layers of makeup, and long and brightly painted fingernails snuggled her bucket of winnings with one arm, while she took a long drag on her cigarette. While exhaling a column of smoke, she mechanically twisted the short stub and lip-stick laden filter into an ashtray full of smoldering butts.

Deciding to waste a few quarters, I selected a Double Diamond machine and sat down. After five or six spins, I won back ten dollars. My cheeks aglow with a modest feeling of accomplishment, I began gathering my winnings into a plastic bucket. I paused when I sensed someone approach. I turned and looked up. Standing over me was a young man, maybe thirty. His narrow face was softly framed by glistening black hair, long and straight, resting atop his shoulders. He was Native American, I was certain. I acknowledged him politely with a smile, a nod, and a casual *howdy*, and turned back as if to resume play. He remained uncomfortably near me. I could feel his dark eyes like lasers burning holes through my brain. My sense of discomfort increasing, I twisted toward him and looked up. "Were you playing at this machine? I'm sorry if I took your spot. I can move."

"Oh, no. I don't play." He smiled, and his ebony eyes wrinkled at the corners. Otherwise, he stood motionless, feet firmly planted. Then he lifted an arm and leaned casually against the machine next to me. "You don't know me, do you?" he said.

"I don't believe so," I answered. No doubt puzzlement was written all over my face. I studied him, wondering if he had seen me at the funeral. But I was sure we hadn't actually met. Maybe he was kin to Poloma.

"I know you," he said, his smile disappearing. His eyes locked on mine as if he sought entrance to my very soul. A chilling sensation washed over me and my chest caved in. In an instant, the entire casino zoomed outward and all I could see were his dark, penetrating eyes. His surrealistic presence drew me under a terrifying spell. Leaning toward me menacingly, he spoke again.

"I'm Tim Rain Cloud. Remember the blue school bus?" His manner and voice taunted. He leaned closer. "The Indian pony merry-go-round? You were on the inside looking out."

A sudden plume of nausea rose into my throat. The room, with a thousand machines and a million blinking lights, spun around me. The confrontation was beyond awkward, or even bewildering. It was terrifying. I was virtually a stranger to these parts, and even among my own relatives I knew almost no one. I hadn't been anywhere in Oklahoma in decades. How could this man claim to know me? Or to know an obscure and personal event from my youth? I swallowed heavily and caught my breath. The spinning sensation subsided. My eyes refocused and I studied the Indian stranger, head to toe.

He wore a western shirt, faded jeans, and sharp toed cowboy boots. I noted his oval turquoise belt buckle, very popular in the southwest. The teardrop by his left eye did not appear to be a tribal tattoo, but rather, the sort of symbolic art common among prison inmates. This guy had done time, I was certain, which made me all the more uncomfortable. I swiveled in the seat and fell back against the slot machine, as if his very presence forced me. My heart raced. I swallowed heavily, unable to speak.

At that moment I felt a tap on the shoulder. Startled, I stood up and wheeled around to face a redhead in a casino uniform, holding a tray of empty glasses.

"Can I get you a drink?" she said, smiling politely.

With the sound of her voice, my head began to clear. The noise of slot machines returned, with their rhythmic tunes and discordant clinking. I stammered, trying to respond. "No thanks. I'm not here long. I'll be on the road soon." She smiled and casually turned away. I spun back in the direction of the Indian. He was gone.

Leaving my few winnings behind, I bounded toward the exit. Heads turned as I roared through aisles of slot machines and gaming tables, and past a crowded bar. Sweat pouring, I burst through the double glass doors into bright sunlight. The security guard scrutinized me until I stopped on the sidewalk and bent over to catch my breath. Hands on knees, head hung low, I felt rattled and confused. I looked back to see the guard turn away and disappear into the sea of lighted slot machines. My head still reeling, I found my way back to my rented Honda, unlocked the door, and fell into the driver's seat. Instinctively, I slammed the door out of sheer paranoia. My face aflame and shoulders tight, I struggled to draw in a breath. A sharp pain gripped my chest. Perspiration flooded my face. Fear gripped me. I thought I was having a heart attack.

I tilted my head back on the leather headrest and closed my eyes. In a few moments, the pain subsided. But my brain was still on fire with questions. *Who was that guy? How could a man that young claim to have seen me up in the Arbuckles fifty years ago?* Five minutes passed. Maybe more. I opened my eyes, feeling more at ease. My heart rate and breathing had slowed.

Sensing movement near the car, I lifted my eyes to the left where a graceful image approached, striding on high heels. A dark-haired woman in short leather skirt and a sheer white top. Obviously, no bra. Long black hair cascaded over her shoulder. She slowed as she stepped close to the driver's side window and rapped on the glass with long painted fingernails. I pressed the button and eased down the glass. She leaned toward me, her firm breasts loosely exposed in the open blouse, and she rested a forearm along the window trim. Her face leaned toward mine. Her dark eyes glistened, accentuated by eyeliner, long fake lashes, and gold tint on her lids. A cloud of cheap perfume wafted into the open window.

"Want a date?" she purred. "I'm available for a couple of hours." Her voice dripped honey. She batted her long lashes and leaned seductively closer. "Got time?"

"No thanks," I answered, clearing my throat. "You're certainly beautiful, and tempting, but I have a plane to catch in Dallas. Heading home to my wife."

"Pity." Her eyes rolled. She flipped her hair as she pushed away from the car and turned back toward the casino. I watched her shapely hips rotate with each long stride, spike heels clicking. I assumed she was offended. But, a few steps away, she tossed a smile over her shoulder, nose in the air. "That *was* the right answer. Good boy."

Puzzled, I started the engine and glanced in the mirror before pulling away. When I looked again, the only person in sight was an old Indian woman with a faded blanket draped over her shoulders. I accelerated out of the parking lot, narrowly missing another car. The driver of a Schneider eighteen-wheeler laid on his horn as I turned in front of him, crossed under the freeway, and made a hard left turn onto the service road.

Still dazed and disoriented, I accelerated southward. Traffic was light. Far ahead, I could see a big rig, twin stacks blowing black smoke. A blue Chevy coupe lingered a hundred yards behind me. Then suddenly two figures stood at the side of the road ahead. Although I approached them rapidly, I could see it was the same Indian with the teardrop tattoo who'd confronted me in the casino, and the old woman I had just seen in the parking lot. The man held up a sign. I figured it would be one of those pleas for a donation, poorly scrawled with a marker, like *Please Help a Veteran;* or maybe *God Bless You for Car-*

ing. Instead, there were the words, clear as a bell, in bold ornate script like a tombstone from the twelfth century: **Don't Write, Don't Tell.** Goosebumps rose on my arms. My thinning hair stood up. I pulled off the freeway, wheels dropping into packed dirt. I slammed on the brakes and skidded to a halt. Dust drifted over the top and settled on the hood. When the dust cleared, I looked in the mirror. No one there. I leaped out of the car and twisted around to scan every direction. The highway and median were silent and empty. It was as if the tattooed Indian and the old woman had disappeared into thin air. In a daze, I climbed back into the car and eased onto the freeway, accelerating to a comfortable seventy mph.

I don't recall crossing the Red River, or much of anything, until I reached the toll gate at DFW Airport. Everything behind me for the previous couple of hours was a blur. I had intended to take a quick drive through Denton. Maybe see the old neighborhood where Spencer and I grew up. Or our high school, which held so many fond memories. But I was too shaken. I had cruised right past it without even a curious glance. Certainly, there had been a lot of development in and around my college alma mater, called North Texas State University back then. I had majored in English literature. I was thinking of a career in journalism, but I wasn't sure what specific kind. I was certain I didn't want to be a war correspondent, which is what Terry and Uncle Luke had suggested. I was no draft dodger, and I wasn't afraid to fight for my country. I just didn't have that *born on the Fourth of July* spirit to go fight a war I didn't understand.

I had moved to *liberal* California immediately after college, but not to get away from friends and relatives or even to help detach myself from the ordeal in the Arbuckles, many years before. It had more to do with falling in love with Meredith, the woman of my dreams. Yet, even there, for several years I had a lingering fear of ruthless people who, if they were inclined to do so, could track any one of us down no matter how far we traveled or how well we hid. Over the years, I occasionally woke up in the night imagining a presence not of this world. But always, when I cleared my head, there was nothing.

However, if the story is to be told, I suppose I'm the one to do it. And I'm certain such a story will be less technical than a travelogue of a Scandinavian river-cruise, which was the sort of stuff I wrote every day. I would need to study legal records, family Bibles, and news clippings from the 60s to jog my memory. And, of course, I would consult at length with Jordan, Terry, and Christine, now that we've reconnected. Christine had already mentioned a journal she'd found among Uncle Luke's legal documents. Of course, that would help. But this was not a biography of Lucas Tatum Greenwood, or any sort of ancestral memoir. It was something else.

Just before noon, I left the rental car at Avis and took a shuttle to Terminal A. Once I found my gate, I plopped into a chair, flipped open my laptop, and started making notes of every detail I could recall from that one week in late December, and its baffling aftermath. It was an experience we four cousins had tried our very damnedest to forget, but it wouldn't go away.

Plain and simple, this was a ghost story.

Part 2: Premonition

Seven

On the morning of Christmas Eve, 1968, my brother and I did our last-minute shopping at the Montgomery Ward department store in Denton, while Mom began baking pies in preparation for Christmas dinner. At the same time Dad pretended to be busy with essential chores around the house.

Meanwhile, something else was taking place in Muskogee, Oklahoma, some two hundred miles to the north. It was the beginning of a chain of events that would impact my life more than I could possibly imagine. A few restless students at the Parkview School were wrapping up class, eager for the early closure. Most were in a queue at the front door, waiting to be collected by parents for Christmas break. Four others, however, sat in the library working on a research project. This particular school had a solid reputation for advanced techniques in instructing students who were either partially or totally blind, and the program drew students from all over the state and beyond. The majority were subsidized by government funding and charitable foundations, but a few came from affluent families who could afford the high-dollar boarding and tuition. Among the latter was a sixteen-year-old Chickasaw girl known as White Dove.

A man and woman appeared at the double doors leading from the entry hall to the library. The square-jawed man in his mid-thirties wore a pale blue leisure suit and a flowered shirt. His short-cropped hair and muscular physique gave him a military appearance. Leading the way, the stiff-faced woman was dressed in a business suit, and her auburn hair was tied back in a bun. She exuded an air of confidence and authority. Tucked under one arm, she carried a black leather binder. A name tag pinned above her left breast read S. Osceola, MD.

The pair stood in the doorway, eyes scanning the room. They were aware that the school was constantly visited by parents, medical personnel, health inspectors, and school board officials. For that reason, they were confident the staff would pay them little attention. However, one teacher noticed them and dutifully stepped in their direction. Janet Dewberry, so her name tag read. "Good morning. May I help you?" she said, smiling pleasantly.

"Yes, please," the woman responded, putting out her hand. "I'm Doctor Osceola. I work with the Oklahoma Tribal Authority, and we're here to pick up one of your students. Her Chickasaw name is *puchi yo-shoba tohbi.*" She paused. "That means White Dove, or something close to that. But I think she's registered here as Whitney James."

Dewberry took her hand and released it after a curt squeeze. "Yes, Miss James is a sweet girl. Easy to work with, and very bright. I'm sure it's difficult for her, having so many names. Is there a problem?"

"Nothing serious, we hope," the doctor answered with a reassuring smile. "Her uncle Overton James, I'm sure you're acquainted with him, said she phoned and wasn't feeling well. He's very protective, as you may know. Besides, she's due at a family Christmas Eve gathering, and he thought it best for me to check her over. Then, if all is well, we'll escort her to the family residence. This gentleman is Daniel Jones, one of Governor James' security guards."

The teacher studied the driver from head to toe before resuming dialogue with the doctor. "Do you have a written order from Mr. James?"

"Of course," Osceola replied. She opened the black portfolio, drew out a single-page document, and handed it to the teacher.

Dewberry perused the single paragraph, lingering on the signature. Looking up, expressionless, she handed it back. "Yes, that looks like Mr. James' signature and seal. Whitney is right over there. She seems fine, but let me get her."

The young Indian female was sitting at a table with two other girls slightly younger. She wore a plaid school skirt and white blouse. Her long, dark hair was tied with blue ribbons in matching pigtails. A book lay open on the table and her lithe fingers glided over Braille embossing. Her dark eyes stared blankly in the direction of the page. Miss Dewberry stepped lightly toward her. Jones cast a shifty glance toward the doctor before he turned, strode briskly into the entry hall, and looked in both directions.

The teacher laid a gentle hand on White Dove's shoulder, and spoke softly into her ear. "You have guests. Let me help you join them."

White Dove closed the book and rose to her feet. The teacher took her arm and led her in the direction of the visiting doctor, who stood with lifted chin and a stiff posture. She regarded both teacher and student with cold, expressionless eyes. With her free arm, White Dove swept a guide stick along her path until a tug on her arm by the teacher signaled her to stop just short of striking the visitor's leg.

"Sweetheart, this is Doctor Osceola."

"Doctor Osceola?" White Dove repeated. "I don't know you."

"No, we haven't met. I'm a specialist. We're going to stop by my office for a few simple tests, and then get you over to your uncle's home for the big party. First, I need to ask you a few questions." Her eyes drifted lazily toward the teacher. "Why don't you join us? We'll try to be brief. Is there a room nearby?"

"Yes, of course. Follow me."

With White Dove on her arm, Miss Dewberry led the visitors down a hallway and into a vacant classroom. She directed the girl toward a chair. White Dove eased down. At the same time, from behind, a hand slapped a cloth over the teacher's mouth and nose. Her startled eyes widened, blinked, and then closed. After she slumped lifelessly to the floor, Jones dragged her to the side. White Dove tilted her head at the bizarre sound of heels squeaking across the polished floor.

Osceola then tipped a small bottle into a folded cloth, dispensing an anesthetizing dose of methoxyflurane. Stepping cautiously behind White Dove, the doctor slapped the cloth over her mouth and nose and held it firmly. White Dove grimaced and her fists clinched, but she quickly succumbed to the vapors. As she slumped, unconscious and limp, Jones scooped her into his arms. Osceola led the way hurriedly out of the classroom and down the hall, away from the crowded front door. They exited through a side door and descended cement steps to a secluded parking area. A dark blue panel van stood with engine running and the side door open. Jones hoisted White Dove into the van, laying her roughly on a thin foam cushion in the floor, while Osceola climbed into the front passenger seat. As Jones jogged away, a large man in coveralls slammed the side door, hurried around to the driver's side, and climbed behind the wheel. Just as they sped away, the school principal and two teachers burst out the doors in a panic, frantic eyes following the blue van as it disappeared out the back gate. Tugging a cap low over his eyebrows, Jones observed from inside a tan Toyota, parked at a distance on the street. While parents came and went, picking up children, Jones drove away slowly.

Never before in the history of this illustrious school had a student been abducted. Within minutes, the event sent a wave of fear and anxiety among staff and students. Official vehicles began arriving—the Muskogee Police Department, Sheriff's Department, Oklahoma Highway Patrol, and, of course, the Department of Human Services. Within an hour, two men in suits arrived from the Federal Bureau of Investigation. They all crowded into an empty classroom for a briefing. The school's superintendent, Dr. Gerald Abernathy, stood with the still-groggy instructor, Janet Dewberry, and fielded questions from numerous individuals.

The drive from Muskogee to the airport in Gene Autry must have taken close to three hours. Early in that tense excursion, the woman posing as a doctor twisted out of her seat and hovered over White Dove. Awkwardly, she changed the unconscious girl into a cotton two-piece track suit, and then tied her hands behind her. She added a scarf blindfold, out of sheer habit, and covered her with a blanket.

Once they arrived at their destination, she and her partner escorted White Dove from a parking area along a cement walkway, through a metal door, and along a corridor with several turns. White Dove was confident she was at an airport, detecting the sound of a jet engine along a taxiway and the more distant sound of a single-engine plane roaring as if taking off. Inside an office, the woman shoved White Dove down into a metal chair, leaving her hands tied and her eyes covered. Immediately, a man eased close and bent over her.

"Hey, little darling," he said tauntingly into her ear. "I know you're confused by all this. We don't intend to hurt you, but we need you to cooperate. If you don't, you might guess what could happen to you. It won't be pleasant, I assure you."

To White Dove's ears, his voice was mellow and confident, somewhat refined. She sniffed, drawing in the fragrance of Brute aftershave that scarcely covered the stale smell of cigarettes on his breath and clothes, or the less offensive smell of Brylcreem in his hair. She turned her face away. "I assume you could kill me," she said stoically. "Or torture me. But I doubt that's your purpose."

The man stood up and eased back. "You're right. I have no interest in torturing you. I don't need or want to harm you in any way. You are, how shall I put it? A valuable asset. And leverage in an important negotiation."

"You do realize that a blindfold is not necessary, right? I'm blind."

The man thought for a moment and then snapped his fingers.

The woman tugged at the knot at the back of White Dove's head and slipped the scarf away from her face.

"What, exactly, do you hope to gain if not some sort of ransom." White Dove asked, smiling in unruffled defiance.

"You sound like an intelligent girl. But that can be a disadvantage if you try to outthink me or fenagle your way out of this situation. You can't, on either point. I ask you to just acquiesce to the circumstances, and you'll survive unharmed. But the issues and reasons are beyond your need to know. At least, at this point."

White Dove's lips tightened and she held her tongue. She did not know this man, but she had heard her uncle speak of numerous unscrupulous individuals in Oklahoma, ranging from entrepreneurs to enterprising politicians. Some were opposed to the advancements of Indian rights and business opportunities. Others wanted a piece of the action. White Dove tilted her head at the sound of the same man's voice across the vacant room. He spoke in a muffled tone.

"Take the van to somewhere in the Arkansas hills and torch it. You," he directed his words to someone else, "follow him in the truck, then bring him back here. There's more work to do."

"I need to go to the bathroom, badly," White Dove said through gritted teeth.

She heard fingers snap and the footsteps of a woman approaching. As she stepped close, White Dove was confident she was the same woman who had abducted her. Same heavy heels. Same smell. Same voice. "Okay, stand up. Let's go." One hand gripped White Dove's upper arm as the woman escorted her out and down a vacant-sounding hall, through a door, and into a cold room with a repulsive odor like industrial waste. The woman untied her hands and helped her into a stall. Then she stood by the door and waited. White Dove could hear the woman's body pressing against the metal toilet panels. When she heard the toilet flush, the woman opened the door and retied White Dove's hands.

Back in the stench of the hallway, White Dove felt a larger presence hover over her. A different man gathered her into his muscular arms and carried her outside. Maybe it was the same large man who loaded her into the van at the school. She had been groggy, then. Not now. Her body rested against his massive and blubbery stomach. She listened to his footsteps and noted his movements. He walked with a clumsy, simian sway. He wore heavy boots that clunked twice as the heel, then the outer sole, met the cement walkway. She felt a light but cold breeze and, at the same time, the warm sun on her face.

The man who carried her was accompanied by still another man, younger, with the same voice she'd heard when she was taken from the school. He seemed to have an athletic gait, moving faster than the fat man. His legs swung evenly and his feet landed softly, rolling with each step. He wore athletic shoes.

The two thugs loaded White Dove into a four-door Jeep Wagoneer. White Dove was certain of the make of the vehicle—the lack of insulation in the panels, the metallic resonance of the door latches, the sound of the engine, and the singing of the tires. One of her older cousins had a Jeep very much like this one. His was red, he had told her. She had no way of determining color, but she remembered red from childhood. A very bold and distinctive color.

In addition to excellent hearing and keen mental acumen, White Dove was well informed concerning Oklahoma's topography. She had traced the details of a three-dimensional map with hills, flatlands, rivers, and lakes. Her uncle had commented often that she knew the state better than a civil engineer. She felt the movement of the vehicle with each turn, and she noted the texture of the road beneath, whether cement, asphalt, gravel, or dirt.

Traveling down from Muskogee was difficult to trace. But, once she heard mention of the town Gene Autry by someone in the building at the airport, she knew her general location and could trace her route from that point, even tied up and lying on her side in the back seat of a moving vehicle. The younger man drove. The heavier man sat in the passenger seat, pushed back near her face. White Dove could hear his labored breathing.

They left the municipal airport driving east on Highway 53, before turning north on Highway 177. They made a left turn onto a gravel road, and the heavier man made the mistake of mumbling *Nebo School.* White Dove heard the name. From there they followed a westward route, then north again, before a monotonous stretch that eventually passed through a small hamlet White Dove was certain to be Dougherty. The highway crossed the Washita River, which meandered southward from that point, following a natural crevasse at the eastern base of the Arbuckle Mountains. After crossing the bridge, they immediately slowed almost to a halt and made a sharp left turn. From there, they followed a narrow dirt road, typically used only by ranchers. It meandered upward, past a Boy Scout campground no longer in use, then narrowed further to a two-rutted lane up the eastern slopes of the Arbuckles.

Lying still in the back seat, White Dove lifted her head in the direction of the driver. "Why are you guys taking me up into the Arbuckles? We're nowhere near Turner Falls. What's the point?" The driver's head snapped to the right, and the two men gazed at each other bewildered. "How the hell would you know where we're going?"

White Dove sniffed in amusement. "It's a gift."

Eight

Two days later on Thursday, the morning after Christmas, I was oblivious to any such events. It was my observation that Texas journalists paid little attention to the hillbilly state to the north, unless it concerned the Red River Shoot Out between the big universities, UT and OU, or a tornado that leveled half of Oklahoma City. If there was any news about a kidnapping in Muskogee, I didn't catch it.

Dad slept in that morning. He and Mom were sick the day of Christmas. Some sort of flu bug, they said, that came on suddenly. Mom had cooked, but neither she nor Dad felt like eating. It was an unusual Yuletide, that's for sure. Spencer and I had Christmas dinner in front of the television, and then I packed gear for my trip. The plan was to meet my cousins at our grandparents' farm and then ride up into the Arbuckle Mountains and camp for a few days. My dad's nifty two-horse bumper-pull trailer, with slant load and double wheels, was perfect for such a cowboy excursion. The nose compartment had space for saddles and tack. I tossed my camping gear into the bed of my Ford Ranger, along with a sack of feed.

So, with a moderate Christmas cheer hangover, I loaded up two horses and headed north out of Denton. As I left the house, Spencer was sprawled on the living room couch watching *Mission Impossible*. And like all our friends, he would simply kill time until the first of the bowl games started on Saturday. The Gator Bowl was popular. Alabama versus Missouri, that year. My cousins were all devoted to OU, this year facing SMU in the Bluebonnet Bowl in Houston. I was more interested in the Cotton Bowl on New Year's Day which, that year, would be between Texas and Tennessee. I planned to be home for that game. But right now, the Oklahoma hills were calling.

Putnam's Gulf station squatted between a 7-Eleven and a McDonalds on the northbound service road of I-35, only a couple of miles from our place. I stopped there to fill up the gas tank and empty my bladder before heading north. As my pickup and trailer rig eased to a stop, I spotted my friend Fred in the workshop beneath what appeared to be a red Chevrolet, perched precariously on the rack. He turned and ducked out toward me, adjusting his cap and dragging a grimy sleeve under his nose.

"Mornin' Russ." He tossed up a hand. "Ain't you going the wrong way?"

"Nope." I slid out of the seat and slammed the door behind me. "Goin' north." I ran my fingers through my hair, which felt odd and breezy after a fresh cut on Christmas Eve. Lately, I wore it in a fashionable collegiate style. But I had no expectations of maintaining that clean and intellectual look on a trip like this. I levered on my brown felt Stetson, right down to my ears, and shoved out my hand for a shake.

"Now, I don't want to go pryin'," Fred said, gripping my knuckles. "But where the hell up north are you headed?" Fred was a strange kid, even if I did consider him a good friend. Skinny as a snake, with an Adams apple that stuck out like the nose of a Studebaker. He casually lifted his knobby elbows and propped greasy knuckles on his hips, waiting for an answer. In a sudden flash, he remembered his job and my purpose for stopping at the gas station.

"Want me to fill 'er up?" he said sheepishly.

"Sure. To the top. How come you're not home playing with your Christmas presents?"

Fred grinned and pointed toward a '59 Chevy convertible on the rack. "That's it, sittin' right there. Dad paid half down. But I gotta make payments on the balance."

"Nice. What's it got? Big block? Four-on-the-floor?"

"Nah, automatic and a 283. Strictly chick bait." Fred grinned. "Just look at those fender skirts. That pretty beast will never see a drag strip. The only rubber burning will be in the back seat, if you catch my drift."

I tossed up a hand. "I get the picture. Your personal love machine. No details required, or requested."

"You got it." He punched my arm lightly with the same fist that had wiped his nose a moment earlier. "You didn't say where you're off to with that pair of nags." Fred glanced at the horses as he shoved the nozzle down my pickup's thirsty gullet. "Can't use but one, unless you're a trick rider. But I think that's a girl thing, ain't it?"

"Going up into the Arbuckles with my cousins," I said. "Deer hunting and a little Daniel Boone-type exploring."

Fred set the handle and let the pump run. "Hunting, I get. But, what's to explore?" He pointed forward in another impulsive segue. "You want me to check under the hood?"

"Nah, it's good. Serviced it last week. But I do need air in the trailer tires. Looks like Barney and Ginger had too much Christmas dinner." I dug the Gulf credit card out of my wallet and handed it to Fred. "I'll check the tires while you do that." I pointed crisply at the pump. "Don't let it run over, now."

"I won't, I promise." Fred's eyes scanned the card. "Russell T. Barnett," he read out theatrically, rocking on his heels. "Got your own card, now. What's the T stand for?"

"Thurman. My dad's name. Got an American Express, too. That was my first."

Fred pulled a *la-ti-da* face and wagged his hips.

"No biggie," I said, waving him off. "But I plan to use it sparingly. Dad says credit cards are the way of the future, but according to him, it's more of a gimmick to sucker you into deep debt. So, I've made up my mind not to let that happen."

"They need to make 'em outa' tougher plastic," he said, waving the card at me. "I've done split a couple in the machine, and customers got really pissed."

"I can imagine. But it might help if you'd stop yanking that handle across like you're breaking down a tire."

Fred ignored my jibe and rested an arm on the pump, giving me a curious look. "Why the Arbuckles? They ain't hardly what you'd call real mountains. Just a bump in the road between Norman and the Red River. Sort of a last reminder of their sorry roots when the Sooners head down to the Cotton Bowl to get their asses kicked."

"I suppose some people would see it that way." I squatted with one heel under a butt cheek and shoved the air nozzle onto a valve stem. A slow stream of air sang its way into the trailer tire. "America's got some crazy high ranges. If you're looking for a big adventure or a new lease on life, like Jeremiah Johnson. You just *ride due west as the sun sets and turn left at the Rocky Mountains.* And hearing the cry of an eagle in the Tetons, or trekking the Appalachia Trail, or stalking elk in the Alleghenies like you're the last of the Mohicans... that's all very special stuff."

"Wow," Fred said. "Did you just make that up?"

I chuckled, before twisting the cap onto a valve stem and flipping the stiff air hose to the other side of the trailer. "No, I read a lot of travel magazines. I did a paper on that, last semester. It's still fresh on my mind. But it's true. And you know what? Oklahoma holds some of America's best kept secrets, and a few are right there in that little bump in the road, as you call it."

"Like what?" Fred said. He squinted quizzically, insisting an answer.

"Wouldn't be a secret if I told you, now, would it?"

"Aw, don't be like that."

"Heh." I waved him off. "It's no top-secret mission. Just outlaw hideouts, dead men's bones, bats, and... shit like that."

"Ghosts, maybe?"

"Nah. I'm not interested in that baloney. Looking for real life, and real history."

Fred nodded musingly as he returned my card with the slip on a plastic clipboard. I scribbled a semblance of my name and handed it back, as I turned and climbed into my pickup. My grease-laden friend stood bent-legged, scratching under his cap with one hand and waving with the other.

I pulled out onto the service road and accelerated up the ramp onto the freeway, aware of the horses shifting around before they settled in at about sixty miles per hour. Passing the *Welcome to Denton* sign at the northern edge of town, I twisted the knob on the radio to 1440 am to pick up Clyde Sebastian's golden oldies. KDNT was Denton's radio station, and Clyde was usually on from noon 'til three. I liked his gig.

Moving to Texas in '58 did not result in detachment from my Oklahoma cousins. I was still close enough for us to get together occasionally. My dad was a building contractor, wanting bigger opportunities than those in a small town like Ardmore. The Interstate 35 corridor, north out of Ft. Worth and Dallas, promised a great deal of expansion, converging in Denton near the campus of NTSU. Denton was clearly a good location. Before we moved, he located a twenty-acre property west of town, with a horse barn. The house was old, but Mom fell in love with it. So, we moved in and started a new life. Spencer and I went through high school in Denton, so that became our hometown. But, whenever somebody asked where we were from, my dad always answered, "Oklahoma, but we got to Texas as quick as we could."

Driving along, I thought about Freddie's mention of ghosts. By high school, I had pretty much dismissed the supernatural, in general. I had never seen an angel—at least, none of which I was *aware*, to draw from that familiar text in the Book of Hebrews. Nor had I ever witnessed a miracle. Our mom was sorely disappointed when I told her I couldn't be certain there was a God somewhere "up there," since I couldn't see evidence anywhere "down here."

The idea of a supreme being, the ultimate source and intelligent cause behind the cosmos, seemed plausible. But not a capricious and vengeful deity like the God described by preachers at church. My dad laughed and said, "The boy's got a mind of his own." Mom didn't buy that assessment, convicted by her own upbringing that it was her duty to raise me and my brother Spencer in *the nurture and admonition of the Lord*. She believed if she taught us right, we would remain on the narrow path to everlasting life. If we didn't prove faithful, it was either her fault, my dad's fault, or both. Since she was the one who took us to church and Sunday School every week, she had concluded that my personal descent along heresy road was my dad's fault. He was just not a spiritual man.

In my opinion, Dad was a good-hearted man and in less traditional terms, a pretty smart dude. But as far as parenting goes, he and Mom were like most other couples. From marriage on to family, they flew by the seat of their britches and learned as they went along. Spencer and I were their subjects in experimental parenthood. And I think Dad assumed that personal knowledge and wisdom were transferred to children by osmosis. That's why he imagined I would be responsible with a credit card. I tried, but like a child in the big department store called America, my hunger for *stuff* sometimes got the better of me.

The Winchester 30/30 on the gun rack in the pickup was an example. I wasn't much of a hunter. I had a 30.06 with a scope, considered the best all-around hunting rifle in the world. But I needed something that would fit snugly in a saddle scabbard. Something easy to draw out on horseback and aim with open sights if there was a need. I didn't buy it to hunt game, but possibly to shoot varmints. And, of course, for self-defense. I considered a Western-style lever action rifle to be reliable and quick against any predator, man or beast.

I had just turned twenty, so I slapped down my American Express card and walked out of Thompson's Sporting Goods with a new rifle and two boxes of ammo. I promised Dad I would pay off any big purchases within three months. So far, I had made good on that promise. But it wouldn't last. He knew it, better than me. Like other guys my age, I had more courage and confidence than brains, and there was a lot of education coming down the pike that a guy just couldn't get in school, even in university.

My dad had grown up poor. His father had been a welder until he had the unusual good fortune to take over a homestead near Paul's

Valley. So, Dad and his brother Harvey grew up on that farm. They were in the Army during WW II, the big one, as they called it, where they served in the Philippine battles of Manila and the Layte Gulf. But their character was molded while plowing rocky soil behind a mule and helping their parents claw out a living during the Great Depression. Spencer and I had heard those stories until we wanted to puke.

Dad found an opportunity with the Works Progress Administration, as a common laborer during the construction of Lake Murray. He also took great pride in having worked on the Hardy Murphy Coliseum in Ardmore, which opened for business in 1937 as the Municipal Exhibition Building. For the first ten years it had no roof, and one year a rodeo bull jumped from the arena floor into the grandstand, charged up the steps through spectators, and leaped off the top row into the parking lot below. No one was injured, but the bull broke two legs and had to be put down. My mother and her sister, my Aunt Dorcas, worked the fairgrounds there, selling hotdogs and chips.

Dad had associated with some famous people in his younger days, although he never got a slice of the *big money* pie. He was a friend of Hardy Murphy himself. They rode together in rodeo grand entries and parades. Their associates included Birdie Pruitt, Gene Autry, Roy Rogers, and Oklahoma's other famous cowboy philosopher, Will Rogers. Like a lot of his friends, Dad loved horses. When we moved to Texas, he determined to have a piece of land big enough to grow grass and maintain a few cows and a couple of reliable saddle horses. But, growing up on a farm, he had enough of plowing and hauling hay.

We had three horses, but Buck, an aging palomino, was Dad's pet and he did not work. The other two, still young and adept at trail rides, were back there in the trailer. Barney was a bay with a white star and four white socks, nine years old and as lovable as a golden retriever. Mom typically rode Barney, because at only fourteen hands, it was easier for her to get into the saddle. I could swing up on him without putting a boot in the stirrup. My mare (named Ginger) was taller than Barney, and a lot faster. A beautiful buckskin, we got her from a neighbor who was training her as a roper. But she couldn't get the hang of backing up to keep a rope taut. Dad concluded that her nature was more typical of a neonatal nurse than a roping horse. Every time he roped a calf, she wanted to go see that it was okay. He said her maternal instinct was stronger than her work ethic. But we found out later that she had chronic tendonitis, and the sudden halt and backup maneuver in calf roping was painful. After the skidding halt, she had to ease forward to walk it off. Otherwise, she was an excellent saddle horse with a good nature and a comfortable lope.

Mom still kept all my childhood photos in neat folders on a bookshelf. One I remember clearly is me sitting on a Shetland pony, my dad standing close by. I must have been about three. Spencer was a baby. But we only started riding seriously in our teens. At school in Denton, I was president of the local rodeo club and I saw a lot of injured horses. That put me off rodeo, in general. My one and only attempt at bull riding ended in a broken collarbone and torn rotator cuff. My mom said that if God had intended me to ride bulls, He surely would have given me bowed legs and a coil spring for a spine. Maybe some guys are built that way; I don't know. But that one short ride knocked me out of football in my senior year.

It also gave me a medical deferment from the draft—not that I needed or wanted an excuse. Like several close friends, I'd tested out of the draft and planned to stay in college and support the war from a distance. As a weekend cowboy, I settled for the occasional gig as a pickup rider. My favorite big event was the Fort Worth Stock Show and Rodeo, which dated back to 1896. My dad, Spencer, and I rode together in the grand entry last February, and we planned to be there again for the next one in two months, come Hell or high water.

As I look back on those days, it now seems like a different century. There I was, driving up the freeway with a Western-style Ruger .38 wrapped in a tooled scabbard on the seat, and a gun rack across the back window of the pickup cradling a rifle and a shotgun, clearly visible from a city block away. The war in Vietnam was raging, as were protests here at home. But where I lived, a full gun rack in a pick-up window was a common sight. Nobody gave it a second thought.

As the previous AM radio station faded, I dialed hurriedly past anything that resembled politics or preaching. I didn't want to hear it. As I crossed the Red River, I drummed my fingers on the wheel to the sound of Jimmy Hendrix's version of *All Along the Watchtower*. I already knew it to be Bob Dylan's lyrics, bemoaning US engagement in a war that didn't concern us and would prove impossible to win. Going past Thackerville, reception dwindled to a dull hiss.

Nine

Leaving the Interstate at Springer, the black-topped FM road leading east was narrow, but in decent condition. I crossed the old
Highway 77 and, after a couple of miles, slowed to turn north
onto a gravel road with deep ditches on either side. I was immediately
forced to zigzag to avoid a pothole the size of a Jacuzzi, trying not to
jolt the horses off their feet. They were already shuffling around, sensing journey's end and eager to plant hooves on solid ground. Soon the
road narrowed to a dirt lane, deeply rutted and high in the middle. I
passed a mobile home, squatting on cinder blocks at an angle near the
front of a small acreage. The only sign of life was a clothes line, sagging
under the weight of diapers and bed sheets. A sign by the mailbox read
Holderman Township, Population Thirty, Including Kids and Critters. A
field of tall dead grass was cluttered with rusty farm implements, and
among them I detected the shape of a vintage Packard. My head turned
as I passed. I assessed it to be a '55, probably with a flathead V8.

Country people seem to enjoy isolation. No roaring noise of engine braking from big rigs; no horns blaring or sirens wailing. Quiet
enough to hear an owl hooting on the barn roof, or a coyote yipping
somewhere along the creek bottom. They enjoy the lowing of cattle
and the cawing of crows, but not the noise of industry. And, on a clear
night, the sky is a breathtaking dome of black velvet, radiant with stellar patterns. In antiquity such a spectacle commanded the attention of
astronomers like Aristarchus of Samos, and more recent artists such as
Giovanni di Paolo and Vincent van Gogh. The thought struck me that
country people don't mind a long drive into town when they need to
pick up a few supplies or pay a bill. It's a refreshing outing full of sights
and sounds as intriguing as a county fair. But they don't want to live
there. Of course, the same distance tends to keep unwanted visitors
away, and that's part of the plan.

Farms in this part of Oklahoma were a bit different from those in
Kansas and Iowa. No sprawling corporate farms here, although that
will happen eventually. For the present, this region is more like what
sociologists characterize as salt-of-the-earth subsistence living. Small
farms lay out of sight and off the beaten path; often in bottom land

near a river, or in valleys between hills where millennia of erosion deposited a bed of rich top soil. In this part of the country the primary crops are cotton, corn, and maize, although some farmers raise sugarcane and make molasses every year. And, here and there you might find a moonshine still, tucked away in a thick grove of trees or in a shed out behind the barn. With each field I passed, I wondered who owned it and what stories it might tell if I whispered the right questions into the moist ear of the earth.

Just past a pecan grove, the road turned left. Three buzzards hopped to the ditch, but maintained watch over the grizzly remains of a dead possum in the road. I eased to one side to avoid collecting carnage in my tire treads. The fields that came into view were bare and striated with the latest plough ruts, laid back for the winter months when the soil rejuvenates before spring planting. A quarter mile beyond that, I slowed to a crawl to ease over a narrow wooden bridge that creaked and wobbled precariously under the weight of the truck and trailer.

It was about noon when I pulled up in front of a familiar frame house with its white shiplap siding and green trim— the Greenwood farm. Our grandparents clung tenaciously to a hundred sixty acres nestled against the southeastern apron of the Arbuckles, between Springer and Gene Autry. It had been the place of family celebrations, reunions, and retreats further back than any of us could remember. And they had eagerly welcomed us on this particular venture.

Grandpa sat in a rocker on the front porch, smoking his pipe. The solid wooden front door stood ajar, the opening covered by a screen door to allow a breeze to flow through the house, but at the same time to keep flies out. Three scrappy mutts let out a chorus of barks as they bumped their way from beneath the porch and scampered toward my truck and trailer. A brother named Dutch and two sisters, Lucy and Ethel, were littermates with an unregistered ancestry of lab, shepherd, husky, and who knows what else. That *something else* showed most in Ethel's red coat. Dutch and Lucy were both black, with brown muzzles and a few patches of white. Dutch also sported a white tip on his tail. Grandma described them as Heinz Fifty-Sevens, a canine concoction, all good-natured but sufficiently courageous to stand against an intruder or chase away a pack of coyotes.

Grandpa's Chevy pickup sat snugly under a metal carport. He kept saying he wanted to build a garage attached to the house like the modern homes in town, but he had not yet found the time nor mustered the energy. My cousin Jordan was already there, I gathered. His 1959 Pontiac coupe was parked at a leisure angle on the patchy front lawn, right next to the metal stakes on each end of a horseshoe pitch. I turned into a well-worn lane that city folks called a driveway, and circled the big elm tree I recalled from childhood. Two swings hung from a sturdy limb. Grandpa had replaced the wooden seats several times, but I noticed that the latest overhaul included chains instead of ropes. Probably a different limb, too. I stopped in a well-worn area in front of the corral.

I was thankful that Grandpa was not inclined to leave broken-down farm implements parked randomly in the weeds to rust and deteriorate, like those I had noticed along the road. He often complained that Old Man Jenkins kept everything he ever owned, and was unconcerned that it was lost in thick patches of Johnson grass and sunflowers, a haven for snakes and varmints. Jenkins had a Model-A Ford and a 1946 Dodge DeSoto that were actually worth some money, either to customize or restore, but he wouldn't part with them. On numerous occasions, so Grandpa claimed, he declined a generous offer, countering with double the figure. That tactic usually caused potential buyers to retreat. On one occasion, a dealer from Fort Worth actually agreed to Jenkins' double-ploy, to which the old man scratched his chin and replied, "Let me think about it." The dealer waved him off and left in a huff.

In contrast, Grandpa had sold his 1951 Massey-Ferguson tractor, along with various unessential implements, and used the money to build a proper indoor bathroom for Grandma with a toilet, tub, sink, and hot and cold running water. He had other farm equipment, and he still mowed and plowed, but he contracted out hay bailing on two larger pastures. He also leased fifty acres to another farmer who customarily rotated crops on multiple fields. Now that it was winter, Grandpa's '64 John Deere was parked behind the barn, covered in a heavy canvas tarpaulin to repel water.

Grandpa grimaced as he pushed out of the rocker and levered on his grey felt hat, which he had worn every winter season for the past twenty years. I recognized it from a distance. The crown bore unsightly blotches where his dirty fingers typically gripped it, and he was unconcerned about its misshaped brim. Hobbling down the porch steps, he paused to stretch from side to side before striding spryly across the lawn and out toward my truck. He lifted a hand, motioning in the direction of the corral. I swung the trailer around and reversed cautiously, glancing from one side mirror to the other. The horses shuffled restlessly, eager to get out and on the ground. The three mutts circled the truck, tails wagging as they supervised my maneuver while dancing sprightly away from moving tires.

At Grandpa's thumbs up, I stopped and set the brake. Climbing out stiffly, I propped my hands on the side of the truck and stretched. A couple of crows took flight from a hackberry tree next to the barn, cawing in agitation as they crossed an open field toward Little Sandy Creek. The dogs encircled me and reared up on my thighs, eager to be petted. Dutch reeked of skunk, or possibly stench from rooting and wallowing in some animal carcass he'd found in the pasture. Whatever the cause, he stank to high heaven. I shooed them all away. But I chuckled at the thought that there's something invigorating about the aroma of skunk and cow manure on a fresh December morning.

Grandpa pushed open the galvanized gate and then turned and ambled toward me. His rosy cheeks lifted into a broad grin as he stuck out his beefy hand. I felt the calluses in his palms and on his fingertips. I anticipated his usual hard squeeze, his way of testing my grip. My knuckles crackled before he drew me close for a hug. He smelled clean and fresh, compared to Dutch. I was warmed at the thought that he had showered and shaved in anticipation of my arrival. It seemed to me that old men could be characterized by their variety of odors. My Grandaddy Barnett, whom I had visited from time to time in the Sunset Acres nursing home, often smelled of urine. The attendants there were not sufficiently attentive. But I had noticed that other old men often smelled of grime, perspiration, and the stale, pungent odor of clothes worn repeatedly without washing. A couple of elders at church, whom I guessed had been converted by the Apostles themselves, wore the same suits Sunday after Sunday, with only a single trip to the cleaners in a year. They probably assumed body odor would be covered by a few splashes of Aqua Velva. But Grandma saw to it that Grandpa bathed at least a couple of times each week. So, for an old dirt farmer, he was typically pretty clean.

Ginger and Barney clomped back and forth in their mobile prison, eyeing me through their front window. I opened the tail gate, slipped inside and unsnapped their harnesses. Each one backed out of the trailer and down the ramp. The pair followed me dutifully into the corral. I unzipped a burlap sack of oats, poured a bucket half full, and dumped it into the feed trough near the gate. Both horses trotted over eagerly and buried their muzzles in the warm grain.

From his stall at the back of the corral, Grandpa's horse Scooter eyed us suspiciously. Once a beautiful animal, as pinto geldings go, Scooter was getting on in years. From a distance, I detected a little gray around his face, as well as exposed ribs and a sagging belly beneath a swayed back. Commonly called a *paint*, that breed of horse apparently originated with the plains Indians. Grandpa had traded a neighbor a side of beef for Scooter when he was a yearling. That was many moons ago. Having been castrated at about ten months, Barney and Scooter considered a mare to be just another horse, so they were never rowdy around Ginger. Scooter was basically a trail horse, never trained for cutting cattle or roping. Over the years, Grandpa had ridden him to check fence lines, and all the grandchildren got their first experience in the saddle riding in circles in Grandpa's corral. In fact, Scooter was the *only* horse some of them ever rode.

On one occasion, so I was told, Uncle Luke rode Scooter up to the rock quarry. Somewhere along the trail, a rattlesnake spooked him. He reared up high and stumbled, and Uncle Luke fell off. Scooter took off down the hill at full gallop. For Uncle Luke, it was an hour's hike back to the farm. When he arrived, bedraggled and sore, Scooter stood contentedly at the feed trough, nibbling leftover sweet feed. He looked up and snorted, as if to say *Where the hell have you been?*

Grandpa often said that he and Scooter would grow old together, just like him and Grandma. And while we all knew Scooter was getting on in years, Grandpa considered him to be as healthy and sure-footed as a Grand Canyon pack mule. He had been up in the mountains so many times he knew the trails by heart. Jordan and I had our doubts.

There at the farm, Scooter occupied the only closed stall. But extending out on the left side, and open from the horse lot, was a covered area with corrugated panels attached to the south side of the barn. I would have preferred my horses to stay in closed stalls, but Grandpa didn't have such luxuries. I had to settle for knowing they could go under a shelter if it rained or turned really cold. I noticed that the water trough was low, so I twisted the tap and let it run awhile. In the distance, a windmill turned steadily in the light breeze. Grandpa folded his arms across the fence rail, studying my every move.

"Bet they're thirsty after breathin' all them fumes on the highway."

"Sure," I said. "But they didn't complain. How's the water these days?"

"Still good. Sweet and clean. It gets a little low during the summer. But never bone dry. This past fall I had to do a little work on the gears up top there." He swept a finger in the direction of the windmill. "Replaced a couple of blades, too. But that old rig jest keeps on turnin'. It's served us real good."

"Scooter need anything there?"

"Nah, I fed and watered him earlier. He's good 'til tomorrow mornin'."

As I switched off the tap, Ginger eased over to the trough and slurped up a gallon. I could imagine a meter on her belly clicking over like a gasoline pump. "You know," I said, "the only thing I don't like about having horses is real cold winter mornings when you have to clomp across hard frozen mud and break ice in the water trough. At our place, Dad keeps a ball peen hammer on a hook just for that purpose."

Grandpa's lined and weatherbeaten face lifted into a broad grin. His blue eyes sparkled. "Yep, I know what cha mean. Country livin' ain't for sissies. Neither's gettin' old, for that matter. But down in Texas it don't get quite as cold as up here. Red River's kinda' like a curtain, know what I mean? 'Course, up in the high country... I'm talkin' 'bout the Texas and Oklahoma panhandles... the winter wind blows straight out of the North Pole. Then, in summer, they tell me it gets so dry and dusty that the prairie dogs dig holes two feet in the air."

Grandpa tossed his head back and chuckled before locking eyes on me, hoping for a response. I smiled and raised my eyebrows. "That's good, Grandpa. I gotta remember that one."

As Ginger meandered in the corral, I heard an odd metallic clunk from one front hoof. I eased up to her and lifted her foot to have a look. Sure enough, she had a loose shoe.

"Grandpa, you wouldn't happen to know a farrier close by, would ya? Ginger needs a little hoof work. Looks like maybe she was pawing at the trailer wall on the way up here."

"Well sir, there's a colored man down the road toward Gene Autry. Name's Orpheus Pratt. Neighborly fella. I consider him a friend. He does some shoein' among other things."

"I remember him. His is the last place on the way up to the quarry. Uncle Luke told us we should always stop for a minute and tell him where we're going and why. I think one or two of the ranchers pay him a little to keep an eye on things. But I never knew how he made a living."

"He's the best around here. Learned from his daddy. Does most of the work along this row of farms, and folks in Gene Autry use him, too. You got any cash?"

"Yep. How much should I pay him?"

"Whatever he asks," Grandpa said, expressionless. "Orpheus is honest. He'll be fair with ya."

I knew my grandparents to be unbiased when it came to racial matters. They never talked about politics, whether they were Democrats, Republicans, Libertarians, or whatever. But I knew they voted. They just kept their political views to themselves. And since neither of them ever used the word *nigger,* I assessed them to be a tad more tolerant than most folks in Carter County, or the whole state for that matter. Still fresh on my mind was the assassination of both MLK and Robert Kennedy earlier that year. And I still had clippings of the JFK assassination down in Dallas. Only a teenager, I wondered if the world could be the same without them, and what would become of a nation where people were bumped off if they were too vocal on sensitive topics. How were we different from less developed countries all around the world, run by thugs and dictators? What's the point of democracy if you kill people to get you own way?

"You know, Grandpa, racial tension is high in some places. Martin Luther King made it clear that black folks are fed up with being denied equal rights."

"Well, sir. I know the man was loved and respected," Grandpa said. He tugged at the straps of his coveralls and drew in a deep breath. The corners of his mouth twisted down broodingly. "But he stirred up a hornet's nest, that's for dang sure. What's the Bible say? If you sow to the wind, you reap a whirlwind?"

"I don't think that's quite what that means, Grandpa. People have a right to stand up for themselves. And in politics, I think sometimes stirring the pot's absolutely necessary. How else could we have become an independent nation? We had to claim our freedom, and fight for it. As I understand it, democracy itself is a pretty liberal and innovative concept."

"Well, son, you may have a point," he responded. "But I doubt you know all the answers to this country's problems if nobody in Washington can figure it out." In Grandpa's assessment, over the years the

USA had progressed out of one big mess into another, over and over again. Lincoln freed the slaves, and then we gave them and women the right to vote. That seems to have created more hatred than we had before. "The Klan and all that cross burning and…" Grandpa looked over his shoulder and lowered his voice, "…horse shit like that." Grandma didn't approve of crude language, so he did his cussin' in private. "That George Wallace," he rambled on, "is gonna hold his ground come hell or high water. We're lucky he didn't manage to screw things up in the last election."

"I think you're right," I said. "Seems like people in Alabama and Mississippi are still trying to fight the Civil War. Sooner or later we've gotta let go and be a united country. But I admit I don't understand all the issues. I certainly don't understand some people."

Grandpa put a hand on my shoulder and squeezed—not hard, but hard enough to make me lock eyes with him. "My friend Jack Bentley's from Mississippi," he said, eyes squinting. "Runs the feed store in Springer. He says all the time that the South's gonna rise again. Talks about Abe Lincoln's war of northern aggression. Some old grievances get passed down from one generation to the next. Maybe get worse over time. But, son, I've learned that you can't solve everybody's problems, and nothin' you say or do'll change how people think. The rivers of politics and religion run deep and wide. If you force it, they'll find a way to make you pay, but they won't change their thinkin.' So, my rule is never step into a battle that ain't yours to fight."

I nodded. "I understand. But this is supposed to be *One Nation, Under God, Indivisible*, and all that."

"That's what we're trying to be. We ain't there yet. And your own children'll still be workin' things out long after you and me are dead and buried. I just want to keep the peace, as far as it's up to me, with everybody. That's in the Bible for damn sure."

Again, Grandpa glanced back as if Grandma were looking over his shoulder. My eyes lingered on his aging countenance as I mulled over the many beliefs he clung to like gold, and the questionable truisms that readily rolled off his and Grandma's tongue. But I respected his wisdom, even if it was sometimes a tad misguided. He had also told us, as did my own parents, that it's hard for youth to appreciate the wisdom of age. You learn a lot from living, but some people are slower than molasses in winter when it comes to change. Minds tend to set hard like cement.

That said, within Grandpa's words I found an erudite spirit that dwarfed the closed-mindedness of the mainstream population. The founding fathers of this nation were visionaries, indeed, but even those sagacious men could not know the rapid development that was to come, with its social and political complexity. They could not foresee the complexity of some of the ideals they espoused. They spoke and wrote from limited perspectives. But for the moment, my concerns hinged on the growing disdain for the war in Vietnam and the swell of racial tension, both problems looming on the horizon like a dust storm sweeping in from the Texas panhandle. Sooner or later, it would engulf us.

I shouldered a bag of grain and tossed it in the trailer, where it would stay dry. Then I grabbed my gear, locked the cab, and followed Grandpa toward the house. I noticed a pronounced limp in his walk. After standing a while, his joints tended to inflame and tighten. Grandma described his gait as a *hitch in his get-along*. The years of farm work had taken a toll on his body, especially his hips and knees.

"You know, ain't no need to lock up your truck out here." Grandpa said over his shoulder.

"I've got guns in there, Grandpa."

"No matter," he said. "It's all safe."

I stopped a moment and turned back toward the truck, staring hard at the guns on the rack. Grandpa kept walking.

"But you done locked it," he mumbled without turning. "May as well leave it be. Come on in."

I smiled and trailed Grandpa toward the house. Across the road, a flock of ducks settling on the surface of a stock pond. It was a mild sunny day for late December, and whatever north wind might have been blowing at the time was blocked by the mountain. As I reached the front steps, I drew in a deep breath of fresh air. Despite the faint tang of the barnyard, there was still something natural and clean about it, untainted by exhaust fumes and dumpster odors. The quiet of the country felt peaceful. My ears strained to detect some kind of human activity. In that almost deathly quiet moment, I thought I heard the rhythm of drums drifting on the breeze from toward the northeast. Not like a marching band, but still, a rhythmic pattern. Then it was gone. I was puzzled, but I shrugged it off.

As Grandpa pulled open the screen door, the aroma of fresh beef stew wafted through the house. I could see straight through to the kitchen where Grandma was setting the table for lunch, which in this neck of the woods folks called *dinner*. In the corner of the living room stood a stylish aluminum Christmas tree with a bright red skirt and a pair of small floodlights aimed upward to illuminate silvery needles. Grandma had already started packing away ornaments, including the star that had adorned the treetop. Family members from both her side and Grandpa's had been there on Christmas day for dinner and the exchange of gifts. In recent years, the number had become so large that they had to draw names in advance. Grandma wanted everyone to receive a Christmas present, and she shuddered at the thought that someone might be overlooked. She always went to town and bought three or four generic gifts, just in case.

The long wall was bisected by a massive stone fireplace containing a few glowing coals remaining from a roaring fire the previous evening. In the interior corner stood an Ansonia grandfather clock made in 1865. Neither her family nor Grandpa's could afford such a clock. It was a wedding gift from Dr. Heinrich Neumann of Little Rock, Arkansas. Over the years, it had become Grandma's ritual to hoist the weights each Sunday morning. The tick-tock of the swinging pendulum was restful, but all of us who occasionally spent a night or two at the farm had to get accustomed to the Westminster chime every quarter hour. Naturally, the head pounding hourly gong was the most annoying at midnight.

I dropped my duffle bag in the living room and followed Grandpa into the lighted kitchen. Grandma's lined face split into a bright smile as she stepped spryly around the corner of the table and threw her arms around me. My face to her perspiring neck, I detected the fragrance of Tea Rose perfume masking the smell of cornmeal and bacon grease. Her long silver hair was tied in a loose bun at the back of her neck.

"Set yourself down," she said. "We're just waiting for the cornbread to brown and we'll be ready to eat." She turned and motioned toward Grandpa. "Sugar, go get that lazy rascal up. His forty winks have long expired."

Grandpa had already settled at the table, but he scooted back, pushed himself upright, and hobbled out toward the bedrooms. I heard the creaking of floorboards under boots as he turned down the hall. Then a door hinge squalled and his muffled voice called Jordan to wake up. A minute later, my sandy-headed cousin trailed Grandpa out of the back bedroom, yawning and rubbing his sleepy blue eyes.

Ten

In certain ways, Jordan was conservative and traditional. But he was also adventuresome and very eager to explore and learn, which in my view made him a walking conundrum. But either way, I loved him as much as my own brother. Previously a Bible major, but now focused on American history, Jordan envisioned himself a history teacher. Like many of our youthful dreams and schemes, that was not set in stone.

"Did anyone get the number of the truck that hit me?" Jordan said, sleepy-eyed. He stretched and yawned as he shuffled into the kitchen. Dragging up a chair, he plopped down next to me. "Need coffee," he growled, eyes glazed. "My mouth tastes like a pigeon pooped in it."

"I never tasted pigeon poop," I said.

"Just an expression. Don't get all technical on me." He tossed me a scolding glance, then grinned.

"Well, I was just kidding," I said.

"Ah, so you *have* tasted pigeon poop?"

I was fully aware that Jordan was cocky and quick-witted. But before I could respond, Grandpa spoke up. "That was a mighty long nap for a man who hardly did a lick of work all mornin' long."

"I packed my gear and drove out here," Jordan jibed. "That was work enough. Besides, the fresh country air makes a man drowsy. I can hardly imagine how anyone can work ten hours without a nap."

Grandpa chuckled. "I already done a day's work before you even crawled outa bed."

Jordan frowned and snapped a retort. "I thought you gave up that farmer John routine; you know, up before dawn and work 'till after dark."

"Lord, no," Grandma interceded. "He's still up at five. Milks ole' Bessie. Feeds the chickens, gathers eggs. 'Course, they don't lay in the dead of winter. But he gets up and piddles around outside, anyway. Gotta feed ole' Scooter. And ever' third mornin' he hauls hay to the east pasture. We got eighteen Angus steers that need *room service* in the winter, don't cha know." Grandma drew her mouth jeeringly. "Loves them cows more than me, I 'spect. But they'll be ready for market next fall. Then he'll raise another herd."

Grandpa sat quiet with a crooked smile while Grandma explained his business and defended his dignity. Everyone knew that in a crowd, Grandpa wasn't much of a talker unless he had a joke to tell, or a few jibes at someone, just for fun. He had talked openly with me out by the corral. But once he was inside the house, he usually let Grandma take over.

A warm aroma of cornbread pervaded the kitchen. An enormous pot of beef stew with carrots and potatoes simmered on the stove. Grandpa bowed his head and recited his customary prayer. "Lord, we give thanks for this food, and ask that you bless it to the nourishment of our bodies, and our bodies to thy service. And, uh, as always, Lord, bless the lovin' hands that prepared it. In Jesus's name, amen."

Grandma patted his forearm lovingly and while seated began her dishing-up ritual, starting with Grandpa on her left and rotating clockwise. Grandpa's seat was, of course, the head of the table. And Grandma's routine was the same in the dining room if there were as many as twelve seated at the table. If there were more, she consented to a buffet-style self-service off the kitchen table. She ran her house with the consistency of a Sunday mass at Saint Peter's Basilica, although as a devout Baptist she would find that comparison repugnant.

"I'm sure you boys will want a little cow salve for your cornbread," Grandpa said, with a mischievous smile.

I glanced at Jordan, who sat pokerfaced. "That means butter," he said. "Grandpa has his own jargon. Moo juice is milk. Cackle fruit is eggs."

"Don't get started with that," Grandma chirped. "The list is a mile long."

"Got it." I said, nodding crisply. "No more explanation needed. I got the picture." Grandpa's quirky terminology fit together like a country jigsaw puzzle. However, as a city cowboy with only a modest claim to country roots, my tastebuds resisted. Certain things on Grandma's table tasted a little strange. The stew and cornbread were delicious. No problem there. But I was accustomed to homogenized milk and margarine. So, genuine country butter tasted awfully *mooey* to my refined palate. But, not wanting to appear finicky, I spread that country cow salve thick on my cornbread and devoured it with a forced smile.

In recent years, each time I visited the farm Grandma considered it her duty to refresh my memory of our ancestry. With me and Jordan there together, her compulsion was even stronger. After she cleared the table, she led us into the hallway to survey photographs which hung in clusters along the sprawling wall. It was easy to follow the burgeoning family's early history. There were a few empty nails, evidence of the ongoing nature of this project. The array was crowned with a couple of badly dulled photos of our great-grandparents, on her side and Grandpa's. But the centerpiece of the wall was Grandpa and Grandma on their wedding day—Bertram and Gertrude Greenwood, June 10, 1913. He was seventeen and his bride Trudy, as she was known, was a year younger.

"We celebrated our fifty-fifth anniversary this past June," Grandma said proudly. "Your grandpa took me to Branson, Missouri to see Presley's Country Jubilee. It was just the bee's knees." Eyes sparkled as she sighed sentimentally. "That Presley was no kin to Elvis, I don't think. Maybe a distant cousin."

To the right was a studio shot of Uncle Marcus, whom everyone knew as Mark, with his wife Hazel and their first two daughters. Frizzy-headed Christine was the oldest. Caroline was two in that picture. Momma Hazel was big as a house, expecting number three. Grandma pointed toward the image of Uncle Marcus. She wagged her head sadly as she whispered, "My dear son, God rest his soul." Next to that was a photo of Uncle Luke in naval dress uniform. He was the youngest, and except for his military service, he had remained near home all his life. Certainly Grandma's pride and joy.

She smiled wistfully as her eyes locked on Uncle Luke's face. Her hand lifted and touched the frame lightly, as she whispered to him, "It's so good to have you home safe. Your nephew Terry, too." Turning abruptly toward me, she added, "Terry's only been back a short while. I have a good picture of him here in this box, with lots more. I had hoped to rearrange 'em before Christmas, but I just didn't get around to it."

"That's okay, Grandma. I remember most of them, but I'll be eager to see them all when you're done."

My retention of long lists of relatives was embarrassingly poor, a shortcoming I would retain through life. But I stopped and drew closer as Grandma lifted out of the box a faded brown photo. Clearly, I could make out a family huddled in front of a canvas tent. She lightly dusted the surface with her apron and gazed upon it with reverence. In the foreground were the muddy ruts of wagon tracks, evidence of earlier heavy rains. Behind them were towering drilling rigs.

Her grandfather, my great-grandfather, was a Cherokee named
Noel Awiakta, whose parents were part of the forced migration from
Tennessee. They settled in the area of Okmulgee, where Noel and his
two sons worked as a rough-necks in the oilfields. Grandma's earliest
memories included cold winter nights in a tent surrounded by oil rigs.
She pointed to a scrawny little girl hiding in the folds of her mother's
skirt.

"That's me," she said, tapping on the image. "My mother and father were Julia and Daniel Awiakta. They changed their surname to
Attaway, hoping us kids would be accepted as white. Truth is, all you
kids have a little Indian blood," Grandma said blithely. "Of course, a
mix of Choctaw and Cherokee and maybe something else. But your
generation has too little to be recognized. Our family didn't make it on
the Dawes Rolls back in 1907. You won't be gettin' any royalty checks,
sugar." She sniffed with a tone of resentment before reaching up and
lightly pinching my cheek. "Don't hold your breath for that. We're
what big-city folks call *poor white trash*. But we know we're not that
white. Maybe they'd say *country trash*. I dunno. They'd call us somethin'
tacky, I'm sure of that."

Grandma rambled on with stories of the old days. She mentioned
that a lot of mixed breeds tried to hide their Indian ancestry because
white folks would shun them if they knew. When somebody asked
about their dark skin color, they would just say they were *black Dutch*,
or they would claim their ancestors had immigrated from Romanian
Gypsies. That seemed to satisfy the bigots. Besides all that, the old tribal leaders scoffed at whites who claimed some degree of Native American ancestry. They said being half-breed or quarter-breed didn't make
an Indian white, so why would it make a white man Indian? As Chief
Tishu Miko once said, those who claim Indian ancestry have only "*a
drop of red in a white river.*"

I bent down and carefully lifted a few photographs from the box,
each still in a frame and glass. Grandpa's family was no less fascinating.
His father obtained a hundred sixty acres in Kingfisher County during
the 1889 land rush, and he cleared the land and carved a farm out of
raw sod. He later purchased this present land, which Grandpa inherited. One photo in particular caught my attention. It was Grandma
and Grandpa in front of this very house. The children were gathered
around, all in their late teens or twenties—except Luke, who was about
ten. But there was a little girl clinging to Grandma's knees. Obviously

not one of her own children, if indeed Luke was the last one.

"Who's that?" I pointed.

"Oh, that's a little orphan girl who stayed with us for a while. Her name's Katy."

"What happened to her? I don't see her in any of these other pictures."

Grandma hesitated, and her eyes lowered. She shook her head remorsefully. "She disappeared one day, and we never saw her again."

That obviously was a sensitive topic. I could see in Grandma's face. So, I didn't pursue it. I turned away and left her to her assortment of family memorabilia. But pausing at the doorway, I glanced back. She was till staring at Katy's picture.

In the living room, Grandpa was settling down in his Lazy Boy recliner. Remembering something I forgot to do when I arrived, I tugged out my wallet and extended a five-dollar bill toward him.

"Grandpa, I brought an Abe Lincoln for a bale of hay. I hope you can spare me that. But I brought two bags of feed. One is oats and the other sweet feed. We'll haul that with us up the mountain, and whatever's left, I'll leave here for Scooter."

"Son, I can *give* you a bale of hay," he said, waving off the money. His tone hinted minor irritation, but the twinkle in his eye said otherwise. "We ain't dirt poor."

"I'd feel better if you let me pay. I still remember when Jordan and I busted up those bales playing fort up on top of the haystack in the barn. So, please. After all, you and Grandma are always giving."

Grandpa nodded and looked away, while stretching out his hand for the bill. "None of it was wasted," he said ruefully. "I managed to fork it up in small batches and pitch it in the feed trough, day by day. Main thing is you boys had fun."

"I also have something for the two of you," I said, calling to Grandma. "A sort of belated Christmas gift."

Grandma left her photos and sauntered in to join us. I handed her an envelope and watched her face as she opened it. My mom had picked out the card. It was a Hallmark, one of those sparkly sketches of a country house flanked by snow-laden fir trees and a frozen pond. Inside the card, she had tucked a hundred-dollar bill. Grandma's eyes misted as she read Mom's hand written note.

As I look back, I cannot recall a time more joyful than Christmas with the two of you when I was young. Now with a family of my own, a husband and two boys who love you both dearly, we think of you often and wish we were nearer. But you're always in our hearts, thoughts and prayers as the center of our roots and the origin of the family values that carry us through life. Love—Phoebe, Thurman, Russell, and Spencer.

Grandma's lip quivered. She floated toward me and enveloped me with strong arms. Her squeeze was tender, but she held me for an uncomfortably long time. I understood and did not resist.

"Thank you, sweet boy," she said into my ear. "I'll call Phoebe later and thank her 'fer this. Your darlin' daddy, too. Thurman's a good man. Our little girl did mighty good to catch him."

Jordan smiled and nodded approvingly.

"Your cousin brought us a nice present, too," Grandma said, looking at me and pointing toward the wall. "That new color TV sittin' over yonder."

My eyes widened as I turned toward Jordan, who lifted a hand to cover a Cheshire cat grin. He and his parents lived close enough to help Uncle Luke keep an eye on the old folks. Sometimes they had to force them into the twentieth century. The previous Christmas they installed a new washer and drier. For many years, Grandma had used a top loading Maytag with a hand-fed wringer, probably dating back to the fifties. There's no telling how many times she got her fingers pinched. But considering it to be fancy, I'm sure she imagined herself right up there with the rich ladies on New York's Fifth Avenue. She had often told us that when she and Grandpa married, she washed clothes by hand with a scrub board in a galvanized tub. So, the new washer last year was a God-send. Now, on top of all that modernization, this Christmas they advanced to television in color.

Grandpa piped up. "Maybe you two boys can hook that up while you're here. I'd do it myself. But if I get down in the floor, I won't never get up again."

"Sure thing," Jordan said. "Shouldn't be very hard. You already have an antenna, right?"

"Yep, the wind blew it over last Spring, but your Uncle Luke climbed on the roof and anchored it down good and tight. It ain't goin' nowhere this time. Unless, of course, we get hit by a twister. Then we'll end up stone dead somewhere in a Nebraska corn field. Won't be needin' no TV then."

"Don't talk like that, Grandpa," Jordan scolded.

"That Luke can do just about anything," Grandma said, totally ignoring Grandpa's remark. "I call him a Jack-of-all-trades, and he always answers back, *but a master of none.* He's as humble as a beggar, that boy."

The RCA color television was a console type, already sitting against the wall next to an electric outlet. The maple cabinet almost perfectly matched the coffee table. There really wasn't much for me and Jordan to do. I removed the rabbit ear antenna that came with the TV, wrapped the short cable around it, and laid it aside. We found a new connecting cable in a paper packet, uncoiled it, and attached it to the back of the TV, then to the antennae connection dangling through a hole in the wall. Jordan plugged the power cord into an outlet. I pushed an "on" button on the front panel, and like magic the dark screen brightened into a kaleidoscope of color. Grandma squealed and applauded when Judy Garland appeared, just as she leaned to squirt oil into the Tin Man's neck.

"We're sure glad you boys are here," Grandpa said, nodding affirmation. "Our old TV went out, and we really look forward to Saturday nights. We like the Jackie Gleason Show, then Lawrence Welk, and after that, maybe Johnny Cash. But we ain't never seen 'em in color."

The late afternoon rolled by quickly, aided by the chores Grandpa assigned to each of us. I inherited scooping the manure out of Bessie's stall, on the north side of the barn. Since we had a late lunch, Grandma heated up leftovers for supper.

At about nine Grandpa settled down in his usual spot and switched on his new color TV. Jordan and I were eager to join him.

"I ain't sittin' up to watch nothin' tonight," Grandma snarled. "I'm ready to hit the sack."

"Well, I guess me too," Grandpa mumbled, groaning as he struggled to get out of the soft recliner. "This cold weather's got my arthritis flarin' up." A sardonic smile turned up at the corners of his mouth and his eyes sparkled. "You know, of all those Itis boys, that Arthur is the meanest."

"You always say that," Grandma scolded. "It ain't arthritis that's gettin' you down. It's too many miles and too many years."

Grandpa wagged his head mockingly. "Old age just gives Arthur more room to play. My doctor... Gardner's his name, Doctor Antoine E. Gardner... he done told me twenty years ago I had arthritis. Hey, and get this. If Arthur Itis teams up with Ruma Toid, they're like Bonnie and Clyde. The meanest pair in the county." Grandpa slapped his hands together and guffawed.

I glanced at Jordan, who shook his head, stifling a grin. "You're in the Oklahoma hills, Russ. You gotta get used to the lingo and the goofy humor."

Grandpa and Grandma went to bed. I watched TV a short while, with the sound down low, while Jordan showered. Then I had turn. The bathroom was located between the master bedroom and Grandma's sewing room. To get there from the back bedroom in the middle of the night, we had to pad quietly through the kitchen and dining room, then back across to the hallway. No matter how stealthy the footsteps, the loose floorboards creaked. To avoid us startling her, Grandma gave us a chamber pot. She said she'd throw it out in the morning unless one of us pooped in it. In that case, the culprit would have to clean it out himself.

At about eleven Jordan and I sacked out. The back room had a pair of single beds. A small table sat between them, on which stood a crooked lamp with a dust-laden shade. A propane space heater stood against the wall, but we saw no need to light it. That night was not really cold. Maybe forty degrees. Jordan and I were cozy beneath flannel sheets and homemade quilts. I lay awake for a while listening to coyotes howl down toward the creek. Occasionally Ginger and Barney snorted or pawed the packed dirt in the horse lot. Scooter was quiet. He was happy in his stall, with a scoop of sweet feed and a short stack of hay in his trough. And the dogs were settled into their cozy kennel, attached to the side of the barn. That's where Grandpa kept them at night. Otherwise, they would run off into the mountains chasing varmints. From their vantage point in the kennel, the dogs had a view across the entire back pasture and the nearest slopes of the Arbuckles. Closer in, they could see the chicken coop, the back of the house, and down the road in both directions. They never failed to bark out an alarm if anyone or anything approached. And now and then they'd start barking at nothing, or what Grandpa called *hoodoos in the night*.

I lay awake for a while before, on an impulse, I whispered to Jordan, "You still awake?" He didn't respond. I repeated, "Hey, are you awake?"

"Yeah, but I was saying my prayers."

"You always pray before you go to sleep?"

"Don't you?"

"No, not anymore."

"Why not?"

"Why would anyone? Unless you just kept doing what you did as a child."

"Well, that's what I was taught to do. Habit, I suppose."

I thought a moment, before tossing more thoughts Jordan's way. "I remember a prayer Mom taught me and Spencer. It went: *Now I lay me down to sleep, I pray the Lord my soul to keep; If I should die before I wake, I pray the Lord my soul to take.*"

"That's the one I learned, but that's not how I pray now. I just thank God for a good day and ask that His hand will be on me as I sleep."

I rolled toward Jordan and switched on the lamp. "Why would God only protect you during the night if you remembered to ask? And if I died without asking God to *keep* my soul, what would happen to it? Those words never made any sense to me."

"Well, I sure want God's protection when I'm asleep and don't know what's going on around me. Don't you?"

I deliberated a moment before answering. "I once read an old Scottish prayer. I can't recall where, but the words stuck. It went, *Laird, protect us from ghoulies and ghosties, and long-leggitie beasties, and things that go bump in the night.* Now, that's a clear example of unwarranted fear. I suspect praying at bedtime got started during the Dark Ages when people were terrified of myths like vampires, werewolves, ghosts, and demons; creatures that lurked in the darkness waiting to get them. If you don't believe in such things, what is there to be afraid of? You just close your eyes and go to sleep. That's how I see it."

Jordan did not respond. I switched off the lamp and rolled over.

Eleven

A rooster crowed at 6:30 a.m. I jolted upright, thinking I was about to be set upon by a banshee from hell, and maybe I should have said my prayers like Jordan said. My heart raced as I sucked in a deep breath, trying to surface from slumberland. As my mind cleared, I eased back down. My head melted into my warm pillow and I drew the blanket under my chin. "I'd like to wring that rooster's neck," I mumbled. "Grandma could have that little bastard plucked, roasted, and on the table by noon."

The rooster's name was Buster. He was a beautifully colored Rhode Island Red, now over ten years old and exceeding the typical lifespan for that breed of chicken. No doubt he had fertilized a lot of eggs and probably had descendants all over the county. So, he had a lot to crow about, besides dawn. Then I heard Jordan's voice. "I could handle that just fine," he said, with little emotion. "Buster's more like a pet, something of a legend around here," he said yawning. "Grandma would probably whack you over the head with her rolling pin."

In the dim predawn I could make out Jordan's vague features, yawning and scratching like a mountain gorilla. I sat up again, reached toward the window, and drew back the musty homemade curtain. "It's still pitch-black outside," I muttered. I blinked and stared northward at nothing. After palming my sleepy eyes, I had a second look. The pitch-black I had just described appeared more like a subtle gray, behind and above the vague silhouettes of the barn and the face of the mountain. I could only make out a few hazy stars. As I flopped back down a second time, I noticed a thin rod of light beneath the bedroom door, casting a faint orb across the linoleum floor. From the kitchen came the clatter of dishes. A drawer opened and closed, followed by the clinking of utensils on the tabletop. Grandma was up, cooking breakfast.

I fumbled around the base of the lamp, searching for the switch. If I were a crime suspect, this lamp would have my prints all over it. I thumbed it on, grimacing in the piercing brightness of a single forty-watt bulb. Jordan swung his bare feet out of bed and stood up, stretching high. He danced across the cold floor, scooped his clothes from a chair arm, and tugged on socks, jeans, and T-shirt.

Compelled by a guilty conscience for challenging Jordan's bedtime prayers, I followed his example. I eased out of bed, half-hearted and mentally unfocussed. A lazy yawn, a slow stretch of arms to the left and right, and a rotation of head loosened tense neck muscles. I figured I was sufficiently awake to dress. I tugged on my jeans just as Jordan stepped lightly out the door to the bathroom. Five minutes later, the pair of us shuffled listlessly into the bright kitchen, more or less drifting toward the inviting aroma of bacon frying in a skillet. It was Friday. The day we planned to head up on the mountain.

Jordan and I both woke up hungry that morning. They say country air does that to you. Not sure that's the cause. I plopped down and drummed my fingers on the tabletop, assuming there was nothing I could do to help. I glanced at Jordan, who was probably thinking the same thing. We both knew that when Grandma was busy, if she needed anybody's help, she'd say so. But Grandma seldom allowed a man to help her in her kitchen. That was her domain and arena of pride; her God-assigned sphere of duty.

She stood over the stove, still in her nightgown and flannel robe, her long hair braided and dangling down her spine. "Heavy frost this mornin'," she said, her voice chipper and melodious. "Weatherman says somebody left the gate open up in Nebraska. Might come a blizzard. I hope you boys brought plenty of warm clothes."

"It's December, Grandma," Jordan whined. "Comin' up on January. We didn't expect to tan on the beach."

Grandma cut him a scolding look and shook her finger at him, real slow. "Don't you smart mouth me, young man. Christmas presents don't buy you a sassy pass."

"I'm just playin', Grandma. You know I respect your wisdom, bein' ancient and all."

Wiping a smirk from her lips with the back of her hand, Grandma tossed another jibe over her shoulder. "Be careful, now. You ain't too big for me to turn over my knee. And I can do it, too. I'm stouter than I look." Her eyes flung another fiery dart his way, trying to hide the crinkle of a smile as she turned back to the stove. Nimble fingers gripped an egg, cracked it on the rim of a cast iron skillet, and deposited yoke and white into a pond of sizzling grease. Three more followed, and moments later Grandma tipped them out together onto a platter, sunny side up. As usual, in a matter of minutes Grandma masterfully created a full country breakfast, including sausage, biscuits, and gravy.

Our eyes turned toward a clatter at the back door. The enclosed porch was the same level as the house, but hollow underneath, and breezy. Like Santa Claus thumping down the chimney, Grandpa stomped the mud and manure off his boots. A rush of cold air followed as he pulled open the back door and trudged across the kitchen floor.

Grandpa's decrepitude was evident. Not just age but many years of farm work. His limp was typically more pronounced when he climbed steps or stood up after sitting for a while. Jordan and I had noted that when the pain was severe, Grandpa hobbled along like Walter Brennan of *The Real McCoys*, fists clinched and elbows lifting with each step. All that was particularly evident this morning. Obviously in pain, Grandpa leaned over the table, supporting his weight with both palms flat while he stretched one leg out straight. He grimaced, bending over slowly, straining to touch his toes. Then he stood up straight, somewhat relieved.

Grandma shook her head. "The doctor says he's got arthritis in his back and both hips." She eased over and sympathetically stroked Grandpa's shoulder. "Of all them Ritis boys…"

"I know, I know, Sugar Dumplin," Grandpa said, moderately irritated. "Arthur's the meanest. You always say that." He forced a smile and patted her hand, as if the moment demanded a gesture of appreciation.

"No, you're the one that always says that. I'm just quotin' you."

Tugging a hanky from his coveralls, Grandpa honked into it, followed by a couple of determined wipes across chafed nostrils. Then he scooted a chair out from the table and eased down.

"Why are you out doing chores this early, Grandpa?" I asked, trying to display sincere concern.

"Oh, I don't really have that much to do. Of a mornin' I mostly jest piddle around 'til I get limbered up. Know what I mean?"

Grandma wagged her head. "You don't jest piddle around. You do what needs to be done, rain or shine."

"Well," he said, "if it's really cold, I might have to break the ice in the horse trough. But it wudn't that cold this mornin'. I've been up since three."

"Couldn't sleep?" Jordan asked.

"Nope, I always sleep sound as a rock. But I got a call and had to drive over to the airport. They don't have staff there at night, and if a plane's due in, somebody has to go turn on the runway lights. So, the airport manager calls me. I do that, plus a few other odd chores. A little extra income, you know. I go in twice a week, 'bout half a day. Then, of course, when they call me. Like this morning."

"I vaguely remember hearing a phone ring. Must have thought I was dreaming. Is that the Springer Airport?"

"No, no. The one over at Gene Autry." Grandpa thumbed over his shoulder. "There's a night watchman there, but he don't do runway lights. I had a second phone line run into the bedroom jest fer that. Can't afford to miss a call by hobblin' and limpin' barefoot all the way out to the hall phone."

All of us grandkids were familiar with the old village of Berwyn, now called Gene Autry. Berwyn was hardly more than a wide place in the road, back in the 20s. I had heard that Bonnie Parker and Clyde Barrow used to come through there to hold up with friends in a little house on the hill near the cemetery. I made the mistake of asking Grandpa how the town came to be named Gene Autry, and he was glad to tell the story, again.

He recounted sagaciously how Gene Autry, the famous cowboy singer and actor, brought his rodeo to Ardmore. He apparently took a shine to the land around the Arbuckles, and in 1939 he bought twelve hundred acres west of town and began construction on a new ranch. He wanted to make it the centralized headquarters for his western show. Somebody suggested changing the town's name to Gene Autry. So, they drew up a petition and nearly all of the two hundred residents signed it, as did the post office, railroad, and county commissioners. Then, after Pearl Harbor was attacked in '41, the illustrious Mister Autry joined the Army Air Corps and sold the ranch.

"So," Grandpa said, "the town got a new name, but Gene Autry never lived here. And the Flying A Ranch was like a dream that never came true." Grandpa's eyes twinkled and he grinned, displaying the gold sliver in his dentures. "Ain't that a hoot?"

"But it used to be an Army air field, right?" I asked.

"Yessir. Until sometime in the 50s."

"What's there now?"

"Well, sir. It's now called Ardmore Municipal Airport. Lots of local traffic. Several businesses, and more comin' in every year. It's right next to the Santa Fe Rail line, so shipments go out by truck and train. All private. Nothing military anymore."

"There was that big crash a couple of years ago," Jordan said. "*That* was military."

"I don't remember that," I said.

Grandpa's head snapped in my direction. "Son, it was all over the news. Even down in Texas. Ah, but you must have been in California." He leaned toward me, a crooked smile lifting. "All starry-eyed over Tinkerbell."

"I suppose you're right." I shrugged, my cheeks red as Iowa apples. "I did have other things on my mind."

Grandma loved the story of how I met Meredith, the girl I planned to marry. Either she or Grandpa reminded me the last time I was at the farm, I'm sure just to watch me blush. Spencer and I were on vacation with our parents in Disneyland. That was just two years earlier, and touted to be my high school graduation present. Depicted often as a bubble frozen in time, Walt Disney's fantasy world attracted people from around the globe, to the tune of nearly ten million each year. No one anticipated Walt's untimely death, but like the USA herself, Walt Disney Productions was set to move forward spectacularly in the name of the founding father. And I was proud as a peacock to be there, to experience firsthand the magic and wonder. As we entered the front gate, my gaze fell on a gorgeous girl with blonde hair in a bob-wave style, brown eyes, smooth tan, and luscious pouting lips. She and her parents fell in line right in front of us. While scooting her hips through the turnstile, she looked back at me and smiled.

School days back then were marred by evacuation drills and hunkering down under our desks, like that would save us in a Cuban nuclear missile attack. Disneyland helped restore hope for a bright future. That first night at the Howard Johnson, Spencer taunted me with repeated choruses of *Love, Love, Love, Russ is in love.* I beat him with a pillow until he shut up. But I can't deny that I fell asleep with that girl on my mind. The next morning in Fantasyland, serendipitously, our families stopped for ice cream at the same time and place. Meredith and I locked eyes and shared smiles as if we were in the lasso of fate. Our parents struck up a conversation and so we spent most of the day together. Meredith and I held hands on the new Pirates of the Caribbean ride in New Orleans Square.

She and her family left Disneyland a day before us, but we said good bye at the main gate on their last evening. She and I exchanged addresses, and as we parted, she kissed me on the cheek with her parents watching. "Take care of yourself, Cowboy. Write me." My face glowed like a neon sign. But I was hooked.

Meredith graduated high school the following spring and started UCLA with a couple of freshman courses. Being a year older, I was a sophomore at North Texas State. She was in every way my dream girl. Every time I thought about her, my head brimmed with the captivating melody of *California Girls* by the Beach Boys. I told Grandma and Grandpa about my plans to fly out to see her in the Spring and talk seriously about marriage. None of that was a secret.

So, with my face aglow after Grandpa's mention of Tinkerbell, I managed to redirect the conversation. I pointed at Grandpa. "Tell me more about that crash at the Gene Autry airport."

"It was an American Airlines charter flight," he said, his tone becoming somber. "Mostly military personnel. Crashed into a hill right up there above Cool Creek. Only a handful survived. That was Friday night, and a bad thunderstorm was rollin' in. The troops aboard were on their way to airborne training at Fort Benning, Georgia. Then over to Nam, I 'spect."

Jordan nodded and his face tightened. "I remember it very clearly, because my dad went with a few guardsmen up there to help haul bodies back to town. Laid them out in the lobby at the city auditorium. Mom and I were there. She wheeled me around so I wouldn't see. But I did see."

"What caused the crash?" I asked.

"Pilot had a heart attack," Grandpa said, his look skeptical. "At least, that's what they reported. Said he slumped over the controls and the copilot couldn't pull up. The plane just nosed down." Grandpa pursed his lips and looked away in solemn contemplation.

"But you didn't really see those bodies," Grandma said, lifting eyes toward Jordan.

"Yep, I did, Grandma."

"No, you didn't. They left you here with us when all that was goin' on in town. They didn't want you to see, so they dropped you off here. Picked you up the next night. I 'spect you just remember things you heard 'cause it was the talk of the town."

Jordan's mouth eased open. His eyes drifted aside, beneath a troubled frown. He couldn't quite grasp how a clear memory could be implanted by someone else's conversation. A heavy silence blanketed the table. As I stared at Jordan's somber face, I tried to remember how we got into that discussion. I broke the silence with a question. "So,

Grandpa, you said you had to turn on the runway lights this morning?"

"Yep. A Learjet landed about four thirty. Two passengers."

"Who were the passengers?" I asked.

"Can't say."

"You mean they were people you didn't recognize?"

"No, I know 'em, alright. Just their binnis is sorta' private, if you catch my drift. I'm not allowed to talk about it."

"Whoooah, Nelly," I taunted. "Grandpa's into international espionage." I guffawed, but Grandma's stern look and a subtle shake of her head told me I shouldn't go there. I abruptly reeled it in.

Grandpa tossed up a hand and wagged his head. "No, no. Ain't nothin' like that. It's jest that one of 'em's pretty well off. Know what I mean? They don't want nobody messin' with 'im, like reporters, and all. We all know how the Paparazzi hound the rich and famous. These boys give me a little extra now and then to help keep things quiet. Well, the head honcho does, anyway. He hands me a wad 'a notes."

"You mean *well off* like a business tycoon? Or *well off* like a movie star?" Jordan quizzed.

"Can't say. But I can tell you that a couple of husky bodyguard types were there waitin' fer 'im. Picked 'im up in a long white limo and drove off in a hurry. Two more guys followed in a new Jeep Wagoneer. The pilot saw me parked over by the tower. That's where the control box is for the lights. I got a key to that. He came over and said he'd probably be sitting 'till after sun-up, so I didn't need to wait around. Asked me what time the service people got there, 'cause he needed to refuel. I told 'im, prob'ly about eight."

Grandpa regarded me and then Jordan with a serious and perturbed face. "Is that enough to satisfy ya'll's curiosity?" His eyebrows lifted, waiting for our response.

"Yessir," we said, nodding in unison. Jordan pulled a face before looking away. I glanced back at Grandpa, whose eyes remained locked in my direction. With no change in expression, Grandpa shoved a jar of molasses in front of me.

"Need to try that, son," he said. "Made by one of the neighbors up the road. Ain't no better molasses anywhere."

"No, no. I'm full, Grandpa."

He continued to stare. "Okay," I said, dipping my head to the side. "I'll try some." I smeared a dollop of butter on an open biscuit, then a little of the thick dark syrup. It was smooth and sweet, almost clinging to my palate. I washed it down with a sip of black coffee; good, but strong. I preferred honey or maple syrup. But at the moment, I thought it best not to say so. Grandpa rotated his head, stretching the taut muscles in his neck. I took it to indicate the passing of a rather tense moment, for reasons that remained unclear. When I saw Grandpa's posture ease, so did mine.

"You boys sleep alright?" he said.

"Yep, I did." I nodded with a forced smile, glancing at Jordan, who copiously smeared molasses on a second biscuit.

"Not me. I woke up after a really bad dream," Jordan said, glancing at me. He licked his fingers clean of goo before screwing the lid back on the jar. "Russ was snoring like a mountain lion. I guess that's what caused my nightmares."

Grandma gave him a scolding look. "I 'spect it wuz them two pieces of pecan pie you ate just before goin' to bed."

"What sort of nightmares?" I asked.

"Strange," Jordan said, lifting an eyebrow. "There was this woman. An Indian woman. She was motioning to me, and…"

Grandma sat straight up, covering her ears with both hands. "O Lordy, I don't want to hear about that."

"No, no. It wasn't anything like that." Jordan waved her down, certain she expected something licentious, as the pastor would call it. Grandma had a thing about pictures, movies, or even talk about *the imaginations of man's fallen nature.*

"Alright, then." Grandma scooted back from the table, stood up briskly, and started clearing dishes.

"No, in my dream this woman was wearing a buckskin dress and a blanket over her shoulders. She was, like, your age, Grandma. But she looked frail and very sad. She was standing in the middle of a sandy road, I think maybe down there by the bridge. She waved like she was trying to get my attention, then pointed up toward the mountains and motioned me to follow. Then a train went by. I saw a track, like, right out there in front of the house. I guess the rumbling was Russ snoring. I tried to count the cars, but I kept looking to see that woman, pointing. When the train was gone, so was the woman."

"The nearest railroad track runs through Gene Autry," Grandpa said. He laid both hands on the table to push himself upright. Easing back on bent legs, he shook his head and cast a challenging glance Jordan's way. "I doubt you heard that. And we don't have no Injuns livin' 'round here. At least, no full-bloods."

"Where'd all that come from?" Grandma said, probing.

"I dunno," Jordan said. "But it gave me the creepin' willies. Before I went back to sleep, I thought I saw her standing in the corner, staring at me. Then she pointed again, up toward the hills. That's all it was, Grandma. Just a dream. What did you think I was gonna say?"

Grandma fumbled, her eyes darted back and forth. "I was afraid it was one of those dreams like you boys have—you know, 'cause of hormones and all."

Jordan shook his head resolutely. "No, Grandma. But if I did, I wouldn't tell everybody about it at the table."

"Well, I never know what to expect. You young'uns are more open about that sort of thing that we were, growin' up."

Grandma pushed her chair squarely into its place, hung her apron on a hook by the pantry door, and dismissed herself. I supposed to the bathroom. She seemed embarrassed, or maybe just tense.

Grandpa spoke in a whisper. A crooked smile stretched the deep furrows in his cheeks. "A couple of your younger cousins… on your Grandma's side of the family, mind you… they wuz out here during summer for a week or so. One of 'em, we call him Bubba, is thirteen and horny as a jackass. Lord have mercy." He leaned forward, eyes widening. "Come to find out, he had one of them Playboy magazines tucked under his pillow. Grandma hadn't been the same since she come across that. Said there wuz this blonde hussy. *Playmate of the Month*, they called her. She had bosoms like a dairy cow, naked as a jaybird, posed real invitin' like, so Grandma said, exposin' every curve and crevice all the way up to glory land. Well, Grandma just flung it in the fire. Wouldn't even let me have a quick peek." Grandpa grinned and rested elbows on the back of his chair. "Told me my eyes were connected direct to my pants, and she knew what happens when an old bull spies a young heifer in heat." Grandpa shook his head, snickering into his cupped hand.

Jordan's purist cheeks glowed like a neon sign. I buried my face in my hands and shook my head. "That's more than I need to hear at breakfast, Grandpa. I think I'll just excuse myself, if you don't mind."

Jordan and I pushed back from the table. I nudged him as I passed. "Forget to say your prayers?" His jaw tightened and his eyes shot fire. But he said nothing.

A short while later, Grandma returned in a tizzy, collected empty plates and shuffled back and forth to the sink. Her eyes roamed anxiously. Grandpa sauntered into the living room, fell into his easy chair, and switched on his new television. He sat grinning and chuckling intermittently as he repeated his own words to himself. "Eyes wired direct to my pants. That's a hoot."

Twelve

The morning was bright and clear, and warm rays of the sun immediately melted patches of frost on the lawn. I trotted out to my pickup to retrieve my canteen and was on my way back to the kitchen to fill it with clean water. Before I reached the front porch, the house seemed to shudder with the thunder of drums and tribal chants. I wheeled around, searching for the source. When I pushed open the front door, the sound blast nearly knocked me over. Grandpa had tuned in KETA Channel 13 out of Oklahoma City, with the early morning news. Whatever event was being covered sounded like an Indian war dance in a John Wayne movie. It resembled what I had heard on the wind the day before, but significantly louder. I swam overhand through the noise as if traversing rapids in the Colorado River, and I covered my ears as I fell onto the couch.

"Turn that down!" Grandma yelled from the kitchen.

Kicked back comfortably in his recliner, Grandpa casually felt for the remote and eased the volume down. He needed constant reminders of his hearing loss, which seemed evident only in certain conditions. At that moment, a commentator's mellow voice broke in.

"Ladies and gentlemen," Bart Richardson began. "We're here at the Seeley Chapel, an Indian Methodist church located northeast of Connerville, in south-central Oklahoma, deep in the heart of the Chickasaw Nation." Richardson went on to explain that this historic church was built back in the days of Indian Territory, but now it was becoming *ground zero* for a resurrection of Chickasaw identity and the homelands of Native Americans in general.

"Just yesterday," Richardson said, "members of the Chickasaw Nation began to flow onto these grounds, now numbering as many as seven hundred. We're told they're here for a meeting with their tribal governor Overton James, known to them as Itoahtubbi."

I leaned toward Grandpa. "Where exactly is Connerville?"

"It's on 377, about forty miles east, as the crow flies," he said loudly. "I don't get over that way much, myself."

The commentator continued. "Chickasaw Governor Overton James was invited to address the congregation. Tribal leaders are here from communities along the Red River all the way north nearly to Oklahoma City."

The camera panned the grounds around the church, which held rows of cars, campers, tents, and a few plains-style teepees near the tree line. Some of the congregants were decked out in traditional dress, brightly colored shirts, skirts, shawls, and blankets. Some men word a feather in their hair or hats. But none bore much resemblance to the Hollywood portrayal of Red Skins. These were clearly twentieth century Native Americans of the Chickasaw Nation, who bore great pride in their heritage. The commentator led the cameraman toward a small group that danced in a circle, holding hands. A troupe of drummers and chanters huddled under a tree, pounding and shouting out a rhythm that filled the air. "They call this the *stomp dance*," he said.

Turning away from the camera, the commentator pointed. "This is clearly an important assembly, but we don't yet know the purpose. Apparently, there is some unexpected news everyone is eager to hear, possibly about new opportunities afforded by recent federal legislation. We await that address from the Governor himself. Please stay tuned and we'll interrupt regular programming at that time."

Within a few seconds Jordan emerged from the bathroom and plopped down next to me on the couch. The previous semester he'd completed a course in Oklahoma's Native American history, and I suspected he was conversant in current politics, as well. He occasionally talked about how Andrew Jackson signed the Indian Removal Act which authorized the forced relocation of five tribes from Tennessee and other southern states to the Oklahoma Territory. Jordan typically lifted a hand to count them on his fingers; the Chickasaw, Choctaw, Cherokee, Creek, and Seminole.

The Choctaw were the first to concede. The Cherokee resisted and tried legal means of resisting, but they were forced to accept the removal. Commencing in late 1838, the government conducted a half year project to move those five tribes along various planned routes to a new location. They all made the journey by foot—men, women, and children—westward past Fort Smith to the new Indian Territory. The region occupied by the Arbuckle mountains would become more or less the center of the Chickasaw Nation, with the Choctaw east to the border of Arkansas.

Considered unique among the five *civilized* tribes, the Chickasaw had already established sophisticated town sites and had a more highly

developed system of governance than most other native nations, and
they had laws rather than loose tribal traditions. The language of the
Chickasaw is called *Chikashshanompa*, similar to Choctaw, and both
came from the Muskogean family of languages that developed in the
woodlands along the eastern side of the Mississippi River. The Chickasaw were more loyal to the American structure than most other tribes,
and since the very early days of immigrant influx they had been cooperative and engaged in business. Once settled in Oklahoma, they set
their attention on development.

"The Chickasaw believe in God," Jordan said, nodding approvingly. "But their version has been interpreted through the lens of ancient
beliefs. It's pretty commonly accepted that the ancestors of American
Indians migrated across the Bering land bridge thousands of years ago.
They believed that God... they called Him Aba' Binni' li'... lives above
the clouds and on earth, appearing in the form of sacred fire. To them,
He was the sole creator of warmth, light, all animal and vegetable life,
and the *unpolluted* people. Under Christian influence, that deity came
to be known as Inki Abu, the Father Above."

Being devoutly religious himself, such details fascinated Jordan.
He explained that among the ancient beliefs there were four *Beloved
Things* above the earth: the clouds, the sun, the clear sky, and He who
lives in the clear sky. Lightning was called *Hiloha,* and the rumbling
noise in the sky was *Rowah*. When it rained, thundered, and strong
winds blew for a long time, the holy people were thought to be at war
above the clouds. Once they acquired guns, Chickasaw warriors would
shoot into the air and make gestures upward to demonstrate they were
not afraid to die. Fire was also respected as sacred. They purposefully
deadened certain trees for the purpose of keeping the annual holy fire
burning. But the white man made it unlawful, thinking such a practice
was devil worship.

Jordan seemed to resent the fact that most Americans thought all
Indians were now living on reservations. It was not true in Oklahoma.
And he thought it shameful that no one knew the great chiefs of the
five civilized tribes. People typically remember only the famous ones
portrayed in movies, like Sitting Bull (whose real name was *Tatanka
Iyotanke)*. He was the Sioux chief who rejected the treaty of Fort Lara-
mie in 1868 and led attacks on various US Army forts. And Crazy
Horse (his Lakota name was *Tasunke-Witko*), was the chief who fought
alongside Sitting Bull at Little Bighorn and killed General George

Custer. The Apache chief Geronimo (called *Goyathlay*) led war parties in the southwest, hoping to liberate his people from reservations. His actions were motivated largely by revenge for the murder of his wife, children, and mother in 1851 by Mexican soldiers led by Colonel José María Carrasco. The true stories of these events, Jordan complained, are seldom told.

In recent years, Overton James had emerged a significant figure in Oklahoma's Native American politics and social development. He was born in poverty, like most Native Americans of his day, and raised by parents Rufus James and Vinnie May Seeley in a little community called Wapanucka. But he had more drive and ambition than most of his peers. After four years in the US Navy Seabees, he earned a bachelor's degree and later a master's degree in education. He taught school and coached in various small Oklahoma communities that were originally Native American, each with its own intriguing history. Most important, in 1963, President John F. Kennedy appointed him to the position of Governor of the Chickasaw nation. A handsome man with a charismatic personality, James stood six feet tall, with a trim build and a bright smile. Anyone who saw him would assume he was destined for greatness.

When the live news returned, the music and dancing had ceased and the crowd had gathered near a makeshift platform with a podium and a single microphone. Governor Overton James rose from a chair and stepped forward.

"By now," he began, with a solemn face, "many of you have learned that my niece, known as White Dove, was abducted on Christmas Eve." The reaction to his words was a blend of gasps and murmurs, indicating that while some were unaware until now, the news was no less appalling for everyone. "She's being held by an unknown group of thugs, certainly for ransom. At this point, we do not know her location, and they have not yet made any demands. The FBI is engaged in a search. But I'm quite sure her captors hope to force a silent partnership with the Chickasaw people that will give them a share of the fortune that is coming our way. And I want you to know, and hear me clearly… my answer is NO!"

James stressed with unflinching conviction that no threats or intimidation could compare with what Native Americans had already suffered. "They think they can offer us a bottle of whiskey for arrowheads and buffalo hides," James said. "They think they can intimidate us all by threatening to kill one of us. They think they can cheat us, the same way the Osage were cheated out of millions of dollars in oil revenue a century and a half ago. They think they can hold our opportunities for ransom by threatening the life a child who is near and dear to me. They are wrong."

The reaction to his speech was mixed. Some cheered. Others stood aghast, that he spoke with apparent callousness and dispassion concerning his niece. James insisted that Native Americans were a strong people. He was correct that their long history in the Americas is nobler than is commonly reflected in school textbooks. The occasion warranted a repeat of recent history, which he elaborated fluidly like a history professor.

"During these turbulent times, the civil rights movement has focused on black descendants of slaves. But we continue to work on rights for our own people. Year after year, the Chickasaw have continued to gather together, believing that our community bond would sustain us. We continue to speak the Chickasaw language and practice traditions along with Christian faith. But we're also Americans, loyal and true. And we deserved recognition."

Recent decisions in Washington indeed pointed to a bright future for the Chickasaw. After the passing of Public Law 91-495, tribal government was finally realized. And their first health care facility had been opened earlier that year in Tishomingo. The Chickasaw communities had come together for the greater good. Women took their place as matriarchs within their families. Elder members of the tribe were still held in high regard for their knowledge and experience. And they were proud that many Chickasaws had stepped forth in defense of the American nation in all its wars, as far back as the Revolution and as recently as Vietnam. James assured the crowd that while some consider him a *puppet* of the white government, he was devoted relentlessly to the interests of the Chickasaw people.

The news coverage homed in on one statement in particular. James said, "I have been working on negotiations for repurchasing the Capitol building in Tishomingo, and I have submitted a formal proposal to the State that it be put on the National Register of Historic buildings." He explained that tribal government would focus on building an economically diverse base to generate funds to support programs and services to all Indian people. That would allow personally owned businesses to flourish and the opportunity to catch up to the white population in terms of service programs and medical facilities, improving the quality of life for all Chickasaw.

When Governor James completed his message, he introduced a guest who thus far had remained seated quietly on the make-shift podium. Carl Albert, Speaker of the U.S. House of Representatives, hailed from the tiny Oklahoma community of Bug Tussle. He was a man who understood the meaning of pulling oneself up by the bootstraps. As an ardent student of true American history, he hoped to construct a genuine solidarity with blacks as well as Native Americans, whose ancestral memory was marred by injustice.

With tear-rimmed eyes, he recounted the Tulsa Race Massacre in 1921, when the Greenwood district was burned and hundreds of blacks were killed. It was a clear case of escalating mob violence stemming from one black youth being accused of attacking a white girl. A later report was that she had lied just to get the boy in trouble. It worked far beyond her expectations. The dead were buried in mass graves. No one was held accountable.

Albert also mentioned the Osage murders during the same period, which had been ignored or swept under the rug. The Osage Reservation in the plains of Northern Oklahoma formed a triangle between Ponca City, Bartlesville, and Tulsa to the south. Like other Native Americans, the Osage were relocated under Andrew Jackson's Indian Removal Act of 1830. The discovery of oil there, just before the turn of the century, resulted in enormous wealth for many Osage Indians. Remarkably, Congress passed a law requiring Osage to have white guardians to manage their oil revenues. The result was a plague of exploitation. White men married Osage women and then killed them and their children in order to inherit their mineral rights. From 1918 to 1931, hundreds of Osage were murdered. Eventually, federal investigators managed to bring a few perpetrators to justice, and laws were amended to protect the rights and property of Osage natives. He added, "I realize no one can possibly convey in words, written or oral, the compelling horror of the experience itself, whether of those who were deprived of dignity and hunted, tortured, and murdered, or those who were forced to drink the bitter potion of slavery. Theirs is a sad saga," Albert said, "that at long last unfurls in a joyful new beginning for a new generation who dares to remember." He endorsed official recognition of the tribal sovereignty of indigenous nations like the Chickasaw. "I want you to know," he said firmly, "I am fully behind the proposition to open gambling establishments in areas traditionally owned by Native Americans, and I stand behind your right to profit from such operations. That should bring jobs to thousands, creating an atmosphere for other innovative enterprises for those who will rise up and take advantage of it. So, what do you say to that?"

Cheers and whoops lifted high into the Oklahoma sky. The rhythm of drums and chants resumed, and dust rose from the feet of exuberant dancers. This was a good day for the Chickasaw nation.

Despite rousing speeches and tribal hoopla, it was not a good day for the young girl named White Dove. Somewhere, alone in darkness, she prayed that someone would hear her voice and come to her aid. But, in response to her dire circumstances and whatever demands had been made for her release, the only word from her uncle was "no."

Thirteen

When the broadcast concluded, Grandpa twisted the channel knob until he found *Days of Our Lives*. He mumbled he was tired of listening to *Injun drums and ballyhoo*, and political speeches that were sure to cause trouble for all the *regular* folks.

Surprised that Grandpa preferred soaps over an important news broadcast, Jordan inhaled to deliver a rebuttal. I playfully slapped a hand over his mouth and dragged him away, but intentionally abandoning Grandpa to his entertainment. With that clever move, the two of us began carting our gear out to the front porch, ready to load up when Terry arrived with the bus. That plan came to a halt when Terry phoned to say he was still packing and wouldn't make it to the farm until noon or later. That provided me the opportunity to take Ginger to visit Orpheus Pratt.

I had left rope halters on the horses. Each had a ring beneath the noseband designed for snapping on a lead rope. Ginger was a highly disciplined horse and responded well to a tug on a rope against her neck, even to a rider's body posture. I didn't hesitate to ride her bareback, using the lead rope instead of reins. So, I hopped on and we moseyed down the road. The morning air was fresh and cool. I whistled a tune to the gentle *rock and sway* of Ginger's pace, loose shoe clunking with each step. After no more than two miles and a few twists in the road, we approached the Pratt place.

The unpainted frame shack sat against a rock bluff, encircled by a wide swath of well-packed bare dirt. Further out to the left, a rusted-out car body and a few pieces of farm equipment were partially visible in tall grass. The property had the exact appearance I had often complained about. But since I needed this man's expertise, I muzzled my critical thoughts. The appearance of his domicile was not a factor. As I approached, I could make out a garage and shop with corrugated sides and roof, set back from the house under the shade of a large sycamore. Double wooden doors stood open, propped with a pair of bricks. I slid to the ground and led Ginger toward the workshop. The clunking sound from the loose shoe seemed more pronounced now.

Two coon hounds, one a black and tan, the other a blue-tick, loped out from behind the house, baying with noses to the air as if they'd treed a raccoon. Ginger's ears pricked, but she didn't bolt. A black man I assumed to be Orpheus appeared from the front screen door and called to the hounds, Mortimer and Sally. They immediately turned and trotted to him, tails wagging obediently. He pointed and they disappeared somewhere behind the house, resuming their sentry duty. I noticed Sally's swollen undercarriage and dangling nipples, and I assumed she had a litter of pups hidden away somewhere.

A stout man with a faded military tattoo on his left arm, Orpheus wore denim coveralls over what appeared to be dingy long johns. His well-defined biceps were evidence of his routine of manual labor. I guessed him to be forty, maybe a tad older. Expressionless, he stepped down from the porch and made his way toward me. As he approached, I eased forward and put out my hand.

"I'm Russ. One of Bert Greenwood's grandsons."

He took my hand and held it firmly as he studied my face. "You're the one from Texas," he said, lifting his chin.

I smiled, returning his studious look. "That's me. I'm told you know a lot about a lotta things. But I didn't expect you'd know that."

A crooked smile lifted on his leathery face. He squeezed my hand as a sign of affirmation, before releasing it and taking a casual step back. Studying my face, he folded his arms across his chest. "Also heard your cousin, the older one, is back from Nam."

"That's right. He'll be here later today. Goin' campin' with me and Jordan."

Orpheus nodded and turned his attention toward Ginger. "Pretty mare," he said, stretching a hand toward her muzzle.

I eased to her side and stroked her neck. "She's got a problem and needs your help."

The black man's callous-laden hand glided along Ginger's jaw and down her neck. Her suspicious eye followed his movements, as he patted her shoulder. "Must be a roper," he mumbled. "Is that why her mane is roached?"

"She was trained for that. But I don't rope. I just like the clean look."

"Yessir. Clean and professional. Not like my old farm horse back there."

I lifted my head to see a swaybacked mare watching us from the corner of a pasture behind the house. A buckskin, as old as Grandpa in horse years. Sections of grey spotted her coat. Her dark mane and tail were long and knotted, full of cockleburs. That was all pretty obvious, even from a distance.

"I was in Korea," Orpheus said, his tone warmer than before. "A corpsman. US Marine Corps. Patched up a lot of boys. Held some in my arms while they died. Weren't none of it easy. But war never is. That's fer damn sure."

He seemed to be a good man, strong and healthy, but there were certain things from the past I guessed he had not managed to let go. His eyes and manner betrayed heavy emotional baggage. And it was obvious he was stuck at a level of subsistence living that was more common to American blacks than most whites realized. It was hard for me to guess which was harder. His life here in the country, or life in a big city ghetto. I had heard it said that if you don't like being poor and white, you should try being poor and black.

"Hope you'll bring your cousin by. I'd like to bat the breeze with him."

"Sure, but he doesn't talk much about it. I imagine he has some hard-core memories much like yours."

"I 'spect so. He might talk with me, though."

"Okay, I'll bring him. We'll see how the day goes."

"Ya'll goin' huntin up there?"

"Maybe," I said.

"I killed a few deer over the years. Don't hunt no more. And them two lazy hounds, they don't hunt neither. More trouble than they's worth." Orpheus chuckled. His perfect white teeth and sparkling eyes overpowered the hard lines in his face.

"I'm sure Terry plans to shoot a deer while we're up there. But Jordan and I are mostly looking for caves."

Orpheus took the lead rope and Ginger followed him into the work shed. I trailed behind. Ginger shuffled and looked around suspiciously at the cluttered surroundings. As we stopped, I eased up close, held her harness loosely, and rubbed and scratched her from muzzle to poll. Her big eyes blinked occasionally. She snorted impatiently, then shifted her weight as Orpheus lifted one foot and then the other.

I noticed a newspaper clipping tacked to a board. The headlines read: *Civil Rights Leader Killed.* I was close enough to read a few lines on the clipping: *American clergyman and civil rights leader fatally shot at the Lorraine Motel in Memphis, Tennessee.* The paper was dated April

4, 1968.

"A sad event," I said. "I mean about Doctor King." I thumbed toward the clipping, expecting a comment from Orpheus. If he heard me, he didn't show it. His mind was now fixed totally on his work. He strapped on a leather apron and stepped to Ginger's left side. Lifting her hoof between his legs, he pried nails out, tossed the shoe into a barrel, and began cleaning and trimming her hoof and underpadding. His movements were smooth and nimble.

"Feet look good. I can see you take care of this pretty gal."

"I try. Costs money, though. You didn't mention your fee."

He dropped the hoof and shifted to the right side, following the same procedure. "I'm fair, but less that you're accustomed to, I 'spect."

"I appreciate that. Everything seems to be higher in the city."

"I hear you. I think we should do all four. That okay?"

"Sure, if you think it best."

Once done cleaning and trimming, Orpheus gave Ginger a pat on the shoulder, just beneath the withers, and ran his hand up and down her neck. He stood close, looking Ginger in the eye. She blinked nonchalantly.

"You're a fine gal, ain't cha? You need me to make them feet feel better? Yes ma'am. I'm glad to help." His gentle hand patted and stroked, starting at the withers and running along Ginger's side. Her head turned slightly as she eyed him curiously. Ears upright, a cordial nicker signaled her approval.

Orpheus turned and clunked through a pile of horseshoes in a box. He never mentioned a dollar figure. He seemed more interested in what we planned to do up in the mountains. He set himself to work, but I could see his mind was churning with questions.

"Spelunkin', you said." Orpheus spoke without looking at me. "Is that the right word?"

"Yes, it is. At least when you explore inside. On this trip, we're mostly interested in locating a couple of caves we've heard about, but never been inside. You know much about that?"

"No sir. Just the ones up by Turner Falls. No secrets about them. But I've heard stories about others. You might discover more than you bargained for."

I waved it off. "If you're talking about snakes, this time of year the rattlesnakes and copperheads hibernate down where it's warm. We're real careful about that."

"Ain't talkin' 'bout snakes."

"What then?"

"Well, sir, some folks say there be ghosts in these mountains."

I chuckled. Orpheus looked at me, pan-faced. I could feel my smile wither, replaced by an awkward frown. "You're serious, aren't you?"

"Yessir."

I shoved both hands deep into my hip pockets, eyes roaming awkwardly. "I don't believe in ghosts."

"I do."

I paused, uncertain how to respond. Then words eased out. "You ever seen one?"

Orpheus lifted his chin in thought. "Hard question. Not sure. Could be."

A sudden chill rushed over me and the back of my neck bristled. I had never experienced anything I considered to be supernatural or paranormal. But I knew many people believed otherwise. And Orpheus was clearly one of those.

In Denton, my friend Brody claimed that his family had a poltergeist. He said now and then it rearranged knickknacks on the mantle right before their eyes. On another occasion, it pushed Brody's mom against the wall in the bathroom. At least, that's what she said. It held her there a whole minute, before releasing its grip and slamming the door on its way out. I told Brody I didn't believe it. So, he invited me to spend a night. We bedded down in the living room and stayed awake till about three. I awoke to the morning clatter of a busy family preparing for their day. The poltergeist was a no-show. Brody said it must have been uncomfortable with a stranger in the house. That sounded like malarky to me.

I brought the topic up to my family. So, Dad thought it would be fun to take us all to Jefferson, Texas, famous for its ghost tours. The first night there, we were escorted through the streets after dark by a seventy-year-old woman with a crackly voice and eyes like Bette Davis. Quite knowledgeable in local lore and gifted in the art of storytelling, she spun numerous yarns of murder, lynchings, drownings, and horrific accidents, all based on *reliable local sources*. Stopping in front of a well-preserved mansion built in the Gilded Age, our eyes lifted to a dark window in a high front gable while *Miss Davis* related how a child was run over by a log wagon in 1886, but his spirit never left home and appears now and then in that very window.

Later in the tour, along an alley next to a boarded-up hotel, we were told that a ghost occasionally appears in the second-floor hall, carrying a martini in one hand, and his head tucked under his arm. Sometimes, a curtain parts in a third story window and a shadowy face looks down toward the street, before a man climbs out and does a swan-dive to the ground. A few paces further, *Miss Davis* swept a hand toward an old well, where the spirit of Lucille van Soter is sometimes seen strolling with her cane and carrying a pale of water. Pointing along a dark alley, *Miss Davis* invited everyone to listen for the sound of Jeremiah Holt peddling his bike home with his poker winnings just before being set upon by a gang of thugs.

Then, after entering a large store packed with dusty antiques, the canned monologue reached a crescendo. "A young woman named Nola McIntosh committed suicide here," *Miss Davis* whispered. "Broke a mirror with her shoe and slashed her wrists with the shards. She came staggering through the aisles, one shoe off and one shoe on, blood trailing along the floor, and fell dead right in front of customers queued up at the cash register. She still comes back every few weeks, looking for her missing shoe. "So," *Miss Davis* invited, "as you meander through the aisles, see if you can detect her presence. Use your flashlights. I'm going to switch off the overhead fluorescent fixtures, but there'll be a lamp at each corner of the building so you can keep your bearings."

That's the stuff that brings folks to town. And no doubt a few folks encountered a ghost that night, at least they believed so. As far as I was concerned, it was all a crock. People have to make a living, some by peddling legends and folklore. But in my assessment, the supernatural and metaphysical were in that murky category of myths like vampires, werewolves, flying witches who cast spells, or occultists who claim to know dark mysteries and conjure up the dead. I was quite certain there were no angels, demons, or spirits anywhere, up there, out there, or anywhere. No miracles, and no mystic experience; nothing beyond the natural. But I was equally confident that the scope of the human imagination is boundless and as unbridled as a mustang running wild in Montana.

Back to the here-and-now, the look on Orpheus' face told me he was a believer, and maybe he knew something I didn't. I cozied one hip up against a workbench, crossed one boot over the other, and folded my arms. "Why would anyone think there are ghosts up there in the Arbuckle Mountains?"

"Some folks laugh when we talk about Oklahoma's secrets," Orpheus said, casting a scolding look my way. "You probably heard stories about somebody dyin' in some suspicious way… maybe got killed, you know, real ugly and messy… and their spirit sort of lingers, trying to find peace. Like a woman hacked to pieces by a jealous husband, but she hangs around there in the house, playin' little tricks, so's to make him pay. That kinda' thing."

"Sounds spooky, alright." I shuffled my stance, trying to relax. "We know about the Wild Woman Cave, but there's no ghost in that story. Now, the so-called Dead Man Cave, that one might be different. But nobody I know has seen a ghost there. I think they just found a skeleton. That's enough to start a humdinger of a ghost story." I chuckled, trying to draw a smile from Orpheus. There was none. "Aw well," I said. "I 'spose time'll tell."

"You probly don't know 'bout all the slaves that died in these parts," he said, his tone somber. "They called this *Injun Territory* back then, but it wuz freedman territory, too. And just like white plantation owners down south, some of the Indians had black slaves. After the Civil War, a whole parcel of freed men started a movement to make this an all-black state. 'Course, that didn't happen. But a few settlements stayed all-black for a couple of generations. Kingfisher was one of 'em. I believe a dozen or so communities like that are still hangin' on, but nobody pays 'em no mind. They're off the main roads. Them folks keep to themselves. And whites mostly stay away."

I was taken aback by what Orpheus had to say. A lot of American history was somewhat fuzzy in my mind. But that portion was totally new to me, and I was born no more than twenty miles from his house. In time I would learn that after the Civil War, from 1865 to 1920, African-Americans created more than fifty identifiable towns and settlements across the country, with thirteen still in existence in Oklahoma. Most were former slaves, and they settled together for mutual protection and economic security. When the government forced American Indians to accept individual land allotments and give up their slaves, most black *freedmen* chose land next to other blacks, and they created cohesive, prosperous farming communities that could support businesses, schools, and churches. It made sense, but it was not something we learned about in school.

However, all that history meant little as I stood there in a garage workshop, just Orpheus and me, a hundred years and several generations later, after a lot of unpleasant events had been swept under the carpet. The current generation of blacks and Native Americans still had a foul taste in their mouths and resentment in their hearts. I could sense it in Orpheus. And I realized that it contributed to the racial conflict currently sweeping the country. The 60s indeed were a troublesome era, and I couldn't deny that it drew a dark cloud over my school days— drugs, war protests, civil rights conflicts, riots in the streets and university campuses, the assassination of JFK in Dallas, and then Martin Luther King Jr. in Memphis. And just this past August, Robert Kennedy was assassinated, and thousands of protesters descended on Chicago during the Democratic National Convention. Some activists hoped to steer the Democratic Party toward a firm anti-war policy, but many simply called for revolutionary social change. On Chicago's North Side, police forced protestors out of Lincoln Park while chants of *the whole world's watching* were broadcast on television to millions of Americans (and no doubt around the world). Journalists spoke poignantly of *long-simmering acrimony between the growing counterculture and the political establishment.*

Orpheus had opinions of his own, and it was clear that he resented what many called *systemic white advantage.* Yet, he had no animosity for white people like me and Terry, or the Greenwood family in general. He was just trying to make a living, feed his family, and get along with his neighbors. And if a ghost came calling, Orpheus would be respectful but unafraid.

Fourteen

Ginger pranced contentedly on her freshly groomed feet and new set of horseshoes, and we made it back to the farm by one o'clock. Terry was still not there. Grandma had left me a bologna sandwich on the table. Next to it laid a bag of potato chips, the opening clipped with a clothespin. She was out back hanging laundry on the clothesline. I wasn't sure where Grandpa and Jordan were. When I finished my sandwich, I lay down on the couch for a nap.

Just after two, the dogs bolted toward the road, tossing skyward a cacophony of howls and barks. Curious but not startled, I got up and moseyed out to the front porch. Jordan and Grandpa were already there. Trailed by a long cloud of dust, a school bus rumbled along the rutted lane toward the farm house. In this quiet rustic setting, the massive blue body had the anomalous look of an alien invader. It turned and circled the big elm tree before coming to a rickety halt. Pneumatic brakes spewed, and dust ascended over the top.

A moment later, the double panel door clattered opened. Terry descended the steps and jumped to the ground like John Wayne stepping out of a landing craft onto a beachhead. His stubbled face split into a wide grin. He lifted his stained cap, revealing a head of thick and gnarled brown hair. With arms widely extended, he stood waiting for a response. Jordan jogged sprightly toward him, spinning around him as they embraced. Terry levered down his cap, leaving it tilted to one side. With one arm stretched over Jordan's shoulder, he lifted the other arm to motion me into a three-man group hug.

As Grandpa would say, Terry was a sight for sore eyes. A first-generation baby boomer and a true war baby, he was among the children whose births helped America celebrate the end of the Big War and the beginning of the Happy Days. My aunt Dorcas (our grandparents' oldest child) had married Harvey Barnett in 1940. They had one daughter, Lisa, born just before Uncle Harvey shipped out and spent three years in Pacific Campaign of World War Two. Aunt Dorcas and little Lisa lived with Grandma and Grandpa while Harvey was away. When he came home, they settled in Paul's Valley, where he got a commissions-only job selling cars for McIntosh Motors. Terry was born ten months later and his little sister Lucille two years after that.

Harvey made auto sales his life's career. I would never forget his plaid jacket and paisley ties, nor his broad toothy smile and hearty handshake. Whenever I saw him, he would draw me close in for a side hug, and then pat my ribs vigorously. He did that with just about everyone. He claimed it helped to create a feeling of trust, which was essential in sales. It must have worked. He sold cars like crazy. But with family, that hug meant something different. Something special.

At age eighteen, Terry was imbued with a strong spirit of patriotism and, like many other American sons, he answered the call to fight for Old Glory. The war in Vietnam was a timely opportunity. Fresh out of high school, he volunteered for Army airborne training. In 1965, on his first tour with the Special Forces, Terry was part of the rescue team sent to Nam Dong. During that early period of the war, two of Terry's classmates, Dennis McAllen and Junior Pickens, were killed in action. The mayor of Paul's Valley honored both with photos and commemorative plaques on display in the County Courthouse. In July of '67, Terry was deployed to heavy combat in the Mekong Delta. He was promoted to E-5 just before he sustained two bullet wounds that got him a Purple Heart and a safe return home. Sergeant Terrance Griffin Barnett was honorably discharged in the summer of '68.

Commonly called the Jewel of Southeast Asia, Vietnam had become a killing field, along with Laos and Cambodia. Many Americans had come home in flag-draped coffins. Some did not come home at all, which was a cause of national consternation. My brother Spencer and I had cried ourselves to sleep when Terry shipped out the first time. But I corresponded with him faithfully, as did Jordan, and he answered all our letters. I suspect we cousins wrote him more often than his own mother.

Of course, after his discharge, we had not seen him until now. He had remained quiet and aloof, trying to reestablish his civilian identity and figure a plan forward. We could not know the wounds that were hidden from view. His sisters, Lisa and Lucille, told Christine that he was never hostile, but clearly distant, reserved, and pensive. He rarely smiled, and so this moment of greeting at the farm was possibly a breakthrough.

The school bus was a short version that had been converted into a camper. It was on the back row of Uncle Harvey's used car lot, but after more than a year it failed to sell. He was willing to cut his losses and give it to Terry. This little jaunt up in the Arbuckles would be a test run. The bus had only a pair of bench seats, one behind the driver and the other at the door. That was sufficient for four people, side by side with an aisle between. Behind the seats was a makeshift kitchen with a propane stove, a sink, and upper and lower cabinets. It was much the same as the galley in a low-end sailboat or cabin cruiser. Behind the galley there were four bunk beds, an upper and lower on each side of the aisle, with the lower legs bolted to the floor. There were no mattresses, but Terry had brought four rolls of heavy egg crate foam, thick enough to provide insulation atop the open bedsprings. At the rear of the bus, behind a curtain, sat a port-o-potty, surrounded by a simple tarp curtain. Terry brought a second tarp to cover the bus entrance to avoid opening the noisy folding doors if someone needed to slip outside at night.

"The dude that did the conversion," Terry explained, "lived in it a couple of years up in the Rockies. A grizzly bear killed him, and park rangers then sold his stuff in an auction. The bus had a few owners and a lot of abuse before ending up in Oklahoma. Dad has given up hope of selling it."

After a brief tour of the bus, the three of us unfolded chairs on the front lawn and chewed the fat for a while. It was a windless afternoon, and the sun felt good on our faces. Our planned campsite was less than an hour away, but none of us felt rushed to get up there. Nor did any of us notice that Grandpa had disappeared and returned several times, carrying tools, including a post-hole digger, bits of lumber, and last of all, a wheelbarrow already loaded with dry cement and gravel.

When there was a lull in our conversation, he invited our attention as he ascended the front porch steps, accentuating his labored effort without a handrail. Jordan stepped up to offer a hand, but Grandpa waved him off. He had seized that moment to draw us away from our catch-up *yammering*, as he called it, to a chore he needed done while he had sufficient help. He wanted holes dug, three on each side of the front porch steps, for six square posts to be set in concrete. Then he wanted the tops cut at an angle to accommodate handrails. He described his great discomfort when climbing steps and the difficulty of keeping his balance when descending. In short, both he and Grandma needed something to grip.

"I want them posts in the ground so the concrete sets good before a freeze," he said. His head rotated upward to survey the graying sky. "The weatherman says we might be in for some cold weather in the next day or so. So, how 'about it? You boys up for that?"

Terry, Jordan, and I were all handy with saws, drills, and hammers, so without hesitation we hopped to it. The job was done in less than two hours, and we cleaned and packed away tools while Grandpa stood next to the steps, his arm resting on the new handrail. By then it was nearly dark. He turned on the porch light and tested the steps and rail another couple of times. He smiled and nodded.

The reward for that chore, Grandma announced, was fried chicken, a hot shower, and a night's sleep in a decent bed. Of course, we figured a good shower would be our last for a few days, so we each made the most of it. I drew the short straw and was last in. The water chilled in about three minutes. I managed to get the shampoo rinsed out of my hair just in time. I toweled off on the cold floor, shivering as goosebumps rippled over my shoulders and down my arms. Still toweling my wet hair, I sauntered into a room full of chuckles. Terry, Jordan and Grandpa sat in front of the TV, glued to an episode of the Three Stooges.

That was interrupted when the front door swung open. Uncle Luke's unexpected appearance brought Grandpa to his feet, and Grandma came galloping in from the kitchen with a squeal and arms flung wide. Uncle Luke immediately led us all outside to see his shiny new Ford truck— an F250 crew cab, dark blue with a matching camper top over the bed. After a round of oohs and ahhs over Luke's new toy, Grandma left us to engage in *man talk* in the front yard and returned to her work in the kitchen with added vigor. Once back inside, I could hear her shuffle about like a short-order cook at a diner. She set another place at the kitchen table. Already the tantalizing aroma of fried chicken drew us in that direction. Terry had invited Uncle Luke to lead our outing, but he was forced to decline. He said he was in charge of a basketball tournament at the high school, with a tip-off scheduled at nine the next morning. We were glad, nonetheless, that he came out to see us off.

"Where's Christine?" Uncle Luke asked, glancing around the room. "I thought she was going, too."

"She didn't make it," Terry answered, eyes lowering. For a moment, the atmosphere thickened. I noted a puzzled frown on Uncle Luke's brow as he studied Terry's response. Terry seemed relieved that he brushed it off and changed the subject.

Uncle Luke had been raised right there on the Greenwood farm.

The youngest of five children, he was the only one to get a college education, and clearly some of his education caused Grandma great stress. Immediately after graduation from Southeastern Oklahoma State, he joined the Navy. That was in the early years of the Vietnam conflict. I was still a pimple-faced teenager when he came home on furlough at Thanksgiving. The four of us cousins admired Luke and clustered around him like groupies at a rock concert. We stroked his uniform and medals and asked silly questions like, *Did you ever get sea sick?* and *How big are the guns on your battleship?*

With a college degree, Luke was able to attend OCS and enlist as Ensign O-1. He then did four six-month tours in Southeast Asia. He was aboard the Bennington just after the Tonkin Gulf incident in August of '64, when the USS Maddox was attacked. He had plenty of stories to tell about the American Navy's air and surface offensive against North Vietnam. He advanced to the rank of lieutenant shortly before he was discharged.

Once back safe in Oklahoma, Uncle Luke applied for a teaching job at Ardmore High. He was accepted, and a year later he became assistant basketball coach in addition to his teaching responsibilities. At the beginning of one semester, he was surprised to see his nephew Jordan grinning in the front row of his geography class. Later on, Uncle Luke found himself coaching Jordan on the varsity basketball team. By that time, I had moved to Texas with my parents, so I missed out on Uncle Luke's formal pedagogy. However, I did spend time with him on holidays when I could get away for a few days. He was an avid outdoorsman. During his first summer after Vietnam, he spent an entire month hiking alone in a wilderness area of the Colorado Rockies. We all assumed he needed alone time to clear his head.

After supper, Uncle Luke went immediately to the big oak table in the dining room and splayed out a large map. It was one of several he had collected, illustrating parks, hiking trails, and caves in a three-hundred-mile radius covering Arkansas, Missouri, and eastern Kansas and Oklahoma. This particular map covered only the Arbuckle region. At the bottom right corner was the insignia of the US Geological Survey, dated 1954. Luke explained that he wanted to review a few things, to make sure we knew what to look for.

The Arbuckle Mountain range is the oldest formation in the region, lying between the Appalachian and Rocky Mountains, and it contains the most diverse mineral resources in the state. A bizarre hump in the mid-west plains covering no more than about five hundred square miles, the Arbuckles contain a granite and gneiss core that geologists estimate to be over a billion years old. The thick limestone top layer is rich with marine sediment and the fossils of sea organisms, similar to other ancient sea beds across America. The range is clearly defined by rows of weathered rocks, the edge of ancient upheavals, now resembling spines on the back of a reptile. The highest ridge is a mere 1400 feet above sea level, which is only a thousand feet above the surrounding farmlands. The intrigue lies in their antiquity and the mysterious network of caves that has attracted spelunkers from all over the nation.

"These caves up by Turner Falls," Uncle Luke said, finger tapping the map, "are well-known. We've all been in them, like every barefoot and bikini-clad tourist." He then pointed as he swept counter-clockwise over the map, a finger landing at each location. "Crystal Cave is located about a half mile behind the bathhouse, Wagon Wheel is right next to the falls, and it's the one you commonly see in photos of the park. Outlaw Cave is located on the same side, on top of the falls, less than a hundred yards back. But up above and to the west, there is a grotto called Bitter Enders, at the head of Honey Creek. It has two openings. And down here," he dragged a finger toward the bottom left of the map, "eight miles west of Springer, on the Chapman place, is the Wild Woman."

That cave I remembered vividly. Uncle Luke had taken me, Terry, Jordan, and Christine there a couple of years back. It was natural and bare, with no accommodation for tourists. It had been explored only by private spelunking groups. There were no lights, no paved walkways or barriers, and no snack bar at the bottom or elevator to the surface like the highly commercial Carlsbad Caverns. We descended cautiously, one by one, through a steep rocky mouth, to the first long and tight room. It was raw, wet, and muddy, and it reeked of animal urine and something dead that we never found. With only flashlights and a couple of carbide lanterns, we inched our way through convoluted corridors. In places, we crawled on our bellies through tight passages carved by millions of years of flowing water. Uncle Luke said we covered about half a mile, and he was certain there was much more to it, but it was very difficult to get to. "You'd have to wriggle along with a safety line tied to your ankles," he said, "in case you get stuck."

The Wild Woman Cave was named in memory of Ethel Hindman, a stunt plane wing rider who was hired to explore it in search of water.

That was back in the 1930s during the Dust Bowl. A photo of her had appeared in the *Daily Ardmorite*. Everybody said she was crazy to do such things, so the moniker *wild woman* stuck. No doubt, many people took that name to mean that a *crazy* woman had lived in or hid out in that cave, or maybe died there, and some even said her ghost haunted the place. None of that was true, but it's the way legends get started.

"There's also another entrance," Luke said, "the size of a manhole, on a bluff overlooking the lower opening. The top one has a vertical drop of about thirty feet, which requires a rope descent. These caves are at a higher elevation than all the others. This entire area is called the Arbuckle Simpson Aquifer region, and there must be hundreds of underground channels cut by water flow. By injecting dye into the water at upper levels, engineers have determined that the Wild Woman and Bitter Ender's caves are connected, and they're part of a much larger system."

Luke went on for half an hour, reviewing details as if briefing a combat platoon before an assault. Jordan's blue eyes regarded him admiringly as he spoke. Terry stood at ease, but listened attentively and nodded whenever Uncle Luke's eyes turned his way. "Over here on the east side of the interstate is the McGalliard Cave, and moving farther east, right up above the farm here, are those little ones, Coon Cave and Dead Man's Cave. We've all had a peek at them."

"Not me," I said, lifting a hand.

"Well, there's really not much to see. They're shallow. Just varmint hideouts. But you can hike up there and see them, if you can find them. If you do, I'd like to have the exact location marked on this map."

"You know they'll be full of rattlers this time of year," Grandpa said, slipping up behind us.

"Yea, but this is just a recon mission," Terry huffed. "We don't plan to actually go inside. If we find a big one, we'll set up a marker and come back in the early summer. But even then, we might find a snake or two. We all know that. And we're always cautious."

Uncle Luke nodded, and continued. "Way out here," his finger slid far to the right, pointing off the map, "is another one called the Mystic. It's on a rocky prairie east of Nebo and Hwy 177. And up here," he swept his hand back to the center and upward, "above the Washita River there is one that some call the Torture Cave. I'd like you to locate it on this trip, and check out the entrance. I've read reports that it's not too far from an old abandoned Boy Scout camp, about here." He tapped the map definitively. "But reports are not always accurate. This is all private ranchland, but we have written permission from the owners. No one should give you any trouble."

Luke's finger drifted to an area high up, near the crest of the mountain, almost due north of the farm. "There is another one up here, somewhere. Ya'll might go see what's there. I've heard stories, but..." Luke paused, pensively. Then he waved it off.

"What's all that over there?" I pointed further north toward Davis, where the map indicated a developed area with roads and buildings.

"That's Falls Creek, the Baptist youth camp," he said. "We have no interest in that area. It's all developed and heavily traveled."

Grandpa interrupted again. "Luke talks all that geology lingo I don't understand," he said. "Anadarko Basin and Arbuckle Uplift. Sounds more like the parts of ladies' underwear." He nudged me in the ribs and winked. "But it's real *interestin'*. I gotta *ad-mit*."

"Sorry to sound technical," Luke answered. "But caves are of great scientific interest. There's a lot to learn from them. For example, piles of bat guano are among the ways of determining the age of a specific cavern. Given the ceiling space above, scientists are able to estimate the number of bats that can hang there. Then, from what we know of the frequency and amount of defecation from a single adult bat and the depth of guano excavated from a specific room, they can determine about how long bats have occupied it. By that, coupled with the consistent growth rate of stalactites and stalagmites and other dating methods, scientists have determined the Carlsbad Caverns to be about four million years old. Amazing, huh? A huge cavern, slowly carved out of limestone by the flow of water laced with sulfuric acid."

Grandma nudged Grandpa in the ribs. I cut a glance in their direction and heard her whisper that according to the Bible, that's all wrong. "God created them caves with the snap of a finger," she said. "Mountains, deserts, oceans, all of it."

Grandpa cupped a hand discreetly over his mouth and whispered, "Mama, there's a lot to know that ain't in the Bible."

She answered, "If it ain't in there, it ain't all that important."

Fifteen

It was no secret that any mention of scientific studies upset Grandma, particularly fossil evidence of the earth's antiquity and archeological remains of ancient civilizations. Several years back, while digging in the garden she found a fossilized trilobite. Uncle Luke explained to her it was a creature from the Paleozoic Era, at least 200 million years ago. He showed her a college textbook with photographs of those, and other fossilized creatures. She argued that all such things resulted from Noah's Flood. They washed up into the mountains by powerful waves in a global deluge that killed all animals except those on the ark, and all humans except Noah and his family. Luke asked her why she believed that. She answered, with an air of self-assurance, "It's in the Bible, my dear son, if you'd just read it."

Luke had studied sufficient history to know that a common but misguided world chronology is attributed to Irish Bishop James Ussher in the 1600s, who used the Genesis ages of patriarchs to arrive at a creation date of 4004 BCE. Luke was also aware that many scholars, Jewish and Christian, recognize the legendary nature of the early Genesis narratives. But there was no point in arguing with Grandma. Doing so, even with the best intentions, would just upset her.

When Uncle Luke had packed away all his maps, with the exception of the one he left with Terry, Grandpa turned and said, "Mama, why don't we open a fresh jar of peaches? That'd be a mighty fine treat at the close of a mighty fine day. Doncha think?"

Grandma nodded obligingly and motioned for me to come with her. I was afraid she was going to complain about liberal universities and the danger of science leading Christian youth astray. But that wasn't on her agenda. I followed her through a tightly stocked pantry to a narrow door I hadn't known existed. She flipped the latch and tugged the door handle, before leaning inside and stretching upward for a string. With a faint click, a light came on. A single bulb dangled from a beam, illuminating wooden steps that descended to about ground level.

"This used to be the toilet," Grandma said. "It was our first improvement from a cold and windy outhouse, before Grandpa built a proper toilet." Bracing herself with one hand on the wall, Grandma began the descent. I followed. Wooden steps creaked under our weight. She twisted to look up in my direction, talking as she eased down the steps. "What we had here was a board seat with a hole, and a bucket I shoved under it through a trap door outside. About twice a week I emptied the bucket in the old outhouse hole in the ground. A little bit of work, but worth it."

Four steps down, another door tilted at about thirty degrees. Grandma bent down to grab the handle, and with a hefty grunt she lifted it open until it fell against the brick wall. "Back in the old days..." Grandma propped a fist on her hip as she caught her breath, "we had to trudge outside through rain and snow. I jest hated that. You boys were just tykes when Grandpa built the new indoor toilet, with plummin' and a septic tank. I had never had such a luxury before."

"So, what's down there?" I pointed into the dark hole.

Grandma's arm waved through the air again, searching for another string. She tugged and the cavern brightened. "We store canned goods here. But this was the storm cellar." She leaned toward me with a capering smile. "Grandpa dug this right off the back of the house, so we wouldn't have to run outside through rain or hail to get into it. The top is our patio. We can still hide down here, if need be."

I was well aware that south central Oklahoma was right in the middle of tornado alley, curving up from the Texas panhandle all the way through Kansas and Nebraska. In such a twister Dorothy and Toto were whisked away to the Land of Oz. But country folks know there's nothing make-believe about the destructive power of a tornado. I lifted my eyes and followed the sweep of Grandma's hand. The walls were lined with shelves full of jars and canned goods. She pointed up to the steel beams and cement. "It stays pretty cool during the summer. And, of course, below ground, it never freezes."

"Wow, looks like a supermarket," I said. "But it's funny you call it *canning* when you put stuff in glass jars instead of cans."

"I don't know how that came to be. You'll have to check one of your science books for that." She shot a critical look my way, then pointed. "The top shelf is all peaches. Grab a couple of those, would'ja, please?"

I stretched up to the top shelf and drew down a cool glass jar. As I reached to retrieve a second one, something glided over my hand. I took a step back, almost losing my grip. Grandma rose on her toes and strained to see. A field mouse leaped across a playground of tin lids and scampered along a section of bare wooden shelves. Grandma tugged off a slipper and drew it back over her shoulder. Before she could take a swing, a dark and slender shape shot out from the shadows and snatched the mouse.

Grandma stepped backward and drew a breath. "Well, I'll be switched. Annabelle's back." She dropped her slipper to the floor and wriggling her foot into it. "No matter how we plug up holes, she still finds a way in here."

Breathless, I observed flexible serpentine jaws working back and forth over the mouse's head, body, and legs. The tail was last to disappear, before the small rodent became a quivering bulge in the snake's long body. The main feature of the show now over, Grandma dragged up a four-legged stool and gripped my arm as she stepped up. Peering into the shadows, she reached with both hands behind a row of jars and lifted up the rat snake. Annabelle was about five feet long and as calm as a lap dog. The tail twisted around Grandma's arm while the forward part of the body rested loosely in Grandma's palm, tongue flicking to taste the scent of the giant who held her. With an adoring smile, Grandma stepped down to the floor. She led the way back up the steps, her carrying the snake while I carried the jars. I had to clutch them against my chest with one hand while I closed and latched doors behind us.

Back in the kitchen, Jordan, Terry, Grandpa, and Uncle Luke all sat waiting. Heads turned and Jordan stood up, a grin stretching from ear to ear. "Ohhh. You found Annabelle." He reached out to carefully uncoil the snake's body from Grandma's arm, then held it up for all to see.

"I thought you were afraid of snakes," I said.

"Just the kind with fangs. Rattlers and water moccasins, especially. Copperheads, too, but their venom won't kill you. Either way, you don't wanna get bit. But this old gal... why, she's just a pet."

"If you wouldn't mind," Grandma said, "why don't you take her out to the barn? It's plenty warm in the hay, and there's enough mice to feed her 'til spring."

Jordan headed out the back door. Annabelle wrapped comfortably around his arm, her head floating to the motion of his steps, forked tongue flicking to savor aromas in the air. I followed with a flashlight.

Upon our return, Jordan and I plopped down at the kitchen table for a bowl of peaches and vanilla ice cream. Terry and Uncle Luke had packed away charts and maps, but remained at the dining room table gabbing in military lingo. They had a lot in common and a lot to talk about, although Terry was cautious and reserved. Grandpa and Grandma were just settling down in front of the TV. Suddenly, the dogs started barking out back. Thinking they'd heard a vehicle pull up, Grandpa pushed himself to his feet, lumbered across the living room, and switched on the front porch light. There was nothing.

"Must be something in the back pasture. Or closer in. The hens are making a fuss."

"We were just out there," Jordan answered, eyebrows twisting upward. "Everything was peaceful and quiet."

"Coyotes and bobcats are always after the chickens. They can sneak up behind you and watch 'til you're gone. Clever little rascals. But I got all the holes plugged in the coop, and the wire is good and tight. I don't 'spect anything could get in, but I could be wrong. Another snake, maybe. But even after a warm day like this, I don't think they'll be coming out into the open. Once they find a winter den, they tend to stay hid 'til Spring. Annabelle's probably already settled in out there in the barn."

Grandpa grabbed his .22 rifle and all four of us followed him out the back door with flashlights. Like the Earp Brothers and Doc Holliday heading for the OK Corral, we strode across the back lawn, hurriedly but with the stealth of a pack of wolves. Grandpa and Uncle Luke walked side by side, flanked by Terry, Jordan, and me. Our beams scanned up and down the sides of the dog kennel. Dutch, Lucy, and Ethel continued to bark, all three facing our direction.

The latch on the gate to the chicken coop tended to squeak, but Grandpa opened and closed it carefully. The rest of us remained outside while he surveyed the floor and upward across the roosts. The hens were all quiet and in place, curious heads turning. The rooster bobbed his head and danced anxiously on his perch. Satisfied they were all safe, Grandpa rejoined us outside the enclosure, and we directed our lights across the yard toward the house. The beams swept left and right as we searched for the glow of eyes and the shape of an intruder.

"There must be something on this side, or maybe out in that direction," Luke pointed, "in the pasture." Terry eased up behind the grape arbor, one arm propped on a cross member, still sweeping the yard and buildings with his light as far as the fence line. Jordan and I had lights, too. My eyes strained to focus with multiple beams crisscrossing, back and forth, in the darkness. But I was sure there was no intruder there.

We were chasing a hoodoo.

We were about to give up when Terry called out, in an excited voice, "Here's what they're barking at." Our heads turned, and eyes followed the light beam to the bare grapevines immediately over Terry's shoulder. There it sat: round and plump, fur thick, and dark round ears erect. A possum. Beady eyes glowed red in the light, and pink nose twitched at the foreboding scent of humans.

Impulsively, Terry grabbed the marsupial by the tail and held it up, expecting it to squirm, kick, or sink its teeth into his hand. It did none of that. It just hung there like an ornament on a Christmas tree, apparently content in the cold night air, and either blinded or fascinated by the bright light in its face.

"Well, lookie there," Grandpa said, stepping closer. "Must have been nibblin' on dried-up grapes left over from the last pickin. Hold him still, and I'll shoot him."

Terry's head snapped in Grandpa's direction, eyes widening. "Wha... What?"

"Just hold him steady and let me get a good aim. You boys keep your lights on him. I'd best take a step this way so I don't hit the butane tank. Okay, that's about right."

I noted Terry's wide eyes, as he ignored Grandpa's instructions and tossed the possum on the ground. It took off running, and Terry quickly stepped backwards just as Grandpa opened fire. The .22 spat out seven or eight rounds as fast as he could pull the trigger. Jordan and I kept lights trained on the possum as best we could, but I didn't imagine that a possum could run that fast. It zig-zagged with every shot, scurrying full speed out across a section of mowed grass toward a barbed wire fence, dodging the old man's doddering aim, and eventually disappearing into a patch of tall Johnson grass.

Uncle Luke buckled over, laughing out loud. Grandpa lowered the rifle and propped one fist on a hip, glaring at Terry's dark silhouette. "Why d'ja throw him down? Dadgummit! I had him in my sights."

"Sorry, Grandpa," Terry said. "I know you're a good shot, but you ain't no William Tell."

Jordan shot me a glance, and we both knew Grandpa was severely pissed off.

"I ain't been to no gol dern Army Ranger school," Grandpa said, tone and volume elevated. "But I've been shootn' a gun since I was six years old. And I can shoot a squirrel in the eye at thirty yards. I can damn shor hit a possum at eight feet, if *somebody* would jest hold him still. Confound it!"

Grandpa turned and stomped off in the direction of the house. We stood speechless, eyes following Grandpa's dark shape, his flashlight sweeping the yard in fretful motions. Remarkably, no hitch in his get-along now.

Sixteen

When the rest of us returned to the house, slipping in through the back door, we found Grandpa still wrestling with his wounded ego and boiling anger. His cheeks remained suffused with blood, but his lips were pale, tightly squeezed against his dentures. Perspiration beaded on his furrowed brow. He had tossed his cap on the kitchen table, and now paced back and forth while mopping his forehead with a sleeve. As we passed by as quiet as Trappist monks, Grandpa dug deep in his hip pocket for a handkerchief, honked into to it loudly, and wiped his rosy nostrils left and right. Still blustering, he refolded the handkerchief and shoved it back into his hip pocket.

Not wanting to rile him further, we left him to settle down in his own time. Uncle Luke kissed Grandma and tiptoed out the front door. Terry, Jordan, and I followed to see him off. He started chuckling again as he sauntered out to his new Chevy truck. In the dim light, I could see the smile on his face as he reversed into the road and drove away.

Expressions like *dadgummit* and *confound it* were about as close to cussing as we ever heard from Grandpa's mouth. Grandma was strict about language, which especially included taking the Lord's name in vain. And of course, she would not tolerate vulgarities that were common in the speech of heathens. She had taught all her children to keep their speech pure and holy like the Good Book says. By adulthood, I venture to guess, they all had relaxed that rule somewhat, although the "F" word, as they called it, was totally off limits. My mother would never use Jesus' name in a flippant manner. And she warned us repeatedly about *blasphemy against the Holy Spirit*, although she could never tell us exactly what that meant. However, she claimed that shit was shit, no matter how large or small the pile, and it's simply human to use that word when life dumps a load of it in your lap, figuratively speaking.

Jordan was probably the only one of us cousins who avoided swearing and foul language altogether. Like Grandpa, he used euphemisms like "gosh darn," "gee whiz," "criminy," or "jiminy whiskers." That's about as far as Grandpa would go if Grandma was in earshot. Her scolding look was enough to cause him to drop his head in shame. I thought it a conundrum that a crusty old farmer like Grandpa could be controlled by a feisty little woman half his weight. That was particularly puzzling since Grandma claimed that Grandpa was the head of the house, just like the Lord intended it to be.

Grandpa fell back into his chair and kicked up his feet, still sulking over the possum and Terry's challenge of his aim. He felt around in the cushion for the remote, and then switched on the new RCA just in time for the ten o'clock news on Edward Gaylord's WKY-TV out of Oklahoma City. The screen brightened and the snow-storm in the center congealed into the face of commentator Dwight Hinkle, who was in the middle of a report on the abduction of White Dove. School officials claimed she was taken by a woman who posed as a doctor and a man she introduced as a driver for Chickasaw Governor Overton James. According to Hinkle, witnesses provided descriptions of the pair, as well as the getaway vehicle, but no one got the license number. Officials were astounded, he said, that such a thing was conducted in broad daylight and the perpetrators did not attempt to conceal their faces. "But thus far, they have not contacted Governor James," he reported, "and there has been no hint of a ransom or any explanation for the bizarre abduction." He added that alerts were posted on major routes in all directions from Muskogee.

"Overton James is a controversial figure in these parts," Grandpa commented, his tone normalizing. "JFK appointed him Governor of the Chickasaw Nation back in '53, and he's stepped on a lotta' toes tryin' to push Indian rights. This kidnapping sounds like a jab at the Big Chief. I understand Indian resentment over relocation and all that. But, geez Louise! I don't see how anybody kept 'em from makin' a livin' like everbody else 'round here. A lot of 'em's got farm land better'n mine."

Guessing it was safe to engage Grandpa in conversation, Jordan responded. "It's like this, Grandpa," he said. "Native Americans resent the white man for all the bad things their people suffered in the past, but they feel like they've been hindered from self-advancement. They're bitter and crushed in spirit. You'd probably understand it had you been born on a reservation in Arizona."

I personally had not experienced life on the rez, so I didn't know whether Jordan was right. But I could see and feel his passion. His face was stern and his lip quivered. It was clear that this topic cut deep into his gut. My earliest introduction to tribal culture was a vacation somewhere around Santa Fe, where we saw cliff dwellings with adobe houses. Spencer and I played hide and seek in rows of bare-walled rooms of red dirt. I remembered watching a dancer in a loincloth and moccasins, accessorized with feathers, bells, and paint. He stepped lively to the beat of a drum and bizarre singing that lifted the hairs on the back of my neck. Spencer clung to Dad's trousers, peering out with terrified eyes. Once we were back in the car and safely on the road, Dad told us that Indians are proud and good people, but a lot of 'em drink too much. He said, "There's nothing more dangerous than a drunk Indian drivin' down Main Street."

My mind drifted to my days in junior high school, down in Texas, when I was in a play and recited the first few lines from Longfellow's *Song of Hiawatha*. Those words rolled over my lips effortlessly: *By the shore of Gitche Gumee, by the shining Big-Sea-Water, at the doorway of his wigwam, in the pleasant summer morning, Hiawatha stood and waited.* I got that part because I told the teacher I was part Choctaw. True, I had dark hair when just about everybody else in my class had blond or reddish-brown hair, blue eyes, and lily-white skin. I knew my hazel eyes and olive skin didn't look Indian, but I was the best option. What I didn't know what that in reality there was little about that epic poem that resembled the real Hiawatha. I don't think the teacher knew that either.

"Like every state in America," Jordan said, "Oklahoma requires school children to take a course in its own history, apart from the broader study of American history. All kids need to understand their roots. And I mean the truth, which is not always easy to find. I suspect a lot of important history is glossed over in schools."

I knew something about the forced relocation of the Five Civilized Tribes to Oklahoma and the sad details of the *Trail of Tears*. But now, in his fourth semester at OU as a history major, Jordan had studied the bizarre twists in the status of Oklahoma Indians. He rattled off data I had never heard before. And I trusted his knowledge and views on that, more so than his religious beliefs.

Jordan droned on about the Land Rush of 1889, which brought fifty thousand non-Indian settlers into unassigned lands of central Oklahoma. That number grew to hundreds of thousands in a couple of decades, primarily in western Oklahoma. In the southeastern area, miners and cattlemen forced Indian transition to White ways. The Dawes Severalty Act of 1887 had promised individual land ownership and U.S. citizenship to American Indians. But the Curtis Act of 1898 dissolved formal tribal governments, cancelled reservation statuses, and nullified tribal schools and judicial systems.

Overall, the allotment of tribal land stripped Oklahoma Indian nations of about twenty-seven million acres. An attempt in 1905 to create the Indian State of Sequoyah failed in the US Congress. The problem over the past fifty years, as Jordan expressed it, was that Indians in Oklahoma felt they had been cheated in multiple ways. They wanted a restoration of some of the benefits held by numerous tribes in other states, like exemptions from state taxes and the regulation of tribal affairs.

"So," Jordan said summarily, "Overton James has done a lot in the last few years to help the Chickasaw Nation catch up. He's served on the Inter-Tribal Council of the Five Civilized Tribes and is the chairman of the State Indian Affairs Commission. He was instrumental in persuading the federal government to establish an Indian Housing Authority in Oklahoma, and with his help just a few months ago in Tishomingo, they opened the first Chickasaw Nation health clinic."

There was still a great deal of tension, Jordan explained, because many locals resent new legislation that gives Indians benefits. But the Indians believe, and rightly so, that past injustices require generous reparations. "Overton James is proving to be a capable politician," he said. "Very effective in defending that position."

Grandpa fumbled with the remote, pushing buttons repeatedly until the television screen went dark. He rose clumsily to his feet and stretched. Grandma had already covered her ears and disappeared into the front bedroom. Despite his aches and pains, Grandpa must have felt better about the possum. Shuffling listlessly toward the bathroom, he brushed his fingertips lightly on Terry's shoulder and chuckled. "Terry, my boy, when I told you to hold that possum so I could shoot him, your eyes looked like two eggs in a slop jar." Grandpa shook his head and chuckled. "That was real funny, and that little critter sure knew how to dodge a bullet."

A pleasant and relieved smirk lifted on Terry's face and lingered as he got up and unrolled his sleeping bag on the couch. Jordan and I shuffled toward the back bedroom and tucked ourselves into the twin beds, trying to stifle giggles about Grandpa's rapid-fire assault on the runaway possum. After we both were giggled out, Jordan rolled over with his face to the wall and was soon fast asleep.

I lay awake wondering about the Indian woman of Jordan's dream the night before. I knew something about that sort of experience, and the kinds of dreams you can have when your mind is fixed on something bizarre. As a child, I'd had an experience when I was sick with flu. I saw plasticene strips growing out of a planter at the doctor's office, like long serpentine vines reaching out to grab me.

A few years later, one of my high school buddies, Larry Hendricks, had a hallucination in geometry class. He sat at his desk, holding one finger out level while the other hand brushed down gently above it. He said there was a parrot on his finger, left in his care by his uncle, who was vacationing on the beaches of Antarctica. I leaned over and pulled at his shirt sleeve, hoping our teacher Mrs. Johnson didn't see. Fortunately, she was busy sketching a hexagonal pyramid on the chalkboard and didn't turn around until after I got him straightened out. Susanne Truitt sat behind him, patting his shoulder maternally. She whispered to me that he had tried some kind of amphetamine at a party the previous night and was still tripping. Eventually, he folded his arms across the desktop, laid his head down, and fell asleep. After school that day, I walked Larry to his car, uncertain he was capable of driving. Meandering behind me, he occasionally ducked and dodged for no apparent reason. He said birds were diving at his head like kamikaze pilots. I scanned the clear sky and saw nothing except a buzzard half a mile away, probably circling over roadkill. No other birds in sight. Larry was hallucinating, I was sure of that. I don't recall anything else like that back then.

I must have fallen asleep while dwelling on those trivial memories. I awoke with a start, lying awkwardly on my stomach with a blanket drawn over my head. I rolled over on my back, as a rapid pulse drummed in my throat. Immediately, I heard movement in the room. My neck chilled and my eyes widened as I tried to adjust to the dark. I lay still, scanning the walls for some hint of reflected light or shifting shadows. There was nothing. I thought maybe Jordan had tiptoed out to the bathroom. But I remembered that Grandma had left a chamber pot in our room, as if we were living in the sixteenth century. Neither Jordan nor I wanted to use it, but maybe he had changed his mind. Or maybe he just forgot. I listened. No sound of tinkling in a pot. I turned my face slowly to peek toward Jordan. He was in his bed, face to the wall, one arm out of the covers.

A moment later, as I gazed blankly in Jordan's direction, an inhuman whisper drifted toward me from a dark corner of the room. I froze in place, ears straining. I heard a faint squeak on the floor, followed by pressure on the edge of my bed. Something scooted lightly across the blanket toward me. I held my breath, waiting, eyes darting left and right, searching for some visible shape. Suddenly, a heavy weight fell hard beside me on the mattress, pressing down. I clawed to prevent myself from rolling toward it. A foul-smelling presence leaned close to my head, and I felt hot breath and sniffing, as if huge nostrils sucked up my scent and blew it back at me. It lingered. The icy fingers of terror skittered up my back and gripped my neck. I lay paralyzed, while the piercing scalpel of invisible eyes bisected my soul. My heart pounded. I tried to swallow, but my tongue and throat felt numb. I held my breath until I thought my chest would implode.

As suddenly as it fell, so the pressure on the bed lifted. A subtle swish, and the presence that had invaded my privacy withdrew like a wisp of stale air. The room went deathly still. I sucked in a long breath, trying to muffle my sound. I sat up straight, at the same time straining to clear my head and think logically. Circuits in my brain ignited as I tried to identify the thing that had just paralyzed me with fear. Maybe it was one of the dogs, checking me out. I didn't recall Grandpa letting them in the house. But I had heard no claws ticking across the floor. The door never opened or closed. It couldn't have been a dog.

I leaned slowly forward, not knowing what to expect. I drew my right arm up to protect my face and tilted my head. I could see Jordan's vague shape, now sitting up in his bed and leaning back in the corner. I stretched out an arm and with trembling fingers switched on the lamp. Jordan's wide eyes stared blankly while he gripped the edge of a homemade quilt and drew it tight up under his chin. His lips were blue, either with chill or fear. His entire body quivered.

"Jordan? Are you alright?"

"I saw it," he said, swallowing heavy.

"What? What did you see?"

"I don't know. It came around the bed on all fours. Lifted on hind legs and hovered over you. Then it plopped down right next to you, turned, and stared at me. After a few seconds, it eased down to the floor and disappeared. That way." Jordan's eyes turned, eyebrows lifting in the direction of the door.

"How could you see it? I felt it right here in my face, but I couldn't see a thing."

"I don't know. I just did."

"Was it one of the dogs? Maybe Grandpa let them sleep inside."

"It wasn't a dog. It looked like a man, with long black hair. But the eyes… when it looked at me, they glowed like animal eyes in a beam of light. Then, when you moved it just sort of disappeared."

Still trembling, I got up and tiptoed to the door, eased fingers around the knob, and twisted slowly. The door creaked as I pulled it open an inch or so. I closed it again, felt around the knob, and slid my fingers up and down the trim and the edge of the door. There was no lock. I paused, my mind racing. My duffle bag lay on the floor at the end of my bed. I grabbed the straps, and in a firm and steady motion I tugged it against the door. I inched my way around the bed and crawled back under the blankets. Jordan lay back, eyes still wide and full of terror. I reached for the light switch. Trying to bolster my confidence, I told myself that shortly when daylight came, I would feel silly, realizing I'd had a bad dream.

"Leave it on," Jordan said.

"Okay. Okay." I drew my blanket to my chin and stared at the door.

My paternal grandfather, Grandpa Barnett, claimed that the ghost of his first wife visited him often. After he remarried, she would occasionally appear next to his bed and wag her finger shamingly. My parents said that was simply his imagination and perhaps a sense of guilt for remarrying too soon after her passing, but they assured him that his vows were "until death do us part," and that he needed to let her go. He said he had tried to do just that, but she would not leave him be.

I had trouble believing that. Early in my teens, I began to doubt all things related to the supernatural, and I refused to be cuckolded by superstition. I was convinced that belief in ghosts, angels, and demons were part of the cause of needless fear and consternation in the entire western civilization. Now an obdurate skeptic, I defined myself as a child of enlightenment and classical rationalism. I openly rejected the paranormal and supernatural. As far as I was concerned, stories about poltergeists rattling the furniture were total malarkey.

However, things change. Even for skeptical and objective minds, new information brings new conclusions. Now, for the first time, I experienced something I couldn't explain and I was both terrified and embarrassed. I propped myself up against the headboard, facing the door. I could not rid myself of the lingering discomfort—no, the fear—that something unnatural was with us. It seemed like a premonition; an advanced warning of something that awaited us up on the mountain.

Seventeen

Sleep eventually overcame me, despite my apprehension. When I opened my eyes again, I had shuffled around in the bed and buried my face deep in Grandma's homemade duck-down pillow. I lifted my head enough to scan the walls and sparse furniture, which were now becoming visible in the cold grey light of pre-dawn. I remembered it was Saturday morning.

The room felt colder than the previous morning. In fact, when I exhaled, my foggy breath momentarily hovered about my face like Casper the Friendly Ghost. I sat up and rubbed my arms briskly before reaching for my watch. I had removed it from my wrist and placed it face up on the side table, which was my habit even at home. I vaguely recalled seeing in the Farmer's Almanac that sunrise would be around 7:30. It was now a little after seven. My eyes drifted across the narrow walk space between our beds. Jordan was fast asleep, his face pressed against the wall. His butt, sporting white Fruit of the Looms, protruded from the bedcovers, hanging precariously over the edge of the mattress. I reached across and popped him with the back of my hand. Startled, he jolted upright, clawing to keep from falling onto the floor. He sat motionless, staring at me.

"Was I dreaming last night?" he said. "I mean, was there something in our room?" Jordan's eyebrows twisted strangely, his forehead appearing permanently furrowed. His pallor and swollen eyes, as well as his tentative voice, reflected intense anxiety.

I regarded him cautiously before answering. "I don't know. It was the strangest thing I've ever experienced. I was scared shitless."

The next five minutes dragged on at a snail's pace. We sat staring at each other in mutual empathy, our minds in turbulence. Eventually I forced myself to get up. My bare feet swung down and landed on cold linoleum.

"Yowee, it's cold," I whined, glancing at Jordan. He had rolled over and eased his feet down to the floor, but he sat staring blankly. "Come on. It's time to get up." I sniffed and lowered my head to catch his downcast eyes. "We're still alive and kicking. No teeth marks that I can find."

Jordan nodded. At about the same lethargic pace, he and I stood up and tugged on our long johns, blue jeans, and flannel shirts, plopping down again to pull on thermal socks. Last of all, hiking boots; laces tied in a double knot.

In the kitchen Grandma was already busy with breakfast. No surprise there. Terry sat hunched over the table, gripping a coffee mug with both hands. Jordan and I pulled up chairs and eased down, both of us with obviously-muted faces.

"What's up with you two?" Terry said. "Rough night?"

"I guess you could say that."

"You sleep okay?" Jordan asked.

"Like a baby."

"No interruptions?"

"No, why?" Terry frowned, tossing Jordan as questioning glance.

Jordan did not reply, but his anxious blue eyes lifted awkwardly in my direction. I hoped that a subtle head shake and a stern look would tell him to drop it. Realizing that on his own, he turned away.

Suddenly remembering that Grandma was not the waitress at a restaurant, I got up and poured coffee for myself and Jordan. Terry smiled subtly and nodded at my innate sensibility, albeit slow on the uptake. His curious eyes lingered on us.

"Smells good, Grandma," Jordan said, lethargically. "What's on the menu?"

"Same as usual," she said. "Eggs, sausage, bacon, hash browns. But no biscuits, this morning. They flopped. Dunno what happened. Turned out hard as a rock. I've got toast in the oven, if you want that with gravy. Or there's apricot preserves and molasses there on the table."

"Sounds great. Any of that," Jordan said, licking his lips. "All of that."

"This would cost you four dollars at the truck stop in Ardmore, but here it comes free with love and devotion." Grandma glanced over her shoulder and winked.

"Where's Grandpa?" I asked.

"He's out at the barn, piddlin' around with the horses, I 'spose. Had his breakfast already."

Jordan and I made an effort to shake off lingering anxiety and get on with the day. As the sun broke through the bare limbs of a huge bois d'arc tree at the east fence line, we began loading our gear into the bus. Terry stepped lively across the frosty lawn. Slung over one shoulder was a large military pack, and his free hand gripped the handle of a soft rifle case, pouches bulging with ammo and a cleaning kit. He had slept with all his gear, as if he were in a military zone. I reminded him of what Grandpa told me, that our belongings are safe out here in the country. No prowlers or thieves. But that didn't matter to Terry. He wanted his stuff close by, no matter where he was.

At the barn, I hoisted a bale of hay and a bag of mixed horse feed into a wheelbarrow. Trudging toward the bus, I struggled to steer the overloaded one-wheeler. Jordan followed, carrying two galvanized buckets with a few light tools for grooming. Neither of us being a trained shoer, we were limited in our ability to deal with hoof problems on a long trail ride. I trusted that Orpheus had resolved any possible issues with Ginger's hooves, but Barney was another matter. If he lost a shoe, my only option was to remove leftover nails, trim splinters, and rasp the hoof. I knew how to do that. Plus, I carried a pick for cleaning debris out of the underside of hooves. Riding in a rocky terrain, there is always the possibility of a bruise, cut, or a small stone wedged in a sensitive place.

Jordan and I loaded our backpacks and sleeping bags into the bus. Without collaborating with Terry, we packed a box of groceries of our choosing, like bread, chips, and peanut butter, along with a cooler of our favorite canned soft drinks—Coke, Barq's Root Beer, and Dr. Pepper. That done, we saddled up Ginger and Barney. Grandma and Grandpa stood on the front porch, as if seeing their last child move away to the big city. Each of us had a rifle in a leather saddle scabbard.

My new Winchester 30/30 was a commemorative model meant to be displayed, not actually used. I planned to wrap the brass in a cloth before shoving it down in the scabbard, hoping to avoid scratches. I should have bought a Marlin. It was cheaper, and all the metal parts were blued and ready for work. But, unlike certain favorite philosophical questions, I didn't think through that decision with sufficient depth. I bought the famous name and the glitzy look.

Jordan carried a double barrel .410 shotgun. Not very powerful, but a good varmint gun. He was a proficient marksman, despite lack of instruction. I practiced a lot at a target range, knowing Jordan spent more time in the woods shooting varmints. I yielded to that practical experience. But we felt no urge to compete. We simply combined knowledge and skills and relied on each other. However, being with Terry made a huge difference. Terry was the only one of us with formal training in weaponry. He was the top marksman in his group during basic training, and the only one who had hunted deer since childhood. He had his hunting rifle and a handgun, a Colt .45 Model 1911. We were in the company of experience and competence.

"You boys look like the Dalton Gang," Grandpa said wryly. "Ya'll be careful up there with them guns." He lifted his eyebrows in Terry's direction. "I'll leave it to you to play drill sergeant and keep these two young scallywags in line." He swept a finger toward me and Jordan, punctuating his warning with a stern nod.

"There's no playing, Grandpa," Terry said. "It's always real. Always serious."

I led Ginger out to the front of the house and stood holding the reins. Jordan saddled up and maneuvered Barney in figure eights just to test his cooperation. Grandma called out from the front porch, "You'll be up there over the Lord's Day, so I hope you'll take a little time to pray and read the scriptures."

"Got my Bible in my pack," Jordan shouted back.

Just as I lifted one foot up into a stirrup, ready to mount up, Dutch, Lucy, and Ethyl let out a volley of startled barks and scampered toward the road. I could see Grandma craning from up on the porch to see what had grabbed the dogs' attention this time. They seemed to bark at anything and everything. They had nothing else to do, and considered it their job.

Grandma's mouth dropped open and her eyes widened. "Land 'a Goshen, is that who I think it is?"

We all directed attention toward the road where, from the cover of sunflowers along the bar ditch, a pair of spindly legs emerged and marched toward us. I could make out the color and shape of denim coveralls, faded and baggy, laboring beneath an alpine backpack with a sleeping bag strapped on top. With a cap drawn down over her brow and eyes to the ground, we didn't recognize her at first. Then she looked up, and bushy reddish-brown hair billowed on both sides.

"My Lord, that's Christine," Grandma said. "What on God's green earth would bring her out here without…" She stopped mid-exclamation, head snapping towards us boys. Wide-eyed and mouth agape, she fired words at us like darts. "Does that young lady plan to go camping with the three of you?"

Without waiting for a response, Grandma stepped briskly down the porch steps and leaped across the patchy lawn. Her arms lifted to greet Christine. Jordan swung out of the saddle, boots thumping on the ground. I stood speechless. Terry's face contorted as he cast a glance back at me and Jordan. "She told me a week ago she wanted to go with us," he said in a low tone, "but since I hadn't heard from her, I guessed she'd changed her mind. So, I didn't go pick her up."

"Christine never changes her mind about anything," Jordan said. "Something must have happened."

Together, with marked reluctance, we strolled over to greet our cousin. Christine, two years younger than Jordan and me, had just finished her first semester in college. She was a stellar student, and what most would call a political radical; a member of Young Democrats of America. Her father Marcus had died at age forty, leaving Christine's insecure and over-protective mom with three girls. Christine was the oldest, followed by Caroline and Catherine.

I stood staring, trying to reconcile the various components of her complex persona. Frizzy hair, parted down middle; freckles across her nose and cheeks, green eyes—exhibiting independence and a fierce determination like no one else I knew. She shrugged out of her backpack. It fell like a huge sack of potatoes onto the patchy winter lawn and rolled over on its side.

Grandma wrapped her arms around her. "Sweetheart, how in the Lord's precious name did you get here?"

"That's a double-barreled question," Christine quipped, forcing a smile over a swell of anger. "I hitchhiked. It was no problem getting to Springer. Show a little leg and a girl can get a ride just like that." She snapped her fingers crisply in the air. "But, of course, you can't show a leg in coveralls." Her thumbs slid up and down the straps. "I had to wait at the truck stop until I found a farmer headed this way."

"But weren't you afraid, darlin'?" Grandma queried. Her eyebrows twisted upward and her tone oozed concern.

"Hell, no," Christine ranted. "I'm sure I was wearin' a scowl that would intimidate a wolverine. Even a horny truckdriver would know better than to mess with me."

"But why?" Grandma persisted. "I don't understand any of that."

"Okay," Christine fumed, fists planted on hips. "Here it is. I told Terry a week ago I wanted to come along on this camp-out. He said he'd pick me up." She shot a resentful look Terry's way and shook her finger at him. "I sat waiting for three hours, and he didn't show. So, I just grabbed up my gear and lit out. I knew the route and figured I could get a ride somewhere."

Grandma's jaw dropped and she gave Terry a long stern look. Then turning back to Christine, she asked the big question. "Sugar, what did your mama think about that?"

"Well … she was at work." Christine's eyes cut to the side. "But I left her a note. When she reads that I'm with Uncle Luke and my cousins, I'm hopin' she won't mind." Christine's head swung left and right. "Where is Uncle Luke, anyhow?"

"He's not going on this trip," Terry said. "He had a prior commitment. I thought I told you."

"You didn't tell me shit; pardon my French, Grandma." Christine's nostrils flared and her face twisted with anger. She took three menacing steps in his direction and pointed a taunt finger in his face. "You said you'd pick me up, and you didn't."

"Okay, okay." Jordan stepped between them. "No matter. You're here now and ready to go. Glad you made it safe and sound. Do you want me to saddle up Scooter?"

"Definitely," she snarled. "I'm not riding in a goddamn school bus with that arrogant bastard." Her eyes fired a volley of darts at Terry.

"Hey, hey," Grandma intervened. "If you go camping while you feel like that, sweetheart, you'd best not go at all. You'd be miserable the whole time."

"Makin' the rest of us miserable, too," Terry added.

Like an involuntary reflex, Christine's middle finger shot upward in Terry's direction. She tried to hide it from Grandma and Grandpa, but they both saw. She punctuated her feelings with a quick jab of her tongue from puckered lips, before folding her arms and turning away.

Grandpa stood motionless and speechless, wide-eyed and mouth agape. He had never seen Christine in a hostile outburst like that.

"I have an idea," I said, on a sudden impulse. I stepped closer and slipped a hand over Christine's shoulder. "Come on, Cuz. You've already had a long morning. You made it safe and sound, all the way out here. And we're as impressed as hell with that. In fact, you proved what a remarkably tough and determined gal you are. I'll tell you straight up, that makes me proud. Why don't you go in and have a shower and grab a bite to eat. A sandwich, or maybe some of Grandma's apple pie. There's one slice left in the fridge that Grandpa had his eye on, but I'd bet he'd give it up for you."

Grandpa pulled a face, then nodded grudgingly.

"In the meantime," I said, "we'll saddle ole' Scooter and get your gear loaded. And we can head out in an hour or so. How's that sound?" I smiled as sincerely as I could manage, hoping for a positive response.

For a moment, Christine stared across the pasture, arms folded tightly. Seconds ticked by in awkward silence. She glanced up at me, her eyes cold but bearing a hint of contemplation. We stood frozen in place like students in an astronomy class, holding our breath and waiting for a solar eclipse to pass. The other two dogs remained at a distance, but Lucy sidled up to Christine and lifted a front paw, stroking her denim-covered leg as if offering her sympathy and support. Christine bent down and patted Lucy's head, pensively at first. I noticed her pluck a tick from behind Lucy's ear, and twisted it into the dirt with a foot. Eventually, her face softened. She turned toward me as her green eyes welled up. One hand lifted to brush away a tear. She drew a deep breath and, looking skyward she blew it out. "Okay, a shower sounds good. So does apple pie."

Terry stepped closer, palms up in a casual surrender. "Look, I'm sorry. I didn't mean for this to happen. I'm glad you made it. And Russ is right. You are a trooper. So, let's start over. Okay?"

Christine nodded, hesitated, and then reached around his waist in a half-hearted side hug. "I'm sorry too. I shouldn't have called you a bastard. But I thought *son-of-a-bitch* would have upset Grandma and disrespected your mom." She withdrew and spun around toward the front porch, trying to hide a crooked smile from Terry's sight.

Terry shook his head, his eyes following Christine. "Same thing as bastard," he mumbled, a trace of a smile lifting. He turned, cut us a conceding glance, and traipsed toward the bus. "That girl. I'll never understand her."

That was Christine's way. Her words were often fiery, far more intense than her intentions. She could be volatile for a moment, spewing like a Yellowstone geyser. Then the steam would dissipate and she would mellow into a cupcake. And beneath it all there was a brilliant mind and a compassionate spirit. She was, as she often described herself, a walking conundrum and a strange piece of work.

Jordan and I shared a quick look, no doubt wondering the same thing. Is this how the trip is going to go? One squabble after another over nothing? We hoped not. But, like marriage, for better or worse, off we go.

"I'm gonna head on up there," Terry said. "It's still plenty early.

Maybe I can get things set up before you guys make it to the campsite. Give me her backpack. No need to weigh down the horse." He lifted his face toward Christine, who had stopped on the front porch. "You got what you need?" She nodded and hoisted up a small bag of personal items. Grandma tugged open the front door.

Terry hoisted up Christine's pack, grimacing as he swung it over a shoulder. "Damn. How'd that skinny little girl carry this thing? Has she been workin' out?" He marched off toward the bus, still mumbling aloud. "Her arms don't look like there's a muscle one under that skin. Just bone and tendons."

Grandpa, who had stood silent with his hands deep in his hip pockets, turned away and made his way toward the barn. Jordan and I trailed him, noting his pronounced limp. We cut each other a glance, confronted with the sad reality of his advancing decrepitude. Behind us, the bus fired up with a billowing cloud of dark smoke. As we saddled up Scooter, Terry rumbled off down the road. He would follow a familiar route around a couple of sections past the Pratt's place and up to the rock quarry.

While waiting for Christine, I slipped inside to catch a bit of the noon news on Grandpa's new television. The meteorologist said that a cold front was moving in from the northwest, and there was a likelihood of rain followed by freezing temperatures within the next forty-eight hours. That was not what we'd hoped for, but this trip was a "go" no matter what.

Part 3: The Encounter

Eighteen

Less than an hour later, Christine, Jordan and I, feet in stirrups and butts in saddles, sashayed along the road to the steady rhythm of hooves on packed dirt and gravel. Jordan had agreed to ride Scooter, since he'd ridden him recently and figured the old trooper would respond better to him. And after adjusting the rigging herself, Christine hopped one foot into the stirrup and swung into the saddle like a professional cowgirl. She and Barney appeared equally comfortable. He was easy to rein and not inclined to buck or run away, even with a novice rider. But it appeared that Christine had more experience on horseback than I'd realized, and that eased my mind. Barney's too, I suppose.

The sun was shining brightly, at least for the moment, but the air was crisp and cool. At the first bend in the road, a foul smell assaulted our nostrils. Ahead lay the remains of a raccoon, covered in an umbrella of feathers. As we approached, the stink hung heavy in the air. Three buzzards hopped away reluctantly, then resumed their grisly banquet when we had passed. I glanced up through the bare limbs of jack oaks. Three more winged scavengers circled lazily overhead, waiting their turn.

"That's pretty disgusting." Christine tugged her shirt up over her nose.

"You should see 'em converge on a dead cow," Jordan said. "Couple a' dozen, squawking, jostling, heads buried in guts, coming out covered in blood. What the buzzards don't eat, the coyotes tear apart and drag off pieces in all directions during the night. Then, after a day or so, the flies and ants take over. Flies leave maggots, which become more flies. All combined, they pick the bones clean. They're like nature's custodial crew."

"I realize a lot goes on that people don't want to see," Christine said, grimacing. "Or even think about. When I was a kid, I thought meat was manufactured, like in a factory or lab. I dunno. But I had a really rough time when I discovered that chickens, cows, and pigs all get slaughtered in sort of a death trap, and then processed in an assembly line. After learning that, for a long time I got nauseated every time we ate at Kentucky Fried Chicken. I thought Colonel Sanders must be a sadist. All those chicken parts dunked into a vat of hot grease. Then we gobble them up like candy."

"Are you a vegetarian now?"

"No. I tried that for a while, but gave up the idea a couple of years ago. But I *am* an advocate of humane meat processing. I accept, reluctantly, I might add, that humans are omnivores, and killing animals for food has always been part of every culture. So, I eat fish, poultry, and some red meat. But I try not to dwell on how it got on the supermarket shelf. That part gives me the willies."

"Good for you," Jordan said. "I was afraid you were caught up in all that liberal mumbo-jumbo before you even started college."

"Well," Christine said, reining Barney closer to Scooter and looking Jordan squarely in the eye, "I've had a couple of advanced placement courses in political science and sociology. And what you call *mumbo-jumbo* is mostly a matter of critical thinking. People poke fun at what they don't understand."

"Oh, is that so." Jordan shook his head, as if brushing Christine's words aside. But his mocking tone invited debate.

"Think about it," she said assertively. "This country was born out of liberal thinking— democracy, freedom of speech and press, abolition of slavery, women's right to vote, and free market trade. That's not old-world tradition or conservative thinking by any stretch of the imagination. At the time, it was highly innovative. And it was criticized by people who wanted things to stay the same. You have a problem with any of that? You call that liberal mumbo-jumbo? *Liberalism* is about exploring and asking questions, being open to new ideas, and being willing to change as we learn. Conservativism is resistance to change, which typically means defending traditions."

"We'll just have to agree to disagree," Jordan snipped.

"How do you disagree? Based on what?"

"I just disagree. All that just sounds like a jab at conservatives."

"I'm not jabbing or stabbing, dear cousin," Christine said, softening her tone. "I'm challenging pervasive irrationality. All beliefs and opinions should be based on some level of intelligent critique. There must be logical reasons to accept an idea or belief. But most people just buy into and defend what they've been taught from childhood."

I lifted both hands, calling a truce. "I can say this. We need to rein in the conversation on those topics. Religion and politics are emotionally charged. It's better to just let it go."

"Brace yourself, Cuz." Christine said flatly. "It's unavoidable. Every topic seems to lead to one or the other. Or both. It's like all rivers flow to the sea."

I responded sharply. "That stuff is debated all day long, week after week, up in Washington. It's about as productive as throwing horse manure at each other and calling it a quest for truth."

"You started college this fall, right?" Jordan said, looking squarely at Christine. He clearly wanted to appear unvexed by Christine's overt progressive thinking.

"I'm at OU, but I thought you knew that. I had my sights set on Chicago, but OU offered me a scholarship. And you both know how expensive private universities are."

"Yep, I do." Jordan nodded and glanced in my direction.

"Me too," I said. "That's why I'm at North Texas. It's right there, a couple of miles from our place. And I'm happy to stay at home as long as Mom and Dad will allow it."

At that point in time, not one of us four cousins could see over life's horizon. Three of my closest friends in high school wanted to be doctors and were already devouring pre-med courses like hungry hounds. When I started, I wasn't sure what I wanted to do, or be. So, I took all the basic courses, hoping for an epiphany before I was forced to select a major. By the second semester in my sophomore year, I was leaning toward some form of writing. I had won an award for a paper titled *The Power of Rhetoric in Motivating Mobs to Action*, mostly about the pejorative view of fascism. I had also kept up with the careers of George Lewis, Frances Fitzgerald, and Sean Flynn, who covered various aspects of the Vietnam War, and I thought that kind of journalism to be fascinating. But in general, I was repulsed by political science.

With only a year left to complete a bachelor's degree, I realized the need for graduate studies. I was torn between NTSU and Stanford. I was inclined to the latter, since my girlfriend lived near there, in the San Francisco area, so I applied. In the meantime, I still needed to take the Graduate Records Exam. All that was on my mind as we lumbered along the road on horseback. I was fascinated by controversy, but I was more in need of relaxation. Behind me, I could hear Jordan and Christine chattering like two squirrels arguing over an acorn.

A mile further, we approached Orpheus' house, which now felt familiar. The hounds, Mortimer and Sally, scrambled from beneath the porch and loped toward us, barking at the horses. Barney and Scooter tossed their heads and shuffled anxiously. Ginger kept a suspicious eye on the dogs, but showed no signs of stress. I'm sure she remembered the dogs from the day before. The barking ceased abruptly at the sound of a whistle from the workshop. The dogs turned and loped back to the house, where they remained. Orpheus appeared at the shop door and waved.

"Thanks for your help," I shouted out. Orpheus nodded and lifted a *thumbs-up*.

Three children appeared on the porch and ran toward us, the two smaller ones stopping at a safe distance. The little boy wore only underpants and a T-shirt. The little girl, maybe five or six years old, wore a dress and house shoes. Her hair was braided into several short pigtails twisting out from her head in different directions. The oldest boy, however, wore coveralls, a tee shirt, and tennis shoes with no laces. He strutted boldly out to the road, sporting a wide pearly white grin.

"Where ya'll headed?" he said, inching closer as we passed.

"Up into the mountains," Jordan answered. "You're Ezekiel, aren't you?"

The boy nodded proudly. "Yes sir. How'd you know my name?"

"Your daddy told me. Tell him Jordan said hello."

"Goin huntin?" the boy asked.

"Maybe," Jordan said, twisting in his saddle as he passed the youngster. "Mostly just exploring."

"What cha'll looking fer?"

"Interesting stuff."

"Caves?"

"Could be."

We moved steadily past, the horses oblivious to the meaning of the sounds that came from our mouths. Nothing resembled a command they should obey, so they trudged forward dutifully.

"Maybe I'll come see ya'll up there," the boy shouted.

"Okay," Jordan said, waving goodbye. "I hope not," he said under his breath. "We don't need a kid to look after."

A black woman in a pink robe and house slippers stepped out of the screen door and onto the front porch. I took her to be Orpheus' wife. Didn't see her when I was there before, but I waved and she returned the wave with a bright smile. Jordan pulled up on the reins, threw his leg forward over the saddle horn, and slid to the ground. He handed me the reins. "Hold Scooter, I'll be right back."

Scooter's curious eyes followed as Jordan jogged lithely back toward the house, turning at a worn path. Once in the yard, he stopped to move a tricycle out of his way. The woman stepped down from the porch to meet him. I had long recognized Jordan's altruistic spirit, and was intrigued to see it displayed in such a casual and natural manner. They talked briefly before shaking hands. Then Jordan turned and jogged back out to the road, slowing to a walk to avoid spooking the horses. I handed him the reins. Scooter began sidestepping away while Jordan tried to lift a foot into the stirrup.

"Whoah, you ornery jackass," he said, scowling. "I'll sell you for dog food if you keep acting up."

Scooter didn't grasp the severity of Jordan's warning. He continued to step away, circling in the middle of the road and eyeing Jordan fretfully as he turned. Jordan wouldn't be defeated. He grabbed the saddle horn with his left hand, took a large step, and vaulted into the saddle in one proficient motion. Scooter stopped dead still, eyes wide in disbelief.

Jordan hauled in the long reins and set his feet into the stirrups. "Okay, let's go." He clicked and Scooter responded submissively. Like any seasoned saddle horse, he recognized authority.

Christine and I had stopped in the middle of the road to wait. As Jordan caught up to us, she taunted. "Hey, what's a nice cowboy like you doing on a swaybacked nag like that?" She giggled, nudged Barney with her heels, and headed down the road at a gentle lope. Jordan and I held to a walking pace.

"What was that all about?" I said.

"You mean, swinging into the saddle?"

"No. That was impressive, but I'm talking about Mrs. Pratt back there."

"Oh, she and Grandma are good friends. Maylene's her name. Grandma told me to tell Maylene she had a few jars of peaches for her when she or Orpheus happen by the farm. It's prob'ly not easy for her to get out at all, with five kids. But then again, that's pretty common around here."

Further along and twenty minutes later, the road curved north and diminished to a sandy lane with two bare ruts and a grassy hump down the middle. Clearly visible were tracks of the double tires on the rear of the bus. We crossed a wooden bridge that spanned Cool Creek just above Cedar Falls. The creek was seasonal, but after fall and a few early winter rains, it was running deep, cool, and clear. The horses eyed the wooden boards that creaked and popped beneath their hooves as we crossed. The heads of rusty bolts jiggled in place. The boards seemed precariously aged, and I wondered how they supported the weight of a bus. No doubt Terry had inched his way across. He was an alert and prudent sort of guy.

Ahead, two mature does appeared from a gully, crossed the lane, and stepped cautiously down into the hollow below the bridge. They were trailed by three younger does, no doubt yearlings, and further back was a young buck with meager spike antlers. If there was an older buck around, he stayed out of sight. A short distance further the lane began to climb steeply, leading above the last ragged tree line. A thousand jaunty sparrows zoomed in and out of bare jack oaks on the rocky slopes. Flat sand and gravel changed to loose rocks and ruts from erosion. The entire mountain was evidence of millennia of alternate seasons of rain and drought, exposing broken rocks of different sizes and shapes—rows of jagged spines and islands of round, smooth boulders.

The climb now made it essential to lean forward in the saddle and slacken the reins, allowing the horses to select their own path. Equestrian experts in a show-jumping arena might criticize the techniques common to western cowboys. Our horses were not being judged on their precision or exact obedience to commands. My dad had told me often that in certain situations it was better to allow horses independence, like on a rugged climb like this— to meander cautiously upward, judging their own footing, and occasionally lunging to accommodate the shifting weight of cargo. All that is even more important on a steep descent, where gravity tends to facilitate increased speed. Horses are better judges of a path than their riders. But to allow and support that freedom, the rider has to maintain balance in the saddle.

I ventured to remind Christine to shift her heels back a bit, keeping her feet, hips, and shoulders perpendicular to the skyline as much as possible. Leaning forward puts too much weight on the horse's front legs, and leaning back—well, you can tumble off backwards and roll down the hill. Christine nodded and complied.

Up the mountainside we went, to explore and to adore. In our present culture, I doubted that one in a thousand young adults has such an experience as this. But we were more than cowboys, or scouts with a wagon train on the Mormon Trail. We were like inquisitive but reverent monks ascending the sacred steps of an ancient shrine.

Nineteen

Soon the rugged lane topped a ridge. Immediately to our right, a familiar trail meandered up to an abandoned rock quarry that was once an ancient ridge. The project had been abandoned because excavators penetrated a natural spring, quickly filling the hole with water. The quarry had remained pristine in appearance, a rock amphitheater almost white in color, primarily limestone, sandstone, and dolomite. The shallow dish at the bottom had become a permanent spring-fed pond.

Off to our left sat the bus. The bright blue paint contrasted rather starkly against the dull and stippled face of an ancient granite cliff. Terry had reversed the bus near the outcrop to create a shelter from the wind. I noticed his indistinct shape squatted next to a fire. He had managed to gather sufficient dry twigs, leaves, and tufts of grass for kindling, and he brought a few oak logs to use sparingly. As we approached, we were greeted by the aroma of T-bone steaks sizzling on a hot plate. Terry had constructed a make-shift stove suspended between two large rocks. Having chopped up several potatoes and an onion, he was busy stirring hashbrowns in a cast iron skillet. Four folding chairs and an aluminum table sat under an awning, extending out from the leeward side of the bus. Terry's combined country upbringing and military training provided skills beyond that of a casual camper. He was a trained and seasoned survivalist. With only basic equipment and supplies, he had created a camping resort. We sat down to a delicious meal, and opened a jar of Grandma's canned peaches for dessert.

"I figured we oughta eat good tonight," Terry said, scratching his whiskered chin. His manner and expression seemed quite chipper. "Then we'll make-do on lighter and easier stuff the next couple of nights. If I kill a deer, we'll have the back strap. If not, I brought hot dogs and canned chili, and of course, bread, bologna and cheese. I know you guys brought stuff, too. So, we won't go hungry. You can count on that. But as a last resort, we've got dried soy beans in sealed packets. It's bland, but a good protein substitute. You guys would eat soybean chili, wouldn't cha? Or maybe stew?"

Jordan and I nodded agreeably, but Christine's face and posture said otherwise. Maybe she was simply full and didn't want to talk about food. Terry got the hint and pointed in her direction. "Christine, you haven't seen the interior of the bus. Why don't you climb in and check out the arrangements. You can have first choice on the bunks."

Christine shook her head with a playful smirk. "You're so kind to the ladyfolk." She turned and sashayed toward the folding door and disappeared up the steps. I knew that deep down, she wanted to get along and be pleasant, despite her recalcitrant and combative nature. But, as Jordan put it, her panties were still in a wad over Terry leaving her behind. Getting over that would take a while. Immediately we heard scratching and rattling inside the bus, a tell-tale sign that Christine was busy rearranging. Terry glanced up and tossed a wink and a smile in our direction.

As sunset approached, Jordan and I decided we should tend to the horses. We unsaddled them and splayed blankets to dry on a large round-topped boulder. The horses didn't work up much of a sweat on the ride up. It was relatively cool and not that far. But if nothing else, it would be good to air out all the tack. We replaced the leather bridles and reins with rope halters and stout lead ropes, and led the horses up to the quarry for a long drink before we tied them up for the night.

Cold and clear, the small and shallow pond had become a watering hole for all manner of resident and migrant species. Cow dung dotted the path that led from the southern rim of the quarry down to the water's edge. But there was no evidence of animals wading. The rocky bottom might have been foreboding. The water was crystal clear. Ginger, Barney, and Scooter approached the water's edge shoulder to shoulder and lowered their heads to drink.

Five minutes later, Jordan unsnapped the lead rope from Scooter's halter and left him standing. He then hopped on Barney's back. At the nudge of heels in his ribs and the sound of a couple of tongue clicks, Barney stepped lively. Instinctively retracing recent hoof prints, he made his way up and over the embankment, and down toward the camp. Jordan didn't need to rein Barney. He just relaxed and enjoyed the leisurely ride. Scooter tagged along behind.

Feeling no urge to hurry, I decided to walk leading Ginger with a single rein. Ginger's muzzle floated casually at my elbow like a large and devoted Great Dane. Reaching the crest of the path up from the water, before descending gently toward the camp, I paused to gaze across the miles of scenery below. Ginger suddenly threw back her head, hooves dancing anxiously. I tugged her forward, but she wouldn't budge. I turned to see her ears perked and her eyes directed toward the upper rim of the quarry. I lifted a hand to shield my eyes from the glare as a kaleidoscope of color in the sunset reflected off the white stone. A chill shot down my spine when I caught sight of a shadowy form.

Jordan must have sensed something. He stopped a few yards ahead, craning to look in my direction. "What's wrong?" he called out.

"I thought I saw something."

"Like what? A cow maybe?"

"No. Smaller, and more like. . ."

"Like what? A coyote?"

"No. A person. I saw a shape standing erect. It was right up there, looking down through that notch in the rocks." Jordan turned and gazed in the direction I pointed. "Then it moved to the right," I gestured, hesitantly. "And disappeared." As I lowered my hand, I noticed it was trembling. I squeezed my fingers tight a few times, embarrassed by the sensation of fear. I tried to fight off images of the *thing* that sat next to me on the bed, back at the farm. I kept telling myself I was too intelligent to allow something like that to get to me. But now I was jumping at shadows and reflections. What was wrong with me?

Jordan scanned the rim of the quarry. After a moment, he waved it off. "Your eyes are playing tricks on you," he said curtly. "Happens easily at dusk. There's nothing there."

"If you say so." The doubt in my response was intentional. "But there was something there. I saw it." I wished Ginger could talk. She'd tell us both what she saw.

As Jordan moved down the path toward the bus, I remained still for a moment, stroking Ginger's neck. My eyes strained to pick up the least little movement among the rocks above. I needed assurance that my imagination wasn't getting the best of me. And after our encounter at the farm, I was surprised that Jordan dismissed this so quickly. As I turned away, Ginger's apprehension seemed to ease. She lowered her head and followed.

Back at the campsite, Terry had reversed the bus up close to the rocky outcrop that was maybe thirty feet high, and somewhat concave at the base. He figured that would provide shelter from wind and rain, which in winter months consistently came from the north. The floor beneath the ledge was solid rock, which meant that the heat from a campfire would radiate outward and retain warmth for an extended time.

We had learned from Uncle Luke that there was no evidence of any permanent residence in these hills by early humans. However, burial mounds along the Arkansas River in Spiro, Oklahoma provided evidence of Caddoan Mississippian cultures many centuries before the arrival of Europeans. There could be no doubt that this very spot had served as campsite for Wichita or Caddo hunting parties. There was seasonal water in the creek not too far below. That had been there long before the quarry was blasted. No doubt, there had been numerous hollows where spring water trickled out of the rocks. That strongly suggested that game had been plentiful here.

Along one edge of the shelter, Jordan stretched up a rope line to tie the horses for the night. Over many years, cowboys who worked large ranches or did long cattle drives developed a variety of techniques for securing their horses near the camp. In this particular terrain, hobbling a horse could be dangerous. A better method was a high line, which Jordan tied to a metal ring on the back of the bus and pulled taut across about thirty feet, securing the end to the trunk of a small juniper (which, in these parts, most folks called a mountain cedar). The rope had to be at least six feet off the ground, with secure loops that would not slip. Each horse was fitted with a halter and a rope tied to a loop in the high line. This allowed them to lower their heads to eat, but there was not enough slack for them to step over and get tangled. Some of the old folks claimed this method came from Plains Indians who, by the 1700s, had become horse cultures with great skills in riding, training, and breeding.

Once our horses were secure, we measured out loose portions of grain in separate buckets, which they gobbled up eagerly. Then each horse got a small square of hay, torn off the bale and tossed onto the ground.

"Where can we stash the rest of this hay?" Jordan called out to Terry. "I was thinking of shoving it under the bus. It should stay dry there."

"No, no." Terry shook his head vigorously. "The fuel tank is under there, and there's a full propane bottle inside. If somehow that hay caught on fire, the whole bus would blow. Us with it. Just stash it under that ledge, not too close to the campfire." Terry pointed and turned away. Then he stopped. "On second thought, there's another light tarp in the bus. You can wrap it in that. But I'd still shove it against the rocks there, away from the bus, and away from the fire."

All chores done, we dragged folding chairs around the campfire.

"If it's okay with you guys," Terry said, "we can take turns making morning coffee. I thought we'd have instant oatmeal for breakfast. Or, you can fix what you want. Potable water is in that cooler." He pointed toward a galvanized container beneath the rear bumper of the bus. "You don't need to open the top. It has a spicket. We'll carry water from the quarry for cooking and washing. That'll be in the big pot by the fire. When you get a chance, have a look in the cabinets in the bus. We've got pots, pans, and utensils galore. We'll use metal plates, bowls, and coffee mugs. We'll have to wash them, but it's better than having a bag full of trash hanging somewhere. That just attracts critters."

Terry had certainly gone all out. He even brought k-rations and snacks to carry during the day. But he said he was holding eggs and bacon for the last morning. Christine stood listening, arms folded and lips taut.

"There's just a few more things you should know. Let's not use the toilet in the bus unless it's a nighttime emergency. There's an army shovel in the tool box. When you need to take a dump, dig a little hole and then cover it up. Paper, too. The best toilet spot is down that way," he pointed west, "just past a big rock."

"I would think the snakes are all in hibernation," I said. "I guess we don't have that to worry about. Right?" I'm certain there was caution in my tone.

"Right," Terry said. "No bugs either, unless we have hitchhikers in the bus. But when you go anywhere in the dark, carry a light. There're lots of critters in these hills."

"That's a fact," Christine suddenly chirped. "I was camping with some friends over at Turner Falls, summer before last. On the very first night, I tiptoed away from the tent to take a pee, and I squatted right next to a skunk. I must have scared him. He sprayed all over my bare butt. Holy moly, did I stink. I swam in the creek and showered twice a day with soap, but when I got home, Mom said I still reeked."

We all guffawed. Even Terry. And it was good to see Christine relaxed and garrulous.

"I've heard," she said, "if not for the spray factor, skunks make good pets. Billy Kates, a friend from school, found a baby skunk and bottle fed it, like you would an orphaned kitten or puppy. Had to have the scent glands removed, of course, but she... I think it was a female...

was as much a part of the family as the dog and cat.

"We'll see if we can find a baby skunk for you to take home," I said.

"Not for me," Christine tossed up a hand. "I'd never trust the little stinker."

Jordan and Terry had been in these hills more often than Christine and I. We all knew if coyotes came around, we'd probably hear them yipping. But their common hunting grounds would be lower down, by creeks and hollows where squirrels are easy pickings. Rabbits are abundant near farms, too, where they have their pick of fresh vegetables. And there were several other critters up here in the mountains, like skunks, possums, and racoons.

"There's always the possibility of a bobcat or even a cougar snooping around up here," Jordan said. "The horses would alert us, I'd think."

"Cougars, in these hills?" Christine said, her eyes widening.

"Oh yeah," Jordan answered. "But they're rare. I've heard that black bears are moving this way out of Louisiana and Arkansas. Growing human population's crowding them out. But I wouldn't really think any would be up on this mountain. There's just not enough cover. Too much open space. And there's not much for them to eat."

Jordan tugged at the zipper of a soft case, dragged out his guitar, and began what he termed an *ancient Chinese melody called Tuning*. Jordan had never taken lessons. He just picked up a few chords from friends, and mimicked strumming styles and chord sequences he picked up from folk artists like Bob Dylan and Joan Baez. Jordan's singing voice was as rough as his guitar picking. But he engaged both with enthusiasm. Once satisfied that his gut-string Epiphone was in tune, he settled on the key of D and launched into *Cotton Fields*, a tune we all knew. It was written by a man named Huddie Ledbetter, better known as Lead Belly. Christine joined in, swaying to the beat and harmonizing to Jordan's rough melody. Jordan made it through a couple of verses and then stopped abruptly.

"You know, sometimes songs don't really make sense," he said, twisting his face skyward. "*Down in Louisiana just about a mile from Texarkana* sounds like the writer was somewhere up north. Ohio, or Michigan, maybe. But Lead Belly came from a little town called Mooringsport, just south of Caddo Lake and close to Shreveport. That ain't nowhere near Texarkana."

The rest of us were all at a loss for words. We stared at Jordan, all wondering if he had a point, or if this was the introduction to a history lecture.

"Besides, you got to get down to Baton Rouge and New Orleans to really appreciate what Louisiana is all about. Know what I mean? The bayous and swamps. Those folks in *Shrezeport,* as they call it, are more like Arkansawyers who rolled down out of the hills and landed in the flatlands next to the Red River."

"Well, a song's gotta rhyme," I said. "And it's just poetry to music. Nothing literal about it. He wasn't writing a geography essay. Besides that, they grow cotton all over Louisiana. Lead Belly got that much right."

"Damn straight," Christine, said climbing to her feet. "Good lyrics are more about the writers' feelings." She stretched out an arm and tugged me into a sort of rockabilly dance shuffle as Jordan strummed and belted out another couple of lines.

I had noticed a shift in Christine's tone and facial expression. She seemed more relaxed, and certainly more garrulous than before. Then I spotted the reason. She drew a half liter bottle of Jose Quervo from under her blanket, twisted off the cap and tossed it back. She then offered the bottle to Terry, who looked up at her with a subtle smile and stretched out a hand.

I figured Terry preferred Christine a little tipsy. Alcohol took the edge off her numerous issues and allowed her to be a friendlier version of herself. Terry took a long tug and passed the bottle to me. I had a healthy sip, but not one to match Terry's big gulp. Guarding the bottle carefully, Christine retrieved it from my grasp and gestured toward Jordan. He was now in the middle of Pete Seeger's *Where Have All the Flowers Gone,* and declined with a crisp shake of his head. Then, reaching the line *when will they ever learn,* he stopped impulsively and reached out for the bottle.

"Yeah, why not," he said "This ain't church camp, now, is it?" He grimaced as he swallowed, and handed it back. "Whew, dogies. How does anybody get used to that?"

"Just like pickles, beets, and turnips," I said. "It's an acquired taste."

"This is true, this is true." Christine lifted an index finger in the nuanced varsity manner. "As one matures certain unpleasant flavors become appealing. Another mystery of life, I should think." She tipped the bottle up for one more swallow. "That's it," she chirped. "We've gotta make this last." She twisted the cap tight and tucked the bottle away.

"More important," Terry said, his tone serious. "I don't want anybody to get shitfaced. There's too much going on up here and too many ways to get hurt. We need to be alert, even at sack time, and up early tomorrow with clear heads. Can't afford a hangover."

"Yeah, yeah. I got it," Christine said, waving him off.

Terry squinted menacingly and shook a finger at Christine. "Don't make me throw you over my shoulder and haul your smart ass to your bunk." Terry cut me a glance and winked.

Christine was quick with a defiant but coquettish response. "You'd be so lucky."

Twenty

Conversation around a campfire can be strangely honest, often mellow, but now and then quite brutal. Jordan couldn't help but reflect on his good times at Falls Creek, the youth camp that Uncle Luke had pointed out on the map. The Southern Baptists were the largest Protestant denomination in America, and this facility had become a Mecca for their children in the region. In that venue, counselors and ministers reinforced ethics and doctrines that were the backbone of conservative and Evangelical theology.

I ventured to tell of my one and only summer camp there with Jordan. The first night in the boys' dorm, a kid in the bunk above me kept reaching down on either side to pop me with a flyswatter. I told him to quit, but of course he didn't. To pester me further, he started bouncing on the mattress, which not only shook my lower bunk but also made an annoying rhythmic squeak. I decided to put a halt to both annoyances. I pressed my foot against the bottom of his mattress, and timing it just right, I pushed upward to deliver a hefty power boost. At that very moment, the group counselor switched on the lights. His eyes immediately locked on my foot pressed up against the mattress, followed by a spectacle worthy of a circus act. My foot launched the kid skyward. He reached apogee just below the ceiling, and with arms flailing he careened headlong to the floor. The counselor dragged me to the camp office and gave me a searing lecture about Christian behavior. He also presented me with a little red demerit badge to take home to my parents. I tossed it into the Red River on my drive back home.

Now years later, that story in the company of cousins led to further reflections on our common and uncommon experiences growing up. During those years, we frequented a place called Turner Falls, located in the middle of the Arbuckles, and just to the west of Highway 77. That was our first visit to caves in that range, although those few were of little interest to spelunkers. Not particularly deep, they were open to the public and marred with graffiti. But the water fall and the swimming hole were quite appealing, and we frequently lounged in the sand and talked openly about the trivia that occupies the minds of teenagers. Like all boys that age, Jordan and I marveled at the female anatomy.

In fact, girls occupied more of our personal rumination than algebra and earth science. We were both convinced that the whole universe was driven by the mystery of feminine allure— compelling but beyond comprehension. Of course, none of us really understood the storm and stress of adolescence, or the complex transition to adulthood. But it was a time of exaggerated bravado and self-confidence, while we frantically pieced together life-skills and prepared for our launch out of the nest.

Things were significantly different now, as the four of us cousins sat around a camp fire. Christine, at eighteen, was the youngest. She was certainly intelligent, but she sometimes behaved like a fly thrashing around in a bowl of soup. In her head, the chaos of freshly absorbed data ranged from the latest fashion in sunglasses to the battlegrounds of psychology, sociology, and political science. She had not been part of our boy-banter when we were younger. But now, as an experienced and vocal young adult, she was willing to engage any and every topic with the gusto of a hunting hound. She pointed out that her parents had carefully guarded her and her sisters from sexual promiscuity, lecturing them frequently about the sacred area between their legs and their moral obligation to preserve their virginity until marriage. To that we each had a response.

"When I was about ten or eleven," Terry said, "I saw my big sister in the shower. And I was blown away by the fact that she had boobs and pubic hair. I was as ignorant as a bag of potatoes and thought she was deformed. I told her she looked like she was turning into a werewolf. I nicknamed her the *large-butted booby-snatch*, which drove her bananas."

"There you go." Christine chided, face twisting to half past ugly. "What does that even mean?"

"That's what my sister said. I told her it was a wild, hairy creature with boobs and the temperament of a wolverine. I don't know where I got that. I think I just made it up. But she was severely pissed off."

Jordan and I laughed out loud. "You're talking about Lisa, right?" Jordan said. "She's a couple of years older than you. And Lucille is the younger one? We don't ever see her."

"Yea," Terry answered, his visage suddenly remorseful. "She's shy. She comes to all the family events, but usually finds a quiet place by herself."

Christine's lips tightened. "Anything to denigrate and belittle women," she barked. "You were a male chauvinist right from the get-go."

Terry's hands lifted in a symbolic apology. "I was just a kid. The world was my play-ground, and people were the object of ridicule. At the time I didn't know any better."

Christine's face bore a congealed frown. "My memory of those days is repulsive," she said, huffing the words through taut lips. "Learning to accept the inevitable menstrual period every goddamn month, I was expected to function normally and pretend I felt just fine." She glanced bitterly at each of us.

"Every boy should experience that, just once," she growled. "Maybe for a year, even. It would change the whole damn world. I'm telling you straight. Or, maybe get pregnant, carry a baby for nine months, and push the little critter out your hoo-ha. That would be the equivalent of a college degree in intensive gender awareness."

"How would you know what it's like to have a baby?" Jordan said, tongue-in-cheek. "I know about flight simulators, but there's no such thing as a birth simulator, now, is there, lil' mama?"

"No, I don't know," Christine mumbled, her face swollen with resentment. "But I will, someday. And I can tell you this. In the Bible story where God curses Adam and Eve for eating the forbidden fruit, I think Eve got the shaft."

"Now, be careful not to blaspheme," Jordan said, wagging a finger in her face.

She slapped it aside. "No, really. I think whoever wrote that fable is the blasphemer. It makes God look incredibly bad."

"How's that?"

"For a start, if God is all-knowing why didn't he see that coming? And why would God get all upset if He knew his most intelligent creatures were going to disobey? In reality, that story casts God in the image of humans, with all our flaws. And then, what about the woman's punishment for believing the snake? Pain in childbirth? And subordination to men for a thousand generations? Give me a break. How does that fit the good, kind, forgiving, loving, and compassionate portrait of God? Surely, God and all his angels could have come up with a plan for human procreation without so much life-threatening pain for the woman. Maybe, she could give birth to a teaspoon-size infant, like a kangaroo, and carry it in a pouch while it grows. What I'm saying is, that story reads like God retaliates against all women because the first one messed up His *perfect* man. It's cruel and unusual punishment, to say the least."

"The lady's got a point," Jordan said, feeling a surge of sympathy. "History paints a strange and conflicting portrait of women. Objects of beauty and desire, possessors of mysterious knowledge and understanding, instinctive love and nurture; yet at the same time they bear the brunt of male disdain and abuse. Property to be bought and sold like goats and cows. But I've read enough to understand that in the ancient world, mothers bore children, ran the household, tended livestock, and gathered crops while fathers sat in a circle planning the next battle with a neighboring tribe. The fathers collected a bride price for their daughters, and then bestowed all their wealth and authority on the oldest son. It was truly a man's world."

"Right on." Christine nodded approvingly. "And it's certainly never been a just world."

"That's pretty heady stuff," Terry said, eyelids flicking. "What textbook are you quoting there?"

"Shut up, asshole," Christine said scornfully. "You haven't read a book in the last five years, except maybe a manual on machine guns, or tanks and shit."

"Heh, hey, now." Terry tossed up a hand. "I think it's time you got off my case. I thought we settled things back at the farm."

"Not by a long shot, Buster Brown."

"Well, it's time. I haven't said or done anything to hurt you."

"No? What about leaving me sitting on the god dammed front porch waiting for a ride that never came? What about that?"

The pleasant atmosphere in our little mountain Shangri-la had suddenly turned sour, and I recognized the need for a segue to a less volatile topic. With no time to think about it, I interjected an off-the-cuff comment.

"You know, my mother never tried to hide herself from me and Spencer. We both saw her naked a couple of times." I paused, asking myself where the hell that came from, unless it was what psychologists deem a Freudian slip of the tongue. "I don't know if that was good or bad," I added, a little embarrassed. "I mean, she covered up, or closed the door, when that happened. But she didn't scold us for looking, or run screaming like she had been violated. She just said something like: *Hey, I need a little privacy, please.* And I had to admit, I would say the same thing under similar circumstances. I didn't want her looking at my junk."

"I have to admit," Jordan said, "I was obsessed with girls when I was twelve. I didn't know much, of course, but I sure thought girls were very special creatures." He looked squarely at Christine, "I'd bet I never told you that when I was in the fifth grade, I went steady with two girls at the same time."

"No shit," Christine said.

"Yep. One was Mary Ann Morgan. I called her M&M, a blue-eyed blonde with a long ponytail, always tied with a bright ribbon. The other was Lucinda Sims, or Lucy, we called her. She had dark eyes and black hair bobbed short and cute. I think her parents were from El Salvador. I can't remember." Jordan leaned back and laced his fingers at the back of his head. His eyes roamed the sky. "There was no one else like Lucinda in our school. Anyway, the two of them were best friends and giggled about sharing a boyfriend. They were like salt and pepper. Totally different, and I was obsessed with them both. My mother wondered why I wanted to buy two identical discs. You know, the kind with your name on one side, and you give it when you're going steady. Did ya'll do that?"

Terry and I nodded, but Christine's brow furrowed as she inhaled to speak.

"So, how long did that little pre-bigamy experiment last?" she chided.

"About a week," Jordan said bluntly. "Until M&M ditched me for Robbie Cookston, a husky kid who went on to play tackle on the Ardmore High football team. Go Tigers!" Jordan pumped a fist in the air. "He had pecs and biceps like a gorilla. Then Lucy moved off to Arkansas. Can't remember why. So, I flew solo after that. No steady girlfriend until high school." Jordan's eyes drifted skyward, lost in memories.

Christine shook her head in disgust. "See? There's that latent urge to dominate and collect women like trophies. I think Freud would probably diagnose that as a nascent polygamous personality disorder or something."

"Did you ever?" Jordan said, eyeing me suspiciously.

"Did I ever what?"

"Ever have two girlfriends? Is that a polygamous... uh, whatever she said... a disorder, if you want two girlfriends?"

"I don't think so. No, I know I never fell for two at the same time. But I know I'm desperately in love with one girl now, and I've had enough experience to know I couldn't live with two. One's hard enough to please. Those Mormon dudes are either supermen, or totally nuts!"

"You got that right," Terry mumbled. "When I was sixteen, we were all girl-crazy. Jerkin' off in the toilet. Couldn't get our minds off cooters and hooters."

"There it is again." Christine snapped a stiff hand in Terry's direction. "It's the constant degrading and disrespecting women. That's what really gets me riled. And who makes up all these goofy names for body parts?"

"Good question." Terry sat up straight. "What do you gals call a guy's junk? Huh? The one-eyed monster and his marble sack? Or maybe his twig and berries, if you want to be insulting."

"That's not quite the same thing," she snapped back. "That's amusing. It's not intended to be insulting and demeaning."

"Bullshit," Terry barked. "I have just a tad more experience than you in the real world, and let me tell you what I see. Women are really no different when it comes to talking crude and nasty, especially when the guys aren't around."

"How would you know that?"

"I've walked in on it, so I know for a fact. And my mother has said so, too. That's pretty solid evidence. I'm sorry if that offends you. But I actually have a progressive mind. Even though women are typically smaller and weaker, I mean in terms of physical strength, I think men and women have equal value, and you women have the right to do and be anything you want."

Christine was quiet for a moment, visibly stunned. "I would never have guessed you believed that," she said.

Not willing to sit on the sidelines, I jumped into the awkward silence. "But there's a grey area where there's constant tension," I said. "I think it's fed by two things. One is sexual energy, and the other is the need for recognition and respect. Women in general are better at some things, and men are better at others. But I also think women get away with a lot that would get a man arrested and thrown in jail. Like grabbing a man by the balls just to be spiteful. No woman gets in trouble for that. And you get by with flaunting your sexuality, like low-cut blouses that expose cleavage or thin tops that reveal nipples with the slightest chilly breeze, or tight dresses and pants designed to display butt cheeks and all that. Short shorts and even worse, if you know what I mean."

Terry leaped back into the debate. "If a guy wears tight jeans that show junk-lumps, like a rock star on stage, he gets charged for indecency. What male school teacher would ever wear his shirt unbuttoned down to mid-chest. A man just can't do that. But a woman can. She can wear a blouse open to show cleavage, or a low-cut dress, bend over and shake it around, and say *O my goodness, don't look, you beast!*" Terry wagged his shoulders, doing his best female impersonation.

Jordan and I giggled. Christine maintained a pan face and folded her arms tightly.

"If a man pees in an alley," Terry added, "and a woman sees it, she can get him arrested for public urination *plus* indecent exposure. If a woman does that... well, she just had to go, and nobody protests, except maybe another woman. And, of course, if men and women are running a marathon with no toilets for a stretch of five miles, and some just have to go, they make an exception for that. I've seen that happen. They pee right there on the side of the road; maybe behind a car. But, Jeeze Louise! Can't you understand? The rules are just not consistent."

Christine blinked and nodded. "I suppose that... or some of that... is true."

"Thank you. But I'm not done." Terry leaned forward. "Here's the problem. Women want equality when, where, and how they want it, but you also want special treatment and privileges too, when, where, and how you want it. And it's very hard for the male half of the population to get that right all the time."

"So, you *are* a misogynist."

"No, I don't hate women. But I think equality requires some adjustments on both sides. Here in the USA, women have it better than anywhere in the world, but they're constantly bitchin' about not having equality. There has to be a balance of behavior, understanding, or respect between men and women. I know it sounds patronizing to say that women's rights have come a long way. But you need to get off the soapbox and just live with your own circumstances which, all things considered, are pretty goddamn good."

"Yes sir." Christine saluted, mocking. Her green eyes glistened like hot coals.

Terry again leaned toward her, glaring. "I'm not your sergeant, and I'm not a sir. But I *am* your cousin who loves and respects you, and I am a couple of years older with a shitload of experience you don't have. What I need is just a thimble full of common courtesy."

Christine teared up and looked away. "Where was the respect when you drove off without me?"

Terry's lips pursed. "Oh, shit. There it is again. That's still stuck in your craw." He drew in a breath, eyes rotating skyward. Then he leaned and looked Christine squarely in the eye. "I guess I have to come clean on this." Terry hesitated. "Your mother told me she didn't want you to come camping with us, even if we *are* cousins. She said if I brought you up here, she'd have me arrested for abduction." His eyes roamed anxiously before returning to Christine's stunned and speechless face. His tone softened. "It wasn't my choice. I apologize. But I'm tired of being your punchin' bag, when it really wasn't my call. And now, Sweet Jesus," Terry's eyes rolled, "we've both gotta deal with your mother when we get back. She's probably on the phone with my mom, as we speak."

After that, conversation fell dead in the rocks. Terry stood up and shuffled around, before reaching for a stick and poking at a few coals in the fire. Jordan was the first to yawn. He stood up, stretching, then ambled solemnly toward the bus steps. Christine followed close behind, her head low and eyes sweeping the ground.

I retrieved a pan of hot water from the boiling pot, washed tin plates and utensils, and packed them in the locker under the rear of the bus. In the meantime, Terry hiked up the hill to the quarry and returned with a full jerry-can of water.

"You did a good job," I said, watching Terry add water to the boiling pot. "This whole rig is impressive. Thank you. And, please," I caught Terry's arm as he was about to turn away, "don't let Christine or her mom, or anything else, get to you. We all respect you for your service to our country, no matter what the protesters say. And, of course, who you are as a person. I love you, Cuz."

Terry nodded, eyes darting left and right. "I appreciate that." He eased back before turning abruptly. "I gotta go pee."

"Me too. Lead the way."

As pee spots go, Terry had selected a marvelous one about forty yards to the west. Unlike the poop spot next to a dense mountain cedar, this was a spot with a view. We stood on a large flat rock and peed over the side of a bluff while looking out across the farmlands to the southwest. Certainly, this was more refreshing than reading graffiti above the latrine in a men's restroom at Denny's. When done, I shuddered at a gust of cold wind, zipped my jeans, and mechanically followed Terry back toward the bus.

After only a few steps I stopped dead still as something touched my shoulder. My neck chilled. In a single motion, I jolted forward and wheeled around to look behind me. I saw nothing. Yet, I sensed a presence just as real and close as the one in the back bedroom at the farm. I could feel it, easing nearer, until stale and musty breath engulfed my face. I held my breath, feeling my heart thump in my throat. My eyes roamed, trying to detect a visible shape. I could not. Then it withdrew. The air about me stirred, as if something moved past me and away.

I swallowed heavy, overcome with the same crippling terror I'd felt before. I turned to shout at Terry, but he had already disappeared up the bus steps. A cocktail of bizarre emotions surged through my veins. Both fear and intrigue. My heart raced, and for a moment I felt lightheaded. I was absolutely certain something had stood and stared me in the face, then brushed around me and departed up the hill. I was petrified, yet I had a compelling desire to communicate. I wanted to see it. I wanted to look it in the eye, just as it had stared at me. But it was gone.

Twenty-One

Terry was right, that he was light years ahead of the three of us in terms of real-world experience. Jordan and I naturally bowed to his knowledge and skills. And maybe now Christine would allow her resentment toward Terry to dissolve into respect.

However, there was another thing. Jordan and I both sensed an enormous turbulence beneath the surface. I had read about post-traumatic stress syndrome. And while I dared not mention it, I could see some of the symptoms in Terry; in his frequent aloofness, and the occasional blank gaze, commonly called the thousand-yard stare. At times, Terry could display remarkable insight and express himself with unusual aplomb, as he had done with Christine. On other occasions, he detached himself emotionally from the world around him, withdrawing into some kind of safe-space in the depths of his brain. You could knock, but there was no response.

We all knew Terry carried a heavy burden. He had come home from a war to find his fiancé Kristal shacked up with a guy she met at a party, and she was now pregnant. A *bun in the oven*, Terry called it. Before that, back in high school, his girlfriend Andrea had a fling with Mister Cavender, her sophomore drama teacher. Totally cuckolded, Terry now had trouble trusting women. And that was part of the tension between him and Christine. Two times cheated on, Terry was hurt and bitter. And even around women he cared about, like Christine, he felt awkward and uncertain.

That was compounded by his experience in Vietnam, which was a different world from anything Jordan and I had ever known. He had said he didn't want any of that to intrude on the sanctuary of family, or the great American ideals which were somewhat stereotypical, if not illusionary. But it could not be helped. The result was an aura of aloofness and rude self-expression that Christine interpreted as male chauvinism. I had assumed that Terry would not trust any of us as a confidant. And I correctly guessed that his problems were deeper than we had detected thus far.

Camping out under the stars, cowboy style, is an uncommon experience among my peers— sleeping on cold and stony ground with only a single wool blanket as a cover and a saddle for a pillow, horse tied to a nearby tree. Jordan and I had done that a couple of times here in these very hills, and once on a ranch west of Denton. Now in this rather unusual home-made camper, we each had the luxury of a metal bunk bed with springs and a foam mattress. We had no reason to complain. As far as I was concerned, Terry's bus was the Holiday Inn.

When I parted the tarp at the door and stepped up inside, I found Jordan packing away his precious Epiphone. Once in the case, he levered it in among Christine's gear under the bottom bunk. Jordan and I each stripped down to tee-shirts and Fruit of the Looms, then climbed into our bunks; he above Christine and me in the bottom bunk below Terry.

Christine paid us no attention. She wore gray long johns and brown thermal socks she had picked up at the Army Surplus Store, accentuated by stylish pink faux fur house slippers from Neiman Marcus. She stood staring into a round mirror with a light metal frame dangling loosely from a hook above the sink.

"God, I look like the wreck of the Hesperus." She brushed a finger over freckled cheeks, chapped lips, and eyebrows badly in need of plucking. Noticing a pimple on her chin, she drew both index fingers together and squeezed it with fierce resolve. "Disgusting," she mumbled. After repeatedly tugging a brush through tangles, she tied her hair into bushy pigtails. Satisfied that this was as good as she could look in this particular place and time, she zipped her belongings into a small cosmetic bag, tossed it under the bed, and scooted into her sleeping bag. Once settled in, she flopped over with her face to the bus wall.

Terry scratched his bristled chin and ran his fingers through a mop of hair, no doubt uncomfortable after the previous protracted military service where his hair was cut short on top and virtually shaved below the hat-rim. He tugged his sweatshirt over his head and stuffed it inside a gaping duffle bag. His taut muscles and lean frame still displayed military fitness. A ragged scar on his left shoulder, and another in his abdomen, told a story he was reluctant to repeat. In the dim light, I could make out on his left arm a distinctive 5th Airborne tattoo— a skull in a red beret with ragged wings curled up on each side.

Christine lifted her head and grunted. "Are you going to run that heater all night?" Her voice was more mellow than earlier, but still abrupt.

"Good question," Terry answered, forcing a warm tone. "I don't think we should risk suffocation. I'll let it burn another hour and then shut it off before I tuck in."

"I think we need the heat," I said. "But I don't like the smell. Can't we open a window? Maybe just a crack to let a little fresh air in?"

"Already did that. The driver's side window is down about four inches. Plus, the folding door will stay partially open. Air should flow around the tarp cover. But, brace yourself. It's gonna get cold in here in a couple of hours. The bus walls are insulated, sort of," he added, "but the top bunks are next to windows. However, heat rises, so I guess it's a tradeoff. We'll see. I think you should keep a blanket handy. Sleeping bags won't be warm enough."

"Mine's got thermal lining," I said self-assuredly. "I should be fine."

"Suit yourself," Terry said. "If you get cold, Christine might snuggle you. But don't crawl in bed with me."

Terry had already felt the blade of Christine's sharp tongue. He didn't need to invite more. Fortunately, she simply rolled her eyes and turned back toward the bus wall. I sniffed and offered an abbreviated smile. With no more than a moment's thought, I heeded his advice. After tugging a blanket out of my pack, I leaned toward a window to grab a peek at the horses. They appeared content, silhouetted against the dying embers of the campfire. A faint glow reflected from the rock ledge that umbrellaed our camp. I scooted deep into my nest and fell asleep quickly.

At about two, I woke up, startled. I must have heard something. The squeak of bed springs, feet shuffling across the floor. I wasn't sure what. I fumbled for my flashlight and aimed the beam in the direction of an odd sound. Christine was up, rummaging through her duffle bag.

"What are you doing?" I whispered.

"I need a blanket."

As I sat up, I realized the temperature in the bus had plummeted. "I thought you had one."

"I do. But I need another. I'm freezing."

"Are you barefoot?"

"Yes."

"You need socks. What happened to your socks?"

"Ahhh!" she hissed. "I pulled them off. My feet got hot and sweaty."

"Just put 'em back on."

In agitated motions, Christine dug and scratched in the bottom of her sleeping bag, until she located the thick alpine socks. She tugged them on, before re-nesting. After stuffing the blanket inside the bag, she flopped and wriggled around like a hen settling onto a clutch of eggs. When I saw that she had settled in, face buried in her pillow, I switched off the light.

"Don't say it." Christine moaned.

"What?"

"Don't say *I told you so*."

"I don't remember telling you anything. That was Terry. You should listen…"

My words were suddenly stifled by a thunderous bang that rocked the bus. It sounded and felt as if a car had crashed into us. Christine screamed and rolled onto the floor, kicking out of her covers, her eyes locked on the metal siding next to her bunk. At the same time, Terry swung off the top bunk and landed heavily next to her. Jordan was wide awake, propped on one elbow and eyeing us all from above.

I grabbed my flashlight and trained the beam on the bus wall. There was a large dent in the metal, about the size of a dinner plate. Another loud bump widened the dent. Christine sat up and scooted back against my bunk. A high-pitched scraping sound then assaulted our ears, as if a tree limb was being dragged along the outside of the bus. More pounding and the dent expanded forward, inch by inch. Breathless and speechless, we held lights on the bus wall, our gaze snapping toward every sound and each new depression in the metal wall. I moved to the window and directed my light on the horses. Their heads were turned toward the bus, ears erect, legs shuffling fretfully.

Terry cleared his throat. "I don't know what it is, but something's out there. If it was a bear, the horses'd be going crazy." Terry drew his handgun and eased toward the front of the bus. Slowly, he pulled the tarp aside. Seeing nothing, he reached for the handle to close the folding doors. Cold metal creaked, followed by a thwack as the panels slammed shut. He tugged the tarp from its hooks and stuffed it in front of the driver's seat. At the same time, we felt another jolt. The bus rocked and swayed. Our heads twisted and eyes darted about in confusion.

"We're moving." Terry mumbled, as if talking to himself. He grabbed the center post, his head turning from side to side. "Yes. It feels like we're rolling."

I rose toward the window to see a tree limb scrape past, leaving etchings along its path. I couldn't recall any trees near the bus. Terry pulled the tarp out of the way, leaped into the driver's seat, and shoved his foot down forcefully on the brake. His flashlight fell to the floor, rolling back and forth with the rocking motion. Then something changed. I sensed acceleration. The bus tilted forward, as if we were descending a steep hill. Christine let out a scream. I remembered climbing that hill on horseback just before we reached the campsite. It was steep and badly rutted. I swallowed heavily as I pictured a wooden bridge at the bottom and a drop-off into the creek.

"Hold on!" Terry shouted.

Jordan fell to the floor, locked his arms around Christine, and gripped the lower bedrail. My arms swirled in the air, searching for a handle, as if I were aboard a crowded metro. Finding nothing, I leaned back on an angle iron bedpost and gripped it with both hands. The sensation swept over me that the bus was airborne. I held my breath in an eternity of silent suspension. My stomach seemed to float into my throat, and my head surged in an ocean of storm waves.

As suddenly as it had begun, the noise and movement stopped. With it, the anxious sensation in my head and stomach dissipated. Jordan released his grip around Christine and rose cautiously to his feet. With tentative steps, we eased toward the front of the bus. Terry slowly pulled the handle and the door squeaked open. One by one, we stepped down and planted feet on cold and brittle gravel. With lights sweeping left and right, up and down, the four of us worked our way along the outside of the bus. We rounded the back bumper, our breathing shallow, trying not to make a sound. Terry led, Colt .45 in hand, flashlight gripped tightly below it.

Our tension eased and we all exhaled in relief. We glanced back and forth at each other's bewildered faces. There were the horses, still tied to the high line. We had not rolled down a hill. The bus had not moved. It was parked exactly where it was when we went to sleep. Each of us shuffled momentarily on anxious feet, shaking away the adrenalin rush and laughing off the terror, now replaced with embarrassment. Our laughter was cut short.

"Look," Christine said, directing a beam of light on the rear window. We froze in place. As we watched, letters appeared on the frosty window, as if written by an invisible finger. An icy tingle ran up and down my spine and my forearms sprouted a garden of goose bumps. That sensation was becoming a frequent one I'd rather have avoided altogether. We huddled together and watched, breathless, as letter-by-letter, words formed on the glass— *Cold... Hungry... Help.*

Visibly shaken, Christine turned and stepped spritely toward the bus door. I shuddered as an icy breeze whistled across my perspiring neck. Terry turned and lifted the light to my face, and to Jordan's. Then he directed the beam on Christine. I glanced at Terry and Jordan and knew in a second that all three of us saw it. A shape, grey and luminous, but in the distinct form of a woman in what appeared to be a doeskin dress. Yes, clearly an Indian woman, with long hair. She trailed close behind Christine, and paused as Christine ascended the bus steps. I swallowed heavy as the apparition stretched a hand to touch our cousin. To me, the gesture represented a plaintive desire to make contact. I felt strangely compelled to do the same. But I hesitated. Then, as if she had touched something hot, the woman quickly withdrew her hand and lowered her head.

Christine disappeared into the bus. We heard her footsteps thump down the aisle, followed by squeaking springs as she fell into her bunk. The vaporous image of the Indian woman lingered at the bus door, glancing over her shoulder in our direction. Her face hung heavy with the look of desolation and despair, like photos I had seen of prisoners of war. I thought for a moment that I saw— a tear. She turned and drifted away into the darkness.

Sleep eluded us the rest of the night, but no one said a word. Christine's terrified face emerged now and then from her cushioned den. She had not seen the apparition that wanted to touch her. She only saw the letters appear on the glass. That was enough. She remained speechless, traumatized. Jordan and I lay quiet, muscles tense, hearts pounding, eyes scanning. In an hour or so, my heart rate returned to normal, as did my breathing. But I remained bewildered. I sat up. Terry remained at his chosen post, sitting stiffly in the driver's seat, watching.

Twenty-Two

I awoke with a jolt to the sounds of clinking and thumping outside. I lifted my head and peeked through a misty window. I didn't know the time, or whether I had slept a couple of hours, or a couple of minutes. It was more or less daylight. I could see movement by the bright flames of a fresh campfire. I knuckled my eyes and looked again. Christine apparently had decided to take her turn at preparing breakfast. She hovered over the fire stirring something in a large cast iron skillet. I rousted Jordan out of his bunk, and after tugging on our boots we shuffled down from the bus.

Both of us yawned and rubbed our faces as we made our way toward the fire, both sporting an eerie hangover from our spectral intoxication. The sky was heavily overcast, and a bone chilling drizzle descended eerily on the mountain. Jordan went straight to the coffee pot, which sat in a cushion of orange coals and bellowed steam like a toy locomotive.

"Morning sunshine," Christine chirped in Jordan's direction, before noticing me. "Ah. Two sunbeams up and glowing."

I was surprised to see her up at all, much less busy and composed. I acknowledged her with a sluggish nod. "What time is it?" I asked, stretching, patting away another yawn.

"Not sure," she shrugged.

"Maybe close to eight," I guessed. "I think the sun is up." My head turned toward the east, and I gestured casually, "But you can't see it through all this."

"No shit, Sherlock," Christine growled. Her brash cynicism suggested a full recovery from the previous night's ordeal. "Do either of you guys have a watch?"

"Yeah, but I'm not wearing it," Jordan answered. "Do you really want me to go check the time?

"No, not really."

"Where's Terry, anyway?"

"I dunno." Christine shrugged. "He was gone when I got up. Hunting, I suppose. You guys want your eggs scrambled, or some other way?"

"Uh, yeah. Scrambled is good. I doubt you can unscramble what's there in the skillet."

"Are you trying to be a smartass?"

"No. That was just friendly sarcasm." I smiled lazily over my shoulder, doing my best James Dean.

"Yeah, sure," Jordan said. "Scrambled is good. Great coffee." He lifted his cup in salutatory fashion. Thanks for doing this."

"Terry made it," Christine muttered. "Fire, too, I 'spose. It was all here when I got up. He was strangely quiet. I never heard a thing."

"Wasn't Terry saving those eggs for the last day?"

Christine shrugged. "If so, he'll get over it. When is our last day?"

"Not sure. After last night, I was about ready to wrap it up now. But, tomorrow, maybe? Day after? I dunno. This trip is sort of open ended."

Both Christine and Jordan looked at me strangely. I felt compelled to ask why neither of them was rattled from our nocturnal adventure. All of us had gone to bed terrified. Now the two of them were as chipper as a blue-jay, like nothing had happened.

"I don't remember anything bad about last night," Jordan said. "Do you, Christine?"

"Like what?" she said. "I was so tired. I just scooted down into my sleeping bag and I was out like a light."

I swallowed heavily, embarrassed and perplexed. I remembered it all with crystal clarity. Goosebumps skittered over my skin as I thought about the writing that appeared on the window, and the Indian woman that stalked Christine. Apparently, they didn't remember that. I considered whether I was losing my mind. Or maybe I had a nightmare. "Yes, that's it," I whispered. "It was a nightmare." That had to be the answer.

I brushed a hand across my mouth. My mustache still retained the flavor of last night's supper. I realized I needed to wash and wake up. I dipped my tin mug into the hot water pot and poured it into a folded washcloth. After a vigorous scrub of my four-day stubble, I poured the remainder over my head and scratched through my disheveled hair.

Breakfast done, Jordan went back to the bus and rummaged through his gear until he found his watch. By eight-thirty we had the horses saddled and ready to ride out. The morning's objective was to search for lost caves. Jordan retrieved the map, which was lying open on Terry's bunk. I watched as Christine tossed the saddle over Scooter's back and cinched it down. She obviously knew more than I had assumed, and that brought a smile to my face. Even when she slipped the bit into Scooter's mouth, she took care not to clunk his teeth. She stroked his muzzle and under his chin groove, rubbing up and down his neck. Most horses like that as much as dogs like to be petted. Scooter leaned into her hand, blinking his eyes contentedly and studying her movements. I was impressed. I glanced at Jordan, who returned the look, bobbed his eyebrows, and nodded agreeably.

"What made you decide to ride Scooter?" I asked.

"Variety, I suppose," Christine said. "Maybe the way he looks at me. His eyes say, *let's be friends.* Should I take this rope halter off and leave it here?"

"Yeah, take it off," Jordan said, "but put it here in my saddlebag with the others. We might need to tie 'em up somewhere."

Leaving the fire to burn itself out, we made a last survey of the campsite. All was as secure as it needed to be. We mounted up and headed out. Jordan led the way up a meandering trail, and then across a rounded knoll to a scrawny clump of jack oaks. By mid-morning the misty rain had stopped, but the cloud cover remained. The ride was pleasant. I tried to shake off waves of emotion as I reviewed the night's experiences, which I now had reason to question. I'd never had a dream with such clarity. But, even now, the sensations lingered. My pulse began to race and my ears throbbed with the sounds I remembered so clearly. While my body swayed back and forth with Ginger's steps, my head pounded at a different tempo. I was lost in my thoughts when Jordan's voice split the morning air, and my head cleared.

"I think that's it right up there," he said, motioning with a nod.

We stopped, dismounted, and tied the horses at three points around a small tree. Stepping cautiously over slippery rocks, we climbed until we approached a ragged hole in the ground.

"Yep, that's it." Jordan said. "This is the one we call Coon Cave." Easing closer, we peered down to a ledge at about two meters below. Beneath that was a vacuous maw surrounded by jagged rocks. The hole was small, maybe shoulder width, becoming tighter as it zigzagged down. It appeared to be just right as a varmint hideaway.

"You plan to go down?" Christine asked.

"I don't think so." Jordan crouched down and gazed studiously into the cave. On an impulse, he picked up a rock about the size of a golf ball and tossed it in. Christine and I stood watching and listening. The rock fell, click clack, as it bounced to the bottom. It did not sound deep. But immediately, a chorus of buzzing noises arose from inside.

Jordan tossed a grin our way. "Rattlesnakes."

Christine took a step back. "Sounds like a bunch of them." She swallowed heavily.

"No doubt," Jordan said. We both bent over, hands on knees, like Santa peering down into a chimney too tight for his rotund belly. "I suspect this cave got its name because a coon hid in there to get away from somebody's pack of hunting hounds. Maybe happened a couple of times. But it's not a cave we could explore. Mouth is too tight, and obviously not very deep. I'm not sure a coon would venture down there in winter, with all that hostile company."

After a minute or so, the rattling ceased, leaving us in the stillness of the mountain slopes. We stood up and turned away.

Back in the saddle, Jordan motioned. "Okay, let's find Dead Man's Cave. I don't think it's far from here. Then we'll head back."

From there we road in circles for almost two hours yet never located anything that resembled that particular cave. Jordan seemed frustrated, and eventually suggested that we give up. The mist had dissipated. The air felt a bit warmer, but heavy clouds blanketed the sky. We were back at the camp shortly after noon.

Sitting around the smoldering coals of the morning campfire, we tore open a bag of salt-and-vinegar potato chips and shared the last of the coffee. Our heads turned as a bizarre round of thunder rumbled from the northeast. Jordan said it was not thunder, but dynamite from a rock quarry in Dougherty. People who live within twenty or thirty miles of that quarry think of Dougherty as Jupiter's battleground— the origin of thunderous noises at given times during the day. Otherwise, the town itself had little to offer. It was scarcely more than a wide place in a road traveled by few. Originally called Henderson Flat, it had never had a population over about four hundred. Around 1900 it was called a *sundown town,* where black people were not allowed to live and could only visit on business during daylight hours.

"Did you know that Kay Starr's from Dougherty?" Christine said sprightly.

"No shit?" I said, not hiding my cynicism. "That's really very interesting. Who's Kay Starr?"

"You never heard of Kay Starr? She's a famous jazz singer. Just completed a new album with Count Basie called *How About This*. I read she's Iroquois and Irish, which sounds like a mighty strange brew. But everybody around these parts assumed she was Cherokee."

"Well, that's because there ain't that many Iroquois around here," Jordan snipped. "I think they were part of the Erie Nation, way up north. But I believe a few relocated to a reservation in the northeast part of the state. There's a lot of history there, too. But unless Miss Starr's people were from western New York, I'd say that's just an urban legend."

Christine and I were rescued from more of Jordan's history discourse when Terry meandered into camp. Surprised, we all turned his way.

"Any coffee left?" he said.

"No, but we can brew another pot," Jordan said. "Thanks for the fire and fresh coffee this morning."

"No, don't bother," Terry said. "I'll grab a beer out of the cooler. I prefer that anyway." Terry disappeared into the bus and returned with a can of Pabst Blue Ribbon. Casually, he unfolded a lawn chair and plopped down before snapping open the beer. We told him we had been up to Coon Cave, but couldn't find Dead Man's Cave. Terry displayed little interest.

"Did you spot a deer?" Jordan asked. "Or anything else worth telling?"

"No, but I found a good hunting spot. Clear antler rubs, and lots of tracks and skat."

Terry scratched around in the bag for the last of the potato chips. Jordan poked at the embers and got the fire going again, adding one additional oak log. He remembered a few more bits of data about the Iroquois. We all listened without comment. Terry watched Jordan blankly before tilting back his head and pouring the last potato scraps into his mouth. Crumpling the bag and tossing it into the fire, he pushed out of the chair and disappeared into the bus. He returned with a packet of Oreos. He extracted a few and waved the bag around, a silent gesture of his willingness to share. We all had a couple. After sucking down the last drop of beer, Terry crumpled the can with a single one-handed squeeze. Then he stood up and stretched. "I'm going back out."

Jordan and I nodded. We all understood that Terry did not need our permission or any level of consent to do whatever he wanted to do. Besides, we understood his need for alone time. Suddenly, Christine jumped to her feet.

"Can I go with you?"

Jordan and I held our breath. Terry hesitated, studying our faces for clues to Christine's mysterious change in attitude. His eyes returned to her. He shrugged. "Sure. Bring your own water. But no food. They pick up the smell."

Christine scampered to the bus and returned with a coat, gloves, knit cap, and a small hiking canteen. Stopping abruptly, she wheeled around and clogged back up the steps. We heard her thumping around under her bed. She emerged with a small backpack, into which she shoved her canteen. The pack might have contained what Grandma would call *unmentionables*. We didn't know, and didn't ask.

Terry shouldered his rifle and struck out in an easterly direction, Christine in tow. Mid-stride, he turned on a heel and walked backwards, calling out to me and Jordan. "By the way. I didn't make coffee this morning. Or a fire. When I left, it was pitch dark. I assumed one of you did."

Jordan and I looked at each other, pan faced. At the same time, a chill crept over me like I had stepped into a meat locker. I recounted mentally that when Christine came outside and started cooking, there was already a fire and hot coffee in a pot. There was a clump of hay in front of each horse. Who did that? I shuddered to think that the spectral woman I saw the night before, and whoever or whatever rattled the bus and wrote us a note on the back window, might also have made our morning coffee. But I'm the only one who remembered all that. I was baffled, and cautiously held my tongue.

Jordan and I watched as Christine skipped along after Terry and the two of them disappeared down a trail between heavy boulders. Jordan kneaded his brow, pursed lips readying to spit out a reluctant thought.

"I've been in these mountains plenty of times," Jordan said, tight-lipped and serious. "And I've stayed with Grandma and Grandpa more times than I can count. And I have never before had any experience like this trip. That thing I saw back down in the farm house…" He pointed and wagged his finger fretfully. "I don't know what's happening, but it scares the livin' daylights out of me."

Obviously, Jordan's memory was suddenly clearing, and it frightened him. But it puzzled me. "I'm not sure what to think either," I replied. "But I saw things last night that apparently you don't remember."

"I didn't earlier," Jordan said, eyes misting, "but it's coming back. It's all pretty scary, and I don't like it."

I was surprised that he didn't just pack up and head back to the farm, possibly thinking that to remain would be testing God's providential care or inviting Satan's presence at our humble campfire.

"I don't believe in ghosts," I said, as sternly as I could put it. "But I can't imagine any type of mass hysteria that would create a hallucination like that. It was certainly real for me. And yes, it scared me too."

Twenty-Three

Terry and Christine crossed the rough double-rutted lane we had followed up to the campsite. Below that, a path led east along the upper side of Cool Creek. Christine struggled to keep pace with Terry until they reached more level ground. Catching up, she could not resist the opportunity to talk.

"I want to apologize for being such a bitch," she said glibly. "And the terrible things I said."

"No talking," Terry said, his tone brisk. "Only whisper."

"Sorry." She lowered her volume to a whisper, which required that she walk close on his heels. "I want to apologize."

"Okay. But try to be quiet. And step lightly, like you're trying to sneak up on something, because you are." Terry glanced over his shoulder with a sardonic smile. "Or like you're getting home at two in the morning, and you don't want to wake your mom."

Terry recognized the change in Christine's tone and demeanor. He thought it best to play into it, without comment. Christine sniggered and drew up a hand to cover her mouth.

"Okay. But did you hear me?"

"I heard. It's all okay. Forget about it. I know the feeling of having something stuck in your gullet and you just can't cough it up."

Terry maintained a heavy pace, with Christine trudging close behind. Their precarious route meandered along a game trail, over loose rocks, and around protruding boulders. He slowed as they approached the edge of a steep decline. He lifted a hand and halted, as if leading a military reconnaissance team. As she walked, Christine blissfully surveyed the rocky ledges and faraway skyline. Awestruck by her surroundings, she nearly bumped into Terry.

"Okay," he whispered, leaning his head toward her and pointing. "We're gonna slip down into that draw and follow the creek to a spot I found." He looked intently into her eyes, his words soft, but strong and deliberate. "First, I want to know why you want to watch me shoot a deer. That doesn't sound like something a liberal environmentalist would do."

Christine answered with equal resolve. "Oh, I don't want to watch you. I want to shoot one myself."

"What?" Terry's face twisted skeptically. "I had the impression you despised guns, and war, and branding cows, eating chickens beheaded in a poultry processing plant, and just about anything conventional. Know what I'm saying? Why would you want to kill a deer? I don't get it."

"I know it sounds crazy, to your ears, at least. But trust me, I'm not off my rocker, if that's what you think. Yes, I do have a passion for nature." Christine paused, fumbling for words. "I just feel a need to understand, and connect, you know, with our ancestors. *All* our ancestors, European and Native American, who lived off the land and survived without supermarkets and pharmacies on every corner. I hear Jordan telling all those stories about Indian history and how they hunted game to survive over hundreds, even thousands of years. I have this sense of spiritual connection with that process of life. Being thankful for a life taken, and of course given not willingly, but relinquished so that others can live. All that is lost in today's culture, and I think it deserves respect. Even more than that. Reverence. I just want to experience it."

"Wow." Terry shuffled his feet, head tilting skyward. "I'm stunned, and impressed." He paused, reflecting, studying her sincere face. "I suppose there's something really special in that." He surveyed the horizon, with the long singular formation that extended west above them; the ravine and creek below; the patches of trees becoming denser as the creek twisted eastward and downward toward the Washita River. He tried to picture the rows of rock protrusions and clumps of ancient boulders that he had seen exposed here and there across the farmlands. All that had been traversed centuries before, by bands of migrant Wichita and Caddo hunters. This was a minuscule section of the vast majestic American landscape with which Christine had the urge to bond. In Terry's thinking, there was something sacred in that.

"You really don't hate me for being in the Army or fighting a war that folks here at home didn't believe in, and trying to change what was really none of our business? You don't really think I'm a baby killer, like all that protest crap and negative publicity?"

"No." She shook her head slowly, resolutely. "I don't. Of course, I don't like war. I hate it, in fact. Really, I do. But I don't hate soldiers. I don't hate you. I understand that a lot of human history is about war, and we can't seem to develop beyond that impulse. I understand that sometimes people have to fight for freedom, or to stop a madman who wants to take over a country, or the world. I understand that small countries are often invaded and taken over by larger neighbors, who justify their actions as political expedience. And I know that America has plenty of dirty laundry of its own. But I'm constantly confused, trying to balance our grand ideals with reality."

Terry hung his head, pondering Christine's bizarre shift in perspective. "Okay. I think I understand at least some of that. That's good to hear." His eyes met hers and his lips pursed momentarily before he spoke again. "You know anything about weapons? Ever shot a rifle like this?"

"Yep. At a gun range. That right there," she pointed crisply, "is a Remington .30/06. A model 700, maybe? And you're using Winchester 150 grain jacketed rounds with a soft point." Christine smiled proudly, lifting her eyes to meet Terry's intrigued gaze.

Terry deliberated a moment. Then he sniffed. "You could have read all that just now, off the box. Big deal."

"Muzzle velocity about 2,600 feet per second," she said, looking Terry in the eye. "But that varies. Did you use the same ammo to sight in and adjust your scope? That's pretty important, if you want accuracy."

A crinkle appeared at the corners of Terry's eyes and a smile stretched across his whiskered face. He sniffed and looked away. "Okay." He nodded. "Let's go hunting."

With a confident swagger, Christine trailed closely behind Terry down a slope and along the edge of Cool Creek. Approaching a thicket, Terry crept slowly. Christine mirrored his steps. Terry pushed aside a cedar branch to reveal a small secluded area that overlooked the creek and the sloping bank on the other side.

"There's no comfortable way to do this," he whispered, "but we have to hunker down behind this rock and just wait. I scouted out this area yesterday. This spot is a natural blind. Elevated position. Perfect view. Just nothing to sit on."

"Understood. I'll make do."

Terry squatted down on a clump of dead grass, maneuvering to cross his legs. Christine mimicked his posture. Terry laid a glove on the top of the rock and rested the rifle stock on it, a steady and padded brace. He leaned forward, easing his right eye toward the scope, through which he methodically scanned the creek bottom, the ridge above it, the tree line, and scattered clumps of brush. He lingered on each small patch of shade. Tilting his head, he chambered a round and flipped the safety on lock.

The first hour seemed like eternity, without a word and without movement.

"What if my legs go to sleep?" Christine whispered.

"That happens. Just reposition slowly and quietly."

"Hard to do, but I understand."

Moments later, responding to a tickling sensation, Christine lifted a hand to her nose.

"Can I get a tissue? My nose is running."

"Just do it slowly and quietly. And just wipe. Don't blow."

"What if I sneeze?"

"Don't."

Christine quietly drew a bundle of tissues from her coat pocket, wiped her nose, blinked and rubbed vigorously, and stuffed the used tissue back in her pocket. Another forty-five minutes passed, seeming to Christine more like a century in purgatory. Various muscles ached, threatening to cramp, and the tingling in both feet escalated to numbness. She wriggled her toes, stretched her neck, and flexed various muscles hoping to find relief. Soon, so she realized, she would need to urinate. As a distraction, she tried listening to her own breathing, or feel the rhythm of her pulse, and she occasionally rotated her eyes upward towards birds twittering high on bare tree limbs. Being quiet and doing nothing was difficult.

Upon a sudden nudge in the ribs, her eyes lifted from picking her nails. Terry's attention was locked on something across the creek. Christine craned her neck, scanning the shadows. Two does and a pair of young deer emerged from behind the tree line and stepped lightly and cautiously down toward the creek.

"Ohhh," Christine whispered. "They're beautiful."

"Shhhh." Terry's *hush* came as a scarcely audible hiss, but Christine heard and understood. Spellbound, and virtually breathless, she watched as the deer lowered their heads to drink. One after the other, they nuzzled the water's surface, imbibed silently, lifting and lowering repeatedly to survey their surroundings. Then, almost in unison, with ears erect, they turned and slipped stealthily up the bank, and into the cover of brush. Just as Christine inhaled to speak, Terry eased a hand toward her in a subtle gesture to be quiet. Frozen in place, she held her tongue, mouth agape. Terry leaned away from the rifle, shifting the stock and cushion toward Christine. She gripped it carefully and eased her eye toward the scope.

At that moment, a buck appeared from shadowy seclusion and stepped tentatively down toward the water. He stopped halfway, studying the area, eyes wide and ears flared. Terry counted ten points on the rack. This was not an old buck, but stout, healthy, and certainly eligible for harvest.

Christine drew the rifle butt against her shoulder, wrapped her fingers around the grip. Peering through the scope, she aligned the crosshairs on her target. Terry raised a finger to the safety and tapped. Christine caught his reminder. Her thumb eased the safety off and her index finger rested lightly against the trigger. Cautious and wary, the buck eyed the other deer as they made their way along an upper game trail, almost invisible in a thicket. The buck looked down toward the water and then turned his head again, his attention on the does. Head erect, he stepped broadside to Christine's view. She aimed the crosshairs just behind the shoulder, mid-chest. After releasing a long, slow breath, she paused— and squeezed the trigger. The thunderous shot echoed through the rocky ridges and sent birds scattering from trees and brush. The buck fell dead.

Terry and Christine rose to their feet, stretching numbness and tingling from their legs. Hearts pounding, they made their way down and across the shallow creek. They approached, and then paused over the dead buck. Christine gazed upon it, entranced, a burning sensation in her face. Her head throbbed with a bewildering blend of conflicting emotions— pride and remorse, triumph and guilt. As she knelt down, her eyes flooded and tears rushed down both cheeks. Her fingers stroked the buck's forehead between still and lifeless eyes. Uncontrollably, emotions seeped through her trembling lips: "Thank you, thank you, brave and beautiful deer, for giving your precious life to me."

Terry sighed deeply and turned away before his face rolled skyward. His eyes welled up and his throat tightened. He felt Christine's joyful pain; her honesty, and compassion. He respected her strength and clarity of will. He thought, but did not say it, that such was the stuff of which a good soldier is made. He was proud to be her kin and to accompany her in this unique moment. He brushed a gloved hand across both eyes, then bent over and patted Christine's shoulder.

"Okay, let's drag him away from here and I'll show you how to field dress a deer."

Terry grabbed the antlers and tugged the carcass across dead grass into the shade of a jack oak. The gnarled tree had a stout limb low enough to toss a line over.

Terry handed Christine his Ka-Bar combat knife, keenly sharpened. She looked at it pensively, then reached toward the small of her back and drew out a similar, but older, Emil Voos Solingen knife with a bone handle.

Terry's eyes widened. "Whoah. Where'd you get that?"

"It was my dad's. He was in Germany during the war. This was his, too." Pulling open her coat, she revealed a leather shoulder holster and lifted out a Smith & Wesson .38 Special, with original wooden grips. Terry took it reverently, as if examining a crucifix heisted from the Sistine Chapel.

"That's a fine weapon. Standard issue for police officers all over this country. So," he handed back the pistol, "you're armed to the teeth, and you made your first kill. Let's clean it."

Terry guided Christine in making an initial slit in the soft skin of the lower belly, taking care not to penetrate the gut or the tarsal gland. The process was challenging, and she cried most of the way through it. But she did everything Terry told her, without protest or hesitation. With all incisions made, she reached in and hauled out the steaming bundle, consisting of heart, lungs, liver, stomach, and intestines. Then, with a few final cuts she removed the penis and testicles in one package.

"Now let me ask you this," Terry said. "This is a nice buck with an impressive rack. Not many hunters do this good on their first try. Maybe you want to have the head and antlers mounted. Not as a trophy. I know that's not your thing. But maybe it would be a good token of your beliefs, and your respect for wildlife in general."

Christine's face melted and her chin quivered. A few seconds passed as she studied the carcass deferentially. She swallowed heavily, nodded, and wiped a sleave across her eyes. "Yes, I think I would. I never would have thought of it like that, until you said it."

"Okay. If you'll carry the packs, I'll carry the deer."

Terry rummaged through his backpack and drew out a large plastic bag. He bundled and tied the legs, then slipped the bag over the carcass, leaving the head and antlers exposed. Christine slipped the straps of her small pack over her shoulders, pack covering her chest, and hoisted Terry's larger pack onto her back.

"That might not stay put," Terry said. "Let's try this." He cut short pieces of nylon cord and tied the straps together beneath Christine's arms. He then emptied the rifle of remaining cartridges and slung it with the strap across his chest. After a moment's struggle to get a grip on it, he hoisted the deer over his right shoulder, bouncing his cargo a time or two to get it settled. He nodded at Christine. "That'll work for me. Let's head back."

The sky was heavily overcast, and evening had descended with little evidence of a sunset. Overhead, a flock of Canadian geese honked rhythmically as they winged in perfect V formation on an ominous southwesterly course. Terry glanced up, wondering if the geese knew something even before the meteorologists in Oklahoma City could agree on a forecast. Frigid weather was on its way. No doubt about it.

Winters in Oklahoma were mild compared to the Northern Plains and Great Lakes area. Snow fell almost every year, but it typically melted away in a few days. There were never long spells of arctic blasts with temperatures below zero. Neither was this like the Rockies or Tetons. There was no danger of getting buried in an avalanche. A winter weather forecast was hardly a big deal. At least, that was true most of the time.

As they trekked upward towards the campsite, Christine jabbered incessantly, assisted by a lingering adrenaline rush. "I've been thinking about the simple process of sighting-in a rifle," she said, breathing heavily. "One thing doesn't make sense to me."

"What's that?"

"I understand the arch in a bullet's trajectory and sighting in at twenty-five yards to get the first point where the round crosses your line of sight. You need to match the crosshairs with the strike point."

"And? What's the problem with that?"

"Well, it's the illogical way they explain how to achieve that. Trainers and manuals all say…" Christine's walking pace slowed momentarily. Her eyes roamed, while she organized her thoughts. She then jogged a few paces to catch up, packs bouncing. "It's like this," she said, shrugging and tugging to adjust straps. "Suppose your first three shots were grouped about two inches low and four inches to the right of the bull's eye. The manual says to adjust up two inches and left four inches. That's, well, however many clicks that might be. But, that's not really what you do."

"What do you mean? That's exactly what you do."

"No, it's not. You can't adjust the barrel of the rifle to shoot higher by two inches, and left by four. That's not possible. The bullet goes where the barrel is aimed."

"That's true. Except for maybe wind, or if the round grazes a leaf or something."

Christine dipped her head, in a moment of frustration. "Yes, but my point is this. You can manually move the whole rifle around to change the direction of the barrel, but you can't adjust the barrel with a couple of twists on a screw. What you actually do is adjust the scope so the crosshairs match the strike point, which is where the barrel is aimed. You don't adjust the strike point to match the crosshairs. Follow what I'm saying? In this case, you adjust two inches down and four inches right. Not up two and left four."

Terry stopped and thought a moment, eyes squinted and lips taut. "Instructions follow the logical process from a hunter's point of view. The hunter thinks of it as adjusting the barrel of the gun, or the strike point to the scope. That's logical."

"Where's the logic in that? You can't bend the barrel. Just like you don't turn a steering wheel left in order to get the car to turn right. You actually adjust your view to match where the bullet is already going to strike."

"We still talk about sunrise and sunset," Terry said, his tone confident. "That's not accurate. The sun doesn't really traverse the sky. The earth rotates, and... well, you know. And on a boat with a tiller, you push left to turn right."

Christine responded without hesitation. "Modern English has a lot of archaic expressions. But high-tech descriptions like sighting in a rifle? No way. That should be precise, and realistic."

Terry turned and resumed his previous pace, tossing a last comment over his shoulder. "When you get elected to Congress, you might want to bring that expert analysis before the Joint Chiefs of Staff. Tell them they're teaching the military marksmen all wrong. And I'm just as sure as shit the NRA will leap into action, ready to amend their century-old methodology to comply with suggestions from Congresswoman Christine Harriet Greenwood."

Christine's eyes widened. Terry's attempt at eloquence and detail struck her as evidence of deeply entrenched bias and total resistance to a fresh perspective. "That's about what I expected," she mumbled. They trekked on a few paces in silence before Terry stopped and turned toward Christine. She almost bumped into him, before halting abruptly.

Puzzled, her eyes darted left and right, studying his face up close.

"Then, on the other hand," he said, with a hint of a smile, "that's a damn good observation. I really never thought about that." Terry turned and resumed his pace along the path, doing a quick hop to adjust his cargo.

Christine drew a hand across her mouth to stifle a grin. *I'm right*, she thought. *He admitted it.* With a contented skip, she caught up. Terry glanced back, a sparkle in his eye. Neither spoke again, but they both bore subdued smiles as they trekked up the hill.

Jordan and I had just made it back from our failed expedition to locate Dead Man's Cave. We had ridden straight up to the quarry to let the horses drink before I unsaddled, fed, and tied them up for the night. Jordan had gathered kindling and made a fresh fire and was busy stacking on more logs, arranging them obsessively in a neat pyramid. Except for a crackling campfire, the camp was in darkness when Terry and Christine rounded the bus and dropped their packs.

Christine was eager to show us the buck and proposed trophy mount. Reveling in her compulsive *fete accompli*, she paced back and forth, recounting details while Jordan scrubbed four large potatoes and tossed them into a kettle of water, not quite to a rolling boil. By the light of a lantern, Terry carved the most useful meat from the carcass. He severed the head with the cape carefully peeled back, rolled it in a bundle, and packed the remaining ice shards inside the roll. The antlers were too large to fit in a cooler, so he wrapped them in a plastic tarp.

At Terry's suggestion, Christine massaged the backstrap with salt, pepper, and garlic while she continued her commentary on the kill. Jordan then cut it into smaller portions, skewered them onto four metal spikes, and racked them over the open fire. Me with a beer and Jordan with a Coke, we sat back and listened to a summary of Christine's sighting-in theory, nodding approval and sharing her sense of accomplishment as we ate. Still chewing, I glanced around. Terry had disappeared into the darkness without a word.

As the three of us cleaned up and packed away utensils, the temperature dropped at a noticeable rate. Before we retreated into the bus, a chilling mist began to fall.

Twenty-Four

A mile or so above the blue bus, and unknown to any of us, an event transpired that I later would piece together from meager evidence. It was easy to imagine the glow of a campfire illuminating the hard and briary faces of two men, whose steely eyes peered through the fur of hooded parkas. DJ, a young ruffian with well-defined muscles, gathered scraps of wood from the hillside. His chiseled face and spry movements marked his relative adroitness and vigor. Coop, older and heavier than DJ, grunted as he leaned forward from his uncomfortable perch atop a rock. A gloved hand gripped a stick and began methodically poking at crumbling heaps of glowing charcoals, rotating fresh splintered wood into the heat. Air rushed in, as if blown from a bellows, and lively flames arose from grey ash at the base of the crude camp fire. A twisting column of smoke ascended, carrying in its arms a chorus of tiny orange dancers that swayed rhythmically, riding the current upward through cold mountain air and disappearing into a canopy of grey mist.

Hidden in a draw, high up in a ragged escarpment, the pair of scoundrels guarded a treasure for whose safety and secrecy they were responsible with their very lives. Hunkered down like a pair of polar bears in a whistling arctic wind, they were warmed mostly by the prospects of handsome payment for their loyalty in these daunting circumstances— camped out on a mountainside in bone-chilling weather. They passed a bottle of whiskey between them and tossed their heads back for repeated long gulps.

Their phantom shadows sprawled across the surrounding amphitheater of ancient rocks, each bending and stretching like the enormous Cyclops of Greek mythology. Empty tin cans lay where they had been tossed randomly among the rocks, evidence of slovenly habits and blatant disregard for both camping rules and the sanctity of the outdoors.

A distressed whimper pricked their ears. Their uncaring faces turned toward the source, hidden in the dark belly of the mountain, amidst calcite teeth above and below, and in the company of bats and deadly serpents. Again, the familiar sound emerged from a recessed orifice partially obscured by a dwarfish cluster of mountain cedars. The men glanced at each other and snorted derisively through stained teeth.

Their attention was soon captured by the graceful shape of a woman approaching from beyond the rim of firelight and gliding silently over a ragged and brittle path. She eased up and perched seductively on a sloping rock. Their faces ruddy with deepening intoxication, the pair of scoundrels rose to their feet and gazed upon her alluring form.

"Aren't you boys lonely and bored up here in the cold?" Each word dripped from her lips like warm honey.

Lustful eyes painted her, from beautiful face to lacquered toenails. DJ started toward the woman, but Coop gripped his shoulder and hauled him backward. Tension rose in their faces as they began to argue over who would have the first turn at her. The woman melted from her perch and sidled up to DJ. Her long black hair cascaded across buoyant breasts as she untied the laces of a deerskin dress. She posed motionless as it slipped from her shoulders, clinging momentarily to her hips before gliding down and settling around her ankles. Her naked body glistened in the firelight, with no apparent discomfort from the icy wind or the sporadic pellets of sleet.

Pushing DJ aside, Coop tugged off his gloves and gestured with a beefy hand, inviting the woman into his embrace. His senses aflame from crown to crotch, the younger man lunged to retrieve her. Coop shoved him back. Then, leaning close and smiling sardonically, he whispered into DJ's face, "I'm tired of taking orders from the likes of you. You ain't shit." His taut finger poked the younger man in the chest. "I know it. Boss knows it, too. And I ain't gonna play second fiddle to you no more. No way, no how."

"Boss didn't say that," DJ answered, lips taut and eyes glaring.

"Yeah, he did. He said you're nothin' but a smart-mouthed young buck with too much ambition."

"Then how come he told me to keep a close eye on you?"

"Beats the hell out of me. He told me you're a dangerous little bastard. Didn't trust you. Said I might need to put you in your place."

"Well then, fat man, give it your best shot."

Coop glared into DJ's defiant eyes. With a sudden tightening of his lips, Coop's arm lifted forcefully as he drove a knife blade into DJ's ribs. The woman observed, expressionless. The younger man's stunned eyes widened as he tilted forward into Coop's arms. A trembling hand clutched his wound while a dark red stream spewed between his fingers. He gazed downward for a moment, riveted and breathless, before lifting his ashen face toward his assailant. Through quivering lips, he forced an insolent response.

"You sorry son-of-a-bitch."

A gunshot split the cold and wet night. Stunned by the deafening noise and deadly impact, Coop's saucered eyes lowered and locked on a trail of smoke rising from the short barrel of a revolver. Pain gripped Coop's chest. Blood rose into his mouth. He knew he'd been shot. But he could not know that the bullet had entered his lower abdomen and spread into a jagged meat shredder that tore its way upward through fat and intestines and lodged somewhere in his right lung. Fear gripped him as he surmised the worst. Gagging, he tried to speak. His dimming vision returned to his partner's steely eyes, and his blood-soaked lips stammered his *ultima verba*.

"Now, that... that's some shit."

DJ squeezed the trigger again. Coop jerked with the impact. Blood spewed from his nostrils. DJ's hand lowered. His grip loosened. The gun slipped from his fingers and fell to the wet and rocky ground. His forehead eased forward and rested against Coop's chest. Clinging to each other like a pair of doomed comrades-in-arms, DJ and Coop sank down into a thorny couch of prickly pear pads. Life evaporated from their muddled eyes and each man expelled a final slow breath. Their skin paled. Eyes fixed. Pupils dilated.

The woman's head tilted dispassionately as she regarded the two lifeless men as if they were no more than sacks of water, meat, and bones. She looked away, surveying the jagged spines of rock that ran parallel, both above and below the hidden draw. The men had called these rock formations *The Devil's Graveyard*. She regarded them differently. Her lips parted into a sallow and sardonic grin as she sniffed in contempt. Then, turning, she disappeared silently into the mouth of the grotto.

An owl watched from atop a leafless jack oak. It had held its position despite the startling gunshot. But now, the echoing volley having disappeared and the night's crisp silence restored, the legendary consort of Athena rotated its head toward movement somewhere else in the darkness. The branch on which the owl perched swayed in a gust of wind, and its feathers ruffled as if tickled by invisible fingers. With a blink of its eyes, the night hunter lifted its wings and whispered away.

Far down below, Terry sat alone in the cold mist, looking out over the pale lights of town. He heard the echo of gunshots. His head turned curiously. He had heard the same thing many times in Southeast Asia, although on warmer nights, and usually followed by more gunfire. He dismissed it with an indifferent sniff. He sat a few more minutes, thoughts wandering. Then, shaking himself into the present moment, he rose to his feet and made his way in the direction of the camp site.

Twenty-Five

Inside the bus and ready to bed down for the second night, Jordan fiddled with a transistor radio, trying to tune in a station. After minutes of sporadic crackle and sizzle, the unmistakable voice of Johnny Cash leaped out of the box singing *Folsom Prison Blues*. The transmission faded intermittently. Jordan gnawed on a stick of Wrigley's Doublemint gum as he continued to rotate the dial. Eventually he came upon the lucid voice of Reggie Muldoon on KATT-FM out of Oklahoma City, reading the weather report. Muldoon predicted rain and sleet until after midnight throughout south and central Oklahoma, with temperatures plummeting to well below freezing. He reiterated that heavy ice was expected by morning, especially on bridges and overpasses.

Jordan and I reluctantly trudged back outside. Fortunately, I'd brought cold-weather blankets for Ginger and Barney. Christine found an old army blanket, and we punched holes in the corners and tied it securely on Scooter. While we were busy with the horses, Terry emerged from the darkness.

Of course, we had been worried about him, but we had accepted that his frequent and unexplained disappearances were to be expected. With no other words exchanged, we recounted to him the weather forecast. Terry nodded agreeably and immediately removed blocks from the bus tires, fired up the engine, and eased the bus back closer to the rock overhang. The intention was to create a tighter shelter for the horses. Jordan and I cautiously pulled smoldering logs out of the fire and moved the rock ring, piece by piece, deeper into the natural rock shelter.

It was a toss-up whether another fire would benefit the horses, or the smoke would asphyxiate them. We gave it a try, and soon we noticed that the arrangement of the bus next to the overhang created a chimney effect. The smoke followed the rock ceiling up and away. We agreed to take turns checking on the horses during the night, and Terry volunteered to take the first watch. The mist had become a light rain as Jordan and I returned to the bus. Terry remained stoking the fire, his back resting comfortably against the rock ledge.

Inside the bus, Jordan hauled out his guitar and belted out a few bars of *Hang Down Your Head Tom Dooley.* But he quickly sensed that neither I nor Christine was in the mood for camp songs. The dismal rainfall brought a return of the chilling experience the night before. Christine acknowledged a vague memory of a terrible nightmare. I was reluctant to inform her that we'd all experienced the same events, and it was no nightmare. Christine stood up and peeked out the window. Terry's ghastly tall shadow stretched up the rock wall, arms moving about as if working a voodoo spell.

"If there's anything out there," Christine said reservedly, "he'll be the first to see it."

I glanced at Jordan, who seemed to ignore Christine as he packed away his precious Epiphone. I lay back in my bunk and threw one arm across my forehead. Christine scooted deep into her sleeping bag. My eyes surveyed the patches of rust and discolored paint on the bus ceiling, and I found myself trying to identify familiar shapes. The first was Dumbo the elephant, with a trunk and billowing ears. Another resembled a witch on a broom. Then I found one that looked like a ghost. With that, I rolled over, face to the aisle.

Within moments, the urge overcame me to ask an awkward but essential question. "Do you guys think we've been hallucinating? Or have we camped in the middle of a Spook Reservation?" Neither Christine nor Jordan responded. The silence was palpable.

After a minute or so, Jordan leaned out of his bunk to peek across in my direction. "I've read about a number of Indian legends," he said, propping himself on an elbow. "Or ghost stories, if that's the right way to describe them. The Cherokees have a legend of a shape-shifting witch they called Spearfinger, with stone skin and a long obsidian spear in place of one of the fingers on her right hand. Spearfinger supposedly roamed the mountains between North Carolina and Tennessee. And even after they captured and killed her, for years people claimed to hear her shrieks and cackles drifting on the wind."

Jordan was quiet for a moment as he meandered through memory archives. "Then there was a Chickasaw legend of three ghosts called White Deer, Blue Jay, and Bright Moon. The story is all about the origin of the deerskin wedding tradition and how those three ghosts punish people who don't adhere to tribal customs. The chief wanted the hide of a white deer as a bride-price. He got it, and with it an angry ghost with two angry friends."

"You know a lot about dead Indians," Christine called out from the bunk below. "Do you know any living ones?"

Jordan sat up, dangling his feet off the edge of his bunk. Christine caught my attention before pointing at Jordan's grimy socks. She pulled a face and waved the air in front of her nose. I grinned, but said nothing.

"I dated an Indian girl for a while," Jordan said. His head tilted, as if reaching far back in time. "That was after I learned not to go steady with two girls. Anyway, I can't remember her Cherokee name, but it meant Daffodil. Everyone called her Daffy. Her parents didn't like me very much. That, I remember clearly."

"That's it?" she sputtered. "Your one and only live Indian story?"

"No, I have another one. I played basketball with a cross-eyed Choctaw named Clifford Cravatt. He could make passes that would surprise you, because you couldn't tell where he was looking. He was also a good shot from half-court. Said he had to close one eye to focus on the basket. Otherwise, he saw two, and only had a fifty-fifty chance at the shot. Besides that, he was pigeon-toed, but that didn't slow him down. He just swayed from side to side when he ran, and that really confused defenders. He was great on the court. A nice guy, too. I don't know what became of him."

Looking straight across to Christine's bunk, I could not ignore her sardonic grin. Our eyes met and we burst into laughter. Jordan couldn't see Christine directly beneath him, but he bent down and gave me a long, serious stare. "What is it with you two?" he said. "Are you laughing at Clifford, or me?"

Jordan was now a sophomore at Oklahoma Baptist University in Shawnee. In some respects, he was the pride of the family, since most of the Greenwoods were Baptists and had married Baptists. But he was the only one who had talked about going into the ministry. He had taken a couple of Bible courses his first year, but after a practicum with the pastor at First Baptist in Ponca City, he suddenly changed his mind. No one knew what had happened. He wouldn't talk about it— not even with me. And we were close, or so I thought. Then, maybe the issue was simply too personal.

His only comment at the time was that academic biblical studies presented more questions than answers. I suspected that many seminarians experienced the same thing. After school and ordination, they return to their congregations compelled to defend specific church doctrines against other beliefs, and sometimes against contrary evidence. I was certain Jordan no longer believed in a recent creation of the world and a literal Garden of Eden. He knew too much about anthropology and the origins of early Native Americans.

From that point forward in college, Jordan loaded up on courses in American history. Since then, if anyone broached the subject, he would prattle in endless detail about the Battle of Little Big Horn and Custer's so-called last stand. He was well informed on the massacre of innocents at Wounded Knee, and he could detail every major battle of the Civil War and the biographies of generals, both Northern and Southern. He knew his stuff. I figured he'd become a history professor.

All that aside, at the present moment, having regained his memory of the bizarre experience the previous night, Jordan couldn't stifle his urge to talk about ghosts and tribal superstition. To some degree, we were all spooked. But I clung fiercely to my hardened skepticism.

"I don't believe in ghosts," I said firmly. "I've never seen anything that would make me think the spirits of the dead even exist, much less roam around at night and scare people, or try to communicate. There must be a logical explanation for what we saw, or think we saw."

"There's a lot I don't understand," Jordan said. "And I haven't met anyone with all the answers. I don't understand homosexuality, but I accept that it happens." Jordan sat for a moment, pensive and hesitant, before unpacking some of his troublesome memories.

"Once, I spent the night with Wayne Dixon when I was about eleven. We were in a foldout couch bed, and the lights were out. He slipped down under the covers, and the next thing I knew he was trying to suck me. Said it was natural, and that I would enjoy it. But I didn't want any part of that. I scrambled out of the covers and started feeling around in the dark for my jeans. I found the light switch, and then I saw his father sitting in the corner, watching. I grabbed my stuff and ran out the front door. It was a terrible experience."

"Well, I must say," Christine responded, "there's a difference between consensual sex between adults and taking advantage of a kid. It sounds to me like the Dixon family was totally screwed up. Where was Mrs. Dixon while Pop was sitting there waiting for a show?"

"I don't recall," Jordan said. "She was a mousy little woman with greasy hair, pale skin, and not much personality. Mostly kept to herself. Wayne had a younger brother named Oliver. I think he slept with his mother, and I think Mister Dixon had his own room. They were a weird family."

We all lay quiet for a moment after that, until I had another thought that I just blurted out without really thinking. "My girlfriend tells me," I said, "that when girls have sleepovers, they sometimes mess around, you know, sexually. But they don't think of that as homosexuality. It's just experimentation, they call it, and no harm done. Is that true, Christine?"

"Now you've gone to meddling." Christine chuckled and sat up straight. "I *will* say this. I don't think anyone can explain the sexual urge at all. It's just there. We're all just wired with certain needs and urges that are hard to control. Trying to psychoanalyze it, especially if we're not psychologists, is just plain confusing. Prison inmates get raped in the showers, but that's an act of violence. It's not the same as a homosexual inclination."

"Like a horse," I added. "I've never known a stud or a mare that needed counseling or coaching. They just do what comes naturally."

"Yep," Jordan said. "We guys get squeezed out of the tube screaming and kicking. In a few years we're over the trauma, and then we can't resist the urge to get right back inside." Jordan chuckled, and leaned over to catch Christine's eye. "But you girls; you're an entirely different creature. None of us will ever understand you."

"You can't compare people to dogs, cats, and horses," Christine said, her tone firm. "We're sentient beings, at the top of the evolutionary chain. Our libido is complex; full of fantasies and constructs of every kind. We're constantly searching for meaning, fulfillment, and ego-gratification. We're all gifted with a vivid imagination. And you guys will never understand women, because we're more complicated than you. Smarter, too. Even dumb blondes. They're smarter than you think."

Jordan let out a long, rumbling fart. "That's what I think of that," he said.

We roared with laughter. I suppose Jordan thought our banter would wilt to silence after his final *coup de grace*, but it continued. All three of us wriggled deep into our sleeping bags and continued jocose grunts from muffled hideaways. The metal beds creaked and popped as each of us squirmed around, trying to settle in. When all was quiet, I could almost smell the smoke of mental wheels grinding. I counted the seconds of silence, waiting for more pearls of wisdom or juvenile snide remarks. I didn't expect another ghost story.

"Then there's Boggy Depot," Jordan said, his voice muffled. "It's got a cemetery and rows of graves from the early Oklahoma settlers, like the ones who died in the land rush. And the local people say you can sit down real quiet-like, and soon you'll see the spirits walking around among the markers."

Christine sat up abruptly. "Jordan, you moron," she barked, now clearly frustrated. "We're to hell and gone past creepy legends and ghost stories. We've seen enough shit here to make a priest piss in the communion chalice. Russ may be right, that there is no such thing as ghosts. But I can't think of any logical explanation for what we've seen. We're not talking about complicated human personalities, or behavior. We're talking about another dimension. A spirit world, and a real and genuine encounter with ghosts."

That was the first indication that Christine fully recalled the events of the previous night. I felt reassured that I was not crazy, but at the same time I was concerned that I had no plausible explanation for it all, and why the others experienced memory anesthesia, and I had not.

All three of us were startled when Terry thumped up the steps and yanked the door open. We sat straight up and froze in place. He clomped up the steps and bumped his way between the bunks. Eyeing each one of us, he leaned toward Christine, his hand gripping the bedrail. "You okay?"

"Fine," she said. "You?"

"Yea, fine." Terry turned away, shuddered out of a plastic poncho, tugged off his wet boots, and climbed up into his bed, directly above me. "I chowed down the rest of the backstrap. I guess you guys all had enough. The cook did a good job."

"Thank you," Christine said. "It's always good to get at least a couple of things right in a long day."

"You guys all sleep sitting up?" Terry said, nonchalantly. "Or did I startle you? If so, I do humbly apologize."

"No, no." Christine lay back and turned her face to the side.

"Thought I should mention," Terry added, "I heard a couple of gunshots up on the mountain. Sound travels in the rain. It was definitely from up top there, somewhere."

"Rifle?" I asked. "I can't imagine anyone hunting at night, in freezing rain."

"No, I think a pistol, but not a large caliber."

"Is it my turn to watch?" I asked, hesitantly.

"No, don't worry about it. The horses are warm and content. The rocks are radiating a little heat. It won't last long, but I think they'll be fine. The temperature's really dropping, though. We should get some sleep, then tomorrow we'll see what we can find. It depends on how bad we're iced over."

"We've been talking about Indians, ghosts, and sex," Christine said, voice swollen, stifling laughter. "Wanna join in the conversation?"

"I don't think so, thanks." Terry snorted stiffly. "I've been up since four this morning, I walked four miles with a loaded pack, and then I hauled a deer carcass back up this confounded hill, listening to some girl jabber on and on in my ear. I think she might be the reincarnation of Daniel Boone, or maybe Annie Oakley. I don't know. But I'm too tired to listen. Like I said, let's just sleep."

Christine smiled and rolled over, apparently content. Jordan and I lay back, wriggling simultaneously into our sleeping bags. Then Terry spoke in a drowsy tone. "You guys were talking about an Indian who had sex with a ghost. Is that right?" Our guffaws were muffled by thick bedding, and we drifted toward the silence of slumber.

Within a few moments, it seemed, we all lurched upright and wide-eyed to a loud thumping along the side of the bus. It was similar to the one that had jolted Christine out of bed the night before. This time, the bus began to rock back and forth, creaking and squawking, as if an elephant was pushing it from the side, trying to roll it over. Christine screamed and covered her head with her pillow. Jordan fell off the top bunk onto the floor. I held onto the bedrail, instinctively trying to ride it out, whatever *it* was. Then, as suddenly as it began, it stopped. All was quiet and still, except for a squeaking sound on the back window. Terry vaulted to the floor and padded toward the rear of the bus, eyes and ears alert. We all clamored out of our bunks and followed. As we approached, the wet rear window sparkled with orange glow of the campfire. Amidst the bright droplets, letters began to appeared one by one, as if written with an invisible finger from the outside. The letters faced inward and were clearly legible: *Two dead. One alive. Go help.* We stood huddled together like orphans in a storm, staring at the six mysterious words. My legs trembled. Not from the cold, but from fear.

The horses suddenly let out a chorus of neighing and the bus began to rock again. Outside, we heard the thunder of hooves. "Holy Smoke!" Jordan shouted. "The horses are loose. Terry, I thought you said everything was quiet out there?"

"It was, ten minutes ago. Things seem to change fast lately."

I bolted to a side window and drew back the curtain. Action erupted before me like a scene from a wild west movie. Terry, Jordan, and Christine all pressed noses against glass, to behold dark silhouettes of Indian warriors galloping around in the rain, riding our horses, Ginger, Barney, and Scooter. In a flash, they were joined by more and more, circling the bus, whooping, firing rifles into the air, and lifting war lances menacingly. An Indian emerged from the darkness, his painted face illuminated by a sheet of lightning as he fired an arrow toward the bus. It torpedoed through the window, the flint head burying deep in the opposite metal wall.

Round and round they rode. Dozens of warriors, it seemed, horses galloping nose to tail, hooves thundering on rocky earth. Heavy sleet pummeled the bus on all sides. The noise swelled as if a barrage of golf balls descended in a protracted volley. Lightening flashed again, igniting the limestone cliff. A deafening clap of thunder sent us all to the floor. We huddled together, trying to muffle our ears and hide our faces.

As suddenly as it had begun, the thunderous assault ceased. All that remained was the crisp but comparatively halcyon rhythm of sleet falling on metal. I lay with my face to the floorboard, eyes blinking rapidly. I glanced at Christine, whose arms shrouded her ears. Jordan lifted his head and craned to see outside, surveying every side of the bus. Terry was the first to his feet. Tentatively, I followed. Jordan found his flashlight and directed a beam through the bus window.

"I think the horses are still there," he said, voice raspy and unsteady. "But they're loose."

We all dressed as hurriedly as weak legs and hands could manage. Within moments, Terry led the way toward the bus door.

"Christine, you need to stay inside."

"The hell I will," she said, shrugging into her heavy coat. Jordan and I followed Terry out the folding door, but behind me I could hear Christine's long, determined footsteps thumping through the bus and down the steps.

Outside, the ground was a battlefield riddled with tracks. Our feet crunched on a brittle blanket of sleet. Behind the bus, the line where the horses were tied lay in pieces, strewn helter-skelter, and two of their winter blankets lay on the ground, covered in mud. The third was flung over a clump of prickly pear. Scooter and Barney huddled together near the back of the rock overhang. Ginger appeared from beyond the front of the bus, snorting and blowing vapor as she approached. I could see she was soaking wet. Of course, they all were. They had been running outside the shelter, where rain and sleet had fallen intermittently for the past couple of hours.

"They got loose somehow," Terry said, his voice taut. "Lightening must have scared them. Big clap of thunder." He laughed nervously, scanning our fearful faces.

I glanced at Jordan and Christine, who seemed to stare right past me at Ginger. I stepped closer and stroked her neck and patted her muscular chest. "Good girl," I said. "Did something scare you?"

"Jesus Christ," Terry said, "She's a horse, not a Pomeranian."

"Yeah, but she's my baby."

I felt silly, but I couldn't deny it. I felt about Ginger the way many people feel about their dogs or cats. Unlike rodeo and ranch horses, she didn't really work hard for a living. Her life was pretty easy, and I treated her like a pet. I liked to think that was pretty common among cowboys. In the old days, a cowboy's horse was his constant and loyal companion on long trail rides, in dust and rain, across swollen rivers, grassy prairies, and parched high plains. His closest and best friend. So, I wasn't embarrassed to show comparable affection.

As I stroked Ginger's neck, I felt my hand slip through something viscous. I directed my flashlight on my palm. It was coated in red. I gasped. My first thought was that Ginger had cut herself on something. A broken tree limb or a jagged rock. I trained the light on her shoulder. My heart leaped into my throat. I stared, breathless, trying to interpret what I saw. A bloody handprint. I sniffed my fingers, and sighed in relief. Yet, I was still confounded. It was paint. I motioned Jordan closer, to have a look. Terry and Christine followed.

I turned the light toward Barney and scanned his shoulder and along his neck. I froze as the beam fell on his eye. Someone had painted a yellow circle around it.

"Those are tribal markings," Jordan said. "Some Indians used to paint their horses for war. There's no single rule for the meanings, but I think the Cherokee believed a yellow ring around the horse's eye brought clear vision. The red hand print..." Jordan paused. "As I recall, they made ochre from iron oxide. But a red handprint meant vengeance against an enemy. And this arrow," he said, directing his light across Scooter's rump, "represents a successful mission."

"But... who did this?" I asked. My voice quivered as I was compelled to acknowledge that someone, whether living or dead, had painted our horses and ridden them in circles to scare the living daylights out of us. I was mystified, and at the same time angry. I strained to force out my words. My mouth was dry and I swallowed hard, trying to regain composure.

Christine tapped my shoulder. As I turned, she pointed. Jordan and Terry also saw it. In the faint orange glow of the dying camp fire, the colorless figure of an Indian woman stood staring at us. Hesitantly, Christine stepped forward. The woman lifted a hand to stop her, before slipping lightly out of the stone shelter and into falling sleet. She paused and pointed upward, toward the top of the mountains. Her chin lifted and her head nodded insistently. After casting a long and intense look in our direction, her eyes lowered and she dissolved into the cold and bleak night.

A gust of wind rustled Christine's hair. She shuddered and lifted her collar to cover her chilled neck. We turned away, back to the shelter of the bus. As we climbed the steps, sleet resumed, pummeling the windows and the roof.

Twenty-Six

L
ike a quartet of Carthusian monks, we returned to our bunks in silence. Our heads were swollen with questions that demanded answers, yet emotional shock left us speechless. While virtually any level of conversation can be cathartic, in this situation, such would only lead to senseless and futile debate. Instead, we attempted to dispel lingering anxiety with a sip of the last few ounces of tequila. Except Jordan. He waved it off, convinced his meager indulgence the night before had been the cause of his nightmares and a disruptor of mental rest.

For the next several hours, it seemed, I rolled back and forth in my sleeping bag, comfort eluding me. My entire body ached, more from tension than the result of excessive lifting, tugging, riding and hiking during the past two days. I fought to clear my head of bizarre images, especially Cherokee ghosts riding rings around our covered wagon in the middle of a desolate prairie. I suspected that for all of us, sleep that night was fretful and sporadic.

In the cold grey of morning, I sat up lethargically. My eyes, still heavy and swollen, roamed the interior of the bus. Terry was asleep, or so it appeared, which struck me as incredibly unusual. Christine cradled the empty Jose Cuervo bottle under her chin as if it were a teddy bear. No doubt it was her only source of comfort as adrenalin dissipated during the night, and fear, disorientation, and exhaustion eventually yielded to sleep.

I eased down to the floor, as quietly as my weary body could manage. Unfortunately, one heel landed with a thump. Terry jerked his head in my direction and stared through murky pupils, trying to determine my identity in a haze of lingering nightmares. His Colt .45 was aimed at my face. Recognizing me as his cousin, he lowered the weapon and withdrew deeper into his sleeping bag.

I padded lightly toward the front of the bus, unable to see through the opaque glaze that covered every window, especially the windshield. I tugged aside the tarp curtain that hung loosely over the exit, to find the folding door closed. Considering the commotion of the previous night, that seemed quite logical. I just couldn't remember which one of us closed it, or when. I gripped the metal handle, which felt blistering cold in my palm. It wouldn't budge. I ran my fingers along the lever arms. They too were cold, but they appeared workable. Then I had a close look at the doors. They were laden with ice and frozen shut.

Terry appeared behind me, knuckling his crusty eyes. "Let's have a look." Stepping down one step, he reached toward the door panels, and with a clinched fist he gave them a series of quick but heavy thumps. Sheets of ice fell, shattering like glass on frozen ground. A thin ribbon of light appeared between the two rubber seals where the panels joined in the middle. Grabbing the lever handle, Terry worked it back and forth until the door sections parted and folded open. We eased down the steps and onto frozen ground, the silence broken by the crunch beneath our feet. All anxiety instantly dissipated, as Terry and I stood speechless before the grand panorama. The mountainside was a wonderland of ice.

The sparse and bare trees had been transformed into thousands of transparent alien fingers reaching down from rigid bodies covered in opaque skin. Various bushes resembled glass spiders on bent spindly legs. The rim of the bus was festooned with dangling icicles. Out across the farmlands to the south, an ice field stretched to the horizon, dotted with an archipelago of white-topped barns and houses. In the deafening silence, the sound of my own breathing seemed as loud as a freight train, puffing vapor into the frigid air.

We climbed cautiously back up the bus steps and trudged down the aisle. Jordan was already on the floor, getting dressed.

"We're gonna need our heaviest winter gear," Terry said.

I shook Christine awake. After a round of growling and indiscernible protests, she swung her feet onto the icy bus floor. Brow furrowed, she peered through a mop of knotted hair and directed a glower specifically toward me. The instant she knew I noticed, her eyes lowered and a trace of a smile appeared. I was learning to accept that such was her way. She was like a honey badger, showing teeth as a gesture of interaction without intent of hostility.

All of us had slept in long johns and heavy socks, so we had a head start in dressing for arctic weather. I wriggled into insulated coveralls, and rummaged through my duffle bag for gloves and a knit cap. The one element of the morning for which I was particularly thankful was that there was no wind. I had hiked in the Rockies in icy winds that seemed to cut through insulation like a knife. In my own world, a cold nose, fingers, and toes were the makings of misery. Had I been born into an Inuit family near the Arctic Circle, I'm sure I would not have survived to my first birthday. Or, at my earliest opportunity, I would have hitched a ride on a seaplane southward to the warm coastal forests of British Columbia. I hated the cold.

Having wiggled into and zipped up our warmest layers, the four of us stepped gingerly out of the bus. My first concern was for the horses, since I was acutely aware they had been run into the ground by an Indian raiding party, who had then stolen away into the darkness. I feared they might have returned and lanced our horses, or shot them full of arrows, leaving them to be covered over by sleet. I led the way, crunching cautiously around the back of the bus toward the rock overhang. Ginger, Barney, and Scooter stood huddled together, as far back under the rock ledge as they could get while still tied to the high-line. Their blankets seemed meager in this bone-chilling air, but they were warm and healthy, eager for morning feed. My face lifted brightly at the sight of Ginger's large eyes, perked ears, and a shuddering whinny that, in horse language, probably meant *Glad to see you. We're cold and hungry, and I personally would like to climb back in the trailer and go home.*

With the events of the previous night looming over us like a funnel cloud in Kansas, we divvied up the essential chores with little discussion. I tended to the horses. Jordan couldn't find kindling that wasn't ice-laden or waterlogged. Instead, he used a wedge of hay. Once aflame, he stacked on a few twigs, followed by the last couple of oak logs. Terry hiked up to the quarry twice to carry water for cooking and washing. Christine assumed the role of cook. Over a breakfast of instant oatmeal and reheated deer meat, we discussed the feasibility of more exploration. We all realized we needed more firewood. That would be challenging in this weather. But we had hatchets and a brush saw. The sun was now up, and shining brightly. The sky was clear. A cold breeze had just come up, but other than that the day seemed accommodating.

Terry informed us that he wanted to explore in the direction of the gunshots he'd heard and see who was camped up there. On his own, he hoisted a backpack and rifle and struck out up the mountain. Jordan, Christine, and I saddled up and rode out toward the west, following a meandering cow trail in renewed hopes of locating Dead Man's Cave. Christine, as before, chose to ride Scooter. The horses seemed puzzled by the crunch of hooves on shards of ice along the trail.

Typically, very few clumps of sideoats or other types of wild grass survive into December. They die back, and like Bermuda and other common lawn grasses they come screaming back in spring. But prickly pear cactus was abundant, and all around us were ice-laden clumps with an eerie plastic appearance, bent to the ground under the weight. Large boulders had become doorless igloos. Depressions and hollows along the path were beds of ice. Leafless limbs of unrecognizable varieties of trees hung low. The only patches of green were the mountain cedars that appeared like tinseled bows of Christmas trees.

I considered for a moment that National Geographic would devour a collection of photos from this very day, this very moment, in these arctic Oklahoma hills. Yet, I realized that professional photographers all over America and around the world have given snowflakes and icicles more than adequate attention. Besides that, I had not brought a camera. So, I settled for the hope of a vivid memory of each fleeting moment and each unique vignette.

Further along, as we climbed steadily, all varieties of flora disappeared, leaving only jagged rocks and rotund hilltops. The higher we climbed, the stronger were gusts of cold wind sliding over the crest of the mountain. After an hour of meandering up and down slopes, we came to a small oval gully, with a single ice-laden tree. Jordan slid out of the saddle. "Okay," he said sprightly. "I think what we're looking for is right up there. Let's tie the horses here and climb up there on foot."

Christine and I followed his lead, moving out of the saddle gingerly, followed by one cautious step after the other, up the rugged slope. Our efforts were productive. The cave entrance resembled the description written by Uncle Luke. Flat rocks provided a series of steps down to the mouth, which was actually large enough for a man to walk into, although slightly bent over.

Jordan descended a few steps. "Okay." His voice echoed in the hollow chamber. "This place is full of snakes, singing like the Mormon Tabernacle Choir. I'm not going any farther, but I'm sure this is the Dead Man Cave. We can mark it on the map and consider our mission accomplished."

Back outside, he wrote notes, consulting a map he had folded into his coat pocket. A nearby boulder was too slippery to climb on, but he found a knoll within short walking distance, and from there he swung his compass left and right, picked visible landmarks, and marked their intersection at the cave mouth. "I have no means of getting exact coordinates," he said. "But I think this method will be closer to accurate than anything we've had before. In spring, I'll come back up here with

Uncle Luke and see if I can bring him straight to it. Then he and I'll check it out as far as we can safely explore."

We made our way back down to the gully where the horses were tied. As we approached the area, I felt a moment of panic. The horses had totally disappeared from view. It struck me that they might have gotten loose and wandered off, or made their way back to camp without us. However, within a few more steps it was obvious that the moisture from their breathing had created a layer of fog that totally filled the gully. We inched our way down the slippery rocks, our footprints still visible from our earlier ascension. Like islands in a fogbank, our three large pets came into view, big dogs with hooves and saddles. They seemed quite content, waiting patiently in the cover of a cloud.

With a sense of accomplishment, we mounted up and retraced our path. The fresh tracks of three horses in dirt and gravel were easy to follow. The sun was now high, traversing the southern sky, and patches of ice had begun to melt. Here and there I detected the musical sound of trickling water. The cow trail we followed skirted the top of a rock ledge that dropped off to a gully full of boulders about thirty feet below. I remembered my apprehension when we crossed it earlier. Jordan reined Barney to the left and upper side of the path, allowing a buffer like a shoulder of a narrow road. I followed, twisting in the saddle to see that Christine did the same.

As I turned, I noticed her leaning out over the drop-off, compelled by curiosity to see what was down there. Or maybe something had actually caught her eye. Either way, her posture appeared risky. "What do you see down there?" I said, trying not to sound concerned.

My words scarcely past my lips when I noticed Scooter inch closer to the edge, no doubt responding to Christine's weight shift. As I drew in a breath to call out a warning, Scooter's right front hoof slipped on an icy rock. In an instant, his foot twisted, buckling at the pastern. I saw it as clear as day. I watched helplessly as he stumbled and dropped to his knees among loose rocks, letting out a pitiful wail.

My brain recorded the next two seconds in terrifying slow motion. Scooter began to roll and Christine instinctively bailed out of the saddle on the upper side, landing hard at the brittle edge of the path. I heard Scooter's right leg snap as he tumbled down across jagged rocks. At the same time, the cinch strap broke and the saddle and blanket fell loose. After two complete rotations, he stopped on his back, wedged in a cleft among several large boulders.

Jordan leaped out of the saddle and ran to Christine, pulling her up and onto level ground. I worked my way cautiously down twenty feet or so to where Scooter lay writhing in pain. He squealed pitifully, rear legs kicking, but he was unable to free himself, much less get up. Jordan had followed me down, and his hand appeared next to mine stroking Scooter's neck. Together we looked into the horse's desperate eyes, that searched for help and relief in his dire predicament. His right foreleg was beyond a compound fracture. It was essentially in two parts, with raw bone protruding. Blood gushed. A mush of sleet and warm blood ran like a river into the crevasse below.

My eyes met Jordan's. We both realized that Grandpa's beloved Scooter was at trail's end. We would never be able to pull him out, much less get him back down to the farm. He stopped thrashing as Jordan stroked his forehead, but he continued to emit deep visceral groans and high-pitched squeals, lessening in volume as he weakened. This was the kind of hopeless situation cowboys of lore dreaded, but had to deal with decisively and courageously. I glanced up at Christine, who stood petrified, her face twisted in horror. Flowing tears left paths down her cheeks, smudged with mud.

A wave of nausea buckled me over. My eyes flooded. I felt overwhelmed with pity for Scooter and Christine, as well as reluctance to act. But I had to do it. With a trembling hand I drew my Ruger. Jordan looked away just before I pulled the trigger. The shot echoed off the side of the mountain and across the frigid plain below. What had seemed earlier like a winter wonderland in an instant had become a lonely hillside of cold, harsh, and painful death. My heart burst at the sight of Christine's face, horrified, and contorted in intense grief. She tilted her head back and emitted a long and bitter wail, like a wolf howling in the night.

We managed to retrieve Grandpa's saddle and bridle, although one stirrup was pinned between Scooter's body and a jagged rock. I drew my knife and cut the leather fender as far down as I could reach. Jordan rolled up the whole rig and tied it upside down behind his own saddle. It was awkward, but the best we could do. After I climbed back on Ginger and twisted my insulated boots deeper into the stirrups, I stretched an arm down toward Christine. She looked up pitifully, with swollen eyes. Locking her arm into the crook of my elbow, she swung up behind me. She slid her arms around my waist and laid her face against my back. Although my coat soaked up her tears, I could feel her spasms of grief. All three of us were abysmally sad, beyond expression. My throat swelled and a furious tear rushed down my cheek, cooling quickly in the wind.

It was perhaps two o'clock when we reached the camp. Terry was back from his reconnaissance. Christine jumped down and rushed to him with a pronounced limp. She flung her arms around his neck, bawling without restraint. I was stunned that she had bonded with Terry so strongly after their overt antagonism just two days before. But it was a moving sight, and I considered it good.

Jordan recounted the details about poor Scooter. I couldn't talk about it. Christine showed Terry her torn jeans and scraped knee and elbows, blubbering through her feelings of guilt and regret. Terry listened and watched with unmistakable empathy.

"I'm glad you didn't get hurt worse," he said softly. "I'd never be able to make peace with your mom if you got all busted up. I may not, as it is." He slipped his arms around her tenderly. "It's gonna be alright. We'll see you through it."

I studied Terry's face, trying to understand him. I noted how compassionately he held Christine, and I respected that. She smiled reservedly and lowered her head. Terry beckoned us all to sit down. We pulled chairs into a circle around the fire, noting the serious look on his face.

"I know you guys are all emotionally ragged. But I need to tell you something else."

I braced myself for more bad news, glancing at Jordan. Our senses were somewhat numb, and we probably wouldn't have been shocked if Terry told us that Oklahoma City and Dallas had been obliterated in a nuclear attack. I didn't know what to expect. My fatigued eyes fixed on Terry's lips.

"I found two dead guys up on the ridge," he said flatly. "They were frozen, lying in a pile of cactus. One had been shot and the other stabbed. That's where the gunshots came from that I heard last night. Looks like they killed each other. I pried a wallet from the big guy's hip pocket." Terry laid it open for us to examine. "Missouri driver's license with the name Cooper D. Hargrave. The younger one didn't have any ID, except a disc on a chain around his neck." He laid that across his open palm. "It's engraved *DJ plus Beth*, like he was still in high school. But I also saw a tattoo on his neck that read *Bethany Forever*. I guess she was his wife."

Terry added that there was a military-style Jeep parked a few yards below the camp, toward the northeast, but he said it wouldn't start. "The battery was flat," he added nonchalantly. "The wind whistled over the top right through that camp. I can't figure why anyone would pick that spot to camp out. We need to go get the bodies and try to figure out what they were doing up there."

"Why don't we just go down to the farm and call the sheriff?" I said. "You found them, but it's not really our business."

Terry stared at me for a moment, thinking. "Okay. That's a good point. But, at least go with me up there and have a look. I'd prefer more witnesses than just me."

Jordan and I agreed to that. We rested for an hour and grabbed a little grub. My first experience of military rations. Not bad. Jordan fed and watered the horses, a bit earlier than usual. I guess that was his expression of compassion for their harrowing morning. Maybe it was to celebrate their surefootedness and dutiful service. Or, maybe it was a manifestation of his sorrow. It was hard to say. In the meantime, Terry tucked Christine in bed with his best effort at words of encouragement. He could not know exactly how she felt, but he had lost a few buddies in Vietnam and he knew the feeling of intense grief.

It was obvious to me that Terry bore deep wounds and searing pain. He tried to hide it, but it was written all over him. Terry said he promised Christine we would all stand with her and explain to Grandpa that losing Scooter was not her fault. It could have happened to any one of us. We all hoped that Grandpa would understand that Scooter, like himself, was not as sure-footed as he used to be.

"Surely, Grandpa knew that when he volunteered Scooter for this mission," Terry said.

I heard his words, but I sensed that Terry's mind was back in Vietnam. He was not thinking like a country boy on an outing in the mountains.

"I'm heading back up top," he said. "You guys follow when you've rested a bit more. And think about whether you want to tie bodies over the saddles and walk the horses down, or make some kind of travois and drag them down Indian style. But don't be too long. We need to get this done before dark, and it's nearly three o'clock now."

Terry hadn't listened to our advice. The dead guys were not our business. But he was making it his business. Maybe he was operating under the principle of *leave no one behind,* and he imagined those two dead guys to be fallen comrades. I was perplexed, but I acquiesced to his decision, doubting that I could dissuade him.

The sun had shone brightly all day. The temperature was above freezing and ice was melting. All around us, water dripped from thawing tree branches and rock shelves. Jordan had a quick nap, slumped in a camp chair in the warm sun. I sat for a while, but I couldn't sleep. I crawled to my feet, feeling like an old man badly beaten in a bar fight. I made Christine a peanut butter sandwich with grape jelly. After rummaging through boxes and packets, I came across a packet of instant chocolate drink and stirred a generous measure into a cup of hot water with a spoonful of sugar. I left it on an upturned bucket next to Christine's bed. She was sound asleep.

Jordan and I climbed on the horses and picked a trail leading up the mountain, this time in a direction neither of us had explored before. Terry had said he had followed a trail above the quarry, and northwest across a more or less flat ridge before ascending to the crest. It wasn't far, but it seemed far.

Twenty-Seven

After an hour's ride, we realized we had not accurately followed Terry's directions. We went too far east and too far north. That became evident when we came upon a dilapidated building we recognized as the abandoned Boy Scout facility called Camp Chapman. Still visible on the outside wall next to the front entrance was a badly weathered emblem, the *fleur de lis* over an outline of the state of Oklahoma. Resisting the urge to explore the ruins, we turned west and followed tire tracks up the hillside. The tracks meander along a narrowing creek bed, and across a bald knoll. At the crest, we spotted a vehicle. It had to be the Jeep Terry had mentioned. The driver's door was ajar, key in the ignition. The hood was partially up. I dismounted and checked, just to be certain. As Terry had reported, the battery was dead.

Fifty yards above the Jeep, we discovered the campsite. We expected to find Terry busy wrapping two bodies in blankets, preparing them to be hauled down to the farm or straight to the County Coroner's office. Instead, they were lying side by side, face up. As we approached, we could see that both were covered in cactus needles. Their faces looked like discarded pincushions. Still wearing parkas, unzipped, their bellies and chests were a solid mat of dried blood around gaping holes. Terry had found them lying face to face, more or less in each other's grasp. He must have rolled them over and separated them. A small caliber handgun rested on one man's chest; a hunting knife on the other. That was not exactly what an investigator would expect to find at a crime scene.

"Terry!" I called out, cupping my hands around my mouth. "We're here. Where are you?" My voice fell flat. Like an anechoic chamber, a bald hill has no potential for an echo. No surrounding cliffs or high peaks from which sound might rebound. I rotated and shouted in all directions. Ginger's ears twitched. But there was no response from anything or anyone around us. I detected no movement anywhere. A few buzzards circled high above. I reined Ginger toward the bodies, so I could have a closer look. A couple of small feathers clung to a bloody coat. The buzzards had been there earlier, but we didn't see them. Apparently, something interrupted them before they could really dive into their repugnant work.

Jordan shrugged, surveying the perimeter. "Yep. That's odd."

We both swung down to the ground, leaving the horses to stand free. "You go that way," I said. "I'll check over here."

There really wasn't any place to check, in my direction. I could see westward up a gentle slope to the crest of the mountain. No trees or brush to hide behind. A couple of long rows of ragged rocks protruded from the surface, running east and west. Slightly lower, I could see the horizon above flatlands, aglow with the setting sun.

Jordan strolled past the campsite, giving a quick kick at a wet pile of ashes. He stepped cautiously along what appeared to be a path curving toward a shallow depression, and I could see the tops of a cluster of mountain cedars no more than four feet tall, but covering a modest room-sized circumference. Jordan disappeared from view, and then I heard his voice. I followed and found him standing over Terry.

Our lost cousin was sitting on the ground cross-legged, arms folded over his knees, his rifle resting in his lap. He was bare-chested, which was bizarre considering the icy breeze that swept over the mountaintop. His face was painted with black and green camouflage. I dismounted. Jordan and I stepped closer.

"Terry? Are you okay, Bro?" I asked. "What's goin' on here?"

Terry lifted a finger to his lips before pointing. Our eyes followed the direction of his finger. As if struck by a sudden impulse, Jordan stepped briskly past Terry and pushed aside the limbs of one cedar. He stood for a moment, gazing downward, before turning toward me, wide-eyed.

"It's a cave." Jordan laughed out loud and repeated, "It's a cave. No wonder nobody's found it. It's hidden from view by these…" He stopped mid-sentence. His head tilted to the side and he stared blankly, straining to hear. He stepped closer, peering into the nothingness of a black hole in the rocks. His face flattened as his attention narrowed.

"Hello," he called out. "Can you hear me?" He glanced quickly back in my direction, eyes wide and alert. He refocused on the grotto and pointed downward. His finger quivered. "There's someone down there. I heard a voice."

I bounded past Terry and over rocks, maneuvering my head in among the cedar branches.

"Yes, I hear you," came an unsteady voice, echoing in the depths. "Help me. Please."

Jordan had a great deal of experience rappelling, and he always carried ample lines and gear in his saddlebags. I stood over the cave mouth listening while Jordan retrieved his gear. He hurriedly strapped on his harness, while I dug out two carbide lanterns. Not the latest technology, such lights were reliable and common among coon hunters in this area. I loaded the bottom of the brass containers with calcium carbide granules and filled the top compartment with water. After adjusting the drip control, I flicked the igniter on one lantern. It brightened like magic. Jordan hooked the spare lantern onto his belt and slipped the other one on his forehead, tugging at the head strap until it was snug. I handed him a flashlight as a second backup and he tucked it in his jacket pocket. On his belt, he carried a hunting knife and his .32 caliber snub-nose revolver, securely snapped into a leather scabbard. I had teased him earlier about that little pistol, hardly powerful enough to kill a skunk and not accurate beyond ten feet. But, in close quarters, it had discernible value. I could see why he carried it. It was simple, light, easy to maneuver, and loud enough at close range to stun any potential opponent, especially in a cave.

When Jordan was ready, I grabbed the two lines and braced my feet against the trunk of one cedar. The red line bore Jordan's weight. The blue line was left slack, intended for anything or anyone I might have to haul up later. I glanced over my shoulder, hoping for Terry's assistance. He was gone.

During his initial descent, Jordan talked to me sporadically. He made me aware that he was placing his feet cautiously, feeling for possible indentions and footholds. For a few moments I could see the carbide lantern flashing back and forth, down and up, with the movements of his head. His voice was clear, and I could actually see the contours of the grotto walls in the lantern's pale aura. He shouted up that he found the initials RNL on a rock, and he remembered hearing of a man named Ray Neal London from Ringling who'd explored a cave back in the 30s. This might be the one he had named Torture Cave.

Soon the light was not visible, and Jordan's voice became indistinct. I think he knew it. He stopped talking and I felt only occasional tugs on the line as he needed slack. After about twenty minutes, I glanced over my shoulder at the ends of the red and blue lines, creeping close. About eighty feet of each had played out. I hoped I would not need to tie on an extension. Suddenly, I felt the lines go slack. No movement. No sound. I waited, my heart pounding, ears straining for any sort of signal from below. I gently tugged the pair of lines. Both were slack. Another five minutes. Still nothing.

As suddenly as the lines had gone quiet, I felt the familiar double tug on both lines. I began to haul them in, keeping both taut. My sense was that Jordan was walking, crawling, and maybe climbing. The red line had constant movement. And whatever or whoever was on the blue line was with, or right below, Jordan. A faint voice drifted up. I dropped to my knees and leaned down. "Hello?"

In the caves we had explored with Uncle Luke, we found numerous curved-bottom channels created by seasonal water flow over thousands of years. They were usually slippery, but manageable. I was confident that Jordan could walk or crawl portions of the cave, even at a steep angle. Both Jordan and his rescuee would require help on vertical sections, and on portions that were very ragged or slick. I had determined that after the first vertical descent, there were at least two more similar drops, followed by a fairly negotiable level or near-level floor that followed a serpentine channel. I was eager to learn whether the ceiling of this cave, at least in places, was high enough for a person to walk upright.

"Okay, we're climbing," Jordan called out. "Take up the slack. Keep the lines taut." I began hauling up the pair of lines together. I felt movement and weight on both. Then the blue line was heavy, but with movement. Perhaps the person slipped and was dangling. My muscles began to cramp. I hoped I could hang on. But I reminded myself that Jordan's job was tougher, and the person on the blue line might be virtually helpless. I shuffled my stance and re-braced, gripping both lines with one hand while I rested the other. I glanced at my watch. Jordan had been down there nearly forty minutes.

"Okay, blue line first, about twenty feet." Jordan called out, much nearer the surface. "But pull slowly." I pulled, lifting dead weight. Not as much as Jordan's 170 pounds. Maybe a hundred.

"Red line," he called out.

I pulled up loose line until I felt weight, then a sharp tug. His voice was closer, but still deep. After about ten feet, again the line was slack. Five, six, seven feet more, and again the line went slack. I waited, listening and feeling the lines. My ears detected whispered conversation and the clinking of metal on rock. Then came Jordan's voice.

"Slowly, haul up the blue line." He repeated, "Slowly." As I pulled, I could feel Jordan ascending and assumed he was assisting whoever was on the blue line. As his line went slack, I pulled and held, aware that he was climbing. At last, I saw vague flashes of light and a form came into view.

"Okay," Jordan called up. "I'm set. Pull her up."

The next sixty seconds were tense. I realized if I simply sat on the ground with my feet braced and pulled up line, hand over hand, the person in the harness would get dragged over rocks, possibly with sharp edges. I chose to place my feet as far apart as I could, straddling the narrow opening, and manage the weight with my arms and back.

Peering into the dark hole in the rocks, I could see the cargo was a girl. I knew I could manage her, even with tired arms and hands. Up she came. I stepped down as far as possible without tumbling in, reached down, and grabbed her harness. I lifted her and laid her gently on a ledge, inches below the surface. Cautiously, I shuffled to get solid footing and scooped her into my arms. Another couple of careful steps up and we were out onto flat ground. As I laid her down, she collapsed, sobbing. Dark matted hair. Face covered in mud. Her feet were bare. Possibly her captors intended that as a deterrent to attempted escape. She wore only a pink track suit, soaking wet and badly soiled. She reeked of urine and feces, and the legs of the track suit were soaked in blood.

Jordan's head and shoulders came into view. I double knotted his red line on the trunk of the cedar that had proved solid, and let him know the line was secure. Leaving the girl, I ran to retrieve a blanket from my saddlebags. When I returned, I found her sitting up. I wrapped her in the blanket and lifted her to her feet, then helped her away from the cave opening. I emptied my canteen into a bandana and cleaned her face as best I could. Glazed eyes fixed, her head tilted to follow my movements. Only then did I realize that she was blind.

"What's your name?"

"White Dove," she said. "It's a bit too long in Chickasaw, so White Dove is what I go by."

"Do you know how long you were in the cave?"

"No. Feels like a year. But I suspect a few days."

I tilted my canteen to her lips and she drank. Moments later, Jordan emerged from the grotto, out of breath and soaking wet. His lips were blue.

"Was it cold down there?" I asked.

"About the usual." We both knew that in this part of the country, caves maintain about 60 degrees in winter. Not a comfortable temperature, but survivable. "The room where I found her had a high cupola," Jordan said, teeth chattering, "and a few stalactites hanging maybe ten feet above my head. She was sitting on this little knoll, with water flowing around her on each side. While I tried to get the harness on her, I fell in a pool. Not deep, but I was on my side," he said. "That's the reason I'm cold. I was okay climbing. But when I stopped, I felt the breeze whistle down the pipe. Also, the carbide lantern went out," Jordan said, rubbing his arms. "The spare wouldn't light. I had to use my flashlight. The batteries lasted just long enough to get us back near the shelf down at the bottom of the chimney. Glad to see a little daylight."

The sun was gone, and the western horizon brimmed with shades of pink and orange. But that, too, was rapidly disappearing. Jordan put his arm around the girl's shoulders. "This young lady was all by her lonesome, rattlesnakes coiled against the rocks in every direction. They were quiet until I got close, and then tails started buzzing."

"Wow," I said, looking into the girl's unresponsive eyes. "We need to get you off this mountain to some place safe. I guess our grandparents' farm will do until we can get in touch with the sheriff. Then we can call whoever you want. But I have to ask, are you the one that has been in the news? Overton James' niece?"

Somewhat hesitant, she nodded. "Yes. I am. I was in the news?"

"Yes, ma'am. You were," Jordan said. "Saw your picture. Knew it was you as soon as put a light on you. I saw that long beautiful hair."

She lifted her hand and tugged fingers through mud and grime. "Not so beautiful at the moment."

"Do you know who these people are? Why they took you?" I asked.

"I think maybe I do, but it's too hard to explain."

"Was it for ransom?"

"Not exactly."

"How did you keep from getting snake bit down there?"

"The woman," she said, her face instantly aglow. "She stayed with me and kept me safe. She told the snakes to keep away, and they obeyed her."

"What woman?" I quizzed. "We found two dead guys up here. Was there a woman with them?"

Before White Dove could answer, Jordan cut her off. Having caught his breath, he had questions of his own. "We saw on the news something about a man and woman who took you from the school.

Did she have a part in this?"

"Not the same woman," White Dove said. Her chin quivered as a breeze tickled her shoulders. "I don't think that woman came up here with the men. The woman down in the cave is one of my people. She said she would bring help." Her face brightened. "And you came for me."

Jordan's troubled eyes met mine and lingered while we attempted to read each other's thoughts. The blind girl was telling us that she'd had company down in that dark cavern. Friendly company, like the old woman who pointed up into the mountains and wrote notes on the bus window. Nothing she told us resembled the visitors who rode our horses in circles around the bus and shot arrows through the windows— visitors who appeared and disappeared in a whirlwind of hyperphantasia. But whoever, or whatever those spectral appearances might have been, it seems they were interested in the girl's wellbeing, and they wanted to impress upon us the urgency of her situation.

I helped the girl to her feet while Jordan rolled up lines. He was particular as to how that was done, and also how the climbing gear was packed into his saddlebag. As I stumbled toward Ginger with the girl in my arms, I remembered that Terry had disappeared. In the intensity of the moment, I had forgotten he was even there. My eyes scanned the perimeter and the upper rim of the mountain. There was no sign of him. At the cave mouth, his behavior had become inordinately strange for a guy accustomed to armed combat. That bothered me, but I tried not to dwell on it. I eased the girl down near the horses, waiting for Jordan.

Jordan approached me from behind and motioned me away from the girl. He glanced back at her before speaking in a muffled tone. "Russ, there was something down there," he whispered. "Someone else."

"How do you know? Did you see something?"

"No, but I felt them."

"Them?"

Jordan hesitated, staring toward the cave mouth. "It was like being on a crowded dance floor, but pitch black and deathly silent. I could feel movement all around me, you know what I'm saying? And the smell. Nothing as pleasant a perfume or cologne. It was musky, like a cocktail of sweat, wet leather, mildewed clothes, and horse manure. I don't know what it was. But it was something. A whole bunch of somethings." He glanced around, shaking away the image. "We need to get out of here."

He stepped lively toward White Dove and scooped her off the ground. I hopped up into the saddle and Jordan eased her up behind me. She instinctively threw one leg over the horse's hips like she'd done that before. Barney had wandered off a few yards and he acted skittish. Jordan had to talk softly to him as he approached. He grabbed the reins just as Barney's wide eyes signaled his intent to gallop off down the mountain. Jordan led him back in our direction and retrieved another blanket from his saddle bags.

"Miss," he said, "stuff this under you as a cushion. Where you're sittin' can be mighty uncomfortable." She hoisted herself up with one hand on Ginger's rump and stuffed the blanket awkwardly between her blood-streaked legs. Giving in to the malaise of stress, helplessness, and embarrassment, but also relieved that her ordeal in the cave had ended, she leaned her head against my back and sobbed. The thought struck me that two girls crying on my shoulder in one day did not make me any sort of hero. It was just a bad day.

Jordan mounted up. We reined the horses back the way we came. We thought it would be easy to follow our own tracks. Just as we started our descent, beams of bouncing lights blazed across the rocky hill top. The silence of the cold mountain evening was shattered by a roar of engines and churning tires. Three vehicles topped the road that led up from the scout camp and thundered in our direction. For an instant we were catatonic, uncertain what was happening or what to do. There could be no doubt that these were the bad guys, partners of the two we had left on display up by the cave. And, for reasons we had not yet ascertained, these guys were after the girl.

Both the horses danced anxiously, eager to turn and run. A gunshot shook us from our stupor and I dug my heels into Ginger's flanks. We took off at full gallop. The girl's arms tightened around my waist. It was nearly dark, and we had to rely on the horses' keen vision. A hundred yards to the south, the trail meandered downward where vehicles could not easily follow. But we sensed that the men, how many I could not guess, would be hot on our heels even if they had to chase us on foot.

From behind us, another round of gunfire filled the chilly air. Bullets whizzed by. Some ricocheted off rocks, and others zipped through brush or struck soft gravel. Jordan galloped past, popping Barney's shoulders left and right with the ends of the reins. Another volley of gunshots. Ginger pulled up, tossing her head wildly and letting out a pitiful groan. I had no choice but to push her, and her hooves slung gravel as she bounded forward in compliance.

"She's been shot," the girl shouted. "I felt her flinch."

Reluctantly, I tugged the reins and we slowed to a walk, at the same time ducking behind a rocky ridge. White Dove reached behind her and leaned back. "Yes," she said, "I feel it, here on her rump." She lifted her hand toward me. Even in the twilight, I could see the thick, glistening blood. Ginger was in pain and was now dragging her right rear leg.

Jordan had stopped lower down, and he turned and galloped back up to our sheltered position. "What do you think we should do?" He said, face contorted and voice desperate.

"I think maybe they turned back." As those words fell from my lips, another round zipped past, proving me wrong. I ducked and tugged at the reins to pull Ginger behind cover. "You take the girl," I said to Jordan, "and head on down to the bus."

"Okay," Jordan said. "But if Terry's not there, I'm going straight to the farm. Then I'll call the sheriff. Buster McCrea, I think is his name. Grandpa knows him. This part of the mountains is his jurisdiction."

"I'll lead Ginger down to the river," I said. "If they keep chasing us, maybe they'll follow a blood trail. We'll try to misdirect them and buy you some time."

Jordan nodded, reining Barney near a big rock to make it easier to transfer the girl. She fell off Ginger into my arms, and then she instinctively reached for Jordan's shoulder as I tossed her over the back of his saddle. Jordan pulled hard on the right rein. Barney wheeled around and they galloped away. The extra blanket we'd given the girl as a cushion fell to the ground. I left it there.

The bus was maybe two miles below our present position, and the farm was on the flatland a couple of miles further to the west. I navigated in the opposite direction toward the Washita River, tugging Ginger with the reins. I wished Terry was with us to tell us what to do. But he wasn't. I had no time to think about him, or what might be going wrong in his head. I could see the pain and stress in Ginger's eyes. She dragged her right rear hoof and winced at each labored step. Gnawing at the bit, she tossed her head up intermittently in resistance. Nonetheless, dutifully she gave in to my persistent tugging and made an effort to keep up with me.

Twenty-Eight

I was aware of the emotional impact war has on soldiers, that having been observed for centuries. However, Vietnam-era military veterans were becoming the focus of critical study by American psychologists. And despite our lack of training in that field, Jordan and I had observed Terry's occasional aloofness, his penchant for solitude, and his periods of detachment from immediate surroundings; sometimes subtle, other times profound. It was obvious to us that something was radically wrong, but we did not know the exact cause or how to address it.

We would later learn that in February, merely ten months earlier, Terry had been promoted to sergeant. That was five months before his discharge. He had been ordered to lead a small team into the Mekong Delta in search of a stash of arms and explosives for a projected VC incursion. Accurate monitoring of VC traffic was nearly impossible, but leads from locals and US military intelligence pointed to a small village just off the Mekong River and near a main road to Saigon. Every village had a communal house or temple called a dihn, which served both a social and religious purpose. It was commonly used as a meeting place for village elders. Some dihns were also Buddhist shrines. If the VC found a cooperative village, the dihn became a storage facility for munitions.

The 5th Special Forces Group was somewhat unique for its use of watercraft, particularly airboats called Hurricane Aircats. That sort of craft was essential in maneuvering the swamps and inlets of the Mekong Delta. Terry's squad had done reconnaissance in a specific area for over a month, and they had observed several sampans operating at night, in and out of one village in particular. They were certain the dihn in that village was a prime target.

Something went terribly wrong in that particular mission. After Terry came home, only limited versions of the event came to light. But it is certain that VC opened fire on the team. One round struck Terry in the shoulder and a second one hit his thigh. The specialist who was with him was killed. Hearing the gunfire after the explosion, the second squad leader led a hurried extraction. Fortunately, the remaining

VC were few. They engaged and killed five. Three others fled.

Terry recovered from his injuries, but he was honorably discharged in June, four months after that event. It was considered a great success, but it left an indelible imprint on Terry's memory. Now, six months later, his nightmares were increasing. Bouts of depression became debilitating. He would often lie in his bed, staring at a plaque on the wall bearing the Special Forces insignia, with its red and yellow stripes and the Latin words *de oppresso liber*, meaning *liberate the oppressed*.

Now and then, as had just happened up in the Arbuckles, he suffered a bizarre blackout which doctors deemed a form of catatonia, during which he retained vision, but was unable to move or speak. Most of all, he was haunted by visions of mutilated children falling upon him from the sky.

Terry later informed us that while Jordan was down in the cave, he must have suffered some kind of episode and wandered off. He came to himself and observed us through binoculars from behind a rock, maybe a hundred yards above. We never saw him hunkered there. But he witnessed the vehicles arrive, and he saw me and Jordan gallop off with the girl amidst a hail of gunfire. He saw three men follow us along the crest of the ridge and down the eastern end of the mountain. He said he heard more gunshots, but when the men returned empty-handed, he assumed we'd gotten away clean. By then he was fully lucid, but he resisted the urge to engage the men in a gunfight.

After that, by Terry's account, the gunmen dragged the two stiff bodies to the mouth of the cave and dropped them in, head first. A tall and slender man with thick silver hair stood at a distance, arms folded across his chest. Assuming him to be the leader, Terry described him as sharply dressed, his shirt and slacks clean and crisp. He wore an expensive looking leather jacket, cowboy boots of exotic leather (perhaps ostrich), and an oval western belt buckle that shined even in the dim glow of dusk.

The group stood for a while and talked, but they were too far away for Terry to catch their words. He saw the leader motion, one arm swinging in a circle, before pointing in a southward direction. The men retreated to their vehicles. Terry said that two climbed into one pickup and three into a more expensive Jeep Wagoneer. It was green, he said. The silver-headed leader drove a new Dodge Charger like the one chased by Steve McQueen in the movie *Bullitt*, but this one was factory blue.

When taillights disappeared down the hill toward Daugherty, Terry climbed to his feet with the intention of heading back to the bus. He realized he did not have his rifle and he stopped, eyes retracing his path as he searched his foggy memory. He had no clue where he'd left it.

At that moment, Terry said, the ground began to shake. He stopped, feet planted firmly, hoping to ride out the apparent earthquake. His eyes locked on the mouth of the cave, maybe forty yards below. That appeared to be the epicenter of the bizarre tremor. But the rumble of shifting earth and the cracking noise of splitting rocks seemed to spread in all directions. Then he heard a terrifying roar that filled the mountain air like a dozen lions bellowing. Out of the cave flew the two bodies. They soared in opposite directions, twenty feet in the air, and fell upon rocky ground like soggy sacks of grain. Blood splattered outward from both. The shaking continued as the rocky perimeter collapsed inward, obscuring the cave mouth but leaving the two perky mountain cedars in place. The quake subsided, as did the rumble of cracking and tumbling rocks.

Thinking perhaps he had hallucinated the entire scenario, Terry shook himself and thumped his head with a closed fist. Once a sense of stability returned, he stood up and made his way cautiously down to the abandoned campsite, stopping to examine the two bodies that were once again fodder for buzzards and coyotes. He was forced to conclude that what he witnessed was real. Not a hallucination. But he had no explanation. An earthquake, so he postulated, might have swallowed the two bodies and buried them deep. But only a volcano spews, and that would be lava, ash, and heated gasses. And a geyser blows steam and hot water. This was something else, unnatural and inexplicable. It was as if the mountain had choked on two unsavory lumps of gristle, and spat them up with violent force. Terry couldn't get his head around it. Bewildered and trembling, he left the bodies as they lay and proceeded southward toward the blue bus. He found his rifle leaning upright against a rock only yards below the cave.

At about the same time, Ginger and I reached a bluff overlooking the Washita River. I hoped her hoof prints and drops of blood would provide an obvious trail for the bad guys to follow. I was committed to an attempt at misdirection, although it proved futile. As we descended, the hard rock and gravel of the mountain skirt disappeared into soft sand which, at the river's edge, became mud. I realized we were now wading through a blend of eroded topsoil and sediment from this mountain as well as farmlands miles upstream. Some of the mud might have originated in the Texas high plains. The longer I stood and stared at it, and felt its grip on my heavy boots, the more anxious I became.

Besides that, I knew that quicksand was common in the Red River, into which the Washita flowed less than a hundred miles to the south. I had heard that such spots were deeper than an average man's height. Once you begin sinking, self-extraction is impossible. How much more treacherous would it be for a horse? I might escape, holding on to the saddle. But Ginger would sink up to her neck, and she'd remain stuck there until she died. That thought compounded my anxiety. I tried to shake it off, as I labored to catch my breath.

A groan from Ginger reminded me that she was seriously wounded and in pain. I had another careful look. Blood was running down the inside of her leg. The hole there was ragged, and larger than the entry wound. It appeared that the bullet went in and out, tearing through muscle without hitting bone or penetrating the abdomen. Her leg trembled and she lifted the hoof repeatedly, trying to find relief.

A sudden rumble like thunder shook the sandy slope. I felt the earth move beneath my feet. Clumps of grass and dirt broke from the edge of the bluff just above and slid toward the river. Ginger's legs churned to resist the wave of earth and gravel that carried us downward. I jolted back at the thought that our pursuers had found us and the vehicles were just above us. But I saw no lights. The rumble was more like an earthquake. I was oblivious to the fact that at the same moment, Terry witnessed the seismic event up close, high above my current position. After a few seconds the tremors ceased, leaving me bewildered. An earthquake in the Arbuckles? That might have been common ten million years ago. But surely not today. What could possibly cause such a thing?

Once in the river, we found footing on a fairly solid bottom of gravel and made our way out to deeper water. Ginger's pain seemed to be eased by the cold water massaging her aching hip and tired muscles. Swimming was easier than walking on solid ground. We followed the flow. I turned frequently to see if there were lights trailing us. There were none. I clung to the saddle horn, allowing Ginger to find her own direction and pace. In the quiet of the deepening darkness and water, we slipped away. For at least a half hour we treaded as the earth-red current carried us along.

Now and then we were able to touch the riverbed, sometimes

mud and sometimes rock. A couple of times we waded only knee-deep through rapids, over rocks, gravel, or sand. Then the current led us back into deep water, where we floated freely in the quiet stream. Eventually we passed beneath a railway trestle. I knew this place. It was clear on area maps. Twisting left and right, I regained my bearings. Just beyond the trestle we labored up the bank on the west side, followed the railway south another half-mile or so, and then crossed over toward the lights of a farmhouse. Ginger was limping badly and weakening fast. I had no option but to take a chance on finding a farmer who was willing to help. The night was clear and the rising moon glowed through a distant tree line beyond the railroad tracks. A small pack of coyotes yipped and scampered away. Their dark silhouettes skipped up and over the tracks before disappearing toward the river.

Between us and the house lay a large pasture of damp earth and stubble leftover from the last corn harvest. There were scant patches of ice from the previous night's storm. We followed a fence line until we came to a crude gate laying open; merely barbed wire on loose posts. The tractor lane seemed to lead directly toward the house.

As we approached, I could see there were no exterior lights; just a faint glow through three or four windows. Leaving Ginger standing in the front yard, I felt my way up the darkened steps onto a covered porch and knocked on the door. Through the adjacent window I could see flashing images from a television. An indistinct silhouette floated in my direction. A young woman tugged the door open and stood behind it, suspicious and cautious. She switched on the porch light, providing her a better view of me than I had of her. I winced in the bright light.

"Ma'am," I said, "I need help." I lifted a hand to shield my eyes. "The story's too long to tell, and it would sound crazy. But the short version is some bad guys were chasing us, and they shot my horse." I pointed back toward Ginger. "I need to get her to a vet, but I don't know one around here."

The woman eased forward into the light. I could make out her plain features and stringy blonde hair, and I noticed her distended belly peeking out from a beneath an oversized sweater. She studied me, one hand clutching the door handle. I wasn't sure how to address her. She was strangely reserved and spoke in phrases, succinct and to the point.

"Who are you?" she said flatly. "How 'bout a name."

I felt my face flush and I nodded obligingly. "I'm Russ Barnett. My grandparents have a farm between here and Springer. The Greenwoods.

You know that name at all?"

As I spoke, she studied my lips, peering critically from beneath twisted eyebrows. When I paused, her eyes painted me up and down, from my lips down my chest, crotch, feet, and back up to my eyes. She may have been uncomfortable with a stranger on her front porch, but she managed to make me feel equally ill at ease.

"Nope. Don't know 'em."

"There's this guy, Orpheus Pratt," I said, stammering. "He's a farrier. Very good with horses. I was hoping I could call him from here. You have a phone, I assume."

"What's a farrier? You mean a shoer?"

"Yeah, he's a shoer. He fits horse shoes."

"I think you need a vet."

"Yes, that too. But Pratt knows some basic vet medicine."

She stared at me blankly. I counted the fleeting seconds. "Pratt, you said?"

"Pratt, yeah. Orpheus Pratt."

"Don't know him either." She lifted her chin, contemplating. "But I think I know his wife and kids. Seen 'em at church. Maylene, I think. A colored woman."

"Yes, she is. Husband, too."

The young woman turned, pushed open the door, and motioned me in. A wave of relief swept over me and my shoulders and neck relaxed. Once inside, I observed two small children in pajamas craning their necks from the couch, studying the stranger invading their space. Ginger let out another distressed whinny. I turned, and through the open door I saw her shuffle her weight. Her right hind leg seemed to give way and her body began to sink downward. The young woman stepped past me and cast a long gaze out the door toward Ginger.

"Looks like she's about to fall." The woman's tone and attention were elevated, and I could detect genuine concern. She stepped back inside. "Ya'll just watch TV," she said to the two wide-eyed children. "Mamma's fine. I need to help this man with his horse." She grabbed a long coat off a hook and tossed it over her shoulders, while pushing me out and drawing the door closed behind her. Once out on the porch, she stepped into a pair of high-topped rubber boots.

"Name's Julie," she said over her shoulder, descending the front steps. "Julie Cobb. Let's get her into the barn. Then you can use the phone."

"Surely you don't live here alone," I said.

"My husband's a truck driver. Long haul. He'll be home tomorrow, maybe. Gil's his name."

I followed, leading Ginger, as Julie made long strides around the side of the house toward a metal building, maybe thirty yards away in the dark. Tall dead grass and weeds indicated the area hadn't been mowed since summer, and there was little evidence of traffic to the barn. With both arms out straight, she pushed open the large metal door, bottom and top rollers grinding. I was acutely aware that a mere two hours earlier, Jordan and I had galloped off the mountain in different directions, literally running for our lives and trying to save an Indian girl at the same time. Now, a cold north wind blew over the mountaintop and winter darkness thickened. I stumbled along dragging a lame horse, following a young woman I didn't know. My mind roiled with anxious questions. I was thankful to have found a caring soul to offer what I needed most at the moment, which was shelter and a phone.

The barn showed signs of neglect. There was no livestock anywhere that I could see. Not even chickens. One lightbulb dangled from a beam, casting shadows as we entered. I could make out vaguely that the first and second stalls were full of farm implements, rolls of wire, and unrecognizable junk. The third stall was vacant, the floor mounded with dirt, manure, and patches of straw. A rat darted across a rail and disappeared at the base of corrugated metal siding. Inside the stall, Ginger immediately collapsed. My eyes welled, but I was afraid to speak. I didn't want a stranger to see me get emotional. I cleared my throat as I knelt beside Ginger and stroked her neck.

"Did you lose power with all the ice?"

"Yep," Julie answered crisply. "Phone, too. Only came back on a couple of hours ago."

"How'd you and the kids keep from freezing?"

"Stayed in bed, mostly. We don't have a fireplace, so I couldn't build a fire. Fortunately, no problems with the butane. The heater in the bathroom worked and I left the stove burners on in the kitchen most of the day. Kitchen was plenty warm."

Reluctantly, I left Ginger in the barn and followed Julie back to the house. I phoned the sheriff's office and reported the chaos on the mountain. I also phoned Grandma, who was watching television. She gave me the Pratt's phone number. Orpheus answered. He had been asleep, but he said he knew the place I described and would come right away. I considered that remarkably kind.

Julie made me a hot cup of instant coffee and I sat with little Brock and Belinda, watching Bonanza on a portable black and white television. My right leg bounced on lively and anxious toes. I sighed heavily, still aware of sore and exhausted muscles in every part of my body. I wondered where Terry was, and whether Jordan and the girl had made it safely to the bus. I fretted over how many thugs might be scouring the hills for her at this very moment. The only consolation was that her life was not in danger. They needed her alive for some twisted reason; for ransom, perhaps, or maybe she was a commodity for sale.

Then I remembered Christine. We had left her alone at the bus. She was probably worried sick. Or maybe Jordan and Terry were now with her. I didn't know. I sat fidgeting in the stranger's living room, waiting for Orpheus, my head churning with questions and concerns.

Twenty-Nine

Several miles to the west, Jordan had ridden hard down the slopes of the mountain, trusting Barney's instincts and vision in growing darkness. He breathed a sigh of relief at the sight of the blue bus. Barney's neck and chest were lathered from the unusually strenuous workout. But he knew where they were, and he turned his head toward the water. Jordan listened for a few seconds, eyes scanning the mountain above. He could not detect anyone following. He acquiesced and let Barney mosey down into the circular amphitheater for a drink in the spring-fed pool.

"Are you okay?" he said to White Dove. Her head rested against his back while both hands gripped the rim of the saddle seat. Whether asleep or in an exhausted stupor, she did not respond. Jordan let it go.

When Barney's thirst was quenched, Jordan reined him away from the water and back on the trail to the bus and campsite. Relieved to have arrived safely, Jordan wiped a sleeve across his perspirant face. In the darkness, he faintly made out the campsite sheltered against the familiar rocky outcrop. Approaching it cautiously, he strained for sounds of Christine's presence. Jordan expected to hear the radio blaring, or maybe clunking and thumping as Christine cleaned and rearranged, which was her uncontrollable penchant. Instead, the campsite and the bus were eerily quiet. A faint glow of light shone in the bus windows. Jordan tilted his head, scanning the area. He heard nothing except the slow clip-clopping of Barney's hooves. He tugged on the reins and Barney tossed his head back as he halted. Jordan swung a leg forward over the saddle horn and slid to the ground. After tying the reins to the high-line, he reached up to assist White Dove to dismount. She grimaced from the pain of saddle burns.

"Stay right here next to Barney," he said softly. "Let me find Christine so she can help you."

He wanted to call out, but he feared the possibility of attentive and hostile ears somewhere in the dark. He bit his tongue, stepping quietly and cautiously toward the bus door. Unnerved, he gripped the handrail and eased onto the first step, then the second, and craned his neck to peer down the aisle toward the back.

"Christine," he said just above a whisper. "Are you there?"

A strange rustling sound came from the back of the bus, followed by a muffled whimper. Jordan paused next to the driver's seat. He could see a pair of bare legs protruding from behind a lower bunk bed. Before he could speak again, a figure stood up and held up a lantern. The light illuminated a ruddy scowling face and a head of short-cropped red hair. A click behind him turned Jordan's head. A man leaned inside the bus door, aiming a gun at Jordan's face. A lanky blond wearing a knit cap with Arkansas Razorback insignia. A third man, large, in bulging coveralls and a hooded coat, appeared a few feet behind the Razorback, scarcely visible in the dark. He leaned close to the door for a moment before striding toward the rear of the bus where Jordan had left White Dove and Barney.

"Come on in and join the party," said the redhead.

The Razorback shoved the gun barrel into Jordan's ribs. Jordan turned and glared into dark eyes, noting dark skin and patchy facial hair, a poor excuse for a moustache and beard. His first thought was that the man was Mexican or Indian. The blond hair protruding below the knit cap was clearly bleached. Eyeing him nervously, Jordan stepped slowly down the aisle, past the seats and galley to the bunk beds. Christine's terrified face came into view, her tear rimmed eyes peering upward. A strip of duct tape stretched over her mouth and her hands were tied behind her back.

"How did you guys get down here so fast?" Jordan sputtered.

"Oh, we didn't come from on top," said the dark-eyed blond. "We've been down here watching you since yesterday. Now turn around."

Jordan studied the thugs with critical but puzzled eyes. The entire episode was complicated and bewildering. Why was a whole army, albeit civilian thugs, after one little Indian girl? This seemed a lot more than a kidnapping. He attempted to jerk his arm away from the redhead's grip. Instantly, the bleached-blond Razorback stepped forward and shoved the gun against Jordan's head. Jordan relaxed and turned slowly, staring point blank into the gun barrel. The redhead tugged Jordan's arms behind him and lashed his wrists together with repeated loops of tape. At the same time, he lifted Jordan's .32 pistol from the scabbard and handed it to the Razorback.

"Now, sit down there next to your girlfriend."

"She's my cousin," Jordan said tersely.

"Girlfriend, cousin, sister, I don't give a shit," the redhead snapped.

He leaned menacingly into Jordan's face. "Sit down." His words were punctuated by glaring eyes.

Jordan eased down to the floor next to Christine.

"Why were you watching us? We didn't even know about that girl until we found her today."

The redhead tore off a strip of duct tape and slapped it across Jordan's mouth, rubbing it roughly with an open palm.

"You can thank your grandfather for that little clue."

Jordan's questioning and offended eyes begged further explanation.

"That's right. Your own grandfather." The redhead smiled tauntingly. "He was bragging to the boss man about his grandsons and their little spelunking expedition. Told him about this big blue camper. We assumed you knew that cave up there, and we figured we'd better keep an eye on you." He knelt down on one knee, threw Jordan's foot across the other, and lashed his ankles together with tape. He repeated the procedure with Christine. "We don't want you two *dear cousins* trying to follow us," he said, leaning into Jordan's face with a contemptuous sneer. "Just stay put. And thanks for bringing the little Indian girl to us. It's good that she was in such tender lovin' care."

Within a few minutes after the thugs left with White Dove, Jordan worked himself free. Retrieving a knife from the cabinet, he cut the tape from Christine's wrists and feet. They stepped cautiously out of the bus. Barney stood dozing, unconcerned. Jordan's shotgun was gone from the saddle scabbard. Having spent the afternoon in miserable solitude, wallowing in guilt over Scooter's demise, Christine had no idea what had transpired higher up on the mountain. All she knew was that about an hour earlier there were several volleys of gunfire, which she took as an omen of trouble on its way. Jordan gave her a hurried summary.

"So, where's Terry?" she said, her voice tense.

"He was still up there when we left. He was okay, I suppose. But something's wrong with him. He was acting mighty strange."

"What do you mean?"

"Terry wasn't himself. I don't know how to describe it. Did you see him take any pills? Maybe smoke marijuana, or anything like that?"

"No, he hates that stuff. He had one short hit from a joint night before last, but he told me to put it away. He said that in Nam, sometimes his buddies got stoned and couldn't function. They would walk into a firefight like it was a birthday party. Stand marveling at the bright tracers and exploding rockets, then get shot to pieces and never knew what hit them."

"Okay. But he's not right in the head," Jordan said. "Here we are, and I don't know what to do next," he added, shuffling anxiously. "I don't have the keys to the bus and I can't go galloping after three armed men like I was Marshall Dillon." Eyes bulging, Jordan marched in circles, desperate for a plan. Christine followed close, blathering in his ear. Suddenly Barney let out a startled whinny and lifted his eyes up the hill. Jordan and Christine turned to look. Terry's silhouette appeared along the dark path from the rock quarry, jogging down the slope, camouflage paint on his face and rifle in hand. Jordan flipped the flashlight toward him as he halted and bent over, out of breath.

"You won't believe what I just saw up there," Terry sputtered.

"Two dead guys?" Christine said, thumbing toward Jordan. "He already told me."

Terry lifted a finger toward Jordan. "But you didn't see what happened while you and Russ went galloping off down the mountain with the girl. Where is Russ, anyhow?"

"I hoped you knew that," Jordan said, clearly agitated. "We went different directions."

"And the girl?" Terry said.

"That's the hard part. I brought her here. Thought it was safe. But they took her, just a few minutes ago."

Terry lifted his ball cap and scratched through sweaty hair. "They? Who's they?"

"The goons," Jordan answered sternly. "Part of the gang, I'm sure. How could I know."

Suddenly as they spoke, their heads turned in unison toward a sound. Somewhere down the hill below the camp, an engine started and revved, followed by the grind of tires on loose rocks.

"Those they!" Jordan said, instantly energized.

The three cousins rushed around the bus to the edge of the bluff, eyes scanning the dark landscape along the southern edge of the mountain. Jordan pointed as headlights became faintly visible through thick trees and brush along Cool Creek, descending along the serpentine road in the direction of Orpheus Pratt's place. It was the only road up to the quarry. The next few moments were full of frantic exchanges of information and ideas as to what to do next. Jordan decided to ride Barney back to the farm and call the sheriff for help. Christine chose to ride with Terry in the bus, and they would try to follow the vehicle that undoubtedly contained White Dove. One vehicle, one girl, and a three-thug escort.

Jordan bounded up into the saddle and galloped off westward along a trail that he knew well, leading to Grandpa's back pasture. It was a shorter route than the road we had followed up to the quarry, but too narrow and soft to negotiate with a heavy and cumbersome vehicle. Jordan also knew a horse's visual limitations in total darkness. He had to be cautious reining Barney down any steep or uneven slopes.

Leaving most of their gear at the campsite, Terry kicked the blocks from under the front tires of the bus, climbed in, and jumped into the driver's seat. Christine plopped into the seat behind him. His dad had warned him about the weak battery, but in all the chaos of gathering camping equipment, Terry had forgotten to charge it. When he pressed the starter button, the battery was dead. No weak turn of the starter, or even a clicking solenoid. Nothing. He pulled the headlight knob. Nothing.

Impulsively, Terry grabbed a flashlight and switched it on. The batteries were fully charged but the beam was faint compared to a vehicle's headlights.

"Christine, come hold this light straight ahead so I can see where I'm going. You'll have to press it against the glass, or it will reflect."

Christine dutifully complied. Terry released the brake, and the bus began to roll. He shoved the lever into first gear and waited as the lumbering vehicle gained momentum. "Here we go," he said, popping the clutch. The engine turned sluggishly and then started, billowing a cloud of dark smoke. He shifted to second gear and the bus rumbled down the hill, bumping and bouncing on loose rocks. He pulled the headlight knob again. The lane ahead ignited in a white orb. The generator was obviously working. Christine switched off the flashlight and fell back into the seat. After crossing the wooden bridge, Terry shifted to third gear and accelerated. Christine held on tight.

"I heard them mention something about a hanger," Christine said. Her voice was unsteady as the bus jostled left and right. "I'll bet they're headed to the airport at Gene Autry. Where, exactly, is that? I've never been there."

"Not that far," Terry said. "I could actually see it from up top there." Terry pointed over his shoulder. "It's right at the southeast edge of the mountains, sort of tucked away in a big curve of the river."

"I guess Gene Autry's hardly a town anymore."

"Just a few houses along the railroad track. A store and a post office and a few up on the hill, by the old school and cemetery. That's pretty much it. Eventually it'll be a ghost town, I guess."

Realizing what he just said, Terry's hair bristled on the back of his neck. Glancing up at the mirror, he read Christine's look and acknowledged, "Maybe more ghosts than people can handle, given what we've seen in the last couple of days."

Christine gazed pensively at the bright skeletal trees that darkened as they flew past. The spectral shape of a dilapidated barn drifted by on the right. "I heard one of those guys say that Grandpa told their boss where to find us. Why would he do that?"

Terry lifted his eyes to the mirror to meet Christine's flummoxed frown. "I don't know," he said, his mind racing. "That sounds crazy."

Within another five minutes, they reached Highway 53, a paved road running east and west between Springer and Gene Autry. Terry turned left and accelerated. In the distance, a halo of lights brightened the eastern skyline. In recent years the small airport had become a hub of business by air, rail, and truck. The buildings were illuminated by scattered streetlamps and security lights. Terry never caught sight of the taillights of the vehicle they were chasing until they crossed the railroad tracks and approached the intersection with Gene Autry Road. Beyond that was the entrance to the airport. Ahead, a white crew-cab pickup passed beneath a streetlamp on its way into the airport complex. Terry switched off the lights and eased to the side of the road. He selected a spot more or less obscured by a group of smaller buildings. The bus sputtered as he killed the engine. They sat for a moment in deafening silence.

"What do we do?" Christine said, just above a whisper.

Terry drummed his fingers on the steering wheel, staring straight ahead. Meandering taillights stopped for a moment at an intersection before turning left and disappearing among freestanding buildings. Terry wondered if they had spotted the bus and were trying to confuse him. Or maybe they weren't sure where they were going.

"Should we...?"

"Let me think," Terry said, cutting her off. Christine held her tongue.

"We've gotta' assume Jordan made it back to the farmhouse and called the sheriff. And we don't know where Russ is. Maybe those guys have him. Rather than just sit here doing nothing, I'm going in there. You wait here with the bus."

Christine propped a fist on one hip and leaned into Terry's face. "Do you really think that's gonna happen?"

Terry peered deep into Christine's determined eyes. "I 'spose not," he said, scooting out of the driver seat. Against his better judgment, he submitted to Christine's refractory nature. "You know, arguing with you is like trying to take a rabbit from a chicken hawk. I'll never be able to explain any of this to your mamma. She's probably pacing the floor right now trying to figure how to get me thrown in jail. Or lynched."

He brushed past Christine and retrieved his rifle, a handgun, and a backpack with ammo. "Here," he said stoically, handing Christine her own Smith & Wesson revolver, tucked securely in its holster. "That's still loaded, but you can stuff a few extra rounds in your pockets."

Christine pulled a mocking face and shook her head. "I know that." She slipped into the shoulder holster, adjusted it like it was a swim top, and then grabbed her coat.

Terry tugged the door lever and hopped to the ground, checking his watch. It was just after nine. Christine grabbed her coat and followed. She gripped the metal handrail and stepped gingerly off the bus, grimacing at the pain in her knee.

"I trust you to keep your eyes open," Terry said. "Stay behind me and try not to shoot me in the back. If we get into any kind of firefight, you'll get more combat experience than you ever imagined. But you'll need to listen to me. If I tell you to do something, do it without arguing."

Christine nodded, drew a deep breath, and blew it out confidently. "Okay, let's go."

Thirty

When Jordan reached the bottom of the mountain, he spurred Barney on at a gallop across the pasture toward the farmhouse. He was unaware of my situation, or the dangerous mission Terry and Christine had undertaken. At a distance, he could see a rotating red light, casting eerie and unnerving images through bare tree limbs. He knew in an instant that the sheriff's department was already there. He would not be the first to inform Grandma and Grandpa of the barrage of gunfire up on the mountain. Someone must have reported it, but as yet they couldn't possibly know all the details.

Jordan galloped around the barn and corral to the front of the house and brought Barney to a skidding halt at the front porch. He leaped out of the saddle, and in a flurry of motions tied the reins to the new handrail and bounded up the steps to the front porch. Barging through the door, he found Grandpa wide-eyed but nestled in his easy chair and Grandma staring quizzically from the kitchen. Two deputies, Chuck Holt and Samuel Jenkins, unruffled at the noise, were parked stiffly on the couch. The sheriff had instructed them to go from house to house along the southern skirt of the mountain to inform local residents of unusual activities on the ranchland above the old rock quarry. Furthermore, dispatch had received a call from Russ Barnett that his horse had been shot. The Greenwood place was the fourth stop for the deputies, so Grandma offered them coffee and a fresh oatmeal-raison cookie. The sheriff had also notified officials in Murray and Johnston Counties to be on the lookout for any suspicious and armed individuals in the vicinity.

Grandpa had already explained that four of his grandchildren were up on the mountain, and he hoped they were not in any danger. Besides that, he insisted on burdening the deputies with complaints about frozen water pipes and loss of electricity intermittently over the course of four hours that morning. But he was thankful there were no lines down, and full service returned when the temperature climbed during the day.

The deputies stood up, greeted Jordan in an official manner, and said they were eager to hear what he might know about the hullabaloo on the mountain. Jordan pulled up a chair and sat down and the deputies eased back down on the couch. Before Jordan could speak, Deputy Holt began to question him.

"I understand you've been camping up on the Lazy S Ranch or somewhere up there on the mountain. It's just about all ranchland, so wherever you were is somebody else's property."

"Yes sir, that's true."

"We're glad ya'll didn't freeze up there. But we need to know if you kids were the ones causin' all the racket and commotion." Holt squinted curiously. "We got complaints, you know." He leaned forward, elbows on thighs, assuming an interrogative posture. Jenkins sat back, arm draped over the back of the couch, quietly observing.

"No sir," Jordan answered firmly. "My cousin killed a deer yesterday afternoon. I think that's right. Seems like a week ago. She fired one shot, and that's it. But a lot has happened since then."

"Yep, like a stray round striking your cousin's horse? Sounds like you youngsters were a little careless with your guns up there."

"No sir. You're barking up the wrong tree. There was a whole drove of scoundrels up there chasing us in vehicles and shooting at us. Look, I've still got duct tape on my wrists from when they tied me up."

Grandpa regarded the deputy with scolding eyes before hoisting himself out of his easy chair. He eased closer to the conversation, folded his arms across his chest, and interjected his own question. "Deputy, have any of you boys ventured to drive up there to check it out? That would be good to do, before you start making accusations."

"Not just yet," Jenkins answered crisply. "We were instructed to notify residents first and then tomorrow, as soon as the sun is up, we'll drive up there and have a look around. But right now, we don't know really what we're lookin' for." His eyes returned to Jordan. "You say these people were in several vehicles, up top there?"

"Yes sir."

"Did you manage to get the license number of any of 'em?"

Jordan leaped to his feet and threw up his hands. "They were shootin' at us, for cryin' out loud. So, we took off in the opposite direction. What would you have done?"

Deputy Holt stood up, assuming a defensive posture.

"Now, now, Jordan," Grandma said. "The deputy's just tryin' to do his job."

Jordan eased back. "Okay, I'm sorry," he waved submissively. "But it's been a hell of a day. Excuse my language, Grandma." He paused to catch his breath. "On the news, there was an Indian girl." Jordan's chest heaved as he started to explain.

"Yeah, we know about that," Deputy Holt said, propping a hand on the handle of his pistol. "But that was up in Muskogee, a long way from here."

"Well, sir," Jordan said, with a perturbed frown, "I can see you guys don't know jack squat. We found that girl up there in a cave. Found two dead guys, too. I guess they had a fight or something. They were probably guarding the cave, and something happened. I don't know. Anyway, I hauled her up out of that deep hole in the mountain, and she told us she was the one in the news. While we were about to bring her down on horseback, a whole parcel of goons with guns came roarin' into the camp up there, guns blazin' and then..." Jordan stopped mid-sentence and turned. "Grandma, I need a drink of water, please."

Jordan sank onto the vacant chair, exhausted and out of breath. Deputy Holt stepped back to give him space. Grandma scampered to the kitchen and returned with a large glass of ice water. She dragged a chair from the dinner table and sat down at Jordan's side. Grandpa eased back in his recliner, without kicking his feet up, but alert and pensive. He lifted his arms above his head and laced his fingers contemplatively. His stern eyes painted the deputies.

"Where's the girl now?" Deputy Jenkins asked.

"Let me explain," Jordan answered. "My cousin Russ, well, his horse took a bullet. But he rode toward the river hoping to misdirect the goons. I took the girl on the back of my horse, and managed to get her down to the bus. And, holy moley, she was a mess. But there were more bad guys waiting for us there. I don't know how they knew where we were camped. But they tied us up, I mean me and my cousin Christine, and they took the girl."

"Where'd they take her?" Jenkins asked curtly.

Jordan's eyes shot fire. "How should I know? I just told you I was hog-tied in the bus floor. Then when I got loose, I rode hell bent for leather down here to call you guys while my other cousin, that's Terry, took the bus rumble-de-bumpin' down the hill, chasin' the guys who took the girl. And Christine, the girl cousin I mentioned, she went with him. All that commotion should have caught somebody's attention. Have you two done anything at all except ask stupid questions?"

"Jordan, honey," Grandma said, in a mollifying tone. She patted his arm lightly. "I know you're exhausted and upset, but these officers are here to help."

Jordan emptied the glass of water in long determined gulps, handed the glass to Grandma, and pushed himself up from the chair. Pacing in circles, he fired a barrage of frustrated words at the deputies. "This was like a whole platoon of armed gangsters, all after that one little Indian girl. The news said she was the Chickasaw Governor's niece. You guys are the law around here. You tell me what's goin' on." Jordan paused, rubbing his face with both hands. "And she's blind. Did I mention that?"

"Ma'am," Deputy Holt said softly, "my radio doesn't have enough range out here. Can I use your phone? I need to report all this to the sheriff."

"Surely. It's right here in the hall." Grandma pointed, but on second thought got up and led the way. The deputy followed her into the hallway, picked up the receiver, and started dialing.

"That dial sticks sometimes, so you may have to do it twice."

"Thank you, ma'am," Holt said. "It's ringing."

It was a few minutes before ten. Jordan plopped down on the couch, taking the spot Holt had vacated. He bent forward, head in hands. Grandma hovered over him, stroking his sweaty neck with a damp washcloth, as if he were still her baby grandson. Deputy Jenkins scribbled furiously in a notepad. Grandpa got up from his easy chair and shuffled nervously in a small circle between the dining table and the kitchen door.

By ten o'clock, portions of the story had made it to the newsroom in Oklahoma City. Holt sauntered over close to the TV. The report was short and simple. The commentator said that the niece of Overton James was found alive in a cave in the Arbuckle Mountains. She was rescued by a group of teenagers on a camping trip, but she was quickly recaptured by a gang of armed men and remains in their custody. Her present condition and location are unknown. He added that FBI agents are investigating.

"FBI, my ass," Deputy Holt said in a huff. "We ain't seen or heard from anybody about all this. We're runnin' around like the Three Stooges, slapping faces, gougin' eyes, and getting nothin' done."

"Yep," Jordan said. "That's what I was thinking."

Holt's eyes shot fire in Jordan's direction as he levered on his hat and stomped towards the door. Grandma's eyes widened, as she lifted a hand to cover her gaping mouth. With Jenkins trailing behind, nodding apologetically, Holt pushed open the screen door, bounded down the steps, and leaped into the squad car. Tires kicking dirt and gravel, and red light spinning, the pair of deputies sped away. Barney, still tied to the handrail, tossed his head and tugged at the reins, his wide eyes following as the strange vehicle disappeared down the road.

Assuming that all the clamor and chaos was done for the evening, Grandma let her hair down and started running a tub of hot water with a healthy squirt of bubble bath. Grandpa settled back in his easy chair to catch the weather at the tail end of the news broadcast. Jordan led Barney to the corral, and dutifully fed and watered him. Without a light, he fumbled his way into the barn and tossed the saddle and bridle over a rack. He returned through the kitchen door, then plopped down in front of the TV. Grandpa had dozed off already and recognized it was bed time. Grandma was in the tub for a while. But when done with her nightly routine, she poked her head into the living room just to say good-night. Jordan was alone, watching Hawaii Five-O.

Back at the Cobb place, Orpheus had dug out a bullet still lodged in Ginger's hip, stitched up three open wounds, and injected Ginger with a strong antibiotic. Despite all that, she was able to climb into the trailer and stand for a relatively short ride. Orpheus took it slow over rough spots. For being self-instructed, everyone agreed that Orpheus was a very capable veterinarian. His experience as a Marine Corps corpsman had given him a lot of basic medical knowledge, and he had adapted it to farm animals without further formal instruction. Of course, he read books. Furthermore, he'd obtained a few instruments and some outdated pharmaceuticals from a vet in town. All things considered, Orpheus knew his stuff, and his lack of proper credentials mattered to no one around these parts.

At around eleven Orpheus and I pulled into the Greenwood farm with a one-horse trailer in tow. Dutch, Lucy, and Ethel sounded their customary alarm in the front yard. That reminded Grandpa he had forgotten to put them in their kennel, but it also announced another arrival. He clamored out of bed as we pulled around the house and circled near the corral. As Ginger backed out of the trailer, we saw the front porch light come on. Grandpa and Jordan stepped out to investigate the clatter.

Still groggy from sedative, Ginger moved slowly. Barney greeted her with a curious nicker, wagged his head and snorted, before suddenly retreating. Orpheus said it was the scent of antiseptic that put him off. We led Ginger into the stall, gave her fresh grain and water, and left Barney to spend the night roaming the lot.

Grandpa and Jordan were both tired and sore, and they made no effort to assist. They just hung over the wooden porch rail and watched. Orpheus and I trekked back toward the house, thinking the long day was done. As we reached the orb of the front porch light, Uncle Luke pulled up in his blue Ford pickup. Hearing another round of racket, Grandma crawled out of bed, retied her hair in a loose bun, pulled a housecoat over winter pajamas, and put on a fresh pot of coffee. She mumbled to herself, "My word, this place is busy as a truck stop. I need to open up an all-night diner."

After exchanging heartfelt greetings, Grandpa, Orpheus, and Luke, along with the two of us youngsters, pulled up chairs around the dining table and sat down to review the events of a long and complex day. Jordan, now rested and composed, related everything he knew, of course, at a slower pace than before. His biggest concern was that Terry and Christine had set out in the bus to follow the vehicle that certainly contained the Indian girl. But, without contact, there was no way to know where they went.

"I'll tell you where they went," Grandpa said stoically.

The room fell into stunning quiet, as all eyes turned in Grandpa's direction. Furrowed brows signaled our concern for what he might know that others didn't, how he knew it, and why he had not spoken up earlier. He sat next to Luke, a decorated naval officer, award-winning teacher and coach, but more importantly at the moment, his dear son. Grandpa bore a painful look as he spoke.

"I'm thinkin' they took her to the airport at Gene Autry."

Jordan's critical eyes studied Grandpa's uncomfortable face. "Why there, and how would you know that?" His acerbic tone was uncharacteristic of Jordan.

"Dad," Uncle Luke said, curious but concerned, "do you know who has the girl? And what they're up to?"

Grandpa drew in a deep breath. His eyes roamed the ceiling. We sensed that he bore a heavy burden, but none of us dared to ask outright. "I don't know exactly what's going on," he said. "But I think I know who's in charge. A couple of nights ago, I got a call to go turn on the runway lights. It was about three in the mornin', which ain't unusual. Ya'll know I got this part-time job there. And some of them operations have shipments comin' and goin' at all hours. If a plane lands late at night, they need lights on the runway. And I can get there in fifteen minutes. That's what I do."

We all nodded, anticipating the meat of his explanation.

"I was there when Victor Thorpe showed up. I think that's the boss man of this gang that took the girl. Now, I don't know him personally, but I seen him there a couple of times, and I seen shipments come in on one plane and fly out on another. Or, sometimes it goes into a truck. I never could figure out what kind of business he ran. Nothin' was ever marked with a company name." Grandpa sat forward and laced his fingers together, nervously twitching and twiddling his thumbs.

"But the other night a guy came up to me, Dunson's his name, and said that Mister Thorpe was just passin' through on his way to a meetin' down in Dallas, and he was expectin' a lady friend. Mary Jane, somethin' or other. He needed it to be discreet. He gave me five hundred dollars as a tip for handlin' the lights, and also to never mention that I *ever* saw him there. More important, he said not to ever mention Thorpe, in any way."

"I don't see why that's related," Jordan said flatly. "That little airport is getting to be as busy as the Wewoka Railyard. People, aircraft, cars, trucks, and trains, all coming and going in just about every direction."

"Yep," I said, looking Jordan's direction. "Has anyone thought about what might be coming and going in unmarked packages? You know that *Mary Jane* is a common street name for marijuana. I'd bet these guys are dope dealers. That guy Dunson, he wasn't talking about a woman. He was talking about pot."

"Well, I don't know about that sort of stuff," Grandpa said. "But I'm mighty embarrassed I didn't see it before. As an innocent bystander, what I seen looked mighty suspicious."

"All due respects, Mister Greenwood, sir." Orpheus spoke softly but firmly. "If you took their money, you ain't really an innocent bystander." Eyes turned toward Orpheus as the searing words fell from his lips. "If the man jest wanted you not to mention him meetin' a lady friend, that's probably not a big deal. But if what you hushed about was some kind of crime, then takin' money fer keepin' quiet about a crime is a crime, too. My experience tells me that if I done that, some of the good ole' boys 'round here would'a done strung me up."

Orpheus had been quiet before this moment. He knew Grandpa,

and they were always on friendly terms. But Grandpa's confession must have struck him as seriously hypocritical, or maybe just seriously ignorant. Either way, it sounded like complicity with white man's greed and chicanery.

Of course, none of us thought Grandpa had a clue about what was really going on. But accepting money to forget he saw Victor Thorpe at the airport was beneath the standard of honesty and integrity that Grandpa had taught his children. It clearly did not measure up to Grandma's standard, a devout Christian whose ethics were grounded firmly in the teachings of the Lord Jesus Christ.

Grandma appeared from the hall. Her eyes welled up and she gazed at Grandpa with embarrassment. For the moment, the atmosphere couldn't have been heavier even if Grandpa had just confessed to bank robbery, or murder.

Uncle Luke eased his arm over Grandpa's shoulder. "Dad, it's okay. If that's the worst thing you ever did, you're still right up there with David, the Shepherd King. A man after God's own heart. You didn't know, not really, what those men were up to."

Grandpa's chin quivered. Grandma got up and threw her arms around him. They rocked slowly, in a moment of intense emotion. Grandpa sobbed.

"Grandpa, did you hear anything else that sounded suspicious?" I asked.

"Well, sir." He brushed away his tears. "I noticed a couple of pickups parked over by Thorpe's hanger, and Dunson said some of the employees were going huntin' out east of Daugherty. Had a deer lease there. And a couple of 'em planned to go up on the mountain. They had permission from the ranchers, he said. That's when I told 'em I had four grandkids campin' up there, and I hoped they'd be mindful of 'em. You know, I didn't want you kids getting in the line of fire. He asked me if ya'll were huntin.' I told him no, they were mostly *spee-lunkin.*"

Grandpa always accented the "spe" portion of the word, which was very much a part of his country brogue. Jordan and I shared a quick glance and tried to disguise our conflicting emotions as Grandpa went on.

"Splorin' caves, I told him, just in case he didn't know what I meant. Just looked at me funny. Never heard of *spee-lunkin',* I 'spect. But I'm the reason they knew you kids were up there. I coulda' got you killed. And I reckon he asked me about huntin' 'cause he wanted to know whether you had any guns. But I didn't think of that at the time."

"But you mentioned caves," Jordan said. "That must have raised a red flag, too. That's where they were holding the girl. Down inside a cave."

"Well, Grandpa, you couldn't have known," I added, hoping to ease his feelings. "But that's water under the bridge, now. In fact, it's water to hell and gone down to the Gulf of Mexico. We just need to figure out what we can do about it."

"I'd have to guess they have at least seven or eight armed men," Jordan said. "Plus the three who took the girl from the bus. One of them said they'd been watching us for a couple of days."

I looked around at all the troubled eyes. "They didn't look to me like any kind of military unit," I said flatly. "Just thugs with guns. But what do I know? I've never been in the military. Never been in a situation like that before, either. I don't mind admitting, it was a terrifying experience. I feared for my life."

"I may as well tell you guys," Uncle Luke said, "I actually know this girl we're talking about, and her uncle Overton James. I interviewed him for a paper I published in the *Chronicles of Oklahoma*, I think maybe Spring of '65. She may be blind, but she's incredibly smart. Scored off the charts on the SAT exam earlier this year, and she's been accepted as a sophomore at Western Michigan University in Kalamazoo. They have a special program for the blind there. Because of Helen Keller's death this year, much more attention is being paid to gifted individuals with auditory or visual impairments. I'm telling you," Uncle Luke nodded assuredly, "this young woman you guys saved is a treasure."

I glanced at the grandfather clock in the corner, and it was close to midnight. I didn't remember hearing it chime earlier. No doubt, the intense dialogue had filtered it out. A sense of urgency grew within our circle. The tension was sliced by a sudden ringing of the phone. Grandma answered, then motioned to Uncle Luke. It was Sheriff Mc-Crea. We all sat quiet, straining to follow the conversation from only one side.

"Sheriff, I think we ought to contact the National Guard there in Ardmore," Uncle Luke said firmly. He paused, obviously listening. "I understand that, but...." He shook his head and grimaced, as if the news wasn't good. "Yes sir, I understand." He leaned our way, stern-faced, scanning the room. "I think we're up for that. There are four of us here, and one more already at the airport." His eyes widened. "Can you actually do that over the phone? Okay. Got it."

Orpheus had strolled casually into the kitchen. He turned the cold-water knob on the faucet and bent over the sink to sip out of his palm. He returned and leaned nonchalantly against a door-jam, arms folded. Uncle Luke hung up and stepped lively back to the dining room. He bent over the table, propping himself on well-conditioned arms, palms flat on the tabletop.

"Here's the scoop. Sheriff says he can't muster a force tonight, and the FBI out of Oklahoma City will take a few more hours. No surprise there. But he deputized me over the phone." Luke rolled his eyes, apparently skeptical. "And he said he'll meet us there with whoever he can round up. So, Orpheus, will you help us?"

"I'm here, ain't I?" The muscular black veteran grinned confidently.

"That's a solid yes," Luke said. "You bring a weapon?"

"Yessir. In my truck. I got my military issue Colt .45 and my .30/30."

"Jordan? Russ?" We both nodded.

"Grandpa, you stay put and be ready to help Grandma with breakfast. Maybe go gather some fresh eggs. We'll be back in a while, and I guarantee we'll be hungry."

Uncle Luke easily and decisively took charge, and we followed his lead. Terry was, no doubt, already on site. Being fresh out of Vietnam, Luke considered him razor sharp and combat ready. I glanced at Jordan, who shook his head dubiously. We both knew this was no time to mention Terry's apparent problem. We had to assume Christine was with him. And while the situation was dangerous, Terry would do his best to keep her from getting hurt.

Thirty-One

The soreness in Christine's leg had not diminished, but she refused to let it show. She pushed herself to keep pace with Terry as he jogged in and out of parking lots and behind buildings, trying to locate the white pickup they had followed into the airport complex. Some of the streets bore names of companies like Lockheed and Grumman, well-known in the defense industry.

Eventually, they spotted the truck in question, parked among several other vehicles in front of a large metal building at the south end of the runway. It appeared to be a vintage hanger, remodeled to accommodate offices and storage. The north end of the structure was a solid wall, except for a single industrial roller door. Remnants of ice left from the storm were rutted with recent tire tracks. On the street side there was a double glass entrance covered by a red and white striped awning. That appeared to be the front entrance. Four light fixtures, spaced evenly from corner to corner, illuminated the parking area. There were no signs of activity outside, and no sounds from within.

Terry and Christine hunkered down next to a utility shed on the opposite side of the street. A row of hollies, still verdant even after a hard freeze, gave them a camouflaged view of the building's entrance. Terry grimaced and knuckled his eyes, irritated by perspiration and grit. The night air was cold and crisp, but they had worked up a sweat searching on foot. A slight wind whipped across the flat terrain that accommodated the industrial complex and airport. Terry tugged off his coat and lay down on it, scanning the building through a compact spotting scope.

"So, here we are," he whispered. "I just can't wait to hear you explain all this to your mom."

"Stop it." Christine slapped him lightly across the shoulder. "I can't wait to get out of that house and as far from her as possible."

"What's the plan?"

"College, of course. At least, for a start. My mom drives me crazy. I don't understand her. I am nothing like her. And my two sisters are *exactly* like her. Always poking fun at other people and conspiring against me.

"So, you're Cinderella with a handgun."

Christine giggled. "And my mom, when she tells a story, it takes twenty minutes for her to get to the point. She'll say stuff like *I was on my way to get my hair done. I'm trying a new stylist, she's over the other side of town in a little strip mall where the Quick Mart used to be. That's a Seven Eleven, now. I used to stop there for a slurpy. Blah, blah, blah.* I just want to pull my hair out, roots and all. You know what I mean?"

Terry smiled and nodded sympathetically. "I've noticed that. I know it's hard to put up with. Don't take offence, but sometimes you go on and on, too." Christine's mouth dropped open. "But," Terry quickly added, "what you say makes sense. At least most of the time."

Christine relaxed, sniffed, and smiled confidently. "Good recovery. Well, at least there's hope for me, right?"

Terry, pushed himself up to scan the perimeter. Still quiet. No traffic. No sounds from the building. He settled back down on one elbow, his eyes roaming.

Christine sat cross-legged, leaning her back against the shed's cold metal siding. "I need you to talk to me," she said.

"What do you mean? Ain't we been talkin?"

"Yea, but I can tell there's something gnawing at your gut. You said you blacked out up there on the mountain. Why would that happen? What's troubling you, really."

Terry laid the rifle on his coat, and plopped down shoulder to shoulder with Christine. She inched forward and turned to face him. Vaguely illuminated by a nearby streetlight, her green eyes searched him for answers to her concerns. Terry's face softened as he perused her freckles, slightly chapped lips, and frizzy hair twisted into a pair of tight braids, secured at the tips with rubber bands.

"I'm really not sure what's wrong with me," he said hesitantly. "It started about a month after I got home. Nightmares, headaches, occasional dizziness. An older buddy of mine from Wichita Falls was in the early deployment to Nam. He told me he had some problems, too. But they began after Korea. Got better for a while. Then worse, after Nam."

"So, it's some kind of depression?"

Terry nodded. Suddenly distracted by a noise, he craned to look through the shrubs toward the building and the parked cars. Seeing nothing, he resettled. "I suppose. I don't know yet."

"What are you doing about it?"

"I'm seeing a psychologist at the VA Hospital. He thinks it's a stress disorder. Happens to a lot of combat veterans. I think they used to call it *shell-shock*. Lots of new studies and theories." He shrugged half-heartedly. "You know, just more shit to deal with."

"Does it happen often?"

"Loud noises and chaos seem to bring it on. Sometimes I get sudden flashes while I'm driving."

"What do you see?"

Terry rotated his head, stretching taut neck and shoulder muscles. On an impulse, he stretched a hand toward her ear. A flicker of light from the streetlamp had reflected a sparkle scarcely larger than a grain of sand. His thumb brushed over it. She lifted and turned her head, revealing a minuscule emerald stud in each earlobe.

"Never noticed those before," Terry said. "Your ears are just about always covered by your hair, a cap, or something. In better light, I'd bet they match your eyes. Green and sparkly."

Christine smiled and sank down, one palm on the ground.

Terry let out a long heavy sigh. With that, he began unpacking his troubled memory. "We were in what's called the Mekong Delta. That's where I got wounded before I was sent home. And there was this little Vietnamese kid," Terry paused, blinking rapidly. "He kept coming to me, mostly for chocolate. But he seemed to want to touch me and follow me around. You know, the way needy dogs do with their master. He was from a fishing village a couple of clicks up the river. But I had this little pendant, or amulet, whatever you call it, from the Mickey Mouse Club back in '55. A little happy face with black round ears. You've seen them, I'm sure."

Terry adjusted his position against the shed, rotated his head, and stretched his neck, left and right. "I don't know why I took it with me to Nam. I just did, and I carried it here in my jacket pocket." Terry patted his chest. "I called the kid Mickey, not because of Mickey Mouse, but Mickey Rooney, one of the original Mouseketeers. The kid reminded me of him. Pug nose, big smile. I gave him the amulet and he tied it on his wrist with a piece of fishing line. He called it his *lucky charm*. Anyway, I hadn't seen him in a couple of days. I told him it was dangerous there, and he needed to go home. I thought maybe he listened. But he didn't. He was stubborn, like you."

Terry smiled, intending no offence, and Christine acknowledged with a smile. Her eyes lowered. Terry continued.

"I think maybe some of those kids just roamed all over the place.

Every village was home, you know. But anyway, during the night we set explosives in this little community temple. They call it a dihn. But the VC were using it to store ammunition. And we were just about ready to blow it to hell, when these gooks showed up, marching a line of kids right inside. Planned to use them as a shield. Figured American soldiers wouldn't risk hurting children.

"When I saw Mickey there, I tried to signal the two trigger men to hold off, but it was too late. The gooks saw me and opened fire. I took a couple of rounds and was lying face up next to a pigsty when the whole place blew. In the rolling smoke and flames, I looked up to see body parts of VC soldiers and children raining down. A child's arm and part of the body landed across my chest. It was shredded and bloody, but there was the little string with that Mickey Mouse pendant."

"Oh, dear God." Christine's lip quivered and she teared up. "That's a horrible memory."

"That's what I see in my dreams all the time. I see his little face, all lit up when I hand him that pendant. Then I see that. It's like, I gave him chocolate, a nickname, a lucky charm, and a hug. Then I blew him up."

Terry shuffled around and stretched his legs. Christine was quiet and pensive. Visibly disturbed. Minutes passed. She sniffed, wiping her eyes with the back of her hand. She found a tissue in her coat pocket, unfolded it, and blew her nose, softly, quietly.

"I know it may seem like nothing, compared to that," she said in a muted tone. Her throat was tight and swollen. "But I really miss my dad." She paused, and her eyes welled up again. "He would always be there for me when my mom was unreasonable or just plain mean. Like you said earlier, sometimes I felt like Cinderella when the two ugly sisters teased and picked on me. But my daddy was my prince."

"I guess I was in Vietnam when your dad died," Terry said. "What actually happened to him?"

"He was kicked in the chest by a horse." Christine's words came out painfully. "Not Scooter. It was a bay mare. Grandpa had traded something for her, I think. But we were at the farm for Thanksgiving, and my dad went out with Grandpa to look the horse over. She was beautiful, but hard to handle. For some reason, Grandpa just *had* to have her, you know. But, anyway, Scooter got too close and she turned and kicked at him.

"My dad was standing right there, and one hoof connected in the

middle of his chest," she pointed to herself, "here on the sternum."
Christine looked away, choking up. "Then… he just collapsed. Grandpa and my mom loaded him in the car. We had a Dodge, I think it was.
A four-door. I remember they laid him on the back seat, and closed the
door while I was still reaching out to him. I stayed at the farm with
Grandma and my sisters while they drove him to the hospital. They
said he died on the way. Doctors called it *commotio cordis*, a severe
cardiac arrhythmia caused by a heavy blow to the chest. It apparently
happens now and then to football players."

"I'm so sorry." Terry leaned close and slipped an arm around Christine. "Maybe that's part of the reason your mom seems so disconnect-
ed, sometimes. She may still feel lost and helpless without him."

"I know I do," Christine said. "That was five years ago. But I think
that's why I want to be independent and self-sufficient. Mom couldn't
balance a checkbook or put gas in the car. She had relied on my dad
to do all those things. A woman shouldn't be so helpless. I miss him
terribly, but not for those reasons. He was just a good man, and he
was good to me. He was sweet and kind and understanding. He never
raised his voice, even when I knew I had done wrong."

While Terry and Christine were engaging in a spontaneous therapy session, the rest of us had become a small posse and were headed
their way. By most standards, we were insufficient for the task, but we
were all willing. The sheriff had managed to find one additional deputy,
Everett Stokes, who was with him in the lead car. Orpheus and I were
in his silver Dodge. Jordan rode with Uncle Luke in his new pickup,
his pride and joy. Still in Vietnam when Luke bought that Ford truck,
Terry had not yet had the privilege of riding in it. Behind us were
Deputies Holt and Jenkins in their black department vehicle.

We drove into the Ardmore Municipal Airport in a slow procession, the sheriff in the lead. He stopped a couple of times, looking for
signs of activity. Most of the airport business complex was locked up
and quiet but with information provided by Grandpa, he had a fair
idea which building was the target. Ahead was the control tower, only
slightly taller than surrounding structures.

We turned a corner onto Grumman Street and cruised toward the
southern end of the airport. The streets were all dry, but we could see
icy patches on the pond, illuminated by one streetlight. The line shack
lay immediately to our left, on the southwest apron. Beyond that, the
taxiway and runway were in darkness. In the distance stood a large

building with exterior lights above several vehicles, angle parked, noses to the building. The sheriff switched off his lights and pulled into a dark vacant lot a block away. Luke followed suit, as did the deputies behind us.

The sheriff's department's vehicles were new 1968 Plymouth Belvederes— black, but with white doors and roof, and a gold star on each side. A large red light and a chrome siren perched on top. They were hardly stealthy in appearance. Even Grandpa, with cataracts and stigmatism, could easily spot one on the side of the highway a mile ahead. But in this situation, sixty yards from a building with no windows, it was doubtful that anyone would notice us unless they came outside.

From their hideaway, Terry and Christine observed a string of vehicles turn the corner and switch off their lights. They scrambled out from among prickly hollies, jogged along the side of a long storage building, and emerged out of the shadows just as our convoy pulled to a stop.

Thirty-Two

Staging for a police raid was likely not routine for Sheriff Mc-Crea and his full-time deputies. In Carter and Murray Counties in south-central Oklahoma, armed gangsters were few and were typically confronted in small numbers or as individuals. There were no more outlaws like the James and Dalton gangs, famous as train and bank robbers back in the late 1800s. Gone was a gang called the Wild Bunch, and the legendary Robert LeRoy Parker and Harry Alonzo Longabaugh remembered as Butch Cassidy and the Sundance Kid. When Grandpa and Grandma talked about gangsters, the name George "Machine Gun" Kelly would come up. That was during the 1920s and 30s, when organized crime thrived in major cities like Chicago and New York, and was dominated by the Sicilian Mafia. But around these parts, Bonnie Parker and Clyde Barrow were no doubt the most notorious outlaws. According to local legend, they had a hideout in the vicinity of Gene Autry and passed through there often.

By the 1960s, that kind of outlaw had virtually disappeared. They remained fascinating, almost heroic, but they represented a bygone era recreated only on the silver screen. Both crime and law enforcement had changed, along with social, legal, and technological development. In the world of crime, bank robbery had become more sophisticated—often clandestine. Drugs and sex had emerged as primary merchandise for illegal operations, and it seemed that more money was laundered and recycled than stolen outright.

For me, and no doubt the rest of our group, active participation in the support of law enforcement brought a mix of exhilaration and sheer terror. We exited our vehicles and eased doors closed as quietly as possible. One deputy, however, stood behind his open car door. He detected movement ahead and threw a spotlight in that direction, illuminating two figures. Instantly, that put me on edge. My muscles went taut and I hunkered down, braced for action. Blinded by the light, Terry lifted his hands, holding a rifle high above his head. Christine, close at Terry's side, lifted one hand to shield her eyes. Before I managed to focus, I heard Jordan's excited voice.

"Those're our cousins. They're with us."

The light went out. Terry and Christine stepped boldly toward the Sheriff's posse, as if arriving at a family picnic. Sheriff McCrea approached them casually. His paunch belly protruded from his unzipped leather jacket and bulged over his belt buckle.

"Are you two with this bunch of greenhorns? What are you doing here?"

"Your job," Christine said, under her breath. Terry elbowed her. "Ow," she whispered, lifting a hand to rub her stinging arm. "I really needed another bruise."

"Yes sir," Terry said, in a disciplined military voice. "We followed that white pickup over there." Terry pointed with the rifle barrel. "A couple of guys snatched the girl from our camp. That's the vehicle they drove." With an index finger, the sheriff pushed up the brim of his white Stetson, stepped out towards the street, and locked his eyes on the truck. His whiskered upper lip twisted left and right as he contemplated.

"So, you reckon she's in there." His squinted eyes turned toward Terry and Christine.

"Yes, sir. I have no doubt."

The sheriff spun around on boot heels. "Okay, gather in and listen up." He spoke firmly, but just above a whisper. "I've done deputized you four... or six, I guess it is now." He swept a hand loosely at Luke, Orpheus, and us cousins. "But I need to remind you all. . ." he paused and nodded slowly, "this is an awkward and very dangerous situation. So be careful, goddammit. I don't want anybody killed, or even hurt, for that matter." He shook his finger stiffly, for emphasis. "You're mostly here for a show of numbers and force. I have no warrant." He rolled his eyes. "The county judge wasn't available. And at this point, I have very little cause for a search of this property—well, except the assertion that the pickup over yonder," he turned and pointed, "was involved in an alleged crime. Ya'll can see how tricky that is, can't cha? We need to be careful as a mule on ice. Now, which of ya'll has military experience?"

Terry, Orpheus, and Luke each lifted a hand. The sheriff nodded in satisfaction. "I know this one was in the Navy." He thumbed toward Uncle Luke. "What about you?" His eyes fell on Orpheus.

"Marine Corps. Korea."

"And you?" He nodded at Terry.

"Army. Fifth Airborne. Vietnam."

"Alright, then." The sheriff nodded approvingly before adjusting his hat. "I think we can up the ante. Ya'll can give out a hearty *Hooah*, *Hooya*, or *Oorah, Semper Fi*. Whichever fits. I'll just stick to my cowpoke, *Yeeha!* But we're all in this together. Heh, and before we jump into the water," he said, "I've got somethin' for everybody."

The sheriff popped open the trunk of his patrol car and pulled out a duffle bag. "These are still in the testing phase and won't be available for another year or so. But it could mean the difference between life or death. They call it Kevlar, a new development in body armor. I ordered these out of a little slush fund the county bookkeeper don't know nothin' about." He grinned wide as he handed out untarnished protective vests, like they were party favors.

Christine nudged Terry. "He reminds me of my mother. Never stops talking." Terry lifted a crooked smile.

We helped each other don the vests, each one with *SHERIFF* in bold letters printed across the back. That made us look official and lessened our own sense of vulnerability. But the air was still tense. Danger and death lurked across the street inside that building. We all sensed it.

"Here's how we're going to handle this situation," the sheriff said. "Me and my real deputies are gonna pull up in front of that building yonder, about thirty yards out, with lights flashin'. Then I'm gonna walk right up to the door and knock. If they don't answer, I'm gonna blow it open with my 12-gauge. I want you," he pointed at Orpheus, "to angle your truck right across there and take a position behind it. You'll have good coverage of that main door. He then pointed at Terry. "And you go with him."

He turned abruptly, face taut as he scanned the rooftop behind them. "On second thought," he motioned at Terry, "since you have a scope on that weapon, see if you can find a way up there." He pointed to the long office and warehouse that extended down the road past the target building. Along there somewhere is where Terry and Christine had been hunkered down, before we all arrived on the scene.

"There's always an advantage from a higher elevation. If you can't get up there, then come back to the truck. Then you," the sheriff pointed at me, "I need you to hunker down with this Marine behind the truck."

The sheriff then instructed Jordan to slip down to a clump of trees in the distance. He drew a gloved finger across his whiskered lip and sniffed. "If you gotta retreat, you can duck into the creek bed and follow it back this way. It runs through this complex from way up yonder." He gestured toward the north without looking.

"Then you," the sheriff pointed to Uncle Luke. "I want you to sneak around back and make sure nobody gets out toward the runway. I suspect there's an exit on that side. If they have that girl with 'em, do not... I repeat... do not open fire."

"Okay, but I'm moving my truck back a bit," Uncle Luke said, stepping spritely in that direction. "I don't want it shot full of holes."

"Why the hell not," the sheriff quipped. "That could be your badge of courage back at Ardmore High School. Whewee! That'd really be somethin' to talk about in class."

Uncle Luke smiled, but shook his head. "No thanks. I can do without that. If I get out of here alive, that'll be story enough to tell." He trotted back to his big Ford and reversed along the road some thirty or forty yards. Then, climbing out briskly, he grabbed a second magazine for his M16 and lit out on a wide circle toward the back of the building.

"And you, Missie," the sheriff shook a finger in Christine's direction, "you back off over yonder behind that building and stay out of sight."

Christine bristled and inhaled to respond. Her eyes shot fire from beneath the curved brim of her baseball cap. Terry spoke up. "She's with me, sheriff. She can shoot the stinger off s wasp's ass at fifty yards. Killed a deer just a couple of days ago. I trust her to back me up."

The sheriff studied Terry's determined face. Nodding with a crooked smile, he cut a glance at Christine. "Alright, then, Annie Oakley. You're in, like Flint. What's that you got in the shoulder rig?"

Christine's coat was unzipped and the sheriff must have caught sight of a leather strap. She reached in drew out her dad's .38 Special. The Sheriff smiled and nodded. "That's what I carry. But that's no good from up there. Can she use your rifle, son?" He looked at Terry. "I'll let you borrow one of the department's finest tools of the trade." He bent down into the trunk, lifted out an M16 assault rifle with a bipod and a scope, and handed it to Terry. "Have fun. Here's an extra magazine. If anyone tries to make a getaway, you two oughta be able to shoot out all four tires before them bad boys can say *Bob's my dead uncle*." He scanned our faces. "Ya'll be careful, now. You hear me???"

During the sheriff's *prep and pep* talk, I glanced repeatedly towards the building we were about to raid, wondering whether any bad guys in there were so blind and deaf, they didn't hear the sheriff's course voice or see the tight cluster of trucks and sheriff's department vehicles parked on the side of the street, right out in plain sight. Of course, there were no windows in the building, at least not along the front, and there was no guard posted anywhere that we could see. Apparently, this gang felt secure behind steel walls and out of sight. My apprehension grew. I kept thinking that this wasn't the way cops would handle such a case on a TV series like *NYPD*. A good SWAT team would surely blow the door with a light C-4 charge. Or, more theatrical, Steve McGarrett on *Hawaii Five-O* would knock on the door, wearing a grey wig and beard and posing as a scientist whose research lab in the building across the street lost power, and he needed to borrow a generator. I wasn't sure anyone would waltz right into that den of timber wolves and asked to talk to the head honcho.

But what did I know? I was just a cowboy college student with zero combat experience. Neither Jordan nor I had ever fired a weapon at anyone, except a human silhouette at Hank's Shooting Range. And Christine—I'm tempted to say that the girl had far more courage than brains. But that wouldn't be fair. I already knew she was plenty smart. Yes, I knew that for sure. Maybe she was too smart, cursed with an exaggerated sense of self-confidence.

Still, what was Terry thinking, getting her involved in all this. He was already in trouble with Christine's mom. What if Christine got shot? How would her mom react? My head was spinning with questions, and I challenged my own sanity for even being here. I hoped it wouldn't escalate into a shootout like Tombstone's O.K. Corral. But, at this point, I had no choice but to muster courage, stay calm, and fire if fired upon.

We all nodded in compliance with the sheriff's instructions. Terry and Christine trotted around the building to search for a ladder or another method of roof access. It was a flat-topped structure with a tar and gravel roof. Lying on his belly, a shooter would have a good angle down and across the entire building front where our yet-unseen opponents were holed up.

Three minutes later, the deputies eased the two Plymouths nose to nose about thirty feet from the front door, stepped out lightly, and left the car doors open. Orpheus steered his pickup a few feet behind them, in the middle of the street, and set the brake. He and I stepped out and took our positions. I glanced up to the rooftop behind me. Terry and Christine were already there. Painters had left scaffolding at the end of the building, and they had easily shinnied up to the roof.

At the sheriff's signal, the deputies switched on the red lights atop their patrol vehicles. The ominous rotating beams illuminated the entire front of the metal warehouse. My heart pounded and my knees trembled. I had not felt this way since the starting kickoff of my first high school football game when I was sixteen. But this was definitely worse. I drew in a deep breath and blew it out forcefully.

The sheriff did as he said he would. Gripping his shotgun with one hand, upright and resting against his shoulder, he strode boldly up to double glass doors marked in bright gold letters—*Golden Enterprises, Inc.* He knocked, then backed off and announced himself with a loud hailer. No one came to the door. He repeated, "This is the sheriff's department. Unlock the door, and come out with…" His second command was cut short by a burst of gunshots from inside, shattering the glass door.

The sheriff and both deputies unloaded a thunderous volley of fire through the opening. Deputy Holt stepped up with a metal pry bar and pounded the glass shards around the doorframe, breaking off all the protruding pieces. The lights inside went out. The sheriff and all three deputies stepped through the opening, flashlights sweeping walls and corridors. Inside, there was a long exchange of gunfire and flashes of light.

A metal door at the south end of the building burst open and two men ran toward the parked vehicles. Both the men carried handguns and fired several rounds in our direction as they ran, bent low. Orpheus and I returned fire. I heard a couple of shots from where Jordan was hiding. He was well covered. One man, wearing a knit cap and a plaid shirt, jerked open the door of a tan Chevy Impala. Without aiming, he fired randomly. I returned fire, and he dropped.

Two others ran from the metal door, shooting in all directions. I heard the zip of rounds passing over my head, followed instantly by the crack of rifle fire from the rooftop behind me. That had to be Terry and Christine. The two runners were both struck and fell to the pavement.

Another thug ran toward the white Dodge pickup that sat reversed into the parking spot next to the Chevy. He fired rapidly in all directions with, as I would learn later, an Israeli-made Uzi. When the magazine was empty, he threw the weapon aside and leaped into the driver's seat. As he pulled out, I heard multiple cracks from the rooftop. Christine had put a round through a front tire, and Terry's three or four shots from the M16 blew the radiator and killed the engine. The pickup halted. Water sprayed from below the grill. Leaving his weapon behind, the driver bolted across the street toward the woods, precisely in Jordan's direction. Jordan sprang to his feet from his hiding place and directed his rifle at the runner's face. The man halted in his tracks and threw up his arms. Jordan instructed him to lie down, face to the ground.

With that, the entire area in front of Golden Enterprises became deathly quiet. No movement outside. Nor was there any sound from inside the building. Jordan hovered attentively near his captive's feet, keeping his rifle trained on him. Orpheus and I crept around the bullet-riddled vehicles to peruse the battlefield. Four men lay dead on the pavement.

One of them caught my attention. Strangely compelled, I lingered over him, studying. He was clearly not a run-of-the-mill thug, but in contrast he was well-groomed, clean-shaven, and nicely dressed. A sharp western outfit, with a leather jacket and a fifty-dollar buckle. His boots were western, with a riding heel. But not just ordinary boots. Expensive, I could tell. Lucchese, I guessed. Made of ostrich skin. Also very distinct was his thick silver hair. He must have been the leader of this gang. But he bled like any man. And he was dead.

Over my shoulder I noticed that Terry and Christine were on the ground, making their way across the street and around the north end of the building. That was the direction Luke had taken earlier. From inside, we heard voices, not stressed or loud, but simple conversation. That was followed by movement of feet on crunching glass as the sheriff and his deputies emerged through the front door with five men in handcuffs. Three were white men with scruffy beards and angry faces. One appeared to be Hispanic, clean-shaven with short-cropped hair. The fifth was an Indian with long hair, a colorful cowboy shirt, jeans, and boots. He glanced at me and sniffed, lifting his chin with a proud and defiant smirk.

The sheriff called us close. "Is everybody alright? All accounted for?" We nodded. "Where's the Ranger and the girl?"

"They came down from the roof and went around that way," I said, sweeping a hand. "I think to check on Uncle Luke."

"Okay. Here's the scoop. We didn't see any girl in there, but we found a room full of cocaine and marijuana. Regardless of what else these boys might be up to, we hit the jackpot on that, no pun intended.

We don't know which one of 'em opened fire on us first, but it was like hanging a welcome sign on the door. They engaged us in an unprovoked gunfight. All of you, and I mean *all* of you, acted in self-defense. I announced our ID, and they opened fire. Got that?"

We all nodded vigorously, appreciating the sheriff's positive demeanor. However, I remained anxious as to what Terry, Christine, and Uncle Luke had encountered on the other side of the building. I was forced to wait for their report.

Thirty-Three

Terry and Christine rounded the back corner of the building and stopped to survey the area. The runway side had a different appearance from the street side. There were several office windows and a double glass door with an awning-covered sidewalk that led straight to a taxiway, which in turn was wide enough for a small commercial aircraft to park and turn around. At a distance to the north, adjacent to the taxiway, a service truck sat next to a large electrical transformer. An aluminum ladder and a large metal container lay on the ground next to the truck. Both truck and container were locked, apparently left there by workers whose project was interrupted by the ice storm. Uncle Luke crouched in the shadows behind the truck, his shoulder resting against a rear fender and his attention directed toward the back door of the building.

He noticed Terry and Christine and waved them forward. Hidden behind a cement panel fence, they sneaked out to the taxiway. As they reached Luke's position, he squatted down and motioned for them to do likewise.

"The sheriff arrested several men, and a couple of others are dead," Terry whispered. "What have you seen back here?"

"Nothing, really. This side has been quiet. I heard all the racket, but I don't think this part of the building is connected to the front. As you can see, there's an armed guard at the back door."

The pair of cousins eased up, shoulder to shoulder, and locked eyes on a tall man wearing military boots, insulated coveralls, and a knit cap pulled down over his ears. On his hip, he carried a sidearm. They observed as he walked his post beneath the long awning, from the door twenty paces to the edge of the taxiway, then he turned and walked back.

"During the gunfire in front," Luke said, "he slipped over to the corner there and had a look. I guess he had no cause to get involved. But, there's something else." Luke pointed. "I want you both to watch and tell me what you see."

The double doors were glass, similar to the ones in the front of the building. These, however, were flanked by large cement planters containing manicured spiral Cypress trees. There was sufficient interior light to reveal a couple of chairs, as one might expect in the lobby of an office building or in a hospital waiting room. A light in the ceiling illuminated the full fronds of an Emperor palm.

Christine turned her head toward Luke. "What's special about any of that? They're just ordinary…"

Terry cut her off with a sharp elbow. "Look," he pointed.

Inside the door, appearing when the guard turned his back, was a familiar figure— an old Indian woman, with a faded blanket draped over her shoulders. As the guard reached the end of his post, ready to turn, she disappeared.

"That's her," Christine said.

"You know that old woman?" Luke answered.

"Yes, we've seen her before."

"Where? What's an old woman doing in there after midnight? At first, I assumed she was the night janitor or something. But she's not working. There's no cart with supplies. She's just there, observing."

"Yep, that's truly odd," Terry said. "What cleaning lady wears a blanket?"

"Then who is she?" Luke said.

"Let me put it this way," Christine said. "We've seen things you would never believe unless you saw it for yourself. That looks like the same old woman who came to us up on the mountain. She wrote notes on the bus window and told us to go help the girl. We didn't even know there was a girl up there until Jordan and Russ found her in a cave. But that old woman knew. And now she's here. I'd bet the girl is in there somewhere."

"But who the hell is she?"

"I'm telling you, man." Terry stared intensely in Luke's face. "She's not real."

Frowning incredulously, Luke pointed. "But there she is. And she knows we're here."

They continued to observe as the old woman's image waited until the guard turned to face her. However, this time she glided through the solid glass and beckoned to him with a slow rotating hand. The guard halted abruptly, drew his sidearm from its holster, and directed it toward her. He cautiously approached, then stopped, lowered the weapon, and peered down into her face. Unruffled, she said something to him the three observers could not make out. The guard paused, as if contemplating her words. Then he stiffly holstered the gun, turned, and meandered aimlessly down the sidewalk, across the taxiway, and disappeared into the darkness. When the three looked back toward the building, the woman was gone.

Luke and the two cousins hurried across the open lawn, still crisp in patches from the recent freeze, and approached the east-facing glass door. As they approached, the woman reappeared as living flesh in the shadows beneath the awning. Christine lifted a hand to touch her, but she retreated, motioning toward the door. "She's in here. I'll lead you," the woman said.

Luke tried the door, but it was locked. While he observed, the door latch turned, seemingly on its own. The woman appeared inside the lobby and beckoned them to follow. Luke's questioning eyes begged Terry for answers. Terry shook his head.

"Don't ask. I told you, none of it makes sense."

They followed as the old woman glided effortlessly along an empty hallway. The runway side of the building was a maze of walls and corridors, with no apparent connection to the rooms in the front. It appeared that the entire building had been converted to a warehouse with offices, the front and back sharing a wall, but no access. The woman stopped at an open door and pointed. The room was pitch black and reeked of a raw witch's brew of mildew and human waste. As they entered, a row of recessed florescent ceiling fixtures brightened. In one corner, White Dove sat in a folding chair, her head bowed, chin against her chest. She was barefoot and wore only panties and a bra. Tape secured each ankle to a leg of the chair, and a strip of tape sealed her mouth. Her arms stretched behind her and were taped together at the wrists. On a small table nearby, a pink tracksuit lay neatly folded. Next to it sat a pair of canvas sneakers; pink with white laces.

The door of an adjacent toilet stood open, with the light on. The globe surrounding the single bulb was dark with dead bugs and dust. Out of caution, Luke stepped closer and peered behind the door. The room was vacant. The toilet bowl was full and overflowing. A plunger lay on the floor, hinting someone's lack of success at unclogging the fixture. The cold-water faucet dripped steadily into a badly stained sink.

Christine stepped close. "White Dove?" she said tentatively. The girl lifted her head toward the sound of her name. "It's Christine. I was with you in the bus. We're glad we found you again, and this time we're gonna get you out safely. Okay?"

White Dove nodded nervously. Her chest heaved with joy. She had been grabbed, tugged, tied up, and tossed around like a bale of hay for days on end. No one had allowed her to use a toilet or clean herself. Her misery was compounded by her menstrual period, onset while in the cave. Her legs were smeared with blood, worse now than when Jordan first found her. A few hours earlier, up at the campsite, Christine was heating a pan of water for the purpose of washing White Dove. That was before the thugs came and took her away. Now, in this room, the clean and folded tracksuit was the only sign of someone's compassion.

Christine motioned to Terry. The two of them began cutting tape from White Dove's ankles and wrists. Once her hands were free, on her own volition she peeled the tape from her lips. Without trying to stand up, she maneuvered her feet and hands in circles to loosen joints and taut muscles. Christine pulled off her coat and draped it over White Dove's shoulders.

"I remember you, Christine," she said. "Where are the two who hauled me out of the cave?"

Terry spoke up. "That would be Russ and Jordan. They're outside helping to round up the bad guys. My name is Terry. I was there too. I'm afraid I was not much help with your getaway, but I saw what happened. And I'm here now."

Luke approached. "White Dove, you may not remember me. I met you at Seely Chapel some time back. I'm Luke Greenwood, the teacher at Ardmore High."

"Yes. Not so long ago. I do remember. Thank you all," she said. Turning her sightless face toward the door, in a stronger voice she said, "Thank you, Lomasi."

"You're welcome, little sister," came a response.

Startled, but at the same time intrigued, the trio turned toward the sound of the voice, which was different from that of the old woman. It was mellow and smooth. A shimmering image appeared before them. A much younger Indian woman with long flowing hair and a delicate band around her head. She wore a doeskin dress, tied at the shoulders.

"Where is the old woman?" Terry said.

She smiled playfully and her chimerical form became the old woman again. "I am whoever I need to be." Her voice crackled with decrepitude. "I can be a wise and aged grandmother children call Lóoliha. Or I can be Lomasi, the young flower with alluring fragrance. Or I can be something else you might not care to see. Her pleasant face twisted into a menacing and sardonic scowl. Now, take the girl and go quickly."

Christine immediately turned attention to White Dove. "Why aren't you wearing the tracksuit?" she asked.

"The other woman washed it. She told me she'd clean me up and dress me, but a little while ago a man came and whispered something I couldn't make out. They left in a hurry. That was before all the gunshots."

"What other woman?"

"The one who took me from the school. I recognized her voice."

Recognizing that there was no time to clean the girl, Christine helped her step into the tracksuit pants. On her own, she shrugged into the top and zipped it up. Luke then lifted her into his arms and turned. "We need to get out of here. Let's go."

Terry and Christine led the way back through convoluted passages, past a custodial closet, and along a corridor toward the exit. Terry pushed the door open and held it wide. Christine trotted out a few yards and surveyed the area. There was no sign of activity.

"Take her and go," Terry said to Luke. "We'll stay and help the sheriff, if he needs us."

Holding White Dove tightly against his chest, Luke clogged along the side of the building and around the cement wall, before angling across open lawn toward his truck. Once there, he settled her on her side in the rear seat, out of sight, and closed the door. He jumped behind the wheel and started the engine.

Terry and Christine hustled back through the building, still keeping their weapons at ready. The sheriff and his deputies had not found a way into that part of the large structure. Maybe it was walled off for a reason. Terry tried the handle of every door he passed. One short hallway had a restroom on either side, one marked "geese" and the other "ganders." Just beyond that was a door with a glass pane and a metal mesh interlayer. He leaned close and peered into the darkness beyond.

"This must be that garage," he said. "I see a metal roller door." Christine nodded, lifting on her toes to peer over Terry's shoulder. He tried the handle. The door opened. As they stepped in, a light came on, controlled by a sensor switch. Terry was right. It was a double garage with two vehicles. On the right sat a dark grey Chevrolet Suburban. On the left was a blue Dodge Charger.

"This is the car I saw up on the mountain," Terry said. He stepped cautiously along the side and laid a palm on the hood. "It's warm. Just got here a little while ago." He felt the Suburban. "Cold."

They left the garage and continued through the corridors, still searching for access to the front portion of the building. There was none. After a few dead ends, they settled on exiting the way they came in. They retraced their steps through convoluted halls, out to double glass doors to the awning. The runway was still dark and quiet.

Out front, Deputy Stokes guarded the four bodies, now covered in a tarp. Deputies Holt and Jenkins, along with Orpheus Pratt, stood over the prisoners who lay cuffed on the ground. They didn't have space to load up five men securely, and were forced to wait for assistance. Jenkins suggested hauling the prisoners in the back of Pratt's pickup. But the sheriff said it was too dangerous. Even a man in cuffs could jump out and get way on foot.

"The Indian, especially," the sheriff had said. "That buck can run like a deer, and even a pack of hounds couldn't catch him. We'll sit tight until we get help." He was now on the radio talking with dispatch, trying to make contact with the Ardmore police. He looked up as Luke's Ford truck made a U-turn and accelerated toward the airport exit.

Terry and Christine had just passed the garage door at the north end of the building on their way around to the front. A loud metallic clacking noise cut through the cold predawn air. Startled, Terry and Christine wheeled around. An engine revved and the gray Suburban shot out of the garage like a bull out of a rodeo chute, bucking off the cement floor and out across a muddy patch of lawn, turning toward the taxiway. Headlights cast eerie bouncing beams off service vehicles and small aircraft parked on the glazed tarmac.

"They're still after the girl," Terry shouted, waving an arm toward the sheriff. At the same time, the runway lights came on. Ordinarily, that would be Grandpa's job, yet it seemed unlikely that he would be there, knowing all the commotion that was going on. Without trying to analyze that conundrum, Orpheus jumped in his truck and motioned to us to get aboard. Terry and Christine came running. Jordan and Christine leaped into the cab with Orpheus. Terry and I climbed in the back, leaning over the cab with rifles loaded and ready.

The Suburban did not turn onto a street. It continued straight north along the taxiway and made a sudden stop near the upper end of the airport. A man jumped out and sprinted across the open apron toward a hanger. We could see a Leer jet taxiing in the same direction, and on first thought, it appeared that the man was trying to catch up.

However, he disappeared into darkness while the jet continued toward the north end of the runway and made a tight circle, clearly preparing for a takeoff. Orpheus stopped, uncertain what to do. At the same time, another jet touched down. There was enough light on the runway and taxiway for us to see that the running man was gone. He had apparently ducked behind or into a building somewhere. And we had no idea who might be on that jet. Terry banged his palm on the pickup cab.

"Forget him," he shouted. "Follow the Suburban."

Orpheus stomped the accelerator and made a hard left turn. Terry and I spread our feet out wide, clinging to the cab top with nothing but our elbows. Ahead, the Suburban's headlights swept past buildings and sign-posts as it sped toward the airport exit.

There were numerous back roads in that area along the southern edge of the Arbuckles, and south toward Ardmore. Orpheus knew them all. So did Luke. But which one would Luke take? I did my best to keep an eye on the Suburban's taillights, moving fast and visible only when passing an opening between buildings. Apparently, Uncle Luke had not been in a hurry. We could see his lights, not very far ahead of the Suburban. I pounded the roof again, leaned to the side, and shouted, "Turn right!" Orpheus responded and headed north on Redwing Road, making a hard left on Buck Hale. It would cross the railroad tracks and eventually lead to Lumberman Road, which ran due west past the Greenwood farm turnoff, and on toward Springer and the Interstate. We could see that Uncle Luke was now at high speed, clearly aware that a vehicle was in chase. We were confident he would not lead the thugs to the farm, which was about two sections to the north. If he couldn't shake them, he'd probably go on to Springer, turn south, and try to lead them right into Ardmore. But we needed to catch up, and Orpheus tried his best.

Within a minute or two, the unexpected happened. As we approached the Suburban from the rear, we saw a flash of gunfire. Uncle Luke's pickup went airborne as it crossed the tracks. The Suburban did the same. Both vehicles appeared unsteady, weaving erratically but continuing to accelerate. At the next section, the road curved ninety degrees left. Luke turned hard. His Ford truck skidded. The rear end hit a dirt bank, leaving the left side fully exposed. The Suburban slid to a halt with lights trained on the Ford. We saw the muzzle flash of two weapons firing repeatedly. Approaching from the rear, we could not risk shooting. Any miss could easily strike Luke's pickup, or its occupants. Orpheus skidded to a stop fifty yards behind the Suburban. We were forced to stand and watch.

At the same time, Luke accelerated, sending a cloud of dirt and gravel into the air. He pulled away, and again the Suburban gave chase. So did Orpheus. Terry and I held on. But the next leg of the pursuit did not last long. Luke anticipated the next right turn, with a steep bank off the road to the west. The driver of the Suburban did not. As he cut the wheel sharply to make the turn, the Suburban slid off the road, rolled down the embankment, flattening a section of barbed-wire fence and landing upside down in a stock pond. With the windows down, pond water flooded the interior. The vehicle quickly sank.

Orpheus slowed to a stop, then eased to the edge of the road so his headlights were trained on the pond. Waves rolled in all directions. Arches of four tires protruded from the surface. The rest of the Suburban was submerged. Headlamps shone eerily through murky pond water. We waited, counting the seconds. Hot metal hissed and bubbles rose from numerous air pockets inside the vehicle. But there was no sign of life. No one surfaced; only the heads of a couple of snapping turtles that popped up momentarily and disappeared.

A moment later, we noticed a small undulating motion crossing the pond. If I had seen it in warm weather, I'd be certain it was a curious water moccasin. But, in frigid water, I had no idea. Maybe a catfish? But it, too, found nothing worth its attention and submerged. As the pond settled, the yellow reflection of our headlights appeared in curious eyes further out in the pasture. A few inquisitive Black Angus approached, stood for a moment studying the situation, then retreated.

After a half hour, Terry and I climbed down from truck bed to stretch our legs. I shined my light down along the banks of the stock pond. Patches of resilient ice surrounded a field of frozen tracks in the mud. I was sure none of us cared to wade out there in the dark. I climbed back into the bed of the truck and sat down. Shortly after, Terry followed. Jordan and Christine remained with Orpheus in the truck's warm cab.

From behind us appeared headlights. As the vehicle slowed, a red rotating light came on. I recognized Sheriff McCrea. Alone, he pulled up close, stepped out, and walked casually over to the driver's window. Tilting his head, he shined a flashlight inside and toward the back, regarding each face. Recognizing us all, he leaned nonchalantly against the door, and drew a packet of Beechnut tobacco from his jacket pocket.

"Well, well, well. The fun never ends, now, does it? How many were in that vehicle yonder?" He flipped the light out across the pond.

"Two, we're pretty sure." Orpheus said.

"Well, sir." The sheriff laid his flashlight on the hood while he tucked a wad of tobacco into his cheek. "I managed to get another couple of deputies out to the airport, plus the Ardmore police showed up. Better late than never, I 'spose. They took them other rascals to the hoosegow. The coroner's on his way to collect the bodies. I 'jest hope he makes it before dawn." The sheriff glanced east, which was still pitch black. "He's kinda' swamped right now. Had to cover for his counterpart down in Love County. Dropped dead of a heart attack last week."

We all nodded in acknowledgement, maybe with a measure of faux sympathy, but we remained quiet and let the sheriff talk.

"So," the sheriff leaned down and peeked into the cab, "if ya'll don't mind, jest hang around here for a while til' I get a tow truck to haul that big Chevy out of the stock tank." He chuckled and batted his eyes before leaning out and spitting into the dirt. "Then we'll see what we have here. You said two, maybe three?" The sheriff's right arm stretched up to rest atop the pickup cab. He propped his left fist lazily on his hip, just behind his gun holster.

"I think just two," Orpheus said, nodding slackly. "That's how many heads I counted through the back glass. That's how many was shootin' from the side windows. I 'spect if there was another one in the back seat, he was hunkered down, trying not to get shot. Know what I mean?"

The sheriff stared at the four tires protruding out of the pond, his fingers drumming on the pickup's roof. "Unless he was injured already. Ain't that possible?"

Orpheus dipped his head. "Yessir. That's possible."

These were all strange circumstances for me, Jordan, and Christine. We couldn't imagine a more exciting ride-along experience. For Terry, it was a piece of cake. No pressure. Little adrenalin rush. Just another day in combat. But the thought was heavy on my mind that Uncle Luke's truck really took some gunfire, and maybe Orpheus needed to go on to the farmhouse and check on Luke and the girl. Orpheus thought that was a good idea.

The sheriff climbed into his vehicle, turned around, and tail lights disappeared in the direction of the airport. Christine went with Orpheus, while Terry, Jordan, and I stayed to keep watch on the flipped Suburban in case anyone surfaced and waded out. By now, that was not likely. But we had two good flashlights and extra batteries, and we all had sufficient ammunition should there be any further trouble.

Thirty-Four

Grandma awoke at the sound of tires skidding to a halt outside, grimacing as bright headlights ignited the front bedroom windows like sunrise. She swung her feet to the floor, shrugged on a winter robe and slippers, and hurried to the front door, mumbling, "Maybe it would be quieter if we moved to town." The headlights went out as she flipped on the porch light. Stepping outside, she immediately recognized Luke's truck. With the bright light at her back, her long shadow stretched out across the patchy lawn.

Luke winced as his feet fell to the ground. He had ignored his own injuries until now. In the weak orb of his flashlight, the batteries almost dead, he paused to inspect the holes in the glossy blue paint. He spotted one low in the driver's door. The bullet had gone through metal and into the seat cushion, narrowly missing his hip. He lightly circled the hole with one finger, feeling the concave indentation and splintered paint. Another round had penetrated the front side window, leaving a larger hole and a spider web of small cracks. "That must be the one that got me," he whispered to himself.

Pain radiated from his shoulder down his arm, but he tried to ignore it. Three holes in the back door sent a chill down his spine, realizing that White Dove was lying in the back seat. Tugging open the rear door, his heart leaped into his throat. White Dove was now face down on the floorboard, her head wedged behind the passenger's seat. Blood splatters on the opposite door panel and window, as well as a trail of blood across the rear seat, were clear evidence that she had been shot.

"Mom, help me here," Luke called out frantically. Grandma scurried down from the porch and out to the truck. Ignoring her own discomfort, she tugged open the door, planted a foot on the running board and lunged up into the rear seat. Sprawled in an awkward position, she strained to help Luke lift White Dove's limp body out of a pool of blood in the floorboard. They managed to drag her onto the seat, where Luke could at least maneuver her out the door.

"Go call an ambulance," Luke said. "Where's Grandpa? He can do that."

Grandma climbed out and ran ahead of him, talking over her

shoulder. "He's at the airport. Got a call over an hour ago. They needed runway lights in a hurry."

Luke scooped White Dove into his arms and carried her up the porch steps, through the front door, and straight to the dining table. Grandma decluttered the table with a single sweep of her hand. Everything went flying— a paperback novel, unopened mail, and a plastic bouquet centerpiece on a crocheted doily. Luke laid White Dove on the bare table as gently as he could. The blood stains continued to expand on the front of her freshly washed pink track suit. Luke unzipped the top to reveal the wound in her upper abdomen, just below the sternum.

From the hall phone, Grandma managed to call for an ambulance. She had to repeat herself, her speech slurred without her teeth. "They'll be here in twenty minutes," she said. "They said there was an ambulance in Springer, on a false alarm, and it was available." With hardly a pause, she added, "Is this the girl Jordan talked about? The one in the cave?"

Luke nodded, his tongue and palate paralyzed from stress.

"Dear Lord in Heaven, I wish you hadn't got my grandchildren involved in this mess."

"Mom, they were already involved up to their eyeballs. Orpheus and I volunteered to help the sheriff, but your four grandkids… they stumbled into a snake pit and had to fight back. It's like they were forced into a tug-o-war, and this girl was the rope. But I must say, they were all beyond restraint. I respect them for their courage."

Grandma scurried to the kitchen and retrieved a pan of hot soapy water, lifted it onto the edge of the table, and wrung out a washcloth. She shook her head dubiously. "Why don't you step back a minute, dear son, and give this girl some dignity while I try to clean her up a bit." Grandma elbowed Luke aside and began scrubbing White Dove's blood-coated torso.

"Don't worry about her dignity," Luke said, pushing Grandma's busy hands aside. "We need to do something to save her life. Bring a couple of towels. Maybe we can stop this bleeding. You can clean her up later."

White Dove, in great pain and stress, groaned and tried to sit up. Blood spurted rhythmically from her wound, but visibly weakening. She fell back and her eyes closed. Grandma dashed off and returned with two bath towels. Luke snatched one from her hand and pressed it firmly against the gushing wound.

"See if you can undo her bra and then lay the towel over her chest. Maybe that'll ease the constriction and help her breathe. I don't know what else to do."

At that moment, Christine pushed open the front door, still on an adrenaline rush from the night's activities. Orpheus followed. "Howdy, Grandma," she shouted gleefully. "Did Uncle Luke tell you…" Her question trailed off and enthusiasm shattered as the gruesome sight on the dining table telescoped into view.

Luke looked up, through tortured eyes. "Orpheus! Thank God you're here. She needs help."

Orpheus bounded across the room, shimmying out of his heavy coat, and shouldered between Luke and Grandma. Christine stepped aside. White Dove groaned and tossed her head from side to side. The former medic hovered over her pale body. As he lifted the blood-soaked towel, the wound continued to gush despite her weakening pulse. He tilted her to one side, far enough to slip a hand under her back and feel for an exit wound. Nothing. He glanced at the wound on her right temple before returning attention to the bullet hole in her upper abdomen.

"This is serious." His head turned left and right, searching. "Mrs. Greenwood, ma'am, I need a couple more towels, please. And how about some isopropyl alcohol, I mean plain rubbing alcohol?" Grandma scurried off again. Orpheus called after her, "Or even peroxide will do."

Christine tugged off her insulated parka, gathered up the coat and gloves Orpheus had dropped on the floor, and carted them all into the hallway to an accommodating coat rack along the wall. The shelf above it had ample space for the hats, gloves, and other accessories of a large family in cold weather. Beneath it sprawled a long plastic tray for muddy boots. A similar arrangement was on the inner wall of the back porch. The necessities of life on a farm.

Grandma returned with more towels and a bottle of common rubbing alcohol. Orpheus sterilized his hands before removing the blood-soaked towel and replacing it with a fresh one. He pressed it hard over the wound. Holding it firmly, he instructed Grandma to pour alcohol over the girl's abdomen and wipe it clean. He then turned to Christine and beckoned her with a nod.

"Missy," Orpheus said. "Can you hold that real tight-like? She's gotta breathe, but we need to block the blood flow."

With a stern and determined face, Christine leaned and pressed both hands on the make-shift bandage.

"Ma'am," Orpheus said to Grandma, "if you like, you can clean that wound on her head. Then put some kind of antiseptic on it. Whatever you got." Turning to Luke, he spoke just above a whisper. "That one on her temple is nothing. I think maybe a shard zipped past and grazed her. But, this one…" He pointed to her chest and belly. "This one penetrated the diaphragm and sliced right on up into the chest cavity. Ain't no indication that a lung is punctured, and I don't think it grazed the heart. But there's a lot of blood. I think maybe it clipped the aorta or vena cava. She needs surgery, like right now. I'm not sure she can make it twenty minutes."

Noticing blood running down Luke's arm, Orpheus tugged at the front of his jacket. "Take that off. It looks like you caught a little lead yourself."

Luke eased painfully out of his leather bomber jacket, which he had worn over the protective vest. The left sleeve padding was soaked. Orpheus felt around the area with fingers and thumb. "There it is," he said, pressing lightly. Luke grimaced. A round had struck him in the shoulder, just behind the socket. "Okay," Orpheus said. "You gotta part with that Kevlar so's I can get in there. Unfortunately, it didn't stop this one. Came in from the side."

Luke's posture cemented, his glazed eyes fixed on White Dove. Suddenly, he was overcome with emotion. He drew both hands up to cover his face. His chest heaved and he began to sob. "Why didn't I think?" he wailed pitifully, spinning around. "When the truck skidded into the embankment, the jolt must have forced her upright against the door panel. That's when they opened fire. "I counted three holes in the left rear door," Luke said. "She was in direct line."

"So… what are you saying?" Orpheus said. "What else could you do?"

"Why didn't I think to put my vest on her before we drove away?" He tugged at his vest with both hands, clawing at the straps, tearing it off, and in a singular motion, heaving it with all his energy against the wall. "Why didn't I think about that? This whole operation was about her. She's the one that needed protection. Not me." Luke staggered toward the couch and sprawled, face down, one leg dangling to the floor. He buried his face in a cushion and wept.

Grandma stroked White Dove's forehead tenderly and a hymn emerged softly from her thin and seasoned maternal lips. "*When other helpers fail and comforts flee, Help of the helpless, oh, abide with me.*"

When Grandma's song faded, Luke gathered his composure, arose, and returned to White Dove's side. His gentle palm cupped tenderly over her forehead. Her clouded eyes opened slightly, staring vacuously upward. A rueful smile lifted on her weak lips and a single tear ran from the corner of her eye. She whispered a prayer, "Ababinili, forgive. They know not..." Her words and smile faded away.

Orpheus came promptly to her side and felt for a pulse. His despondent eyes lifted toward Luke, and he shook his head. White Dove was dead.

Thirty-Five

A little after six, the morning of December 31, the front door pushed open. Grandpa entered, smiling, oblivious to everything that had happened on the mountain, at the airport, at the farm, and on the road in between. He was unaware that the Indian girl he had heard about on television lay dead on his dining room table. Puzzled by a room full of sorrowful faces, he stopped in his tracks. Orpheus and Christine sat on either side of Luke, trying their best to console him. Grandma sat solemnly, head bowed over the edge of the table, hands folded in prayer.

As Grandpa shrugged out of his coat, his eyes fell on the blanketed body. His breath halted and his mouth dropped open. Blood drained from his face. "O dear Lord." He staggered forward on buckling knees. "Who is that?" He caught his weight with one hand on the back of the couch.

Grandma spoke softly, her voice melancholic. "That's little White Dove, the girl in the news. Jordan and Russ found her in a cave late yesterday evening. Well, Papa, a lot happened during the night. You just came from the airport. Didn't you see all the hullabaloo there?"

"I noticed some activity down at the south end," Grandpa said, "but there's construction going on all the time at that place. I didn't give it a thought. Then, while I was lockin' up the control room, two yahoos went tear-assin' down the road. One chasin' the other, it looked like." I remember thinkin' to myself, this airport needs a crew of full-time night watchmen."

"Dad, that was us," Luke said stiffly. "We were helping the sheriff. What were you doing there?"

"Why, just like always. They called me to switch on them runway lights. Planes always comin' and goin'. That place is gettin' real busy. Hardly even notice Gene Autry anymore. Development is like an ant hill, growin' and coverin' up everthang around it."

"Was Victor Thorpe on one of those planes?"

"I don't know," Grandpa shrugged. "They never tell me who's on board. Or what they're shippin'. Just what time to switch on the lights, and whether I need to wait and switch 'em off."

Luke beckoned Grandpa to come sit with him on the couch. It then took a few minutes to give Grandpa an abbreviated version of all that had transpired over the course of the last twelve hours. Luke and Christine each contributed, trying to summarize in simple terms.

Grandpa's eyes roamed the room. "Where are the boys?"

"We're not sure," Christine said. "They were working with the sheriff and should be done any time, now. They didn't get hurt. They're all okay."

"Papa, you want me to fix you some breakfast?" Grandma's voice was as weary as her eyes.

"Oh, it don't matter much. With all these goins on, I sorta' lost my appetite. I guess a cup of coffee'll do fine. Thank ya, Sugar."

Grandma turned listlessly toward the kitchen. In unhurried mechanical motions, she filled the percolator with water from the tap, slipped the stem into the basket, spooned in six rounded teaspoons of coffee grounds, and set the pot on the stove. When she struck a match and turned the knob, a blue flame danced under the grate. Over the years, Grandma's routine had become innate and unconscious. One independent motion followed another, with hardly a thought. She reached into the upper cabinet to the right of the sink and drew out Grandpa's favorite coffee mug, bearing a hand-painted logo and picture of their honeymoon spot, Niagara Falls.

As she hovered over the sink, her ear caught the sound of barking from the kennel out back. She spontaneously stretched out a hand toward the checkered curtain and drew it apart. Her mouth dropped open, and her eyes widened. Breathing halted. The pan she had washed slipped from her fingers and fell to the floor with a startling clang. She wheeled around, away from the kitchen window, waving her hands above her head. "Dear Lord Jesus, help us." She called out with a shrieking voice, "Papa, hurry. Come quick."

Thinking Grandma had been overcome by grief, or suffered one of her dizzy spells and fell onto the floor, Grandpa rolled over the arm of his easy chair and hurried to the kitchen. Christine pushed ahead and was already at Grandma's side, but she could not detect a problem. Grandma stood trembling, her back to the kitchen window, elbows lifted at her side, hands gripping the front edge of the sink.

"What is it, Grandma? What's the matter?"

Grandma slowly loosened her grip, lifted a hand, and pointed over her shoulder. Christine leaned close to the window, drew the curtain aside, and peered out across the back yard. A crescent moon hung low in the western sky. In the pale early dawn, the back pasture appeared to be covered with heavy fog, hovering over the ground. Her eyes widened as the fog began to move like rolling water, flowing toward house.

Grandpa, curious but unruffled, pushed open the screen door and stepped out onto the back porch, surveying the yard. Suddenly, he gasped.

"Ya'll better come have a gander at this," he shouted. His heart pounded and knees quivered.

Luke and Orpheus quickly joined him on the porch, eyes transfixed and faces tense. What Christine first observed to be fog or mist had become a pale grey tide of featureless figures, standing erect. Farther out, a horde of similar opaque images rolled down from the foothills and across the back pasture, advancing on invisible feet across a ploughed field, and swarming like ghastly large insects, or aliens from another world.

Grandpa stood with Luke and Orpheus at his shoulder, frozen as the spectral mob glided silently forward. Some passed through fences and farm implements as if they weren't there. Some emerged from the well and spread out like an overflow of spring water. Others rose to the top of the windmill and descended the other side. Still more dissolved into the barn and emerged through the empty corral. The dogs cowered in their boxes as the river of human shapes penetrated their kennel and spewed out the other side, flowing resolutely toward the house. By the chicken coop and grape arbor, water bubbled up from the ground and took shape, as if gopher holes had been pumped full and overflowed. Each spreading wave congealed into recognizable human shapes with distinct features—face, hair, and the garments of a particular time and circumstance, and the appearance of specific races, young and old, male and female. They stood erect, pulsing with asynchronous rhythm, eyes directed toward the small group standing petrified on the back porch.

Luke stepped back, fumbling for the handle of the screen door. Grandpa and Orpheus followed, each looking anxiously over his shoulder. Advancing in unison, the front line of uninvited guests stepped up onto the porch and gathered around the door, eyes darting from one person to the other.

Christine and Grandma had remained at the kitchen window. Hearing strange noises at the front door, Christine ran through the dining room, where White Dove lay in state, and halted abruptly in the middle of the living room. Swaths of grey, undulating shapes appeared at the windows, faces approaching and retreating, wide inquisitive eyes peering through the glass. The entire house filled with phantasmal guests, appearing to be individuals but at the same time an amorphous spectral cloud— a collective mind and spirit.

A little girl in a long dress and a barefoot boy in coveralls stood inside the front door, flipping the light switch on and off as if fascinated by electricity. A man and woman in night clothes switched on the television and gazed at transitioning scenes of vehicles passing along a roadway. The grandfather clock struck seven, and two youthful appearing men with long hair and feathered headbands disappeared inside it. The pendulum stopped and hands spun round and round. Again, the clock chimed, but at a more rapid rate—eleven, twelve, thirteen times. Hands over her ears, Christine stepped gingerly backwards into the kitchen. The clock stopped. The pair of young men emerged from the clock and congealed into a faceless cloud of rolling shapes. Curiously, they followed Christine into the kitchen, pressing shoulder to shoulder and stacking to the ceiling. Some hovered over her, as if floating on their bellies in a pool, eyes directed downward.

Suddenly they halted, as still as death itself, faces directed inquisitively toward the back porch. A familiar-looking Indian woman appeared. Christine pushed past Luke, certain the woman was Lóoliha, the wise grandmother who led the boys to the cave and, just a few hours later, escorted Christine, Luke, and Terry into the building where they found White Dove bound and gagged.

The old woman had described herself as a shape-shifter, able to assume a variety of forms at different times—perhaps an alluring young woman, a warrior on horseback, or an observant owl high in a tree. She had not made those associations clear. She paused, turned toward the spectral crowd, and beckoned with a hand. From their ranks appeared the vaporous image of a young girl. She, too, had a strikingly familiar appearance.

"That's... that's White Dove!" Luke sputtered, pointing with a trembling finger. "How can that be?" He wheeled around and cast a telescopic gaze toward the dining room, straining to see through the spectral fog. White Dove's lifeless body remained on the table, hidden beneath a quilt. But now it was surrounded by faces and forms, hovering and stroking as if they all knew her. A young black man with a noose around his twisted neck, his eyes sullen and resentful, stood with hands folded solemnly. A young Indian boy, whose ankles were clasped in metal and bound together with a chain, reached out an arm to touch White Dove's homemade covering. Nuzzling the bare and pale feet that protruded from the death shroud, a little white girl appeared, dress torn and ragged, strips dangling from her shoulders, hair matted and face marred by scars. A young Indian boy, face mutilated and body riddled with holes, tilted sympathetically, as did an Indian mother, her arm draped protectively over two children.

At the back door, Lóoliha slipped an arm around a graceful spirit form that resembled White Dove and escorted her forward. "May we come in?"

Stunned by her question, blood drained from Luke's face. His skin rippled. The house was full of apparitions. Why ask permission now? Grandma shot a terrified look at Grandpa, whose hands lifted and eyes widened. His jaw quivered, but he could not frame a response. Grandma looked at the old woman and nodded, beckoning with a hand. "Please come in."

Lóoliha escorted an indistinct spirit through the kitchen and into the dining room, stopping by the corpse. Luke's bewildered eyes followed the old woman.

"Who are all these... people?" Luke asked, stammering.

She turned toward him, lifting her chin with undaunted pride. "We're the spirits of many tribes and races, all bearing the marks of injustice. You have our stories. Read them. Among us are men, women, and children of all races. Some were killed by their own kind, out of greed. Some were hanged for someone else's crime; or for no crime at all. Some of us..." she looked over a shoulder with a slow sweep of her hand, "...were killed by mobs in Tulsa and buried in a mass grave. Others were murdered for their land and oil rights. But, know this. No spirits of evil men are among us. They are not welcome. They are held in chains of darkness in another place. We roam free. Our special place is there." She turned and pointed up the mountain.

"This small mountain as our shrine," she said proudly. "Our common grief is poured into the earth in these many caverns, connected like veins, flowing with our blood and tears, our painful memories, and our unrequited suffering. Our place of mourning, refuge, and consolation, we have named Ghost Cavern."

"And you alone speak?" Luke said.

An Indian with the look of a chief stepped toward Luke, his form coagulated to apparent flesh and blood, yet transparent, chimerical, and other-worldly. "No, my friend. We all speak." An ancient-looking black man stepped forward. He wore ragged long pants that clung precariously to emaciated hips. His legs were bowed, head and shoulders bent low, chest sunken, and skin stretched tight over a cage of uneven ribs. He turned to reveal his scar-laden back. He eased toward Orpheus and spoke.

"What a fine man you became, my grandson. I am proud of you." Mechanically, others echoed his words. *I speak. I speak. I have a story.* Their combined voices increased in volume until it became a roar, declaring their individual suffering and unjust demise. The old woman lifted a hand. Voices subsided.

Grandma's eyes fell on a young girl with light-colored hair who seemed to look at her longingly. "Katy?" The girl's head tilted curiously. Grandma's lips quivered and her eyes welled up. Tears rushed down the lines in her weathered cheeks. The girl glided forward. Her shape brightened and became clear. "Don't be afraid to remember me, Mama. Fear the living. Not the dead." She retreated.

"Why do you come here now?" Luke asked again, with tumescent boldness. His hand lifted and stretched out to touch the old woman. She reacted as would a bird, easing away just beyond his reach.

In unison, the motley apparitions spoke. "The great Spirit sent us."

With that, they began to merge into a swirling wind, increasing in velocity like a tornado until the roar was deafening. They disappeared into walls and furnishings, which then pulsed like living flesh, breathing and throbbing with a rhythm of a heartbeat. Faces appeared and retreated, all watching and listening. Then, as quickly as it began, so the room quieted.

The old woman spoke again, pointing toward the body of White Dove. "This one should not join us yet. Within her is greatness." With a gentle hand, she pushed forward the spirit that had huddled at her side. It lifted from the floor and floated silently toward the table. Opaque faces and attentive eyes emerged from all around the room to observe. Some hovered near lampstands, above furniture, beneath the ceiling, or around doorframes, and a few cowered in dark corners.

The solitary spirit disappeared into White Dove's body. Her chest immediately heaved and she drew in a long breath. A hand lifted and tugged the burial shroud down to reveal her face, followed by her shoulders. Her eyes opened, and eyelashes fluttered.

"Where am I?" White Dove asked. Her head turned toward a bright lamp on the side table, and her pupils constricted. She sat up, panting. Fingertips lifted to touch her dark eyes, sparkling with life. She could see. At the same moment, a thousand other eyes brightened and smiles stretched across spectral faces, delighted at the wonder of restored life and restored vision.

A red light flashed across the ceiling and all the faces turned towards the front of the house, much like a deer would look up when startled. Christine and Orpheus also turned. Christine stepped to the front window. "It's the ambulance," she said, nodding slackly.

The faces in the walls and ceiling retreated. The woodwork and furniture resolidified, leaving only the old woman and the newly revived White Dove. The woman leaned close and kissed White Dove on the forehead. Ancient fingers stroked young skin and long black hair.

"We must go, now," she said. Itoahtubbi will come for you." The old woman turned toward Luke, then Orpheus, and nodded cordially. The same with Christine, Grandma, and Grandpa before gliding briskly through the house and disappearing through the kitchen wall.

Grandma followed, out onto the back porch, eyes lingering, ears straining. They were gone. All of them. There was nothing. Grandpa joined her, stepping from the porch down onto the patio. His eyes swept the horizon. The dogs were quiet, and the chickens were settled on their roosting perches. Solemnly, he turned and moseyed out onto the lawn and around the house. His head continued to spin with numerous disconcerting thoughts. He drew his pipe from a coat pocket.

The ambulance had taken longer than promised. In fact, it had taken nearly two hours rather than twenty minutes. Inside the quiet and hollow-feeling house, Christine pulled open the front door. A lanky young man, barely in his twenties, stood on the porch, shaking his head apologetically. His pimpled face and a burr cut, waxed upright in front, seemed a stark contrast to the faces that had surrounded Christine for last hour. Leaning to one side, Christine could make out a second guy, stouter and likely older, at the back of the ambulance. He had just unloaded the gurney. Christine threw up a hand and stopped him, calling out.

"It's okay. It's okay. She was not as bad off as we thought."

He nodded and waved.

The younger attendant on the porch shuffled his feet, puzzled.

"Oh, that's good," He said, nodding diffidently and scratching at the stubble on his head. "Yea, that's good. We were told the victim had a gunshot wound, and we were afraid we were too late."

"I know," Christine said, blocking his way to the front door. "But it's okay." Again, she waved him off, forcing a cheerful face. "Thankfully, she had a *miraculous* recovery." Christine smiled. "Sorry you made the trip for nothing."

The young man turned, eased down the steps, and returned to the ambulance. Walking straight to the back, he motioned his partner to replace the gurney.

"I don't know what that was about," he said. "You should have smelled that house. Musty, or something. I don't know. Strange."

His partner craned his neck to see Christine disappear and close the front door. "Yeah. Some of these old houses are like that. But, she's a real cute chick."

Grandpa sauntered up on other side of the ambulance, smoking his pipe. He overheard the comments and stepped toward the pair. "Howdy, boys. This the end of your shift?"

"Yessir," said the young man with the burr cut. He shuffled nervously. "Twelve hours. It was a long night."

"Yep. Same here," Grandpa said. "Sorry for the trouble. At least you can get home a little early, have breakfast, and hit the sack." His face rolled towards the dawn sky, brightening over the eastern tree line. "Maybe this'll be a nice, quiet day for us all."

Part 4: The Afterglow

Thirty-Six

White Dove eased demurely from the tabletop, drew the bed quilt about her, and planted her bare feet gingerly on the cold wooden floor. Grandma had given up trying to wash her earlier, when Orpheus and Luke franticly worked to stop the bleeding. Clearly, the urgency of her massive chest wound had taken precedence. All that was irrelevant now. White Dove awoke as she had died, with bare feet and exposed breasts, wearing only panties and soiled tracksuit pants. But she was alive, and her body bore no sign of a lethal wound. Most important, her sight was restored. However, her lower body and legs remained streaked with mud, blood, and feces; some of that as much as three or four days old.

Grandma escorted White Dove to the bathroom and twisted open the hot water knob on the tub faucet. Although Grandma was proud as a peacock to have indoor plumbing, her bathroom remained a museum of antiquity. Minuscule blue and yellow flames danced in a free-standing space heater. The vintage cast iron tub sat atop rusty claw feet, its porcelain interior marred by orange stains and scattered black pits. The newest addition was a row of vanity lights on a long faux brass cover. It was out of place above the antique mirror and other rustic appliances and fixtures, but Grandma was proud of it. She stretched an arm over the cold tub rim and levered a round rubber stopper into the drain. Steaming hot water slowly rose in the tub, misting the mirror and windowpanes.

Behind Grandma, White Dove's bare belly pressed against the rim of the sink. One hand rose to wipe away the haze in the center of the mirror. The antique glass bore unsightly de-silvered patches around the edges, and cast a distorted reflection. Yet, Grandma had refused to replace it. The single sink beneath it stood on four wooden legs, with all the pipes and connections exposed.

The resurrected young Chickasaw rested her palms on the sink's edge and leaned closer, curious and mystified, studying her own features. She picked up a washcloth and wiped the mirror again. She had not seen her face since early childhood. Although she had become a beautiful young woman, she mused over her changed appearance; she pursed her chapped lips comically and then stretched them apart in a wolfish, submissive grin. She rotated her head to examine her teeth. Then she touched the tip of her nose and eased it left and right. Lightly brushing the same finger along the arch of one eyebrow, she tilted her head side to side, following her touch with curious eyes. She raked rough and splintered nails through her knotted hair. Her crinkle of a smile faded as her lips began to quiver and her eyes welled.

"What's that brown grit in your hair?" Grandma asked.

At the sound of Grandma's voice, White Dove's composure returned. She drew her fingertips to her nose and grimaced. "Must be bat guano. Quite a few of them swooped in and out of the cave, and I'm sure they roosted on the ceiling above me. I don't know how big the chamber was but the ceiling seemed high. Jordan said maybe twenty feet. I could only guess, gaging from the rustling noises as the bats moved about and the echoes of my own voice. I got so bored and lonely, I sometimes talked to the bats. And now and then I felt something fall on my head. Bat poop and a little acid rain, if you know what I mean."

"I can't imagine what that was like. I'm sure you were cold."

"Actually, the first night wasn't too bad. "That tracksuit," she pointed to the soiled pink stack in the floor, "is fairly well insulated. I think it's cotton. Certainly not waterproof. After I got wet, I was cold. At first, I was wearing shoes, like canvas sneakers. They fell off somewhere. Maybe in the cave. But I remember that Christine put shoes on me at the airport. They must be in Luke's truck."

"I'll go look for 'em once I get you clean and dressed," Grandma said. She swished a hand back and forth in the tub, testing the water's temperature. "I think that's about right. I'm sure you're ready for a nice hot bath. Need me to help you?"

"No. I can see now, remember? But you can stay and talk to me. I'm not embarrassed. I've been humiliated beyond description."

"Sweetheart, did they abuse you? I mean...?"

"You mean, did they rape me? No, they didn't. They wouldn't dare. I heard the boss warn them that if they touched me in any way, other than to carry me or control me, he would personally cut off their privates... but, that's not the word he used... and feed them to the buzzards."

Grandma drew a hand over her mouth and giggled. "I'd bet that put the fear into 'em."

"The men all stank to high heaven, and they had very bad breath. And that awful woman who pretended to be a doctor." White Dove's eyes rolled up in disgust. "She stank too, and tried to cover it up with cheap perfume."

White Dove eased down into the tub. Her eyes closed serenely as she lay back. Grandma sat down on the toilet seat and rested elbows across her knees. White Dove recounted her ordeal from the start, and Grandma listened intently. She said she'd never tried to escape, particularly in the cave. She remembered the descent by rope and harness, and she'd felt the cave walls as she was lowered. They were slippery and impossible to climb without help. The cave floor was damp and uneven, and the man who took her down there nudged her left and right, up and over rocks, until they came to the place where he left her. He gave her a cluster of bananas and a jar of oily peanut butter, but no spoon. When she got hungry, she scooped out a few globs with her fingers. She depicted how she sat on a knobby cave floor with a wall at her back and a shallow channel of cold water on the floor to her right, only three or four six inches deep. She drank water from a small trickle down the wall on her left, that then flowed into the deeper stream along the floor.

She said the man gave her a hint that she could relieve herself in the water and wash there, and it would exit down a hole in the rocks a few feet beyond. Just like her ancestors, who drank upstream and washed downstream, nature provided a toilet system.

She mused that her defecation doubtless meandered through a long and convoluted conduit, eventually floating out of the ground in some farmer's pasture. The grass would be greener, or the corn or barley crop taller, because she had helped fertilize it. "I found myself giggling out loud," she said, "when I imagined someone shopping at the supermarket and picking up a packet of corn with the label *White Dove Natural Nurture*. Then, after I giggled about that, I cried. I truly thought I might die down there. And squatting on slippery rock over a small trickle of cold water wasn't that easy. Nothing to hold on to. I slipped and fell a couple of times. I now know the humiliation of wallowing in my own poop, like a pig. The thought is disgusting."

Grandma's compassionate eyes surveyed White Dove's body. "You know, the scratches and bruises you had before are totally gone. There's not even a scar where that bullet went in. And your cheek and temple... why, land sakes, sweetheart, your skin's just as smooth as a baby's bottom. But what happened to..."

"You mean this?" White Dove sat up and stretched to the foot of the tub to retrieve a ragged lump of lead and copper. She passed it to Grandma.

"How'd you get that?"

"It was lying on the table when I woke up. I knew immediately what it was."

"You're certainly a miracle," Grandma said, her voice bubbling. "I'm a firm believer that the Lord still works wonders, for those who can see." Grandma's eyes beamed. "I ain't never seen anything like that." Her face suddenly fell flat, as a conflicting reality pricked the balloon of her conviction. "Dear sweet Jesus forgive me, but ghosts worked that miracle, not the Lord." Grandma's eyes welled up and her chin quivered. "I truly don't understand that." Her head shook slowly, in serious cognitive dissonance. "Maybe those were angels, not ghosts. That would make more sense to me. But why didn't *they* get another chance? All of them looked so pitiful. That's too much for this old, feeble mind to ponder."

"I've never seen an angel," White Dove said. "But I was raised believing in the spirits of our ancestors. And, unfortunately, those spirits never saved anyone from bad people. There are lots of ruthless killers in our history. But I saw something when I woke up on that table. I heard a voice call my name, *puchi yoshoba tohbi*. I opened my eyes and there was my great-grandmother, standing over me, smiling. She reached out a hand and lifted me up. Her own grandmother was among those who died on the Trail of Tears."

"And all the others? Do you remember them?"

"No. I don't remember seeing anyone else. Only her."

"We saw them, Sweetheart. Hundreds of them. All around you."

White Dove shrugged. "I don't know about that. I felt a warm presence and I saw something like a bright cloud of light. But I saw no one else."

"Let me put some shampoo in your hair," Grandma said, refocusing on immediate needs.

"Thank you." White Dove's dark eyes moistened. "I know this entire ordeal must be confusing for you. But you're very kind, and your grandchildren are my heroes. The one called Luke, he's your son?"

"Yes, he's my youngest. He was in the Navy, but now he's a school-teacher and coach at Ardmore High."

"I remember him. I met him at a tribal event; I think maybe in Tishomingo. He shook my hand and spoke very gently, and then he danced with me. He had such a cordial manner and intriguing voice. It was nice to see his face when I woke up here in your home."

"I have some clothes one of my granddaughters left here. Maybe a little big. And there may be some Tampax in there, too."

"I'm done with that. I left a lot of myself in that cave." White Dove drew handfuls of hot water up to her face and let it trickle through her fingers. She marveled at her recovered sight, but felt a tumescent surge of pity for those who had endured so much to help her.

"What caused it?" Grandma asked. "Your blindness, I mean."

"They called it retinopathy. I had problems from birth, and my mother was not one to depend on doctors. I could see, for a while. And I never forgot the look of a person's face, or my mother's smile and laughing eyes. I remembered sunlight and stars at night, storm clouds, and a rainbow. I remembered colors like red, blue, green, and yellow. You know. Everything that's beautiful to see. While I was blind, I tried to picture those things when I touched or heard something. But it was not the same. I'm so thankful I can see again."

In the living room, Orpheus and Luke shared a parting handshake before impulsively easing arms around each other. Luke's fists gently thumped Orpheus' back. In a matter of hours, their mostly-casual acquaintance had deepened into a fraternal bond. Their minds had been led back in time to days of war, fear, pain, and death. Orpheus retrieved his coat and gloves from the hall rack and slipped quietly out the front door. Luke stood on the porch and waved, eyes following as Orpheus climbed into his farm-worn pickup and disappeared down the road.

Moments later, Christine and Luke sagged down at the kitchen table, yielding to exhaustion. Weary eyes crinkled as they stared at each other, musing on the bizarre and harrowing events of the night. Luke planted his elbows on the table, and rested his head atop finger tips.

"I just can't get that image out of my head." His voice was soft and pensive.

"Which image?" Christine said. "There's so many to choose from."

"White Dove lying on that table with blue lips and pale skin, a gaping hole in her chest. In that moment, I felt weak and helpless. Life is so fragile."

"I hear you. But that could have been any one of us… or all of us, for that matter. We're all lucky to be alive."

Thirty-Seven

Terry, Jordan, and I were at the pond until mid-morning. We stayed until a deputy arrived, leading a tow truck and an ambulance. They said they didn't need our help, for which we were grateful. Fact is, we didn't need to stay there at all. Nothing happened. No one in the Suburban came to the surface. We had been night watchmen at a drowning site, waiting for someone to recover the bodies. However, we were stuck there, on foot. We asked one of the deputies if he could drive us to the farm, or if dispatch would be willing to call the farm and ask someone to come pick us up. The deputy said they didn't run a taxi service. Grudgingly, we hoisted our packs, shouldered our rifles, and set out along the road like a small squad of demobilized troops after a war.

Fortunately, we got a ride from a farmer named Homer Bentley. He had been to Springer to the feed store and was on his way home. As he slowed and rolled down his window, we could see he was a little reluctant to stop for three guys carrying guns. I suppose we looked pretty rough, with mud up to our knees and a week's bristle on our faces. Apparently, he saw the official vehicles in the distance and figured we were part of the good guys— not fugitives moseying along the road out in the open, trying to look innocent. We gave him the short version of the story, and since it was only about five miles to Greenwood place, he said he didn't mind turning around and driving us there.

Terry had left the M16 with the deputy and Christine still had his 30.06. Weaponless, he thought maybe Bentley would feel comfortable with him in the cab. Jordan and I laid our guns in the bed of the truck, shoved aside a roll of barbed wire, then hopped in and sat on bags of horse and mule feed with our backs to the cab. Bentley pulled away slowly, still glancing curiously toward Terry and eyeing me and Jordan in the mirror.

We were relieved to get back to the farm. It was end of an ordeal that felt longer than it was, but with the reward of knowing we'd saved a life and helped capture some bad guys. The fact that I had killed a man did not register in my head until later. We ascended the front steps at the farmhouse, whistling the tune from *Bridge Over River Kwai*. Jordan pushed open the front door and began talking, expecting a welcoming crowd. "Well, that was an exciting end to the Christmas holidays, don't cha think?" Jordan stopped, confronted by an atmosphere as thick and heavy as molasses.

Luke lifted his head from the couch and stared at us blankly. Christine shuffled wearily in from the kitchen with a cup of coffee and a cold biscuit with butter and strawberry jam. Grandpa had just switched on the television, and he looked up from his easy chair, unruffled by the calamitous entrance. Eyes vacant and face expressionless, they were all impossible to read. The three of us glanced from Luke, to Christine, to Grandpa, searching for some measure of joy over the good ending to a vexing and dangerous experience. Jordan's shoulders slumped and his hands hung limp at his sides. "You guys look like you've seen a ghost."

Grandpa, Uncle Luke, and Christine exchanged quick glances. Suddenly, in unison, all three buckled over in laughter. What appeared to be a solemn atmosphere quickly erupted in raucous and bawdy laughter like a Viking banquet. Uncle Luke rolled off the couch onto the floor, his face buried in a folded arm and his shoulders heaving. Grandpa tossed his head back into the headrest, wagging his head left and right. His belly bounced in spasms and tears poured from the corners of his eyes. Christine staggered toward the dining table, fumbling for a parking spot for her biscuit and coffee cup before dropping to her knees and toppling over onto the floor.

It seemed like one of those all-night parties, when guests are dog tired and someone says something that gets everyone to giggling—then the giggles swell into infectious, uncontrollable, rolling-on-the-floor belly laughter, and nobody can stop. The three of us watched, pan-faced and totally flummoxed. Eventually, their mirthful spasms subsided. Christine sat up, still sporting a broad grin, and mopped the tears from her cheeks. Clinging to a dining chair, she managed to stand up straight.

"What have you people been smoking?" Jordan said. "Christine? You didn't pass a joint around at this time of day, did you? Grandpa, this girl is dangerous. I hope you didn't let her corrupt you."

They all laughed again. Grandpa managed to rock himself up and out of his La-Z-Boy. "Son, we're all as sober as a supreme court judge. I don't know what you boys were doing all morning, but we had a hell of a time here at the house."

We stood speechless. Terry shook his head and eased over to Christine, reaching around her with both arms. She responded, slipping one arm over his shoulder. She continued to chuckle while Terry searched her sparkling green eyes for an explanation. I reached out a hand to Uncle Luke and helped him off the floor. He stood up for a moment before falling back on the couch. I plopped down beside him. It seemed that no one was willing to offer an explanation.

The sound of a door opening turned heads and our eyes zoomed in on Grandma as she emerged from the bathroom. She eased aside and gestured, as if announcing the arrival of a debutante. I stood up while Jordan and Terry leaned closer. Our mouths dropped open.

White Dove stepped forward, backlit by a bright row of vanity lights. Like an angel emerging from heaven's gates, she radiated life and beauty. Her freshly shampooed hair, long and black, was combed out straight, and cascaded over her shoulders. Her head bowed as she checked the buttons on a freshly ironed floral pinafore, and then she glided across the floor with stately poise. I noted, with amazement, that she was not hesitant, nor did she need to feel her way with an outstretched hand. Padding lightly into the living room, she lifted her head. A radiant smile split her face and her dark eyes sparkled. It was instantly and resolutely obvious to us all that she could see.

Jordan fell back against my chest, stunned and speechless. His skin immediately went sallow and his knees buckled, as if he himself had witnessed a miracle.

"It's okay. Don't be startled," she said, lifting her hands in a settling gesture. Glistening dark eyes darted from face to face, her gleaming smile offered as a balm for our troubled senses.

Luke turned and pushed the front door closed before leaning back and crossing his arms. His pleasant smile reflected the radiance of White Dove's presence. I nudged Jordan forward. His knees quivered, as did mine. My mouth was parched, and I could scarcely swallow. White Dove embraced us both, thanking us for her rescue. Terry stepped behind Christine and sat down heavily on the arm of the couch. His brow furrowed, displaying both doubt and confusion.

"Let us explain as much as we can," Uncle Luke said, stepping away from the door. He dragged a chair in from the dining table and swung a leg over it, resting crossed arms on the back. He motioned. "Come, sit. This is heavy... very difficult to describe."

White Dove sidled up behind Uncle Luke and rested an arm on his shoulder. "Grandma's busy fixin' a big breakfast," he said, glancing at his watch. "I know its noon, but we've all had a long day and night. I confess, I feel like I'm in a huge time warp. And we're all hungry as a bear. Right?"

The three of us nodded apprehensively, moving closer. One by one, we sat— or leaned— and extended Luke our attention. He spoke to us almost as if we were children, in a calm and comforting manner. He explained the chase along the road and the gunshots into the side of his pickup when he skidded into the ditch. He stood up and showed us where he was hit by one round. Fortunately, he added, it was an in-and-out type of gunshot that tore tissue, but the bullet didn't hit anything important. With that, Uncle Luke drew a deep breath and slipped his arm around White Dove's waist. He looked down at her, his eyes full of emotion, and explained he did not realize she had been seriously wounded until he pulled up at the farm and climbed out of the truck. Orpheus tried to save her, he said, but within a few minutes, she was gone.

I tilted my head back dubiously, feeling a rush of skepticism. I braced myself for one of those claims of an out-of-body experience, or some other fantastic tale. I had heard such things before and seriously questioned their reality— the light, and a voice saying *Go back, you're not ready yet*. I simply didn't believe it. Jordan looked at me, a hard frown cemented on his brow.

"I know what you're thinking," Luke said, with compelling clarity. "But what happened next was certainly beyond belief and reason. It was not the sort of thing to report to the local news, nor to explain in a classroom. And I doubt that it could ever be shared in church, no matter how you twist it to make it sound inspirational. It was, in every way, unbelievable, but I'm absolutely sure it was otherworldly… and miraculous."

With that, White Dove stepped away from Luke's side, directing our attention completely to herself. She repeated what Jordan already knew well, that her people were very religious and referred to God as Aba'Binni'li, who created all things and resides in the sun, sky, and clouds. She described, in her own words, the plight of her ancestors and the many examples of injustice against them.

"As they died," she said, "one by one, their spirits gathered in special places," pointing over her shoulder toward the mountain, "like the cave you found up there. Those men you fought last night dumped me there as their captive. Ironically, they were not aware that in that dark cavern, I was surrounded by a powerful band of warriors, chiefs, holy men, and wise grandmothers, like the one who spoke for me earlier today. The spirits decided together that I was the one to be raised up as an advocate for them and all the oppressed in this region's sad history."

I listened to White Dove with great interest, as did the others, but my brain was enmeshed in a thick web of doubt. I noticed that Jordan also maintained a questioning frown. He couldn't get his head around her bizarre story, which was even harder to believe than the ghost raid on our campsite, the phantom in our room the first night, and his bizarre dreams. But, more than White Dove's commission as an agent of social change, I couldn't grasp how she was brought back to life. Was this a Lazarus sort of resurrection? Or was it merely a near-death experience? And what was I to think of her instant healing and restoration of sight? Was White Dove's name called out by the ghost of an Indian grandmother? How could that be? Was this miracle worked by the combined power of a thousand ghosts? And if they could do that, why had they not done so for themselves?

I considered that perhaps this was a rare opportunity in the spirit world. Maybe this was like a ghost lottery, and White Dove had won the grand prize! I trembled, not fearful but baffled, with a deep and visceral misgiving that, at the same time, yearned for both acceptance and comprehension. I felt silly resorting to explanations that I would normally reject, had others presented them to me.

When Luke and White Dove had expressed themselves fully, there seemed no appropriate way to wrap up the conversation. We more or less dispersed, one by one, to different places— one to the bathroom, another to the kitchen. I stepped out on the front porch and then meandered around back to check on Ginger and Barney. I ran my hand over the stitches in Ginger's rump to see if they were real.

When I returned, my cousins were all sound asleep. Terry was on his belly in the floor, head turned, cheeks resting on folded arms. Christine was stretched out on the couch. Jordan, had collapsed on the bed in the back room, head back, mouth agape. Luke came shuffling out of the kitchen, rubbing his eyes with one hand, a cup of coffee in the other. There was little or no conversation. White Dove was in the kitchen with Grandma, helping her with chores that had defined Grandma's life. In that moment, I realized that, amidst all the bewildering events, we had forgotten to tell Grandpa about Scooter.

When I sensed Grandma was about ready to call everyone to breakfast, I nudged Terry and Christine, called them to the back bed room, and shook Jordan awake. Despite my best effort, I came away from that spontaneous meeting elected to break the sad news to Grandpa. After all, I was the one who'd shot Scooter. Christine said she'd go with me.

Grandpa had gathered his pipe and a packet of Prince Albert tobacco and limped out the front door to the front porch swing. We could see him there through the window. He struck a match and held it to the pipe. After a couple of puffs, billows of smoke circled his head. He touched a finger to his tongue and daubed the match head with saliva before tossing it off the side of the porch.

Christine and I stepped hesitantly out the front door and crossed the porch toward the swing, where Grandpa eyed us suspiciously. Christine shoved her hands deep into her jeans pockets and leaned against the porch rail. Glancing back through the front window, I noticed Terry and Jordan watching from the living room. I sank down next to Grandpa. Before I could begin with my rehearsed apology, he blew out a long puff of smoke and studied me with dubious eyes.

"I noticed Ole' Scooter didn't make it back to the farm," he said. "I 'spect you plan to tell me what happened."

I glanced at Christine, whose wide eyes rolled. She looked away, and her fingernails dug into the wooden porch rail as anxiety mounted.

"Yes sir," I said. "That's what this is about. I'm sorry we didn't tell you earlier, but all the excitement over White Dove sort of overshadowed it, and we needed time to think about how best to tell you. First, you should know that…"

"Heh," Grandpa waved me down. "I don't have the patience for a long introduction, son. Jest spit it out."

That caught me off guard, but I understood and nodded. "Well, Grandpa, Scooter's dead." Grandpa stared straight into my eyes, and did not flinch. "He slipped on some loose rocks and broke a leg." I glanced at Christine as she brushed a tear from her cheek, but kept her eyes fixed on Grandpa. "It was bad. Real bad, Grandpa. Scooter was in pain. He fell down off the trail where we couldn't get him out. He couldn't get up, and we couldn't move him. So, Grandpa," I sputtered, choking up. "I had to shoot him."

Grandpa's eyes drifted across the porch floor before he shook his head slowly. Then he lifted his chin and stretched his neck muscles left and right. I got up from the swing and paced. Grandpa's attention settled on Christine, whose sad face told him more

than her words could ever explain. He read her thoughts and motioned her to him. She leaped toward him and fell into his arms.
"Grandpa, I'm so sorry. I'm the one who rode him that day, and I feel
like it was my fault. Maybe I didn't rein him the way I should have."

Grandpa's voice quieted to a whisper, "There, there, sweetheart."
His words were exceptionally tender and compassionate. "Scooter and
me, we done rode a lot of trails over the years. All over that mountain.
He knew the dangers better than you. He'd been snake bit twice, and
he got stuck up to his belly in quicksand over by the river. Had to leave
him there a couple of hours while I went to borrow a tractor. I used
long cables and a lifting harness and finally drug him out on his side."
Grandpa shook his head. "I thought he was a gonner, that time."

Christine stepped back to the porch rail, chin quivering. I returned
to the swing next to Grandpa and sat bent over, elbows on knees, head
hung low. Grandpa was quiet for a minute before taking another puff
on his pipe. Smoke lifted on a cool breeze. He gestured in Christine's
direction. "You know, if that rascal hadn't been pesterin' that bay mare,
your daddy…" He paused and swallowed heavily. His words then
seeped painfully through tight lips. "My son Marcus… would still be
alive." He choked on those words, and his forlorn eyes roamed the
ceiling.

Christine again sank down next to Grandpa in the swing. They
embraced and cried together.

"I forgave Scooter for that. That mare was a temperamental bitch,
pardon my French. Never should have bought her. Traded a flat trailer
for her, actually. Surely, the worst deal I ever made."

"Whatever happened to her?"

"I called the man I got her from and he came and picked her up.
Brought me my trailer back, plus a hundred dollars. That was for my
grief, I 'spose. Didn't help none."

"Sounds like he meant well."

"Yep. 'Spose he did. So," Grandpa coughed and sat up straight.
"Scooter was old. Older than me, in horse years. His time was up soon
anyhow." Grandpa cut a glance at me. "Course, that don't make it any
easier for you two, 'cause you feel responsible. But I trust your judgment, Russ. You showed him mercy and kindness like the Good Lord
taught us all. And, my bet is that old boy had the time of his life up
there with ya'll and them other two ponies. He was glad to get out of
that old corral out back and go clompin' along up in the hills where the

coyotes yelp and the air feels cool and fresh. His last days were happy. I'm sure of it."

Christine and I both knew that Grandpa had let us down gently, while inside he must have been aching *something fierce*, as he would say. Scooter was not just an old farm horse. He was Grandpa's pal. Those few moments with Grandpa felt interminable. His grief swelled in my chest and I could scarcely fight back the tears. I stepped off the porch and out into the yard to walk it off.

We were spared further wallowing in grief by Grandma's call to the table. It was now early afternoon, but none of us had eaten in over thirty hours. Grandma had been watching for us ever since the other guests left, planning to feed us well. But, in White Dove's company in the kitchen, she was not herself. While her maternal nature reached out to White Dove, Grandma still seemed distracted and distant.

We gathered around the kitchen table, where Grandma had laid out everything buffet style. The plan was familiar. Same thing at every big family gathering. We would load our plates and sit at the big table in the other room. If there were too many, out came the folding chairs and card tables. Either way, it was always good.

On this unusual occasion, an afternoon breakfast, we had eggs, both fried and scrambled, sausage and bacon, fried tomatoes, biscuits and gravy, pancakes and maple syrup, toast, and jam. I took note of the jars, labeled peach, apricot, and strawberry. She had made a breakfast fit for a king. Well, in realistic terms it was fit for hungry cowboys, spelunkers, deer hunters, volunteer deputies, and damsels rescued from distress. She asked Jordan to offer a prayer before we began, since she thought of him as the most dedicated to the Lord in our group. White Dove immediately lifted her hands to invite a circle around the table.

Grandpa sat on the front porch a while longer and was the last to come in. We were already seated when he dished up a plate and pulled up a chair. We had left his place open at the head of the table, as always. His eyes were red, and I was sure he'd had a good cry when no one was watching. Jordan asked White Dove what she liked for breakfast. She said, "Anything but peanut butter and bananas." That brought a round of laughter. Peanut butter was on the table, but White Dove didn't touch it. Instead, she buried her pretty face in pancakes and syrup. Breakfast together brought the room a renewed sense of joy. That was something we had not felt since Christmas. That was only a week earlier, but it seemed like a distant memory.

As we ate, Jordan suddenly remembered. "Hey, ya'll. This is New Year's Eve! Did anybody bring fireworks?"

Thirty-Eight

An hour or so later, I went out to check on Ginger. Jordan and Terry had already driven to Springer to pick up a few Roman candles, and were out back setting up a launch pad for a fireworks display later that night. I had left Grandpa in front of the TV, and Grandma, Christine, and White Dove were busy in the kitchen, washing and packing away dishes. White Dove waltzed around the other two women as if she had grown up in that very house, joyful for life itself. Christine, in contrast, slouched resentfully over the sink, scrubbing a month's worth of stubborn grease from the bottom of Grandma's cast iron skillet. Doing woman's work gave Christine opportunity to launch into a tirade about antiquated social paradigms and the traditional subordinate status of women.

"Have either of you heard of Gloria Steinem?"

"No, who's that?" Grandma said, drying a handful of forks with a stained and badly frayed dish towel.

"She was a Playboy Bunny, but she rebelled and became a voice for civil rights and gender equity. I'm intrigued by her views on the role of women in society. She's started a war against male dominance, which is what history scholars call the *patriarchal paradigm*. I think we'll see some interesting changes in the near future, and I want to be part of it."

"Like what?" Grandma said, cautious but curious. "What's wrong with the way things are? A husband and wife, lovin' each other, each doin' their part to make a family work… that's the way God made us. Read your Bible. It's all in there."

"I don't want to sound rude, but slavery, beating a child, polygamy, and stoning a wife for adultery… that's all in the Bible, too. It seems like Christians pick and choose what they want to believe, and then find a Bible verse to support it. Not very honest, if you ask me."

"Child, I don't know what Bible you read, but mine's pretty clear."

"Grandma, I'm happy to sit down and read those passages with you any time you like. But my point is, times have changed and cultures have developed. Some of the old ways and beliefs just don't fit anymore."

"I don't understand."

"It's like this, Grandma. Back in the 1800s, about eighty per cent of the US population lived and worked on farms. But today, that number is less than twenty percent and declining. People are learning to do other things to make a living. Science and technology are the way of the future. Back-breaking labor will be done by people who have no education or advanced skills."

Grandma propped a fist on her hip and answered firmly. "I've always believed if you trust and obey, the Good Lord will provide, no matter what."

"What did you and Grandpa do during the Depression and the Dust Bowl? That hit parts of Oklahoma pretty hard. A lot of farms dried up and blew away."

"We stuck it out right here. I used to drive our little Model A Ford over to the Santa Fe rail line and gather up lumps of coal that fell off the train. We needed fuel when we ran out of firewood. I think bein' on the south side of the mountain kinda' helped. Folks in the Panhandle, and out there in the wide-open plains from Texas up into Kansas, they suffered the most. A lot of 'em just packed up and left."

"Yes, and lot of them were good church-going Christians, too. How'd God let that happen?"

"Well, all I know is the Good Lord carried us through. Them that had faith did okay."

"My people had faith," White Dove said cautiously. "When the whites overran the land, many converted to Christianity or, like the Chickasaw, adapted their traditions to accommodate Jesus. But believing did not save them from evil men. As you know, our history is very sad."

"Why are you telling me all this? Are you two gangin' up on your poor ole' Grandma?"

Christine rested a hand on Grandma's shoulder. "No, Grandma. But we want you to understand that your family has not abandoned you just because they have different religious beliefs or use a different laundry detergent. We value your wisdom. But at the same time, we have to grow with social development. You know, go with the flow of changing times."

Grandma lifted her eyebrows and directed a taut finger at Christine's nose. "Is it developing? Or is it going to hell in a handbasket?"

"Change doesn't mean falling apart or goin' downhill. You vote, don't you?"

"Yes ma'am, I do." Grandma nodded firmly.

"Women got that right in 1919. Change for the better, don't you think?"

"Yeah, but that's just one thing. And God's Word's the same yesterday, today, and forever. It don't change."

"Today, women can get an education and build any career we want, just like men. We were not made to be second fiddle just because our parts are different. And a wife should be the husband's full partner in marriage, not just his subordinate side-kick."

"Well, I believe that's the role the good Lord assigned us, and I've tried to accept it with grace."

"Our world is changing faster than ever before. And I'm telling you right now, that young woman there…" Christine wagged a finger loosely toward White Dove, "…you just watch. She's bound for greatness."

White Dove nodded sheepishly. As Christine and Grandma continued their debate, something caught White Dove's attention. She turned her face toward the front of the house and slipped quietly in that direction. Christine noticed her standing near the front door, as if expecting someone. Moments later, the dogs thumped out from beneath the front porch and ran barking toward the road. Christine skipped through the house to join White Dove, just in time to see two black Buick Electras pull up side by side in front of the house. A Lincoln Continental followed, and parked neatly between the Buicks. The official-looking motorcade seemed out of place on a dirt farm road, and the intrigue was sufficient to coax us three boys back into the house.

The driver of the Lincoln jogged dutifully around to open the rear passenger door. A husky black man with a shaved head and a crisp blue suit, stepped out and surveyed the area. Upon his confident nod, out stepped Overton James, the Chickasaw Governor. Perceiving no threats, the driver and three bodyguards remained by the cars while the governor's personal bodyguard escorted him toward the house and up onto the porch.

Grandpa elbowed his way past Christine and White Dove, pushed open the screen door, and stepped forward to greet him. "Well, sakes alive," he said, grinning. "Look who's come to our house. Welcome, Mister James. I'd recognize your handsome face anywhere. Come right on in."

Grandpa held the door open while the bodyguard entered, fol-

lowed by the governor. They were greeted by our wide eyes and awkward smiles. White Dove, who had sensed their approach before the
dogs heard them, skipped into her uncle's arms. James looked down
into White Dove's bright, responsive eyes. His gentle fingers encircled
them, brushing away a joyful teardrop from her cheek.

"My, my, what beautiful eyes you have."

"All the better to see you with," she replied, laughter in her voice.

"We live in a world of wonders, and unexpected miracles do occur,"
he said, wheeling around toward us all. He and White Dove laughed
and embraced again, and our small group applauded.

At age forty-three, Overton James was a handsome and charismatic
man. He stood just over six feet, topping me, Jordan, and Terry by a
couple of inches. His thick dark hair was cut and combed stylishly. He
had dark gleaming eyes that exuded warmth and intelligence. And his
smile— well, that was the center of his charm. He had a bright film star
smile with gleaming white teeth and an engaging manner that simply
drew people into his aura. Grandpa was right. This distinguished man
was easy to spot in a crowd.

White Dove beckoned us forward and introduced us one by one.
I felt awkward shaking hands with such a man. In his eyes, I saw two
different worlds. One was the centuries of Native American culture,
with many tribes and nations, all funneled into the federal government's written plans and defined plots of ground, which ultimately
meant some degree of subjugation. Second, I saw in Governor James
an image of American politics stretching from a local mayor right up
to the White House, with all the wheeling and dealing, baby-kissing,
handshaking, and backstabbing that goes with it.

After the introductions, White Dove recounted our specific roles in
her rescue. "These two," she pointed at Jordan and me, "found me and
hoisted me out of the cave. And these two," she motioned toward Terry
and Christine, "helped rescue me the second time from the airport,
and she…" lingering attention on Christine, "lifted my spirits with her
confident words and vision of a bright future." White Dove glanced
around the room and did not find Orpheus. "Mister Pratt's not here,
but he tended my wounds." The Governor nodded gratefully with each
comment.

"And this one," pointing at Grandma, "she bathed me and gave
me clothes. And this one," she smiled brightly as she pointed to Uncle
Luke, "he's my knight in shining armor. He carried me in his arms from

harm's way to safety." Luke bowed sheepishly, with courtly aplomb. White Dove quoted a portion of Matthew 25 with a sweeping hand that included us all. "I was hungry, and you fed me. I was naked and you clothed me." She giggled as her words continued to flow. "I was captive and you set me free."

I cut a glance at Terry to see if he'd detected the same discretion in White Dove's words as was apparent to me. She'd whitewashed a few details and left out a few others. And she offered no hint that she had died and was resurrected by an indescribable power. I posited that she intended that detail to remain our secret. Essentially, White Dove declared us all honorary members of the Chickasaw nation. Governor James extended a hearty thanks, and he announced that in a few weeks he would organize a gathering where we would be duly recognized. But, as any politician would, he said a few things that were beyond the scope of White Dove's rescue.

"There is great potential for Native American prosperity here in Oklahoma, with plenty of job opportunities and many developments that will help bring our people up to par with the rest of America. As you know, we have made modest progress in terms of medical care. A couple of new clinics are already operational. And, a couple of years ago, we started running bingo parlors in a few towns." He paused as if expecting a round of applause. He received none, but we all nodded approvingly.

"However, a huge breakthrough began with a Chippewa couple named Russell and Helen Bryan, up in Minnesota. It was a simple tax issue that went all the way to the US Supreme court. The bottom line is this. Native reservations and territories are not subject to state or county taxes, nor can local governments regulate native activities on their own reservations. We envision a new era for Native Americans all over the country, from Florida to Washington State.

"That also means a certain vulnerability to organized crime. And this episode, of which you unfortunately were a part," he gestured toward Uncle Luke, then us cousins, "was just a taste of what unscrupulous people will do to get a slice of somebody else's pie. They tried to force my hand, but I would not be forced. On behalf of my family and our great Chickasaw nation, thank you all."

Christine leaned close to White Dove and asked whether her uncle knew anything about the ghosts. White Dove shook a finger discretely and whispered. "He knows traditions, but we should not speak of that here."

The Governor added, almost as an afterthought, "I have the task of persuading this generation of Chickasaw, and other nations if they'll listen, to stop wallowing in a cesspool of misery, despair, and resentment and jump into the spring water of purpose and prosperity. It's there, waiting for any American who will claim it."

As the Governor and his entourage shuffled out of the house and down the porch steps, two additional cars pulled up, trailed by a panel van marked KETA Channel 13. Clearly, they had come from Oklahoma City. A troop of journalists bounded out, wide-eyed and eager, with notepads in hand and camera crews in tow. They rushed toward the Governor, who drew White Dove close under his arm. An attractive young woman with short blonde hair shoved a microphone in his face.

"Governor James, we understand that the men who abducted your niece have been apprehended. What details can you add?"

"I know you're all doing your jobs," he said. "But this is private property and these good folks don't need all this clamor. Let me make a brief statement. My niece survived the ordeal." He nodded at one of the bodyguards to escort her to the Lincoln. "We're taking her home. Some of the perpetrators of this crime were killed during her rescue, and those who are alive are in custody at the county jail. You can approach the Carter County sheriff about that. The reason for her abduction was never made clear, but that's over now. As a joyful note, somehow, the traumatic experience resulted in the restoration of her sight. So, we're doubly blessed. Thank you." He pushed past reporters and stepped into the back seat of the Lincoln next to White Dove. The convoy pulled away, leaving us with a maelstrom of emotions, memories, and unanswered questions. The reporters immediately turned their attention our way.

Uncle Luke motioned us toward the house as he made a singular comment. "In deference to the James family, and because of the ongoing investigation by the FBI, we are not authorized to make any comments."

As Uncle Luke turned away, Grandpa stepped off the porch with his double-barrel shotgun and fired one round of buckshot into the air. The reporters scrambled to their vehicles and left, tires spinning in the damp sandy road.

That evening, we all gathered on the patio to watch Terry's fire-works exhibit. A meager ten minutes, but it was good family fun. The ground was still damp from the ice storm, so there was no danger of fire. From there we gathered around the TV to watch the ball drop in New York's Time's Square. Sleep came easily that night, and no one had nightmares. At least nothing scary enough to tell. We remained dazed and exhausted.

On New Year's Day, I drove Terry and Jordan back up to the camp-site to clean up and retrieve the gear we had left behind. Grandpa load-ed Christine's pack in his truck and took her home, thinking he might be able to smooth things out with her mom. He also promised to take her trophy buck to a taxidermist— someone he knew in Ardmore. He said he'd cover the cost, in honor of Christine's heroism.

A short while later, I dropped Terry off at the airport in Gene Au-try. The bus was still parked where he and Christine left it. None of us had any good ideas as to how to buff out scratches or patch the holes in its sides and windows. Jordan and I each agreed to foot a third of the cost if insurance didn't cover it. Of course, the first problem was the dead battery. Fortunately, I carried a jumper cable in my pickup. After a few minutes, the starter whirred and the engine started, with a huge puff of blue smoke. Terry chugged away with a parting wave and headed home to Paul's Valley to face his dad. He would have to explain how the bus appeared to have been used for target practice.

Jordan and I drove leisurely back to the farm, where he helped me hook up the trailer and load Ginger and Barney for my trip back to Texas. Barney was tired from his hard run down the mountain, and Ginger was sore from her wound. Jordan and I left the farm at the same time, as Grandma waved tearfully from the front porch. Grandpa lifted a hand and grinned, flashing the gold sliver in his dentures.

Terry, Jordan, Christine and I were all enrolled in college classes for the Spring semester. Mine would commence on Monday, January 6.

Thirty-Nine

I kept in contact with Uncle Luke and my three cousins for the next several months, mainly to be assured that everyone had recovered from our ordeal without too much lingering emotional stress. I was also especially interested in the legal process regarding those who had kidnapped White Dove. In July of 1969, seven months after our frightful and life-threatening escapade, Grandpa and Uncle Luke attended a trial of four defendants apprehended during the impromptu sting operation led by Sheriff Buster McCrea. Neither Uncle Luke, Orpheus, nor any of us four cousins were compelled to testify.

The case involved double jeopardy— specifically, dealing in illegal drugs and kidnapping. In the first trial, which was held in Federal Court in Muskogee, all four defendants were convicted on felony drug charges. Each was sentenced to ten years in prison. Sheriff McCrea assured the court that he conducted the sting based on a solid and reliable tip. The target had been a building leased by Golden Enterprises, located at the Ardmore Municipal Airport. The owners of the building were a firm in Oklahoma City who reported that the name on the lease was an M. J. Hemphill, not among those killed or arrested at the site.

The second trial was held in Oklahoma State Court, Carter County, located in Ardmore. Judge Quincy Townsend presided. Charged with kidnapping, one of the defendants agreed to testify in return for a reduced sentence. That defendant, Tim Rain Cloud, was a Kiowa Indian from a reservation in southwestern Oklahoma. His actual given name was Taima, meaning *born during a thunderstorm*. Rain Cloud commented that such a name was ominous, predicting his inalterably destructive path in life. That was no excuse, he said; but it was a factor he had found to be beyond his control. As a previously convicted felon, he faced a life sentence for a third felony conviction. Thus, his court-appointed attorney convinced him to plea bargain for two ten-year sentences, served concurrently, with the possibility of parole after seven years. Rain Cloud conceded.

During the trial, he stated that he was an orphan, raised by an aunt and uncle, and he left the reservation at age sixteen in search of work. After repeated terminations for substance abuse and inappropriate conduct, he and two other Kiowa boys robbed a grocery store in Law-ton. Because the store was next to the US Army's Fort Sill, the case got special attention. He was convicted of armed robbery at age eighteen and was paroled eight years later. Sadly, he seemed destined to become another statistic in the national dilemma of criminal recidivism.

Rain Cloud's involvement in the kidnapping of White Dove was minimal. He had been recruited by Taggard Hall as a bodyguard and general roustabout. As a Native American with long hair and an an-gry face, he proved useful in the intimidation of individuals who were targets of Hall's drug and racketeering operation. Rain Cloud testi-fied that while two other employees of Golden Enterprises held White Dove hostage in a cave, Hall learned from Bertram Greenwood that his four grandchildren were camped out up in the Arbuckles somewhere above Gene Autry, with a primary interest in spelunking. Since their location was dangerously close to the cave where the girl was stashed, he instructed Rain Cloud to take a couple of boys up there and try to scare them away. He didn't want complications or collateral damage to sully their scheme.

Rain Cloud testified that on Saturday, December 28, 1968, around midnight, he and a couple of his pals from the reservation sneaked up to the campsite in question on the southeastern slope of the Arbuckles. They rocked the bus back and forth, using steel poles for leverage, and scraped sticks along the side. The next night, well after midnight, they again slipped into the camp and painted the horses in random Indian symbols. "We rode 'em in circles around the bus, whoopin' and hol-lerin," Rain Cloud said, unable to stifle a wide grin. He added, "We were sure they would pack up and leave after that, but they didn't."

Rain Cloud chuckled out loud and the judge reprimanded him for not taking his situation seriously. He said, "I'm sorry, Your Honor. But when I think about stuffin' feathers in my hair and shootin' store-bought wooden arrows at that bus, I just can't help myself. Flint arrow-heads are a dime a dozen." He tossed his head back. "It was like a Hol-lywood movie set, Indians circlin' a wagon train on the Oregon Trail. Those kids were so scared."

The prosecuting attorney, Alvin Dunson, ventured to ask Rain Cloud if he had anything to do with hiring an Indian woman to help with his charade. He said the victim, Miss Whitney James, who was commonly called White Dove, had mentioned being protected during her ordeal by an old woman. She called her a *shape-shifter*, as in Indian lore. "Maybe," the attorney said, "she was one of your recruits from the reservation, just there to make an appearance as added intimidation. After all, the victim was blind at the time, and she couldn't identify any individual participant."

Rain Cloud said he knew nothing about an old woman. If the campers saw an old woman, maybe it was someone who lived around there, perhaps scouring the hills for herbal medicine. "But if so," he said, "it was not my doing."

Dunson asked Rain Cloud whether he had ever seen a shape-shifter, or knew anything about such a thing. The poised and confident Kiowa said that a *skinwalker*, as it is sometimes called, is a person endowed with the ability to transform into the body of a bear, wolf, or eagle, all for purpose of protecting the community. He added, "I don't think the nations that settled around here believe in that kind of thing. Maybe some do. But it's just a legend." He turned his eyes toward the judge. "Your Honor, there's a difference between the real world and tribal superstitions. I am not an ignorant redskin, stuck in the sixteenth century. I don't believe in shape-shifters and ancestral spirits and shit like that."

Toward the end of his testimony, Rain Cloud added, looking at the judge and then the jurors, "I blame no one for my problems. I know I could have made an honest living had I tried harder. I know what I did was wrong, and I accept the findings of this court. But I speak directly to the honorable Chickasaw governor, and to his niece, and to all his family. I ask your forgiveness for my part in this crime. I meant the girl no harm, and I was careful not to bring harm to the campers."

Victor Thorpe, the man Grandpa thought to be behind the kidnapping, was never indicted. Evidence was lacking, of any connection to White Dove's abduction or the drug ring that operated under the auspices of Golden Enterprises. However, he was subpoenaed and questioned. A portly sixty-year-old man with a bald head and a precisely trimmed red Van Dyke beard, he had an appearance that anyone could easily identify in a lineup. He typically dressed like a lawyer in a dark pinstriped suit, a pocket watch on a fob tucked inside the vest.

None of the defendants had ever seen him personally. They only knew there was a *big boss* somewhere. Taggard Hall, according to two of the defendants, was the one who phoned Overton James, speaking on behalf of his boss. Hall had been killed in the shoot-out at the airport. During the trial, photos of Hall's associates and co-conspirators were projected onto a screen. Hall was the man Terry had seen on the mountain— the flashy dresser with long thick silver hair; the one who drove a Dodge Charger. He was the one to whom Grandpa had unwittingly divulged his grandchildren's campsite.

The remains of the two thugs named Cooper and DJ were collected and cremated. The only perpetrator missing from photographs or any list of names was the woman who'd posed as a psychiatrist at the school when White Dove was kidnapped. That woman, so detectives concluded, was an alleged business associate of Victor Thorpe. Her name was Mary Jane Fitzgerald, of Muskogee, Oklahoma. She was last sighted boarding a Leer jet at the Ardmore Municipal Airport around two in the morning of December 31, about the same time as Sheriff McCrea and his volunteer posse raided Golden Enterprises.

The owners of the building had never met Fitzgerald, and their data concerning her proved to be false. The only photograph of her was the driver's license on file, and that was forged. Likewise, the social security number on file belonged to a woman in Kansas who'd died in 1943. Neither could the owner of the Learjet be identified, but the pilot who flew it on the night in question was determined to be a Colombian national. He had filed a flight plan with the FAA, landing first at Cancun and then on to Cartegena, Colombia. Investigators with the FBI and DEA identified the woman as Monica Juliana Giraldo, related to the Giraldo drug cartel known to operate out of Cartegena. Thorpe denied any knowledge of, or any association with her.

Uncle Luke phoned me after the trial to report Rain Cloud's testimony. He asked me whether I thought that might explain our delusions of a paranormal encounter up on the mountain. For the next few days, my head was swollen with doubt. Maybe that one joint Christine had passed around caused hallucinations, and maybe that intensified the prank Rain Cloud and his cronies played on us. Maybe we saw an old woman up there and assumed her to be a ghost.

But those possibilities did not account for Jordan's nightmares, or the creepy thing that breathed in my face at the farmhouse and, later, up on the mountain. They failed to explain White Dove's claim that a woman came to her aid in the cave. Nor could anyone explain the phantasmal collective that invaded the farmhouse, witnessed by Grandma, Grandpa, Uncle Luke, Orpheus, and Christine. They were certain that White Dove had died of a gunshot to the chest, and an hour later she stepped down from the table alive and unscathed. With her sight restored! How could Uncle Luke, or anyone, account for that!?

In October of that year, I received an invitation to a Chickasaw Festival at Seeley Chapel, Oklahoma. I eagerly drove up from Denton to join the gang in a celebration, hoping also to learn more about Chickasaw customs. My younger brother Spencer accompanied me on that trip. Each of us four cousins, along with Uncle Luke and our friend Orpheus Pratt, received a decorated eagle feather which, among Native Americans, is a sacred gift representing respect. Governor James made a speech recognizing us for bravery and compassion.

White Dove, celebrated as a miracle girl because of her recovered sight, was also honored as the Chickasaw Princess for that year. We met Governor James' wife Evelyn and his daughter Ranell Harry, who lived in Tulsa and had been princess by default each year since '63. She had represented the Chickasaw Nation during President Lyndon B. Johnson's inaugural parade.

Uncle Luke had already earned respect as a friend of the Five Nations. His work as a schoolteacher, coach, and volunteer with the Oklahoma geological research team brought him in contact with many significant people of all races. But, in particular, he developed ties with the Chickasaw Nation. He had pointed out that nearly all the members of his own family had at least a trace of Native American blood. However, he understood that adoption into a Native American tribe represented friendship, loyalty, and trust—all more important than physical bloodline.

As the festival progressed, Jordan and I played stickball with a group of youngsters while Terry found himself chatting with tribal elders about Vietnam. Christine fell in line with White Dove in a traditional stomp dance. Even when she was blind, White Dove had loved to dance. With her sight recovered, she found dancing even more enjoyable. Her head tilted as she drifted away with the rhythm of drums and shakers. Luke observed her from a distance, mesmerized. That wonderful day seemed a fitting conclusion to a bewildering and terrifying ordeal, not just for White Dove, but for all of us involved in her rescue.

Part 5: The Reckoning

Forty

With the Arbuckle experience still fresh in my mind, I moved to San Francisco in 1971. As expressed by Mac Davis, I left Texas and Oklahoma in my rearview mirror, with no remorse and no parting sentiments. At the time, I was convinced that in order to become a successful writer, I had three choices—New York, Chicago, or the west coast. Of course, I didn't have to live in any of those places. I just needed solid contacts there. But contacts were easier to develop and maintain by living there.

My parents must have thought I'd had some kind of sailor's dream of chasing the sun, the sand, and the sea—that I imagined myself aboard the schooner Tiki III, navigating the blue Pacific with Captain Adam Troy, on a heading to southern islands like Fiji or Samoa. I did eventually learn to sail, but it was not an obsession and not what drew me to California. My sailing skills never developed beyond crewing with friends on a moderate-sized sloop in the San Francisco Bay. On my one and only day trip out into the Pacific, around the Farallon Islands and back, I was seasick most of the way.

Plain and simple, my strongest attraction to California was Meredith. We had fallen in love at Disneyland as teenagers, a story my Grandparents liked to hear repeatedly, and we maintained a long-distance relationship for four years. Tragically, shortly after we became engaged, her parents died in a car wreck on their way up to Lake Tahoe. I flew out to be with her for the double funeral, and on that same occasion we worked out a plan for going forward together. I committed to continue my education at Stanford so I could be with Meredith through the process of grieving, and to assist her in assuming the responsibility of running a business. Circumstances demanded that we learn together, and I'm certain that enhanced our bond. Of course, our wedding was conducted in the dark shadow of her parents' death. My parents came out to support us in that complex situation. However, apart from the hard work of grief, we had cause for double celebration.

Meredith was heir to a small fortune. She inherited a solid nest egg of investments, as well as a twenty-acre vineyard and winery in Palo Alto.

California is home to hundreds of competitive vineyards, and Meredith already knew a lot about the process of wine production. She proved to be a hard taskmaster in providing me on-the-job training, and I learned as quickly as I could. We decided to change the name from *O'Banion Family Winery* to the more upscale *Vineyard Amour Complet,* and she made appropriate amendments in both management and marketing.

Within a year, business had doubled and Meredith easily sponsored me through graduate school. After that, besides helping her manage the vineyard, I accepted a position with *International Travel Magazine* as staff writer. We raised our children on that acreage, with ample profits for their education and our comfortable life. Our son, Russell Jr., is now a meteorologist studying climate change in Anchorage, Alaska. Our daughter Elizabeth, who in childhood was our little princess from toenails to tiara, now teaches sociology at Berkeley. In my leisure time, I grow exotic plants and enjoy outings with my granddaughters Susan and Cherie, Elizabeth's two little blonde angels.

Today, we have a staff of twelve at the vineyard and we produce fifteen varieties, ranging from sparkling wines to various whites and reds. We have our own labels for Cabernet Sauvignon, Merlot, and Pinot Noir, as well as whites, including Viognier, Chardonnay, and Riesling. Our home is on an adjacent two-acre property, and we can walk or ride a golf cart from the house to the winery and vineyards. I continue to work from home as a free-lance writer for periodicals like *Global Traveler, Travel and Leisure,* and *Destinations.*

All that aside, I am proud of my humble roots and feel a strong attachment to the state that was once official Indian Territory. I have in my library a copy of a *National Geographic* that includes a photo of Grandpa Greenwood and three other old codgers playing dominoes around a turned-up barrel at the general store in Gene Autry. And, even now, every fall I settle in my recliner in front of a big-screen to watch the Red River shootout between the OU Sooners and the University of Texas Longhorns.

No one cares or asks why I root for the Sooners. Nor does it matter to most of my friends that Oklahoma holds some of America's best-kept secrets, like beautiful lakes, springs and waterfalls, mountains and plains, and inspiring stories of survival like Steinbeck's *The Grapes of*

Wrath. To an Okie, such matters are important. But beyond the pro-
motional trivia, what gnaws at my gut is that the Sooner State holds
a number of dark and sinister secrets which were my misfortune to
discover, up close and personal.

Over the years, Meredith was acutely aware that I reacted to any
mention of the camping trip in '68 almost to the point of phobia. If
a memory of that experience crossed my mind, I broke out in a cold
sweat. I especially shunned television documentaries that involved the
paranormal. I declined to read ghost stories. Even the movie *Ghostbusters* was out of bounds for me. I simply didn't want to go there. My
children taunted me, "Come on Daddy, watch *Ghostbusters* with us.
We ain't afraid of no ghost."

Ironically, Meredith understood my need to attend Uncle Luke's
funeral in the fall of 2015. She thought it would prove cathartic and
help put my mind at rest. But when I got back home, she then struggled to grasp my obsession with writing about events I had refused to
deal with over our many years together. The bizarre encounters at the
casino had rattled me to the core, and I didn't want to discuss it with
her. I cloistered myself in research and contemplation for nearly three
months.

Beginning with the notes I made at the airport, I typed a hundred
pages of basic outline and a rough draft. During that time, I phoned
Jordan and Christine, both of whom claimed to have suffered depression and a siege of nightmares after the funeral. I was not able to reach
Terry, but I suspected that our quick jaunt up into the hills with Jordan
might have triggered a recurrence of his post-traumatic stress disorder.
If so, I didn't want to compound his problem with a truck load of
questions.

I also wondered whether Terry and Christine had remained connected. At Uncle Luke's funeral, I gathered that both of them had
spouses. Yet, as I was leaving the farm, I saw Terry drape an arm over
Christine's shoulder. It appeared a tad more intimate than two recon-
ciled cousins. I wrote Christine about that, and her response blew me
away. She disclosed that she and Terry got married after college, and
were together for twenty-one years. Intrigued, and happy for them, I
begged for more details.

While planning an academic tour in England, which was part
of her undergraduate studies, Christine applied for a passport. That
required a birth certificate which she obtained without her mother's

knowledge, assuming there would be no problem. In the process, she discovered that she was adopted. Understandably, she was outraged that her mother had never disclosed such an important fact. The primary reason was that the birth mother was a seventeen-year-old named Jennifer Dee Brewster, the younger sister of Jordan's mom, Lydia Brewster Greenwood.

As in classic small-town stories of hidden shame, Jennifer had become pregnant after a tryst with a boy she met on a school trip to Galveston. Her parents pulled her out of school until after delivery, and insisted that she put the child up for adoption. At that time, Marcus and Hazel Greenwood had been married four years, hoping to raise a family but with no success at pregnancy. Doctors concluded that Hazel was infertile. They adopted infant Christine to raise as their own child. Three years later, Hazel got pregnant. She gave birth to a healthy daughter, whom they named Caroline; and eighteen months later, she had a second daughter, Catherine.

When Christine made that significant discovery, she paid Terry a visit. She had stifled her feelings for him because she thought it inordinate for cousins to have an intimate relationship. He confessed that he had fallen in love with her even before the Arbuckle adventure. They married in May of 1970. Christine was the mother of Heath and Hanna, whose photographs Terry showed me at the farmhouse after Uncle Luke's funeral.

Christine explained that in the early years of their marriage she was okay with Terry's career as a police officer, but they drifted apart when he became an undercover detective and symptoms of PTSD returned. In general, their breakup was a common story in American law enforcement. Eventually, both remarried. Christine's second husband was a banker by the name of Howard, whom I'd never met. The woman who accompanied Terry at Uncle Luke's funeral was his second wife, Sue.

I never learned whether Christine reconnected with her birth mom, or whether she even cared to do so. My personal hope has been to maintain a simple and basic family, with uncomplicated relationships. That hope has been fulfilled, so far. However, my obsessive research into Uncle Luke's relationship with White Dove, as well as dredging up other details from the past, have created in me apprehension and trepidation beyond my ability to cope.

Forty-One

On a sunny Tuesday morning, Meredith and I drove east from Palo Alto, across the bay on the Dumbarton Bridge, and along a route we hoped to be less congested and more scenic than others. Our daughter Elizabeth wanted us to meet her and her husband (our son-in-law David) for lunch, since they and our two granddaughters were not able to join us for Christmas dinner. Dr. David Lochridge is an economics professor at Berkeley. He and Lizzy met when both were at grad school. Early in their marriage we had an agreement with David's parents to alternate Thanksgiving and Christmas gathers so neither family feels slighted.

Somewhere along Interstate 880, we found ourselves stuck in heavy traffic. Meredith tuned in a radio station that played oldies, thinking that a little nostalgia might enhance my patience. The mellow voices of Peter, Paul, and Mary compelled us to sing along—*Where have all the flowers gone, long time passing.*

My thoughts returned to Jordan strumming his guitar by a campfire in the Arbuckle Mountains. I mused on my frizzy-headed cousin Christine, ever resolved to change the world, and my older cousin Terry, the Vietnam veteran with PTSD who'd hoped to become a cop and put an end to crime. I more or less bundled them together with the rest of our family, *long time passing*, with whom I shared humble roots in the Oklahoma hills. Having struggled thus far to write the story of our paranormal experience in 1968, with limited resources and conflicting witnesses, I became acutely aware of my fretful dilemma.

Back home that evening, with a measure of reluctance, I decided to share specific details with select professionals, hoping for some helpful insights. After all, lunch with our daughter and son-in-law reminded me that people with three or four degrees in a specific field have knowledge beyond urban legends and folklore, and typically such people can distinguish between fiction and reality. The story I was attempting to tell seemed to hunker at the blurred crossroads of superstition and the paranormal. Whether anything about it was verifiably real, I remained uncertain.

Among my close friends was UCLA psychology professor, Dr. Milton Aldridge, and I was confident he would chat with me about this dilemma. Not being a church-goer, I didn't have a close relationship with any clergy, but I was at least acquainted with Meredith's minister, the Reverend Angela Cox of the United Methodist Church in Palo Alto. To get a fair perspective, I decided also to interview Dr. Josh Radcliff, and evangelical minister who had taught a course at San Francisco State that he called *Mysteries of Faith, Death, and Dying*. He held a Doctor of Ministry from a conservative theological seminary in the upper Midwest. His opposition to gay marriage and his disdain for Bruce Jenner's transition to Catilyn Marie, along with his unabashed defense of biblical inerrancy, had led to his dismissal from SFSU. However, he was still in the area and agreed to see me. I figured I had nothing to lose by listening to his views. Last, I approached the Roman Catholic bishop with whom I had played tennis a few times— scholar and author, the Most Reverend Miguel Gutierez.

As I expected, among these distinguished professionals, religious beliefs and professional scientific perspectives ran amok. Their responses varied and theories clashed. Both the psychologist and the Methodist minister were certain that my cousins and I had suffered a form of delusion, no doubt triggered by stress and physical exhaustion. The practical joke played on us by the Kiowa ex-con complicated matters, as well as the gunfight at the airport for which three of us had neither training nor experience.

Aldridge and Cox also said that a puff or two on a joint and a shot of tequila might have compounded the delusion, but those were not critical factors. They also agreed that while White Dove had experienced a rare, but not impossible, recovery of sight, that might have resulted from physical and emotional trauma. However, they insisted that White Dove's death on the table was apparent, but not clinically factual or verifiable. In their view, literal revivification after a limited space of time was simply untenable. How that perception arose among several witnesses might be mysterious and fascinating, they said, but it was certainly not valid.

The Catholic bishop challenged the ghost stories, although he claimed a belief in miracles, visions, spirits of the dead, demon possession, and exorcism by a qualified Catholic priest. However, in his view, my depiction of the events raised serious doubts. The cave story, he said, resembled the tradition of Jesus descending into Hades to preach to imprisoned spirits, as recorded in 1 Peter 3:19. He could not imagine

God empowering the dead to raise the dead or to perform any sort of miracles. If that were possible, then all the dead would be active in the world of the living, resuming former lives with greater knowledge and wisdom. To him, the very idea was absurd. He assessed that my cousins and I had somehow misinterpreted a number of experiences, and over time they'd solidified as misguided assumptions and false memories.

In contrast with the other clerical assessments, the evangelical minister emphatically denied the existence of ghosts or apparitions. He referenced the story of the rich man and Lazarus in the Gospel of Luke, maintaining that there is a great gulf fixed between the living and the dead, preventing any form of contact or ghost appearance. Furthermore, he said our collective delusion was the work of Satan. He quoted a passage from 2 Corinthians 11:3 which suggests that human sin resulted from the corruption of Eve's mind by the cunning ways of the serpent. He punctuated his assessment by assuring me that if I would accept Jesus as my personal Lord and Savior and denounce all association with evil, my nightmares would cease, the fog of uncertainty would lift, and the power of the Holy Spirit would protect me from further disconcerting experiences. He also said that I should not publish the story, claiming its contents to be an instrument of Satan to sow seeds of doubt among true believers. "If you saw anything," he said, "it was a demon, not a ghost."

Still trying to evaluate this soup of conflicting opinions, it dawned on me that I should also consult a medium or spiritualist—someone who actually believed in ghosts and at least claimed to have communicated with them. After all, intellectuals are in favor of reaching out to whatever intelligence might reside out there in the far reaches of space. So, for those who believe in a realm of the conscious dead, why wouldn't we want to know what the dead know? I located Rosiland Kitzinger, whose book *With Us Still* explained her theories and included transcripts of dialogues with the dead. During an hour's consultation—for which I paid a hundred dollars—she told me that apparitions have energy fields much like electronic impulses from a satellite or a cell phone tower. They're everywhere—all around us, but invisible.

With training, she said, the living can learn receptivity. She also told me that sometimes the dead are not aware they are dead, and their lingering energy congeals into a visible or audible form in an attempt to communicate with the living. I related to her our ghost encounters in the Arbuckle Mountains, as well as White Dove's revivification. Her demeanor changed dramatically as I spoke. It appeared that my stories made her rather nervous. She said none of that paralleled her own experience, and she could not offer further advice. She escorted me out rather abruptly.

***

Back at home I continued my research. I found a few news clippings covering the trial of Tim Rain Cloud and the other thugs involved in White Dove's abduction. One article caught my attention. After sentencing, Rain Cloud never spent another day in prison. Handcuffed in the back seat of a squad car, and in the custody of two officers, he was on his way to the state penitentiary in McAlester, Oklahoma. Somewhere along the route, he escaped. Both officers reported that he was there, occasionally conversing with them, but when they arrived at the prison he was gone. The cuffs, still locked, lay in the seat. They had never stopped along the way, so he was never left alone in the vehicle and he had no opportunity to exit. He just disappeared, they said, into thin air.

I came across a photo of Rain Cloud that sent chills up and down my spine. He looked exactly like the Indian who confronted me at the WinStar Casino, on my way home from Uncle Luke's funeral. Surely that was not the same guy, I thought. Unless he hadn't aged a bit in nearly fifty years. Or, as I suspected concerning the old woman and the hooker, perhaps I imagined the encounter. Maybe I'm far more predisposed to stress related delusion that I'd like to assume. Or, even more disturbing, maybe the Rain Cloud look-alike and the two women are the same individuals we encountered back in '68. Maybe they're ghosts.

***

Other than personal observations and the testimony of those at the farmhouse, most of the information I gathered about White Dove came from a journal that Uncle Luke left among his official documents. Christine had found it when she and Jordan's wife Poloma were cleaning out the house, preparing it for sale. Despite the bulk and expense, she mailed me a photocopy.

Luke had recorded his daily thoughts and reflections, dating from the first time he'd met White Dove. He wrote that he recognized her special intellectual gifts from very early, and it was no marvel that she had mastered Braille as a child and remembered everything she read. However, she was also able to memorize oral speeches, lectures, and sermons and repeat them verbatim. After she recovered her vision, her eidetic memory became evident and did not diminish over time. She mastered various additional learning techniques and could apply them simultaneously. She enlisted a cadre of volunteer readers who rotated, each reading to her three hours each day—encyclopedias, journal essays, advanced textbooks. She could read one book and listen to another at the same time. When she lay down to sleep at night, she often played tapes of classic novels. She was particularly fond of James Michner.

Uncle Luke recorded in his journal that he had proposed to White Dove at a tribal powwow in Tishomingo. He wrote that when he asked Governor James's permission to marry her, the answer was negative. The Governor said that he personally, and the Chickasaw nation as a whole, respected Luke immensely. He did not consider marriage between whites and Chickasaw problematic. But for Luke and White Dove, marriage was impossible and unthinkable. Despite Luke's challenge, he would not explain further. He sent Luke away with the hope that he could find happiness without White Dove. Evidently, Luke's love for her was irrepressible, so he and White Dove eloped and she never returned to her own family or community. From that time forward Luke called her Dovie.

The deeper I delved into Uncle Luke's journal, the more mysterious it became. He expressed great pride that Dovie made the most of her second chance at life, recording a detailed list of her accomplishments. She graduated magna cum laude from OU at age twenty-two. She went on to complete a *juris doctoris* at the Pritzker School of Law at Northwestern University in Chicago. After passing the bar exam in the states of Oklahoma and Illinois, she was granted federal board status, as well. She soon became a legal advocate for the Chickasaw nation.

Luke spoke in detail of their upscale home on a twenty-acre plot southeast of Ardmore. It was situated near the Executive Airport, facilitating White Dove's business flights on behalf of the Chickasaw people. He also recorded his disappointment when she told him she could not bear children, resulting from another physiological disorder like her blindness. He found it puzzling that uterine or ovarian health had not accompanied her miraculous revivification and restoration of sight.

According to Uncle Luke's notes, they were married thirty years before Dovie died of multiple myeloma. None of our family was notified when it happened. Luke and I had spoken by phone on numerous occasions, but he never mentioned Dovie's illness or death. I learned about that at his funeral.

However, I found a page in his journal where Uncle Luke depicted Dovie's declining state of health and her desire to visit Ghost Cavern one more time. He recorded how he took her up into the mountains on the back of a four-wheeler. She guided him intuitively up above the rock quarry until they came upon a crevasse she identified as the mouth of the grotto. A cluster of thick mountain cedars guarded the spot like sentinels at a castle door. She slid off the four-wheeler, drawn irresistibly toward the rocky depression. She crept forward as if she could still see the mouth of the cave beneath the boulders that camouflaged it.

Luke recorded that White Dove described subterranean tunnels, chambers, and waterways which her eyes had never seen. Then she lifted her arms and began to dance in small anemic steps, singing softly. He stood trembling as he beheld her metamorphosis. She relinquished flesh and bone and assumed a chimeral form, in which she quietly descended into the earth where the cave mouth once gaped. Luke noted that her ears must have been attuned to the sound of running water, and perhaps the chant of sacred songs from other ethereal voices. He wrote that Dovie had a most radiant look on her face, and she just slipped way, back to her home in the depths of the earth.

I never found any notes by Luke on the mélange of events during that week in 1968 that had been so troubling for me—events all four cousins had promised not to divulge to others or even mention again. Totally stumped, I decided to research White Dove using the names by which she was known in specific contexts—Whitney James and *puchi yoshoba tohbi*. To my consternation, I could not find evidence of her education, either in primary and secondary school or in university archives. Nor could I document her alleged involvement in politics. There was no record of her marriage in any of the counties in and around Chickasaw territory. And, there were no medical records or evidence of her birth. The Chickasaw Princess for 1969 was listed as Kay Holly, not Whitney James. It appeared that, as far as the Chickasaw Nation was concerned, White Dove never existed.

Uncle Luke and Christine had claimed to witness the cadre of spirits who assembled at the farm to assist in White Dove's restoration to

life. They witnessed what neither Terry, Jordan, nor I had seen personally. Of course, Grandpa and Grandma Greenwood were also there, as
was Orpheus Pratt. But they're all deceased. Orpheus died from can-
cer in '89. The probable cause Agent Orange. I was unable to locate
his wife or children. Ironically, Overton James passed away the same
month as Uncle Luke. None of the James family members responded
to my letters or phone calls.

I was aware that Uncle Luke did not witness the Indian war party
that raided our camper bus, nor did he share in any of the other paranormal experiences that haunted me and Jordan. And after attending
the trial of Tim Rain Cloud, Uncle Luke said he was certain the rest of
us had suffered a traumatic delusion. Despite those anomalies, what he
recorded in his memoirs seemed rational and legitimate. But none of
it could be verified. And I now wondered whether Uncle Luke himself
lived out the remainder of his days in a state of psychosis. Christine
browsed through Uncle Luke's photo albums. The only picture of him
and White Dove together was when they first met at a powwow in
Tishomingo. She was only sixteen. But there was nothing after that.

Like a bolt of lightning, it struck me that Uncle Luke never married White Dove. He must have loved her so intensely that he could
not live without her, and he fabricated stories of their life together and
her personal accomplishments. I considered the possibility that White
Dove died on that table at the farm and was never resurrected. Rather,
her ghost came to live with Uncle Luke and remained with him until
he died. I began to think I should complete my own version of the story with that as its conclusion. But as I suspected, that was not the end.

Forty-Two

By Superbowl Sunday 2017, I considered my manuscript complete and ready for editing. I had contacted Ian and Sharon McNeal, an editing and agent team, who agreed to review it before pitching it to a publisher. Trying to clear my head of all the details, with which I had been obsessed for fourteen months, I cozied myself in front of the TV in my hide-away den, ready to watch the big game between the New England Patriots and the Atlanta Falcons. That would be broadcast live from the NGR Stadium in Houston. Uninterested in football, Meredith chose an afternoon of bridge, wine, and cheese, with friends. Needless to say, she provided the wine.

Our plan was to go out for dinner later that evening, win or lose at bridge or football. I watched the first half with abysmal disappointment. For several years, I had been a fan of Joe Montana, the 49ers' *Comeback Kid*. But lately my loyalty had shifted. Now fascinated with Tom Brady and the Patriots, I fully expected a spectacular performance in this Superbowl LI. For that reason, I could not believe they had done so poorly in this climactic game. Late in the third quarter, Atlanta was ahead by twenty-five points. Even a tie seemed out of reach for the Patriots.

Disgusted and losing interest in the game, my thoughts returned to my manuscript. Like most writers, I worried that I might have neglected or misstated certain important details. Since this project had led me to question my own sanity, I now had to consider that there might be much more hidden away in dark recesses of my mind, or out there somewhere in documents I had not found, or in someone else's memory. And, there was no one alive I could talk to who witnessed White Dove's resurrection— except Christine.

I must have fallen asleep thinking about it. The doorbell rang. I awoke with a jolt and a chill at my neck. The TV was flashing on and off. There must have been a brief power-outage in the area, and I slept through it. I crawled out of my recliner and shuffled foggily into the entrance hall. Through the front door's opaque glass, I made out the distorted images of a man and woman. I hoped it was not Jehovah's Witnesses peddling end-times propaganda, linking current politics with the end of the world as we know it. I reached for the door handle, preparing a *no solicitors* speech. As I tugged the door open, my jaw dropped. Before my astonished eyes stood my dear cousins Terry and Christine. For a moment I was speechless, my legs weak and face tingling.

"Good Lord, what a surprise. Come in." I swept my hand heartily.

Smiling warmly, both paused to embrace me before stepping across the threshold. Their touch felt warm and familiar. Yet, something seemed different... something I could not describe. Terry's bearded face looked precisely the same as I remembered him at Uncle Luke's funeral. Christine's scattered freckles were hidden beneath a thin mask of makeup, but unlike before, she appeared tanned and relaxed. The frizzy hair I remembered was in a stylish short undercut, swept back on top, and certainly attractive and sophisticated. Their casual jeans with light jackets were appropriate for travelers in California's unpredictable winter.

Without prompting, they glided curiously through the tiled entry hall, eyes scanning the walls and high ceiling. I escorted them as they explored the house past my study and library, the dining room and kitchen, outside across the patio, and around the pool. Christine headed further out to a spot with a view of the winery and vineyard. Terry and I followed, virtually wordless.

In the distance, four of our workers were busy pruning. Although it was Sunday, Meredith and I had agreed to give them a week off with pay if they finished that essential chore by Valentine's Day. They weren't going to make it, I calculated, but we planned to honor that promise even if they were a few days late. It had been a good season and Meredith's policy had always been to generously share winery profits with the staff and vineyard workers.

Surveying the property, Christine cut her laughing green eyes toward me. "You certainly landed with your butt in the butter, dear cousin. This is a wonderful place."

I chuckled. "I did, yes. But it all followed true love. Unexpected fringed benefits, I guess you could say." I led the way back toward the house, puzzled that Christine and Terry were together without their spouses. I asked about Sue and Howard.

"We left them behind," Terry said cannily. "It was something we both needed to do."

A serene smile lifted on Christine's lips. "Life's short and full of surprises. Sometimes we can relax and just go with the flow. Sometimes we have to take the bull by the horns and make things happen. You know, before time runs out."

My eyes darted from one to the other as I pondered their puzzling comments. Their words seemed more like riddles than observations. Enigmatic, to say the least. Christine segued to their daughter Hanna, who had married and settled in Reno. No children. She was still a flight attendant, now with Virgin Atlantic, mostly working flights in and out of Las Vegas. "We haven't seen her in a while and we figured we'd better reach out. Know what I mean?"

"Of course. We see Lizzy and the girls often," I said, "but Junior is way to hell and gone up in Alaska. Seldom hear from him. We're planning a cruise this summer and hope to see him then. His wife Lydia is pregnant with their first child."

Terry and Christine nodded approvingly. Terry, in his typical stoicism, thought long before speaking further. "About the story you're writing," he said, leaning toward me, "and our big adventure up in the Arbuckles. I'm curious about how you handled the ethereal part of all that. You must have come to some sort of conclusion. After all, you're an inquisitive and critical kind of guy."

"By ethereal you mean other-worldly," I said, somewhat hesitantly. "You're asking about ghosts, right?"

My dear cousins smiled casually, without a nod or verbal response.

"Well, in fact, clear and definitive is the hard part," I said, clearing my throat. As I tried to frame an answer, I found myself fumbling with words. I felt awkward and very ill at ease. Since Terry had posed the question, I directed my response toward him.

"I recorded everything I could find, and my honest assessment of it all. But there are just too many unanswered questions and too many details that don't make sense. Particularly the parts you and I didn't actually see with our own eyes. For example, things that Christine, here, told us." I motioned and directed my eyes toward her. "And of course, Grandma and Grandpa."

"I'm sure you understand." My eyes returned to Terry's unemotional and aloof face. "Christine here is the only surviving witness to a number of things you and I didn't see. I wanted to tell the truth with some measure of personal conviction. But I struggled when I realized how much I didn't actually experience myself, can't prove, and certainly can't claim to understand."

"Ah, the truth." Terry nodded incredulously. "I've heard people quote Hemingway on that important concept. *There's no one thing that's true. It's all true.* Others quote the Bible, *I'm the way, the truth, and the life.* Not being a literary type, I've always had trouble with statements like that. I suppose Hemingway meant that whatever happens is real, and we shouldn't over-analyze the *whys* and *wherefores.* The catch is how we perceive and interpret what we see and hear... and read. But, of course, that tends to determine what we believe, and how we live. I guess that's the meaning." Terry stared at me, searching my thoughts.

"I understand that. At least, I think I do." I was cautious and diffident, feeling Terry's eyes grilling me. I glanced again at Christine. She studied me in the same intense manner.

"Much of what people believe isn't true at all," I said, folding my arms across my chest. "People let themselves be misguided and misinformed, I suspect because it's easier than thinking for themselves. God only knows the reason. Or maybe God doesn't know, or care. We latch onto a specific belief, and we call it *truth.* Like, some people argue that if you don't believe in God and a final Judgment, when you die, you miss out on all the good stuff."

"Of course, yes," Christine said, nodding crisply. "And, worse, you'll go to hell and suffer eternally when you could have avoided it. You have to consider whether disbelief is a risk worth taking, so they say. People also say the Devil's in the details, right?" She bobbed her eyebrows, smiling sardonically.

"Exactly. But I keep wondering if there is an afterlife at all, and if so, whether it's determined by what you believe and how you live as a mortal."

"Ah, Russ," Christine added, "these are the sort of questions most people never ask. There is much more to know, and experience, and it's so very, very close."

I stood for a moment, my eyes darting from Christine to Terry, and back again. Her comments gripped me firmly and I could not hold back.

"My question to you, Christine, is simple. Are you sure you saw White Dove brought back to life? Are you sure you saw Lóoliha, or Lomasi, or whatever she was at the moment, and all those other ghosts you described in detail? I have no one else to ask. Grandpa and Grandma are dead. Orpheus is dead. Uncle Luke is dead. And very important, White Dove is gone. Dead for real this time, we assume. Her people apparently never heard of her. A huge part of our story now rests on you."

"Fact is," Christine leaned toward me, her green eyes penetrating my thoughts, "we're all part of a passing parade. And we all want to know whether there is an immortal soul, a spirit, our distinct person-hood, within ourselves. And if so, where is it ultimately bound? What happens when we march on past the grandstand and turn the corner? Is there a different crowd waiting there?"

Terry slipped an arm over my shoulder, picking up Christine's cadre of questions. "Does a person simply cease to exist at death, in the nothingness of Erewon? Or is there more? Will you stroll in fields of Elysium, dear cousin? Will you find peace in Valhalla? Nirvanah? Xanadu? Heaven? Or is all of that myth? Mere human fantasy? Big questions." Terry bobbed his eyebrows and smiled.

I shuddered at his uncharacteristic fraternal gesture, as much as his philosophical discourse. At the same time, I was mystified at Christine's calm presence, in contrast with the mercurial traits of her youth. But her summary question cut into me like a hot knife through butter.

"I'd bet you want to know the answer, don't you, Russ?" Christine said. "What if our spirits have another mission, right here among the living?"

It seemed that she had been holding back and knew things we had never discussed— things she had discovered, that she had never shared. For a moment, I was lost. I had no answers, no comments, and no further insights.

My cell phone rang. Compulsively, my eyes drifted downward as I drew it from my shirt pocket. I didn't recognize the number, so I shut it off without answering. When I looked up, Terry and Christine were gone. I swirled around, searching for them, then bounded along the driveway toward the road. Maybe they had taken a taxi or Uber and it had been waiting for them nearby. But, still, I would have noticed a ve-hicle. For a moment I staggered in bewilderment. Terry and Christine seemed to just disappear. They had mentioned they were on their way to Reno and couldn't stay longer. They were in a hurry, they said. To catch the next flight, I guessed. I hated that they left me dangling. Even with the bizarre dialogue, I wanted more. Our visit was far too short.

I checked my phone again as I meandered back across the patio, through the kitchen, and into the den. I plopped down on the couch, trying to collect my thoughts. As I switched on the TV, I was pummeled

by a commentary on what they called the most spectacular comeback
win in Superbowl history. I pounded the arm of my recliner with a
fist. I was elated, but outraged that I had missed the plays, catches,
and runs, the fumble recoveries, the interceptions, the touchdowns,
the field goals— whatever they did to close the gap and win the game.
I found zero consolation in knowing I would see all the highlights later
that night on the news. That's just not the same.

I was still fuming when Meredith bounded through the front door,
squealing victoriously after winning her bridge tournament. Needless
to say, she was eager to celebrate. She threw her arms around me, hop-
ping up and down like a high school cheerleader, her blond hair bouncing. As she settled down, she dispatched a sortie of complaints about
her partner's stupid mistakes, saying they were lucky to have come out
on top. I told her briefly about the visit from my cousins and the Superbowl I'd missed. Waving all that aside, I turned attention to dinner.

I suggested the Greek restaurant *Evvia Estiatorio* as a good place
to dine and celebrate. Meredith wanted to drive, since her BMW was
waiting at the front door. I acquiesced. As I climbed in and closed the
door, my cell phone chirped again.

"Just switch it off," Meredith said. "We need to unwind and have
some fun."

I glanced at the phone. "It's Jordan, I'd better take it. He'll understand if I can't talk long."

Meredith turned out of the driveway and accelerated down the
road, hinting that I had ignored her advice again. My thought was that
Jordan was calling to tell me about their recent vacation in Italy. Or
maybe he'd also watched the Superbowl and wanted to rag me, since
he didn't like Tom Brady. Whatever the reason, I was glad he called. I
grinned as I answered.

"Hello, you old coot. Don't tell me it was a lucky win."

Jordan was silent for a moment, before a lackluster response. "No,
no, I didn't watch the game."

"You didn't? Geeze Louise. You missed a hell of a comeback." I
listened for a response, but Jordan was quiet. "Anyway, how are you?
Everything alright?"

"Well, no. Not good."

Jordan's voice was raspy and weak. I was reminded of that call in
the early hours of the morning when Uncle Luke had passed away. But
I surmised that Jordan had come down with the flu or something. I

didn't want to ask, so I waited and let him speak.

"I have bad news, Russ." Again, Jordan was quiet.

Ice water shot through my veins. "Pull over and stop," I said abruptly. "Please, Meredith."

Seeing my face go pale, Meredith pulled into a strip mall parking lot and stopped. "What's up?" she said, anxious eyes locked on my face.

I shook my head and shrugged, waiting. "Not sure," I said. "Something's seriously wrong." I switched the phone to speaker.

"It's Terry and Christine," Jordan said, hesitantly.

"Yes, I already know. They're finally back together."

"That's an odd way of putting it. What do you mean?"

"They came by to see me this afternoon."

Jordan hesitated. Then he hit me in the gut. "Russ, Terry and Christine were both killed in a plane crash. They're dead Russ. Our Terry and Christine are dead."

I felt the blood instantly drain from my face. My scalp tingled. "What? No, Jordan. That can't be. They were just here an hour ago. Was that the flight to Reno? They said that's where they were headed."

Meredith lifted a hand to cover her mouth. Her eyes welled up. So did mine. I stammered through futile and empty comments.

"My God, Jordan, we walked together along the edge of the vineyard, talking. It was a captivating visit. Strange, in some ways. But it was delightful to see them. I can't believe they're gone." I choked up, but I managed to sputter out a question. "How. . . how did you find out?"

Jordan did not respond. I waited, assuming he also was emotional and needed a moment. An indescribable chill ran through my veins. Eventually Jordan spoke, more direct in tone.

"Russ, I know you've been under serious stress for months. I wonder if maybe you need to see that counselor you told me about. Maybe get some help to work things through."

"What do you mean? I'm upset, naturally, but I'll deal with it."

"No, no. I'm talking about what you just said." Jordan paused. "Your visit with Terry and Christine, earlier today. It sounded... well, frankly, it sounded like someone talking to his dead wife at the cemetery. Are you actually seeing things, buddy? Maybe you're talking out loud to your cousins because you've been writing about all of us. I dunno. It just didn't sound like you."

My face ignited. Jordan's words and tone were profoundly disturbing. In fact, odious and insulting. I reacted defensively. "No, Jordan. You're reading me all wrong. I can handle death. We've all experienced plenty of grief over the years. But I'm telling you, man, they were just here. They stopped by on their way up to Reno to see Hanna, they said. We had a remarkable conversation. A bit strange, but too short. They were in a hurry. And it's just mind-blowing that they could be here one minute, and an hour later they're dead. Life is so unpredictable."

"Russ, Russ. Stop." Jordan paused breathlessly. "Listen to me."

I waited, puzzled but curious, wondering what Jordan needed to say.

"The plane crash, Russ, was last Monday. Terry and Christine were both killed. They've been dead a week."

I felt my breath and spirit empty out into the floorboard, like the flush of a powered toilet. My stomach knotted up and I felt as if I were sinking into a black hole a mile deep. I feared I might vomit. Then, I felt a warm stream flood my Dockers slacks. My eyes lowered as I realized that my bladder had emptied involuntarily. Meredith's eyes followed mine. Stunned, she lifted a hand to cover her gaping mouth. I switched the phone to speaker.

Jordan continued. "The two couples, Terry and Sue, along with Christine and Howard, were with a small group of friends. They spent a few days in the Bahamas, then Key West, before heading to St. Thomas. Someone in the group was an executive with Fairfield Investments and had access to a corporate jet. I think they said a Cessna Citation. It went down in a storm off the coast of Puerto Rico, just north of San Juan. The authorities said there were no survivors. Twelve passengers, plus the pilot and copilot. They recovered all the bodies. It was on the news, but... well, you know. They had to identify each one, before they could inform the next of kin. I got the call just a little while ago."

Hearing that, Meredith made a slow and cautious U-turn in the parking lot, eased out onto the road, and headed home. Neither of us had an appetite after that call, and we'd certainly lost our desire for celebration. Back at the house, I showered and changed clothes. Then, dutifully, I carried a bucket of warm soapy water out to garage and cleaned the seat in Meredith's BMW.

A short while later Meredith put on some light jazz. A group called *Fourplay*, as I recall. We had a glass of wine and sat on the couch in dim light. Meredith listened as I shared memories of Terry and Christine. In her usual manner, Meredith draped an arm over my shoulder and lightly brushed her fingers through my hair, trying to ease my embarrassment at peeing in my pants. She noted that a serious emotional shock can cause bizarre physical reactions.

Meredith had never met my cousins, but she knew how special they were to me. Each had a remarkable life. And while Terry had retired as a decorated police detective, Christine had a stellar career in education with her heart set on politics. Recently, she'd held two town hall meetings and was in the running for Oklahoma State Representative. I'm sure she would have won.

Terry said it best. In a world of many traditions and social perspectives, it appears to matter little what one believes or does not believe. What matters is *how* you live, how you treat people, and how well you cope with things you cannot control, explain, or understand. But it also seems that we only find time to reflect deeply on occasions of devastating loss.

I've tried to live my life in harmony with Edith Piaf's famous French lyrics— *No regrets, no, I regret nothing.* I discovered over time that such was not really possible. Sometimes I imagine myself in the hereafter, sitting down with Grandpa in the shade of a live oak enjoying a summer breeze. Grandpa would smoke his pipe and I'd sip a glass of Grandma's lemonade, as we shared memories of our brief sojourn in this terrestrial realm. But I also dream, sometimes, of exploring territory not seen in the flesh. There have been moments when I imagined myself in a limitless spirit form; in ways more substantial than dreams and visions. And, strangely, I'm always left with more questions than answers. Having heard the testimony of people I loved and trusted who claimed to have witnessed an incursion of ghosts into the realm of the living with the specific purpose of restoring life to only one, I am forced to consider that ghosts might be real.

In light of that, I ask myself questions like those posited by Terry and Christine. What will be my role in that hinterland of the unseen, if there is such a place? Or, will I dissolve into nature, my molecules and atoms eventually intermingled with many others to become a tree, a field of wheat, a salmon in the stream, or a bear roaming a hillside? Will my essence find its way down a river to the sea, to be portioned out into myriad new creatures in the vast and dark abyss? Because of the trace of Choctaw or Cherokee in my veins, I wonder if my spirit will traverse vacant plains following a herd of buffalo. Will I run with the ancestors, fleeing the incursion of hostile invaders? Or will I choose to ascend the slopes of the Arbuckles to reside in the company of other unsettled spirits, seeking peace and satisfaction in the heart of a haunted cave? Or, will I return again as someone else? If so, to what purpose? To whose aid shall I come? Or, am I now on a journey of inquiry, learning, and growing, and the afterlife is but another phase of a timeless but existential venture?

As far as I know, the mouth of Ghost Cavern in the Arbuckles remains closed. Perhaps there is a connection between that cave and a similar legendary abode of the dead, the Well of Souls in Jerusalem, beneath the Dome of the Rock on Temple Mount. There may be many others where spirits of the dead await a great Battle of Armageddon when all evil deeds will be avenged. If such legends are true, human spirits must be everywhere, all around us, watching and waiting for their moment.

I have been apprehensive about divulging these details along with my personal reflections. I have suspected we shouldn't speak of matters held secret by the dead. Maybe that's the reason I was warned not to write or speak. Having done so anyway, I now suspect Uncle Luke and White Dove might have more to tell me, if I ever see them again. So will Lóoliha, the wise Chickasaw grandmother who seems to be an auteur of all spirit affairs.

Christine and Terry had more to say to me, no doubt, but the chirping of my cell phone caused their sudden retreat. And now, my certainty grows stronger that no matter where they are, or how many there are like them, they are indeed out there. Ghosts, spirits, or wandering souls— what we call them matters little. They will appear when they are ready, and I'm certain they know exactly where to find me.

And make no mistake, they'll find you, too.

Acknowledgments and Disclaimer

This story and its principal characters are fictional. No literal association should be made with Overton James, Carl Abert, or other real persons living or dead. The author extends gratitude to the Chickasaw people and other Native American tribes and nations mentioned in this story, with due honor and respect to all who have suffered and died unjustly.

The author also acknowledges and thanks personal friends, whose shared outings in the Arbuckle Mountains inspired this story.

THE RE-ATTRIBUTION OF THE BRITISH RENAISSANCE CORPUS

BRRAM

ANNA FAKTOROVICH

RICHARD VERSTEGAN

of RESTITUTION of DECAYED INTELLIGENCE in ANTIQUITIES

ANNA FAKTOROVICH, TRANSLATOR

BRRAM

20-Volume Series
Proves with computational linguistics, handwriting and biographical analysis:

6 GHOSTWRITERS
Created All British Renaissance Texts

WILLIAM SHAKESPEARE PERCY

SONNETS TO THE FAIREST COELIA

THREE LETTERS

ANNA FAKTOROVICH, TRANSLATOR

GABRIEL HARVEY

SMITH

ANNA FAKTOROVICH, TRANSLATOR

WILLIAM SHAKESPEARE PERCY

THE THIRSTY ARABIA

ANNA FAKTOROVICH, TRANSLATOR

WILLIAM SHAKESPEARE PERCY

HAMLET

ANNA FAKTOROVICH, TRANSLATOR

First translations of inaccessible books, with annotations, introductions

https://AnaphoraLiterary .com/Attribution

WILLIAM SHAKESPEARE PERCY

FAIRY PASTORAL

ANNA FAKTOROVICH, TRANSLATOR

WILLIAM SHAKESPEARE PERCY

FOREST TRAGEDY

ANNA FAKTOROVICH, TRANSLATOR

WILLIAM SHAKESPEARE PERCY

CUCK-QUEANS' AND CUCKOLDS' ERRANDS

ANNA FAKTOROVICH, TRANSLATOR

WILLIAM SHAKESPEARE PERCY

The APHRODISIA

ANNA FAKTOROVICH, TRANSLATOR

WILLIAM SHAKESPEARE PERCY

FEDELE and FORTUNIO

ANNA FAKTOROVICH, TRANSLATOR

WILLIAM SHAKESPEARE PERCY

LOOK AROUND YOU

ANNA FAKTOROVICH, TRANSLATOR

www.ingramcontent.com/pod-product-compliance
Lightning Source LLC
Chambersburg PA
CBHW030405030726
47497CB00002B/493